# Charlotte Vale Allen

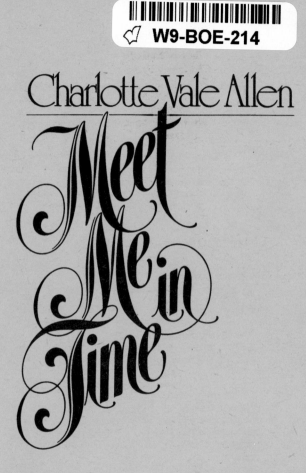

# Meet Me in Time

Ⓑ®

BERKLEY BOOKS, NEW YORK

*For my brother Bill,
and for Dorothy.*

Untitled poems by Helen Wolfe Allen printed with her permission.

This Berkley book contains the complete
text of the original edition.
It has been completely reset in a typeface
designed for easy reading, and was printed
from new film.

MEET ME IN TIME

A Berkley Book / published by arrangement with
the author

PRINTING HISTORY
Warner Books edition / January 1978
Berkley edition / June 1983

ISBN: 0-425-05964-2

# PART ONE

## *1939–1958*

Lover
   meet me in time
      as the ocean rarely meets the shore
      so gently no wave breaking
        marks the joining.

   meet me in time
      where the wild waves
        crash into the darkest
        caves and seek out
          the farthest corners.

   where the sea wears
      holes in the beach sand
      and leaves its eternal
        mark in rock.

   where the winds
      whip and twist
      and gnarl the
      oak trees.

shake me, wash me
   make me new
   and old and
     more than
       what I am.

# One

"She is not like the others were. You have noticed this?"

Ray looked up from his reading. "Sorry darling?"

"So quiet," Lisette said. "She cries so little. You have forgotten how Gabrielle cried? And Dana? My God! He screamed without stopping. But this one. Look how she sleeps."

He looked down at the baby in the basket at the foot of the bed.

"She's supposed to sleep," he said.

She shook her head and took the book from his hands.

"You don't listen," she said, putting the book down on the night table on her side of the bed, then fitting his arms around her. "What I am saying to you is Glenn is a *different* baby from the others."

"And that's bad?"

"I have not said it is bad." She smiled. "You see how you don't listen!"

"Well, now I *can't* listen." His mouth curved into a responding smile as he lifted the hair back from her face, tracing her eyebrows with his thumb. He gazed into the luminous blue of her eyes, deeper tonight, darker blue.

"Two more weeks," she sighed, resting her head on his chest. Perhaps it was something only a mother might recognize, this matter of the differences between children. Gaby, eleven, and Dana, nine. As babies they had been very similar, except for the matter of his screaming. Dana's deafening screams had frequently stunned his older sister into surprised silence, a look of unchildlike indignation lifting her pale eyebrows. This indignation prompted Gaby to hang on to Lisette, to drag at her arm or leg, in a direct attempt to shift Lisette's attention away from Dana to herself. Two-year-old Gaby had asked in very clearly enunciated tones, "Why do you need him?" pointing an accusing finger at the infant Dana.

"Perhaps," she said now, after a moment, "it is only that I have forgotten about babies. Nine years is a long time. I try to remember but I find I have forgotten many things."

"Only certain things," he said tenderly, stroking her arm. He found it impossible not to touch her, daily more in love with the sound of her voice, the look of her. The sight and sound of her was as potently arousing as it had been at the start, but more so now after all the long weeks of abstinence. For a few seconds he experienced a brief flaring of resentment at his own impatience and her damnable fecundity: a few rash minutes that resulted in a third child; three children when it hadn't even occurred to him—at the beginning—there'd be any. Of course that had been positively imbecilic of him, and he'd grown quite attached, in his fashion, to the children because they were proof, somehow, of what he put into loving her.

"I am sore in the breasts," she said, lifting herself off him. "Perhaps I will not nurse her for so long as I did Gaby and Dana."

"Don't do it then," he said sensibly, concerned about her. She was still so lethargic much of the time. "If you put Glenn on a bottle, you'll be able to get a bit more sleep. We both will."

"I will think about it," she said, again looking down at the baby. "I have the feeling maybe it will not make so very much of a difference to her if it is a bottle or the breast."

"You give so much of yourself to the children," he said, so that she studied his face closely, feeling the blackness swirling about her feet, threatening to rise up, engulf her, that ominous heavy feeling that had been overtaking her regularly since the baby's birth. "And tomorrow?" he asked. "You're speaking again?"

"At two o'clock. I must remember to prepare everything, take enough pamphlets, although there are not so very many women now. Everyone is preoccupied with this war. They think of nothing else."

"We'll get into it right enough," he said knowingly. "No doubt at all since Hitler's been taking over Europe; it's inevitable."

"You think so?"

"I know it. Absolutely."

"You would not go, would you, Ray?"

"They wouldn't have me even if I cared to go. I'm too old."

"Good. I wouldn't wish to have you go."

"No bloody fear," he laughed. "Turn the light out, will you, darling? I'll be damn glad, I can tell you, to get shut of this morning segment."

"Perhaps soon they will let you do the bandstand show. Then you will be happy, eh?" She tried but couldn't see his expression in the darkness.

"It's only logical that since Moore's left, I should be the one to do that show." His voice was filled with conviction, determination.

"Of course," she agreed, closing her eyes, thinking again about the baby, how different she was, easier.

He lay back thinking about the show, planning to drop a few subtle words in the appropriate ears, but carefully. Lisette sighed and he put out his hand to touch her cheek. She sighed again and settled against him. Two more weeks. It felt like years to him since they had made love properly. It had been a hell of a strain, waking up in the mornings when it was still dark, to look at her asleep and want so badly to do something about the accumulating weight of his hunger that he had to hurry off guiltily to the bathroom for a cool shower; cold water to shock away the heat, shrink his flesh.

His parents were out. They were out a lot of the time. Dana didn't mind. He sneaked upstairs and found the two little books of Lisette's poems. They'd been published a long time ago, way before the two of them were even married. She didn't like people reading them, she said. So he had to get the books and then go hide in his closet with the flashlight to read them. He thought they were very good. The ones about breasts and thighs and YOU were sort of silly, but the others were really very good and he liked them, read them over and over. He'd probably read the books twenty zillion times at least.

He didn't think he'd write poetry. Plays, or maybe books. But probably plays. He loved the idea of having all kinds of people all saying things in plays that would get put on the radio. Maybe Ray might even play one of the parts. *Maybe*. He wasn't so sure he'd let Ray be in any of his plays. One thing for sure, Gaby wasn't ever going to be in any play he ever wrote. He opened the closet door and listened. Gaby was still downstairs practicing. He closed the door and leaned back against the wall in the dark. Gaby was so stupid. There were some girls he really liked. Why couldn't he have had Julienne for a sister? Or Lucy? Gaby was always acting so important.

The closet was getting too hot and stuffy. He got up, crept out, returned the books to Lisette's desk, then stood deciding what he'd do next. He went to have a look at the baby.

He liked her, which was a big surprise. He put out his finger and chuckled softly as the baby's fingers wrapped themselves hard around his finger. He'd known there was going to be a baby. Lisette had said so for one thing, and for another, he'd been watching, seeing her stomach get bigger and bigger. He'd have known if she hadn't sat them down to say, "You will have a new baby sister or brother." He'd known all the time. The big surprise was how much he liked this baby.

He picked her up and sat down on the side of the bed, playing with her hands, then tickling her feet, saying, "Does that feel funny? I bet you'd laugh if you could." Very carefully, he touched the top of her head where it was all soft, the hole where they'd put her brains in. You could easily hurt an infant if you weren't very, very careful with them. So he always was.

"Glenn, Glenn," he whispered, then laughed, watching the baby's mouth get all puckery. She was nice and soft and her skin was a pretty color.

Maria came along the hallway and stopped in the doorway.

"You wanna give her the bottle?" she asked, smiling.

"Sure," he answered eagerly, holding out his hand.

"You be careful, eh? You don't wanna drop her." She gave him the bottle.

"I'll be careful," he said seriously, pointing the nipple at Glenn's mouth, smiling as she started to drink.

Maria came back a few minutes later to take the baby, change her, and get her ready for her nap. Dana went downstairs to look up *Breasts* in the big medical dictionary, studying the cross-section view with all the little lines on it, reading what it said, but it didn't tell where the milk came from or how it came out. He'd have to ask Lisette about that.

Someday, he thought, stealing a couple of graham crackers before going out the back door, he was going to have his own baby. A girl baby, it would be. Just like Glenn. He didn't know if he wanted to be the mother or the father, though; because as far as he could see, it was fun being either one.

Lisette came hurrying in, late.

"She's pretty hungry"; Maria said, "been making a lot of noise the last half hour."

"Bring her down to me. Then maybe you would do the potatoes while I nurse her, eh?"

"Sure," Maria said easily, loping off up the stairs to get the baby.

Gaby sat in the armchair watching Lisette nursing, thinking it was just disgusting the way her mother did that. She'd do it right in front of anybody. She'd even done it a couple of nights ago in front of *guests*. It was just mortifying. And when she'd said, "Why do you have to do that all the time in front of everybody?" Lisette had smiled and answered, "I did the same with you. You were not bothered," which made Gaby mad because Lisette always said things like that. Gaby was quite sure she said those things just to get Gaby's goat.

Why did they have to go ahead and have another baby anyway? It was bad enough they had to have Dana. They were *old*, for heaven's sake! She knew for a fact Lisette was thirty-eight and Ray was forty-seven. That was old. It was amazing they could still even *make* babies, she thought. And she couldn't imagine them doing *that* to get a baby. Every time she thought about what they'd had to do to get that baby all the blood rushed right into her face and she had to close her eyes and tell herself not to think about it, she wouldn't think about it, it was too awful and she'd never, never do anything that sickening with a man.

"Someday you will change your mind about that," Lisette liked to tell her.

"I never will!" Gaby always declared. She crossed her arms angrily over her chest, glaring as Lisette shifted the baby to the other breast. Gaby groaned and Lisette looked over.

"Something is wrong?" she asked.

Gaby shook her head.

Dana crawled out from behind the sofa to lean on the arm of the sofa and watch, asking, "Where does the milk come from? I looked it up but it didn't explain that."

"A woman's body makes the milk," Lisette said. "Inside the breast."

"But it has to come from somewhere," he persisted.

"I cannot tell you precisely," she said. "I have not a medical degree. I am finished. You would like to burp her, then return her upstairs, Dana?"

"Sure I would," he said.

Lisette fastened her clothes and watched Dana gently rubbing the baby's back. She patted him on the head and went out to the kitchen to see to the dinner.

"Only six women today," Lisette told Ray over their predinner drinks. She sipped at a glass of wine, making it last. "It makes me frustrated, so few. But still, six is better than no women at all."

Thoughtfully, he looked into the depths of his glass. "Why not let it go for a time?" he said. "Stay home, get your strength back, perhaps work at your writing." She looked so tired, he thought, taking hold of her hand. "It frightens me to see you in such an exhausted state."

"Someone must keep on," she said. "If I stop, the others will become discouraged. Elizabeth cannot manage on her own. She becomes too embarrassed when the women wish to ask questions."

Gaby, who'd been closely following this exchange, crossed her legs, lifted her chin and said, "It seems to me that someone who goes around telling women not to have babies if they don't want them, showing them how not to have them, isn't setting a very good example by having a baby of her own. Isn't it just a little *hypocritical* of you?"

Lisette looked over at her wondering how she could have had such a child. At some moments she hated Gaby.

"That will do, Gabrielle," Ray said. "One does not speak in that fashion to one's mother. And you're intruding on our conversation. Surely you have schoolwork to do?"

"I've already finished," she countered. "And when're we going to have dinner? I'm *starving*. I don't see why, if Dana and I have to sit here and watch you drink, we can't have drinks too."

"Dana?" Lisette looked over at him. "You would also wish for a drink?"

"I wouldn't mind," he said with a smile. He'd been sitting pretending to read the book on his lap but, in reality, following every single word that was said. He'd become so good at it, half the time no one seemed to notice he was even there.

"Very well!" Lisette said, getting to her feet. Dislike of Gaby at that moment was burning a hole inside her. She felt a sudden irrational dislike of all of them, even Ray, and an overpowering desire to simply walk out the front door and never return. "You shall both have drinks, of course," she said, her voice remaining calm despite the dreadful fluttering inside. "What will you have, Gaby?"

"Scotch!" Gaby declared, her eyes lighting with excitement. This was very grown up. She was going to have a drink just like papa's.

"Scotch," Lisette repeated, noticing her hands were trembling. "And for you, Dana?"

"Could I have some of that wine you're drinking?"

"But of course!" Dana would, naturally, exercise good sense, caution. She poured a measure of scotch into a glass, and some wine into a goblet then returned to present each child with a drink. "Salut!" She smiled at them. "You must absolutely have whatever it is you wish." She wanted to strike them, but returned instead to sit once more on the sofa beside Ray, resuming their interrupted conversation.

Ray, if he wondered what she was doing, neither said nor looked so. He rarely questioned her actions concerning the children. She wished he would. Letting her eyes drift, she suddenly saw an image of the four of them hitting each other, screaming: a chaos of windmilling arms and legs. He continued to drink his scotch, trying to pinpoint where they'd been in their conversation. "Ah, yes." He remembered, patting Lisette's knee. It irritated her. She didn't move. "About staying home," he said. "I do wish, darling, you'd think about it. It's time you got back to your writing. And once we're into the war, there'll be no problem of superfluous babies, after all. There'll be a shortage of men, rather."

"Perhaps," she said, covertly watching Dana and Gaby sampling their drinks. "I have said I will think on it." These children, wanting so much, demanding so much, giving so very little. Gabrielle greedily gulped down the scotch. Dana savored each tiny sip, appreciatively turning the goblet between his fingers. What would she become, Gabrielle, with her histrionics, and her erratic talent? Dana, inevitably, would write, and perhaps be very old by the age of thirty; he would be someone to whom the world came much too soon. So shocking the things Gabrielle could think to say! Hypocritical? How was it she dared to speak this way to her mother? Accidents occurred, even with the very best of intentions. Would she ever understand about passion? She looked again at Dana. Yes, you will. To you, this baby is of interest, worthy of attention, affection. Not proof of parental hypocrisy. You do not make judgments, but merely see everything. A small man of nine. A shrew of eleven. God help me! I feel I hate these children and this man who will only offer his support too rarely.

I am being too emotional, she told herself, taking another swallow of wine, again noticing the tremor in her hands. What is wrong with me? I am not this way normally. I have no hate. But now I am filled with despair. How did it come to this?

She remembered that first night with Ray. He had been so eager yet so hesitant. It had touched her, his desire to please. He'd been so unlike the others who'd sought only to use the various parts of her for their own gratification without any apparent recognition of her totality. How could she have failed to love someone who cared so very much for her pleasure, her words and thoughts, her company?

Gabrielle vomited violently and had to go to bed without

dinner. A hot water bottle was prepared for her assaulted stomach. Dana calmly finished his wine, asked for more, was refused and continued reading until dinner was ready. By the end of the meal, Lisette was exhausted; she felt as if she were teetering on the edge of an emotional abyss. She would wake the baby for her feeding. That done, she would at last be able to rest, until the baby woke again, wanting another feeding. Just thinking of it, she wanted to cry.

In bed finally, she said, "Ray, Gaby defeats me. When she speaks to me in that fashion, I wish so much to strike her I must force myself to think of her age, who she is so that I do not strike her. I would not have dared to speak so to my mama and papa. Perhaps we are too liberal, too easy with them." Help me! I have a wish to die, to close my eyes and be gone from here forever.

"You shouldn't allow the things she says to bother you," he said, eyes on his book. "She's just a child, after all."

"*Zut!* Nothing very much bothers you."

"Gaby is Gaby," he said, refusing to be provoked. "She'd be precisely the way she is no matter how strict we were with her. I daresay she'd be considerably worse."

No good, she thought, sinking back against the pillows; hearing and seeing Gaby saying, 'Isn't it just a little hypocritical?' So hurtful, selfish. If we had not had these children . . . I would have used mama and papa's money not for the house but for trips we two could have taken. So many things. But it is wrong to think this way. I do love them. I made them, they are mine. But they would make it impossible to love them.

"You're not crying about what she said, surely?" he said, distraught. "Really, you mustn't let the thoughtless things they say bother you so. They're only children." Unnerved, he put his arms around her, attempting to embrace her.

"You remove yourself!" she accused, caught up in the tears but finding no relief in them. "You don't see them, hear them, feel. Gaby is heartless," she cried, "without feelings, without thought for anyone but herself, for anything but this *music.*"

"I do nothing of the sort!" he argued, stung. "I simply see no point whatsoever in being victimized by children. You know you're the only one who matters to me. And you're worn out. The birth and this incessant bloody nursing. I've never seen you this way. This isn't you."

"What is me?" she asked, feeling frantic. "What?"

"Not this," he said, regaining some measure of his composure. "Not breaking down because of some imbecilic remark of Gaby's, not railing at me for supposed omissions. Tell me what you want of me. I can't bear this." He actually looked as if he were suffering. It softened her, broke the spine of her anger.

"I don't know," she said, drained. "I don't know."

He dried her eyes, that grieved expression clinging to his features.

"You need rest," he said. "You're completely worn out. I'm not unsympathetic, darling. I simply don't know what to do for you."

"There is nothing to be done," she said, closing her eyes under the tender onslaught of his caresses. His fingers stroked her breasts; his tongue sought to ease the pain. "I am sorry for . . . all of this."

"Shh, shh," he murmured, continuing to caress her.

She kept her eyes closed, thinking again of that first night and how he'd turned from the band to smile at her. His smile, his eyes made her forget everything. And then, later, during the break, he'd come down from the stand to talk to her. Gerard had departed outraged, leaving her there on her own. After the dance, she'd gone with Ray to his hotel, touched at the sudden loss of his impressive composure and certainty. She'd guided him, teaching him the ways in which to love her. She opened her eyes, raising his head from her breasts.

"I love you," he whispered. "You know how much I love you. When you're unhappy, so distraught, I feel helpless."

"It will pass. It was just a moment."

As she'd done during the weeks before the baby's birth and these weeks since, she made love to him, feeling lonelier than she'd ever dreamed it possible to be. It was like pain inside wanting him, giving him love but being unable to receive it; making slow, deliberate love to him as he whispered endearments, stroking her hair, her spine.

Ray went to sleep at once, after. She lay back tracing her lips with her forefinger, the taste of him slowly leaving her mouth.

* * *

Having made her decision to try staying at home for a while, she turned over the pamphlets and samples to Elizabeth. Looking let down, and uncertain, Elizabeth said, "You're right, of course. It's too much for you now. But it's going to be so difficult without you."

"You will manage," Lisette told her, fond of Elizabeth. "I know that you can."

"Oh, I'll manage," Elizabeth smiled. "Until one of the women asks some question I'm too embarrassed to answer. You're so good at it. It never bothers you. I wish I had your ability, your openness."

"You will be fine," Lisette assured her, although she had considerable doubts. Elizabeth was so English, so rigidly private, so dismayed by her womanliness. "Simply answer the questions and don't think about yourself when you respond. You must try to be clinical, not personal."

"I'll never be able to be that way," she said, then smiled. "But I'll try."


Dana came home from school and marched directly upstairs to the bedroom to say, "Can you explain metaphors to me? What's the difference between a simile and a metaphor?" He held out his English textbook to her. "And how do you decide what rhyme-scheme you're going to use? And what about the meter? Do you decide all that first and then start writing? Or do you start writing and then decide on the meter and the rest of it?"

She looked at his small, perfect face and told herself to remain calm, and tried to answer his questions appropriately. Her insides were fluttering again as she said, "Always, when I first began writing, I used ABBA. Later on, when I became freer, blank verse seemed more fitting." She continued on with her explanation, then reached out to embrace him, suddenly wanting more than anything else to hold him, but he held himself away, seeming to suffer her kiss.

"Thank you very much," he said, retrieving his textbook. "I think I'll go do my homework now."

He'd only just left the room when Gaby began practicing

downstairs. Lisette got up and closed the door, then lay down on the bed with the baby. Opening her clothes, she fit the baby to her breast. She couldn't bring herself to stop nursing just yet, seeing the end of it as some oblique punishment she'd be directing at the baby. Gaby's music pounded in her ears through the several closed doors between them.

"I will go mad," she whispered aloud. The music itself was not unpleasant, but Gaby's interpretations, her heavy-handed articulations and mightily underscored bass notes seemed like some kind of subtle torture purposely directed through the house, up the stairs and past the door, at her mother. How, she wondered, could anyone who was so delicately lovely play with such a total lack of feeling?

It was only her first day at home and already she had the sinking feeling this wasn't going to work. She'd no sooner finished nursing the baby—she was just fastening her clothes— when Dana was back, knocking at the door, then opening it; staring fascinatedly at her breasts for as long as they remained exposed to his view, asking, "I forgot what you said. Tell me that again about the meter."

Gaby came pounding down the hall to push Dana out of the way.

"I need a new music pen and some score paper. I have to have five dollars. What d'you think *you're* doing?" she demanded of Dana.

"Drop dead!" Dana said casually, going to sit on the side of the bed beside Lisette, reaching over to play with the baby's hand.

"You will both stop!" Lisette said evenly. "Gaby, tell me again what it is you need?"

"I *told* you!" she said impatiently. "Five dollars. For a new pen and some score paper."

"Papa just gave you money for your music paper."

"That was *two weeks* ago. All right," she said angrily. "If you're not going to give it to me, I'll just have to quit doing my homework. Then I'll fail and you'll be very happy."

"Take five dollars from my bag," Lisette said, too tired to argue. "Please, both of you will go out now. I wish to put the baby down for her sleep."

"There's only a ten and some ones," Gaby said.

"Take the ten and bring the change back to me. Please, Dana," she gently eased him off the bed. "I will talk with you later about your writing. Later."

Gaby, the ten dollars in hand, paused in the doorway to say, "I don't know why I can't just have the ten dollars. I'll only need it next week."

"You will bring me back the change," Lisette said firmly, getting up to close the door. She leaned against it for a moment before pushing herself away and returning the baby to its basket.

Tomorrow, she told herself, it would be better. They were simply not accustomed to having her at home. Once it became familiar to them, they'd stop making so many demands.

Three months later, it remained the same, and she was still nursing Glenn because those half hours had become a refuge, regular breaks in the day when she could take the baby and escape up to the bedroom for a bit of peace. She'd written nothing in all these weeks at home. She worried about the family planning group disintegrating without her presence to keep everyone focused and active. Elizabeth called regularly to bemoan her failure to answer properly the women's questions. "I go cold," she said. "I look at their faces and make up absurd answers. I do wish you'd come back."

She worried about things over which she had no control, worried constantly, even during those hours when she should have been sleeping. Her head ached from lack of sleep, from the endless nonspecific fears circulating in her brain.

Ray, in his understated and quietly aggressive fashion, succeeded in getting that hungered-for promotion at the station and was now the master of ceremonies for the bandstand show. This much was an improvement because the hours were better. He wasn't required to be at the station until four-thirty in the afternoon.

When he told her, jubilantly relating the details, her only thought was that perhaps the atmosphere in the house might now change. And on the first day of the changeover, they slept late while Maria got the two other children breakfasted and off to school.

The baby's crying woke Lisette and she got up to nurse her while, with a groan, Ray sat up feeling about on the floor for his slippers. She watched him go into the bathroom, heard the sound of the toilet, then the shower. When he came out, he smiled at her blankly and went downstairs. She finished with Glenn, changed her, put her down and went, yawning, into the bathroom to find the towel Ray had used wetly abandoned on the floor, sprinkles of talc here and there, a gray ring around the sink. She picked up the towel, used it to wipe out the sink, then pushed it into the hamper, angered by his lack of consideration.

By the time she got downstairs, he was on the telephone, a cup of coffee perched on his knee. Maria was now upstairs making the children's beds. With a sigh, Lisette reached for the frying pan and began to prepare Ray's breakfast, listening to his half of the telephone conversation.

"Yes, quite. Quite. No, indeed. No. Oh, absolutely! We'd be delighted. What time? Fine. Looking forward. Yes."

He hung up, saying, "Dinner. With Sheffield and his wife. Saturday at seven. I expect there'll be a good group of people there, some interesting sorts. Coffee, darling?"

Why didn't you ask me if I care to go? she thought, scowling, feeling sickened by the sight of the two eggs in the pan, yet watching the edges solidify with a fixed stare. She was startled when his arm came around her middle and he lifted the hair from the back of her neck to kiss her there.

"Do you want some coffee, darling?" he asked again.

"Thank you, yes."

"I much prefer these hours," he said, still holding her. "Don't you, darling? So much more one can get done."

She sighed and leaned back against him, mechanically basting the eggs.

"You know we are already to be out Thursday and Friday?" she asked. "Now this will mean three nights in a row we are out late."

"Very worthwhile," he said, releasing her to pour more coffee into his own cup and some for her. "I'll note it down in your diary when I go up to dress."

"You are going out?"

"A few people I thought I'd see."

"Oh!"

"Had you plans?" he asked.

"No, no. I had thought only that you would be here."

"I've made a date for lunch with one of the chaps from the news department."

"I see." She buttered the toast, put the eggs on a plate, and carried the plate to the table. She sat down with her coffee to watch him eat, trying, all the while, to put words to her feelings. She wanted to say, I want you here. I don't care to go out Thursday, Friday, Saturday. I wish to stay alone with you. Instead, she said, "Please do not give Gabrielle music money this week. She has taken money from me and not returned the change."

"Right," he said, biting into a piece of toast. "Have you enough? Or shall I give you a check?"

"I have enough," she said. "You will be home when?"

"Directly after lunch." He looked up at her. "Are you sure you didn't have plans? I could cancel the lunch."

"No, no. I have no plans."

He looked at her a second or two longer, wanting to ask again when she planned to stop nursing the baby. She looked as worn down as she had three months ago. He smiled and took another bite of toast as she lit a cigarette.

She looked at the telephone thinking perhaps she'd speak with Elizabeth later, find out how things were going. She yawned again, so hard her jaw cracked.

"Why not go back to bed?" he said. "I'll be on my way shortly."

"Perhaps," she said vaguely. "Ray?"

"Mmmm?"

"Nothing. I will talk with you later." She got up carrying her cup and the cigarette and wandered through to the living room to stand looking at the mess. Gaby's music was strewn all over the top of the piano. One of Dana's notebooks peeked out from between the sofa cushions. There were several empty glasses on the coffee table and two very full ashtrays. The sight of the room depressed her. She went back upstairs to sit on the side of the bed and finish her coffee and cigarette.

*       *       *

Within minutes of their arriving home from school, Dana and Gaby were having an argument. Lisette stood at the top of the stairs, listening.

"You just keep out of here while I'm practicing!" Gaby shouted. "You know very well this is my time. You can't come in here!"

"You don't *own* this house!" Dana shouted back. "This is my living room too and if I want to sit in here I'll sit in here and you can't stop me! So there!"

There was the flat, smacking sound of a hand hitting flesh. A brief silence. Then Gaby screamed. The front door opened and Ray walked in to see Dana with his hand wound into Gaby's hair, pulling for all he was worth, and Gaby, red-faced, screeching and kicking at Dana's shins.

Lisette continued to stand at the top of the stairs, waiting to see what Ray would do. He stood for a moment, looking at the two of them.

"Bugger off, the both of you!" he said sharply. The children sprang apart. "Bloody monsters!" he said to himself, making his way to the dining room to fix himself a drink.

In the downstairs hallway, both children stopped to watch him go. Then Gaby again kicked Dana in the shin, as hard as she could. Dana kicked her back, then snatched up his books and went racing up the stairs two at a time. Lisette stepped aside to let him pass.

"I hate her!" he cried, flying down the hall. The door to his room slamming loudly. Below, Gaby began on her scales. Noise.

This must end, Lisette thought, turning away finally; despair clotting in her throat. It was time—again, again, always—to nurse the baby. She lay against the pillows convinced she was going mad.

Ray came in with his drink and stretched out beside her, jiggling the ice cubes in his glass.

"What was that bloody fracas about?" he asked, contemplating his drink.

"Nothing, everything. I have no idea. They hate each other. I hate listening to them. It is impossible, this business of staying at home. I will lose my sanity with all this."

"If you're not accomplishing anything, if you're not happy,

perhaps the best thing would be for you to get back to your work outside. I merely suggested you stay at home because I thought it might be some sort of solution. Obviously, I was wrong."

She couldn't seem to concentrate on what he was saying. The sound of his voice washed over her melodiously. Then she remembered. They were going to talk.

"Ray?" she interrupted.

"What is it, darling?"

The door burst open and there was Gabrielle. Lisette's fists clenched. Ray's hand closed around her wrist.

"You've got to tell that brat that the living room is *mine* during my practice hours! You tell him to stay out of there and stop bothering me!"

"Not now," Lisette said, her voice threatening to go out of control. "We are talking. And you will *knock*. You do not come into this room without knocking first!"

"Daddy?" Gaby appealed to him.

"I believe your mother just told you not now, Gabrielle. Off you go."

Angrier now than before, Gaby banged the door shut and stamped off down the hall.

"Sorry," he said, looking at his watch. "I must fly. I'm on in forty minutes." He got up and leaned over to kiss her.

"I will wait up for you," she said quickly. "We must *talk*."

"All right, darling." And off he went, leaving his dripping glass on the night table. She picked it up and, in one swallow, finished the half glass of scotch. Then she sat staring at the empty glass for some time before realizing the baby had fallen asleep.

Gaby and Dana at last quiet in their rooms and Glenn asleep in the basket at the foot of the bed, Lisette stood naked before the cheval-glass studying herself, seeing the effects of child-bearing on her body. Her breasts were still swollen from the prolonged nursing. Her belly was round and soft no matter how hard she sucked in her breath and tightened her stomach muscles. Faint stretch marks showed on the flesh at her hips, and the sides of her belly. Up close, standing inches from the mirror, she could see that the quality of her skin was changing, going slack here and there. She'd lost all the weight gained during the pregnancy. In fact she weighed less than she had in many years, yet her body looked old. Her legs were too thin in comparison to her torso. Her neck was too long. And her face, she thought, holding her hair back with both hands, her face, too, was becoming old.

The sight of her face sent tears into her eyes. She moved quickly away from the mirror, pulled on her robe and sat down on the bed gazing down at her shaking hands, trying to think.

When Ray came in finally, she was sitting up in bed, waiting for him.

"You did wait up after all," he smiled, starting to undress. "I'm glad."

"I told you that I would. You had a good evening?" she smiled back at him.

"You didn't listen?"

"I forgot. I am sorry."

"No matter," he grinned. "There's so much more *scope* with this show. Infinitely more. I'll be having guests on. And you know they're talking now of four hours a week of on-the-air theater, getting in scripts, having a look-through, the lot. Very exciting, actually. Room to move in any number of new directions. I quite like the idea of the plays."

He went off to the bathroom and she rearranged herself under the bedclothes, slipping off her nightgown. She was so nervous her hands were wet. The fluttery interior feeling took hold of her. What was she doing? Every smile, every word came from some automatic place in her brain that sent out words and smiles meaninglessly.

He returned and she moved over close to him.

"I've been damned worried about you," he said unexpectedly. "I shouldn't have made that lunch date today. I'll not do that again. D'you want me to call back and cancel Saturday night?"

"No. That will not be necessary."

"Be sure," he said. "If you're not up to it, we simply won't go."

"I will be up to it."

"We've got to get you back to yourself," he said, as if he, too, had prepared the things he wanted to talk about. "It seems to be taking you an awfully long time to recover from having this baby."

"So it seems," she said, waiting to hear what else he'd say.

"You know I'm frightful at this sort of conversation," he said apologetically. "But I'm worried. Tell me how you are. What was it you wanted to talk about?"

"I have been deciding," she said, beginning to find him familiar, recognizable. "Tomorrow, Glenn will go to a bottle, and into the nursery as well. It is enough, the time she has been in here." She looked up at him to see his response.

"Good. Very good."

"Then there is Maria," she said. "I think we must dispense with her and find someone perhaps older, more experienced, who will tend to the house, see to the children, cook for them sometimes."

"Quite right! You *have* been thinking! What else?"

"I am going back to my work. More than before. I have been speaking with Elizabeth and if I do not go back, she will abandon it. She cannot keep it up on her own, and I don't wish to see all we've done lost. It is useless my remaining in the house. I accomplish nothing. Nothing. Gaby must every day find some new dreadful thing to say to me." She was starting to tremble, feeling the rage. "And Dana has no understanding that I require time alone, to myself. They take me over when I am here. I have the feeling they would crush me." She gripped his arm. "If I stay home one more day, I will go completely mad. I know it."

"You're planning to be out all day, every day?"

"No, no," she said quickly. "But I must have sufficient time away, for myself, to do something of value. The writing is finished, Ray. I have no more introspection for the writing. It is gone."

"It all seems to make good sense," he said. "As long as you don't grind yourself down more."

"It's them!" she said feverishly. "Gaby and Dana. They are driving me mad!"

"Lisette, they're *children!* I grant you Gaby's a shocker. But in time she's bound to come around. And Dana's not a bad little chap. The point is you've let them assume far too much importance. In any case, I think you've probably made

a very wise decision. Obviously, the best thing right now is
for you to put a little distance between yourself and them. I
can't bear to see you trying to surrender yourself to what you
see as your role as 'mother.' It's not the sort of thing that works
for people like us, darling. Had you been the sort of woman
intent only on playing out her life as a mother, I doubt very
much we'd be where we are right now."

"Where is it we are right now?" she asked.

"We're moving forward. Surely you can see that. One doesn't
halt one's progress and turn oneself over to one's children. My
parents most certainly didn't. And I daresay they did a successful job raising their children."

"I daresay they did," she said softly, suddenly unsure of
everything. Ray's family had been such cold, remote people.
Ray, too, on the surface might seem cold and remote. It was
because she possessed such a deep knowledge of his interior
aspects, his private aspects that she failed ever to view him as
cold and remote.

When they'd traveled to England expressly for the purpose
of meeting his family, she'd suffered serious doubts as to the
wisdom of her marriage to this man. It had been the only time
in all their years together she'd been sufficiently removed from
him to see him as others might: someone often arrogant, someone abrim with ambition, someone of the so-called "upper
class" who let things fall where they might, confident some
hired underling would do the picking up. That was the super-
ficial view. The view privately was of someone with passion,
someone with unsuspected sensitivity, someone with the rare
ability to focus on a point and strive ceaselessly to get there,
someone who could, in bed, devote himself entirely to her
pleasure; deriving so much pleasure himself from these devoted
acts that he had no need to insist on a return of attentions.
She'd been chilled throughout that visit to his family home,
both by the unrelentingly damp, cold weather and by the upper-
class stoicism and superficiality of his family. "One does,"
"one says," "one thinks," "one would." Ad nauseam. Until
she'd hissed at him behind the closed door to their bedroom,
"Say *I*, say *me!* You are not '*one.*'" It had frightened them
both so badly, they'd agreed to cut short their visit in order to

return home and reacquaint themselves with each other.

She touched his face lightly now, questioningly. "I am not ugly for you?" she asked in a whisper, still daunted by that encounter with the cheval-glass, and by her own emotional up-and-down swings.

"Don't be absurd!" he said emphatically. "You're *beautiful!* Good God, what a thing to say! You can't believe that!"

"I am not so sure any more what it is I believe."

"Well, damn it, you're not *ugly!*"

As if to actively demonstrate precisely how absurd this thought of hers was, he took her in his arms, eagerly searching her mouth, his body urging against hers. She felt all at once lighter, freed in good measure from the weight of a number of her skittering, insubstantial fears.

"Do you remember?" she asked. "That time we went to visit with your family. How they frightened me? You remember?"

"Perfectly."

"For months, I have had the same feeling here, in this house."

"Bloody hell! Why didn't you tell me?"

"I don't know why. I have been feeling so frightened."

"Surely you're not still frightened?"

"Less. Much less. Hold me," she whispered. "I have been so afraid you would lose your desire for me, your love."

"Never! *Never!*"

She laughed softly, knowing it was true, and made love with him as if it had been a very long time since they'd touched, since anything but the voices of the children had penetrated her interior. His hands on her, his mouth, were extraordinarily stimulating; overwhelming. Their exchange of kisses, caresses removed her from her self at last, bringing her back into him, rendering her strong again, and ardent; capable of loving him as she had at twenty-three.

There was a moment the next morning, as she and Maria were moving the baby into the nursery, when she felt terribly sad again, and uncertain, as if what she was doing in removing the child from Ray's and her room was something far more than merely a physical relocation. There was an accompanying sense of loss. She would not allow herself to succumb to it, and quickly readied the crib while Maria stood playing with the baby.

She put Glenn down for her nap, sent Maria off to do her chores, then went downstairs to telephone Elizabeth. There were many things to do: an advertisement to put into the newspaper for someone to replace Maria. She seemed able to breathe more freely. She dialed Elizabeth's number. This family would now begin to grow properly and not be allowed to overwhelm the two people who had created it.

# Two

Two months after her thirteenth birthday, it happened. Gaby was upstairs getting ready for her bath when the blood started down her leg. She saw—instantly sickened and terrified by the sight of it—and erupted into convulsive sobbing, holding her arm over her mouth because she didn't want anyone to hear her, or to know.

Terrible. Just terrible. It was the worst thing that had ever happened to her. She'd never believed anything this awful would actually happen—not to her. Now she felt like dying and sat in the hot water appalled by her body, by what was happening inside and outside to her body. Hair growing *there*. God! And her nipples—the very word made her cringe—pushing out. If she grew a great big bosom like Lisette, she'd kill herself, she would. Oh, God, it was all so horrible!

She didn't dare invade her mother's supply of napkins or tampons, convinced Lisette knew exactly how many there were. So she went about for the remainder of that evening and all the next morning with wads of tissue stuffed inside her underpants, gritting her teeth. At lunchtime, she bribed Annette, one of her classmates, with fifty cents to go into the drugstore and buy a box of sanitary napkins.

"If you ever tell anyone," Gaby warned her, "I'll kill you!"

"What's the matter with you?" Annette wanted to know. "Everybody has periods, you know. I've been having them for almost a year already. The people in the drugstore don't care. Why don't you just say you're buying them for your mother? What're you getting so worked up about?"

"Just do it, please!" Gaby said, giving her the promised fifty cents along with a dollar bill purloined from Lisette's handbag. "Unless, of course, you don't want to be my friend."

Annette saw the fear in Gaby's eyes—never mind all the threats and promises—and felt sorry for her. She shrugged, took the money and went into the drugstore, returning with a large brown paper bag.

"Here." Annette pushed the bag at her. "You didn't have to pay me, you know. I would've done it anyway. I just don't understand why you're making so much fuss. I could understand it if you had the kind of mother like mine who'd rather die than talk about stuff like that. But your mother's terrific, for Pete's sake!" Annette was thinking about that time she'd gone home with Gaby for dinner and how nice Gaby's mom had been, how interested and kind, so kind, that when Gaby had gone up to her room for something, Annette had asked Gaby's mom, "Could I come back another time and kind of talk to you about some stuff?" Gaby's mom had known right away what kind of stuff and said, "But of course. Come at any time. I will be happy to talk with you." So Annette had gone back one afternoon when Gaby was having a late class and Gaby's mom had made coffee and told her all kinds of things and answered every single question without going all peculiar or even getting embarrassed. Gaby's mom was terrific. "I don't get it," she said again.

Gaby couldn't have explained her feelings to anyone. They were too complicated. She said, "Thank you," and draped her arm around Annette's shoulders. "You're just about the best friend I've ever ever had."

"Sure! Swell! Just don't ask me to do this every month."

After school that day, Gaby sneaked into the house and upstairs to her room with the telltale bag, to close herself in and open the box, feeling as if she'd suffocate looking at the thick, white, gauze-covered pads; like things you'd put on some terrible injury. She actually felt ill when she realized she hadn't anything with which to keep the pad on her, and she positively wasn't going to go out and buy something. She'd use safety pins. She hid the box at the very back of her closet, making sure lots of things were piled in front of it so no one would see it there.

She wore the disgusting things for four more days until at last it was over, the whole time feeling as if every single person in the whole world could tell by the way she walked what was happening to her. She wished she were dead. She hated having to grow up, having to become a woman. If Lisette found out, she'd probably make some speech about how wonderful it was being a woman, and talk about *sexual intercourse* and *masturbating* and other repulsive things. Gaby would die before she'd let Lisette find out and then have to sit and listen to yet another of Lisette's "little talks."

Dana noticed that Gaby had started pulling at her blouses and sweaters so they bagged in front and, for a time, wondered why on earth she was making herself look so untidy, until one evening, during the before-dinner drinks when Gaby happened to stand for a moment in profile near the lamp and he saw, through the fabric of her blouse, two small bumps on her chest. He thought, Isn't that interesting? She's growing breasts. He wished she were the type of sister he could ask to let him have a look. She wasn't. But Julienne didn't mind. At recess one morning, she lifted her sweater and vest and allowed Dana to have a look.

"Could I touch them?" he asked.

"I don't care," she said, looking around to make sure nobody could see. "Just hurry up! I'm freezing."

Gingerly, he touched her tiny breasts, deciding he didn't care for breasts, after all. He said, "Thank you very much," and helped her rearrange her clothing. He couldn't understand why Gaby was going to so much trouble to hide hers, unless, perhaps, she didn't much care for them either.

That same evening, he had a look at Glenn's chest while Mrs. Petrov was giving her her bath, and came to the conclusion that Glenn would probably be the sort of girl who'd find her breasts very interesting when she got them. Glenn was so funny.

After the bath, Mrs. Petrov tried to get Glenn to sit on the toilet and Glenn ran away, naked, laughing with Mrs. Petrov in pursuit. Dana went out into the hall to watch, laughing at the sight of Glenn flying down the hall. Mrs. Petrov caught up with her and picked her up. For a second there, Glenn looked as if she couldn't make up her mind whether to laugh or cry. Then she laughed. Dana really liked that about her: you could never tell what she was going to do. Sometimes now, he put babies in some of the plays he wrote.

It was Ray's idea to send Dana to St. Andrew's. He thought about it for months before finally bringing it up for discussion with Lisette.

"He and Gaby are constantly at each other's throats," he said dispassionately. "It's easy enough to see how a daily diet of the two of them could drive someone quite mad. I think the sensible solution would be to send Dana to boarding school. I've investigated and I think St. Andrew's sounds far and away the best place."

"But what if Dana does not wish to go away to school?"

"Dana likes the idea of anything that's new and different. Rather takes after me in that area. I haven't any doubt he'll be delighted at the opportunity. They have a first-rate theater and offer quite a number of courses in drama and playwriting. I expect he'll leap at the chance to go there."

"Do you suppose Gaby will be jealous?" she said, attempting without success—as always—to anticipate Gabrielle's reactions.

"I can't see why she should. After all, she's been attending the Conservatory all this time. Dana deserves as much of a chance to develop his abilities as she's had."

"Very well," she said. "I will leave it to you to speak with him of this."

Dana listened carefully, then smiled, and said, "That sounds very good. When would I go?"

"I see no point to disrupting your school year. It seems to me best to plan on starting you fresh come September."

"Do they wear uniforms there?" Dana asked. "I don't think I like the idea of uniforms."

"One dresses for dinner. I take it the classes are informal. Naturally you'll come home during school holidays."

"Does that mean somebody else is going to get my room?" he asked warily.

Ray looked bemused. "Why should anyone have your room?"

"Okay," Dana said, the wary expression departing. "Just so long as I can keep all my things the way I like them. I don't want anyone coming into my room when I'm not here and changing things around."

"Indeed," Ray said vaguely, going off in search of Lisette; wondering about Dana's odd passion for order.


"It's just going to be wonderful around here with you gone," Gaby gloated. "It'll be pure heaven to have some peace and quiet with nobody sneaking around spying on people."

"You're so stupid," Dana said scathingly. "You're just jealous because I'm going away and you're not."

"Why should I be jealous of a stupid boy like you? They're only sending you away to get rid of you. Nobody can stand you."

That hurt. "You're a bitch!" he snarled. "A stupid, jealous bitch. Bitch, bitch, bitch!" He stuck his tongue out at her and ran away.

Seething, Gaby charged upstairs, desperate to shout and kick and scream at somebody. The only one around was Mrs. Petrov, getting Glenn dressed to go out for a walk. Mrs. Petrov was practically a moron, Gaby thought. She couldn't understand half the things the stupid woman said. Disgusted and frustrated, Gaby slammed into her room and flung herself on the bed, pulling at her hair.


Lisette treasured Mrs. Petrov. A young refugee in her early thirties, she came each morning at seven-thirty, left every afternoon at four. In between, with Glenn tagging along after her, she cleaned the house, prepared breakfast for the children and a midday meal—should anyone be home for one—and seemed to have a wonderful time playing with Glenn. She even volunteered to toilet-train her, saying, " I do this for young sister. I do for you, uh?" Lisette accepted her offer gratefully. She didn't think she had sufficient patience to attempt the job.

Certainly, Mrs. Petrov wasn't beautiful, but she worked very hard and didn't need to be told what to do, didn't require constant supervision as Maria had. Despite the fact that her cooking left something to be desired in terms of seasoning and variation, she did make excellent borscht and Glenn happily gobbled up everything Mrs. Petrov put in front of her. She was a clean woman, very efficient and industrious, and surprisingly light-hearted and imaginative with Glenn. She admitted to Lisette one afternoon, "I lose one baby, maybe make one more sometime. Nice. She nice baby. Pretty."

"She is very happy with you," Lisette said, smiling.

"You ever lose baby?" Mrs. Petrov asked sadly.

"No."

"Bad feeling," Mrs. Petrov said, then brightened. "I make one more."

For a short time, Lisette feared Glenn might form an overstrong attachment to Mrs. Petrov. But Glenn seemed to have no difficulties recognizing her mother and made a beeline for Lisette the instant Lisette came through the door. Laughing, she threw herself at Lisette's legs, her arms reaching, saying, "Up, up, mama!"

Lisette couldn't resist her. She seemed so much more of the earth than Gaby or Dana, more immediate, more open. Often, sitting for a few minutes on the sofa holding her, she thought about how Glenn had come to be: in hasty passion, without time to think or prepare, in the middle of a party they'd been giving for some of the people from the station. Their eyes had kept meeting, and Ray had slowly worked his way to her side, taking hold of her hand, to whisper, "Let's go upstairs." They'd hurried, giggling, up to the bathroom, because their bed had been buried beneath the coats belonging to the guests.

"This is madness!" she'd whispered, feeling weak in the knees.

"You're so bloody beautiful!" He'd bent her forward, clutching at her breasts as they made a frantic connection. After, Ray quickly tidied himself, bestowed a last kiss on her mouth, then went hurrying back down to the party, while she unearthed the douche, knowing absolutely how ineffective it was.

It had all been worthwhile. Glenn was a nice baby, and

pretty. Now that Dana was going to be going away to school, perhaps she'd have more time to spend with Glenn, and with Gaby, too. Gaby seemed to be becoming even more secretive and hostile. Lisette decided it was because Gaby was ready at any time to commence her menstrual cycle. It is the hormones, she told herself, needing some valid explanation for Gaby's behavior.

"I want a lock on my door!" Gaby demanded. "I'm sick and tired of people just walking in when they feel like it. It's *my* room after all."

"No locks," Lisette said strongly. "But everyone will knock first. And *you* will remember also to knock first. You must stop entering our bedroom without knocking."

Gaby made a face, muttering under her breath, "You don't know anything. You're so stupid."

"No locks," Lisette repeated, choosing to disregard Gaby's contemptuous asides.

"Well," Gaby conceded grudgingly, "everybody just better make sure they do knock, *Dana*."

"What're you doing that's so secret?" he asked coolly.

"None of your business! Just keep out of my room!"

"She's probably just in a bad mood," Dana said, with an air of knowing superiority, "because she's having a period."

Gaby turned scarlet and started screaming incoherent threats at him. She leaped to her feet, her clenched fists waving in the air.

"That will do, the both of you," Ray said, thoroughly disliking the way these two constantly baited each other.

Lisette simply stared at Gaby, surprised. Finally finding her voice, she asked, "Dana, you have been spying on your sister?"

"I have *not!* I just happen to know that that's probably what's making her behave like such an idiot. She's got breasts now, you know."

*"I'm going to kill you!"* Gaby screamed. *"Tell him to shut up!"* She turned beseeching eyes on Lisette, thinking she'd murder Dana, she really would.

"Since how long are you having periods?" Lisette asked quietly.

*"None of your business!"* she screamed, flying to the door. *"I hate you, ALL OF YOU! And I hate him the MOST!"*

She went sobbing up the stairs, and slammed the door to her room so hard the entire house seemed to shake.

In the ensuing silence Lisette asked, "Dana, you did not spy on her?"

"I did not," he said truthfully.

"Then how did you know this?"

"I just knew, that's all. I figured it out for myself. I don't see why she had to have such a big fit about it. I mean, it's nothing unusual."

"But you know Gaby is . . . It was unkind, Dana. Did you intend to be so unkind?"

"I don't see that I did anything so unkind."

"Ray," she turned to him, exasperated, "please make him see that he was unkind to Gaby."

"One doesn't," Ray said soberly, "simply blurt out whatever's on one's mind, Dana. You know perfectly well your sister is very high strung. The two of you simply don't give each other any rest. I think an apology's in order here."

"What for?" Dana asked, feeling unjustly accused. "I didn't call her names or anything. All I said was what I said."

"I hope," Ray said patiently, "that as you grow older you will learn to demonstrate a little awareness of the sensitivity of others, particularly women. Now you will go upstairs and apologize to your sister, and tell her to return downstairs for dinner."

"No!"

"Go ahead, Dana," Lisette said quietly. "Do this! I will see to the food."

"*No!* I didn't do anything wrong and she doesn't *have* any sensitivity and I don't see why I should have to apologize. She's the one who started screaming and telling everybody how much she hates us. All *I* said was she was having . . ."

"We are perfectly well aware of what was said," Ray cut him off. "You will go upstairs at once and make your apology."

"Or what?" Dana challenged him.

"Or I will withhold your pocket money for a fortnight. During that fortnight you will not be allowed to go out or to listen to the radio. And, if you persist in defying me, you will not go to St. Andrew's."

Dana's expression turned to one of sheer disbelief. "It's not fair," he said, slowly getting to his feet. "It's really not fair!"

"It is fair! In turn, Gabrielle will apologize to everyone for her remarks. Off you go now and tell her to come down directly after you've made your apology."

Dana turned and went out.

Ray followed Lisette into the kitchen, and exploded.

"What in the bloody hell is *wrong* with those two? I've never seen anything *like* it! Out to kill, the both of them. Little sods."

Quietly gratified, Lisette poured him another drink. "I will go to my grave wondering about that."

"No bloody talk of your grave, *please*. Don't you dare leave me alone with those two!"

She looked up at him and he laughed.

"Sorry, darling," he apologized. "That was the last bloody straw. Given half a chance he'd probably have told us he's examined her discarded napkins or something equally as appalling."

"No, no," she said. "You don't do this enough. It is good for me to hear you can be angry with them."

Muttering to himself, Dana went up the stairs. It wasn't fair, not fair at all. He trudged down the hall to knock at Gaby's door.

"*Go away!*" she screamed from inside. "*Go away whoever you are!*" She hated them all, and wished she could die, just die.

Dana knocked again, thinking, I hate you. You're a stupid, stupid girl and a troublemaker and I *hate you*. Nobody in the whole world could like someone as stupid and horrible and mean as you.

She threw open the door and stood there quivering, red-faced, fists clenched so hard her fingernails bit into the palms of her hands.

"*What do you want?*" she shrieked. If he'd never been born, her life would have been so perfect.

"Ray said I'm to say I'm sorry and that you're to come down right now and apologize to everyone."

"I WILL *NOT!*"

"Oh, yes you will," he said with a smile. "*Oh, yes you*

*will."* His voice was light, but the words heavily underscored. He stood a moment longer smiling at her, then, feeling he'd scored a definite victory, went off to wash his hands before dinner. She wouldn't dare disobey Ray. If Lisette had said it, Gaby would've just gone slamming back into her room. But she wouldn't dare disobey Ray. She was always hanging all over him or talking about *"my father,"* like he was God's half-brother. "My father's on the radio, you know." Dana dried his hands and went downstairs to make some notes while the whole thing was still fresh in his mind.

Gaby, in a murderous mood, came down to insinuate herself onto Ray's lap, winding her arms around his neck, and whispered her apology into his ear. Ray patted her saying, "Go apologize now to your mother and we'll have done with all this."

In the kitchen, Lisette enfolded her into one of her insufferable embraces. Gaby could hardly stand it when her mother did that. She hated being touched, especially by Lisette. She mumbled out her apology and moved to get away but Lisette kept on holding her, and stroked her hair, saying, "Gaby, you take everything so badly. It was not Dana's intention to humiliate you. You did this to yourself by the manner in which you interpret the things that are said."

"Oh, he *meant* it, all right!"

"I think not," Lisette said, feeling Gaby's eagerness to escape. "Why did you not tell me?"

"I just didn't, that's all."

"For how long?"

Gaby groaned. "A while. Three or four months."

"You have everything you need, Gaby?"

"I've got everything I need," she said, desperate to get away. If she didn't, she'd start screaming again.

Lisette released her. Gaby dashed out. Lisette watched her go, then put down the wooden spoon she'd picked up and went upstairs to stand beside the crib for several minutes watching Glenn sleep. She wanted, suddenly, to talk to another woman; be with another woman, and thought of Elizabeth, wondering about her.

\*     \*     \*

They had an appointment to address a group the next afternoon. Elizabeth usually started the session by giving a brief talk, then Lisette would take over for the questions and answers and show and explain the devices.

It was always a surprise to Lisette how strongly Elizabeth felt about the family planning work. For someone so reticent, surely it had to be extremely difficult to have to stand and simply listen to the questions and answers. She couldn't begin to imagine how Elizabeth had coped alone during those months Lisette had stayed at home.

Small and matronly, Elizabeth wore "sensible" clothes, "sensible" shoes, had what appeared to Lisette to be a "sensible" husband and three "sensible" children. Yet Elizabeth was devoted to the cause and worked tirelessly, lining up the groups of women, arranging for someone's living room in which they'd hold their lectures. Occasionally, they hired a small hall, but primarily, they spoke to the women in living rooms.

When it came to the questions, Lisette hadn't any qualms, felt no embarrassment whatsoever in responding truthfully, factually. The questions were usually much the same, although occasionally there would be a woman with a problem having nothing at all to do with birth control. Many of them attended because they hoped to find answers for sexual questions. Lisette tried to offer counsel, bothered by how ill-informed women seemed to be.

Elizabeth was very disappointed with the turnout. "I'd counted on at least twice as many. It hardly makes sense to talk to five women."

"If we help five, we have done a good day's work." Lisette comforted her. "Come, we will start."

At the very end of the session, when Lisette asked, "Are there more questions?" a young woman who'd sat silently through the entire session raised her hand looking discomfited.

Lisette, as she always did, asked, "What is your name?"

"Margaret," she answered in a nervous voice. "I, um, wanted to ask you about the, um, diaphragms."

"Yes?"

"I can't quite understand how you, um, put them in."

"When you go for a fitting, your doctor will instruct you in this."

"I don't know," she said, looking terribly ill at ease. "I mean, if I just knew... I don't know... If I could see how it's done..."

Lisette lifted her head and looked at the faces of the other women.

"You would also," she asked, "like to see how it is done?"

They all nodded.

"I see." Lisette reached for her handbag. "I will show you then."

Elizabeth looked horrified and put her hand on Lisette's arm as if to stop her.

"Elizabeth," Lisette said gently, "sit with the others. I will make a demonstration."

"But you *can't!*" Elizabeth whispered frantically.

"Nonsense. Everyone wishes to see, to know. There is no harm in showing. Sit with the others. Please." Raising her voice, she said, "When we are able to establish permanent centers, we will make certain everyone is shown privately how this is done." She removed her own diaphragm from its container and lubricated it.

Elizabeth sank onto the sofa between two of the women and watched Lisette unfasten her skirt, step out of it, then remove her half slip. Elizabeth was positive everyone in the room could hear how loudly her heart was beating. She chewed on her forefinger as Lisette next removed her underpants, then dropped down on her haunches, exposing herself fully, and invited the women to watch closely as she inserted the diaphragm.

"You can all see?" she asked, not looking up, somewhat fearful of what she might find on their faces.

Hearing murmured responses, she risked lifting her head to see that they were all—including Elizabeth—seriously intent on looking, watching.

"How do you get it out again?" Margaret asked.

"Like this," Lisette said, and removed it, then got to her feet.

She set down the diaphragm, wiped her fingers on a tissue, then got dressed. By the time she was smoothing down her skirt, the women were chattering together, intimately, like old friends. Elizabeth, though, looked perplexed as she began collecting the remaining pamphlets.

Margaret approached Lisette to say, "Thank you." She took Lisette's hand and held it. "That was very important. Thank you."

As she and Elizabeth were getting into Elizabeth's car, Lisette said, "You have time to come out for coffee?"

"I was going to ask you," Elizabeth said.

In the coffee shop, Elizabeth gazed down at her hands as Lisette lit a cigarette. Finally she looked up to say, "I could never have done anything like that."

"I did not think that *I* could do that," Lisette admitted. "But I am glad. Someone must care enough to show, to make everything real. It is not my body that is important. It is what we try to do that is important."

"Do you know," Elizabeth said slowly, the familiar blush rising into her cheeks, "I've never *seen* another woman before?"

"This upset you?"

"Not upset. It made me feel something of a charlatan, going about crusading when I haven't any idea, really, what I'm going on about."

"You can believe many things without having to experience everything."

"I admire you," Elizabeth said softly. "You are so—contained."

"Elizabeth, come! I am not admirable. For one moment, I felt a fool, thinking, 'What am I doing? How can I be doing this?' But then, when I looked at the faces of the women, I thought to myself, 'We are all the same.' We *are* the same. What does it matter about my being a fool? It does not matter."

"I've always hated sex," Elizabeth admitted, looking down again at her hands. "I've done all this work for the wrongest possible reasons. I feel quite quite ashamed."

"You have no reason to be ashamed. None. What we do is not about sex."

"But it *is!*" Elizabeth argued, meeting Lisette's eyes. "Of course it is! What else is it about?"

"It is about babies, making them, not making them."

"That's sex!"

"For you," Lisette said quietly, "it is sex. You would like to talk about it?"

"Oh, I couldn't."

"Perhaps you could. I am willing to listen. Perhaps, also, you would be willing to listen to something I wish to speak about."

"What?"

"You are so good with your children. They are so respectful, so loving with you."

"You're mad!" Elizabeth laughed, forgetting herself. "They're proper little buggers, the lot of them. They drive me potty half the time. Why d'you think I'm always so anxious to get out of the house? If I spend more than an hour or two with them, I start coming apart at the seams, shrieking at them like a fishwife. So good with them! That's marvelous! I don't know a mother alive who can bear her children one hundred percent of the time. Part-time is fine. Full-time and I'd probably end up institutionalized!"

"I thought it was only me," Lisette said, surprised. "You are serious?"

"Utterly, totally. I do love them, of course. And I'm sure, in their hearts, they love Roger and me. But I love them best when they're sound asleep and can't make faces if I want to kiss them, or make rude remarks about some idea I express. I expect I'll love them best of all when they have children of their own and bring them to visit. I'll adore every moment of that, knowing they'll all go home at the end of the visit."

Lisette shook her head, pleased and reassured, yet still doubtful. Elizabeth's children were so mild, so very ordinary compared to Gaby and Dana.

"I feel better for hearing you say all this," she said, taking a sip of her coffee. "Have you ever the feeling that you are completely alone, that no one feels as you do?"

"Oh, yes." Elizabeth lost a good measure of her previous élan. "Almost every night of my life, when Roger comes to bed. It's dreadful."

"What is dreadful?" Lisette prompted. "How he makes love with you?"

"Sometimes," Elizabeth said cautiously, "sometimes, you know, I'm quite excited. But then suddenly it's over and I feel angry, and left out."

"Roger, he is open-minded about making love?"

"Open-minded? How?"

"He pays attention to all of you?"

"All of me? You're not serious! I don't think Roger knows there *is* more to me."

"Then you will have to show him. I will help you. I have some very fine books you will read. And I will tell you. You know how to masturbate?"

*"Lisette!"*

"If you wish to find out, to experience, you must start with yourself, Elizabeth. Do you know how?"

"My God!" Elizabeth was scarlet, fumbling for one of Lisette's cigarettes. "No," she said boldly. "Tell me."

"Fine! I will tell you."


By the end of the war, their group had succeeded in obtaining city funding to set up a small center downtown, staffed with volunteers and several sympathetic gynecologists who each gave a few free hours a week. Elizabeth often volunteered to take over the question-and-answer segments of their joint sessions. The only reference she made to their afternoon at the coffee shop came on a similar afternoon in '44 when, over coffee, she said, "It worked, finally. I thought you'd like to know."

"That is wonderful!" Lisette smiled.

"It is," Elizabeth agreed. "That's why I'm divorcing Roger. I've found someone who *is* good for me. I'm grateful to you, Lisette. I'll never be able to tell you how much, so I'm not going to try."

"If all is well, then I am happy for you."

"Wouldn't it be lovely," Elizabeth said, her voice laden with irony, "if we could be with our daughters the way we are with our friends?"


There was talk going around the radio station—now that the war had ended—about television, and Ray confided he hoped it would come soon.

"Tremendously appealing," he said, "this idea of television." He had an ambitious, detached look to his eyes. Lisette knew at once he'd set his sights on moving still higher.

"I'm quite looking forward to an opportunity to branch out,

perhaps be one of the people in on the ground floor. So many of the others are up in arms, terrified they'll lose their jobs. They lack vision."

"I cannot form an image of it," she confessed. "In my mind, I see it like a small film. But I think you would be beautiful in films."

He laughed and hugged her against his side. "Just you wait," he promised. "It's bound to happen. I can feel it."

"Ray, what would you think if I told you of something I'd done?"

"That would, of course, depend on what it was you did, my darling."

"If I told you that a few years ago, before a group of six women, I took off my underclothes and showed how to insert a diaphragm?"

"You did that?" His eyebrows lifted. "You actually did that? When?"

"Perhaps two years ago. You are shocked?"

"I'm not shocked. I'm not quite sure what I am. I'm trying to visualize it."

"And what is it you see when you try to visualize?" Her hand stroked his chest, back and forth, back and forth.

"Truthfully?"

"But, of course, truthfully."

"Truthfully." He smiled as he took hold of her arms above the elbows. "It's too bloody erotic. You are the most outrageous woman!"

She began to laugh.

"What's so amusing?" he asked.

"I thought perhaps you might be angry."

"Come *on*, darling! Now if you told me you'd taken off your knickers two years ago in front of six *men*, I'd be bloody furious. But six women. It's erotic, *erotic*. I hope they enjoyed it. Wish I'd been there."

"The point was not eroticism."

"Nevertheless, that's what I think."

She smiled. "Dana comes home tomorrow. I must remember to have Mrs. Petrov air his room, ready the bed."

"Why are we suddenly talking about Dana? Tell me more about the other. We can talk about Dana any time."

"I did not think you would find it so stimulating. That is not why I told you."

"Why *did* you tell me?"

"I think I am jealous," she said softly. "Always you have something you aim for while I do always the same, the same, the same."

"Well, let me tell you something, madame," he laughed. "You can go on doing the same the same the same forever as far as I'm concerned. Bloody erotic."

"I am serious, Ray."

"Darling, I'm doing the same thing I've always done," he said. "Just fancying it up a bit and hoping to do it with a bit of makeup. But it's the same. And you worked damned hard for that group. Damned hard. Everything's the same."

"I suppose you are right."

"There's nothing new under the sun," he said, quoting in mellow tones so that she laughed.

"I think," she said, "you are crazy. I, too, am crazy. That remains the same."

Dana made an entrance. She could only see it as that: a grand entrance, with his coat slung around his shoulders in cape fashion and a bag in each hand. He wore a soft corduroy suit, with a cashmere sweater-vest and a fine linen shirt. It had been three years. He'd changed tremendously.

"You look very well," she said, embracing him. "You have grown even taller."

"I guess I have," he said, freeing himself. "Who's home? Is everyone home?"

"Gaby is upstairs. Ray is at the station." She recalled Ray saying nothing changes and thought he was wrong. There was a change here. She could feel it.

"Hope you don't mind but I promised to meet a few of the boys for dinner. You don't mind, do you?"

"No," she lied. "I don't mind."

"We'll have dinner together tomorrow night," he said, racing up the stairs with his bags. "Promise."

She stood at the bottom of the stairs thinking of the dinner she'd planned as she listened to the exchange in the hallway above. Gaby opened the door to her room, and greeted him with barely concealed condescension. Dana, in an undertone, answered, *"Bitch!"* his tone acid.

"I am fearful Dana has become homosexual at this school," she told Ray late that night, having stayed up in order to have this talk with him.

Unfazed, he said, "I think we all of us had that sort of encounter at school, darling. Not all of us became homosexual as a result. It's simply something that happens."

"Something that happens. You had this experience?"

"I thought I'd told you. I didn't mind the 'friendlier' aspects of it all that much. I did mind getting buggered about, though. Put a stop to that straightaway, I can assure you."

*"Don't!"* she whispered, repelled by the image. "You *never* told me of this. How could you allow Dana to go off to this school if you knew of these things?"

"I think you're overreacting," he said. "Whatever Dana turns out to be, I can promise you his experiences at St. Andrew's won't in any way be responsible. I daresay he'll face a few rough patches if he is homosexual. But your anticipating that won't do anything more than upset you needlessly. After all, it *is* Dana's life."

Shaken by his imperturbability, she said, "I will never be able to be as you are! Never! You display your feelings for me, but rarely for the children. Don't you care what becomes of them?"

"Of course I care! Simply because I don't happen to demonstrate my caring in the same fashion as you doesn't mean I'm without feelings."

"I am sorry," she backed down. "We won't speak of it further."

"I'm not sure I care for being accused of being cold-blooded. If I'm able to be objective about the children, it's because I work at it. It might be a wise idea if you worked a little harder at it, rather than attacking my way of dealing with them."

"Please, I have no wish to argue. Please."

"All right," he said curtly, picking up his book from the bedside table. "Good, fine." He flipped through the pages, then slammed the book down. "Damn it!" He got up and stalked into the bathroom, then emerged to pace back and forth at the foot of the bed while she watched, shaken. At last he came around to her side of the bed to sit down.

"Look, I know—you've told me for years—I'm not the sort of man who articulates his feelings. All right. I'm not. You know it. I know it. Stop expecting me to be something I can't be. I *do* have feelings. I *do* care for the bloody children. But I *can't* live their damned lives for them. My feelings first, last, and always are for you. The children can go to hell for all I care! I'm not going to have some hypothetical problem of Dana's stand between us. Not his or Gaby's or Glenn's. I don't know how in hell I can be held responsible in any way if Dana's homosexual. My having had boyhood experiences doesn't make me an authority on schools. Or on boys."

"I know it," she said in a low voice, reaching for his hand. "It is not that I blame you. I have no wish to place blame. I am unhappy about it, that is all."

"Don't attack me," he said miserably. "I'm *not* responsible. I don't happen to believe homosexuality's an illness or something for which one should blame the parents. One simply is. Or isn't. You take everything, anything that has to do with the children . . . so directly, so . . . personally. I do the best I can. We both do. I loathe this sort of disagreement. It hasn't anything to do with us. Not with *us*."

"I do not find it so easy to separate 'us' from the children, Ray. Maybe . . . I don't know. We will forget it now. Come to bed. It's very late."

"You said a while back you were jealous of my career," he said. "I don't suppose it's ever occurred to you that there's a small spot of jealousy inside me, a part of me that's jealous of your ability to give so much of yourself. I'd be the way you are if I could. But I simply can't. It's too far along in the game for changes of that sort. I love the way you are, always have."

"I love you. Come."

Ray spent some time the next afternoon before leaving for the station, talking with Dana about of one of Dana's scripts.

"I'll take it along," he offered.

"That'd be swell!" Dana enthused. "Be sure to tell me how you like it."

Ray passed the script on to the producer of 'Circle One,' who read it, liked it and subsequently purchased it. Dana was ecstatic.

"Thank you!" he said happily. "I'm so pleased you liked it well enough to pass it along."

"Congratulations," Ray said, looking a little uncomfortable. "Jolly good show, Dana!"

Witnessing this exchange, Lisette knew at once something was amiss. Ray only said things in that silly, too-British fashion when he was unsure of himself. And when she later asked him, "Did you read Dana's script?" he looked pained but admitted, "I didn't actually. I had intended to but I thought another opinion might be best."

"But you did intend to read it?"

"I did."

She let the matter drop. It didn't seem worth arguing about.

# Three

Dana flew up the stairs and into the room, laughing.

"Eric! Congratulate me! I've sold a script!"

Eric's mouth lifted into a smile. The two boys flung their arms around each other, laughing, laughing; waltzing around the room, jumping up and down; laughing.

"Isn't it great?" Dana couldn't stop laughing.

"Fantastic!"

The laughter ebbing, they stopped to catch their breath, arms still around each other; eyes meeting, their heads moved slowly closer together. Dana thought, You're happy for me. I'm happy about that. He closed his eyes, accepting Eric's mouth. A moment, then Eric had stepped away and was laughing again, saying, "We've got to celebrate! Let's go get some of the others and go out, do it up!"

"Okay! Do you realize now that I've sold one, it'll be easy to sell more?" Excitedly, Dana threw his suitcases on the bed. "I'll work out the kinks, clean them up. I *knew* I could do it."

"I knew you could, too," Eric said, sitting on the side of Dana's bed, watching Dana unpack.

"Did you?" Dana turned his head to look at him. "Really?"

"Of course. You're a first-rate writer. I wish I were as good at design as you are at writing."

"You're just as good as I am. Better," Dana argued.

"Well, never mind that now," Eric smiled, letting his hand trail over one of Dana's cashmere sweaters. "Hurry up and get unpacked and we'll go round up some of the others and celebrate!"

Dana duly hurried, marveling over his good fortune in having a roommate like Eric. Eric was exceptional, and, no matter what Eric said, really talented. And so wonderful to talk with.

For some unknown reason, an image of Lisette came to his mind. He studied her image, experiencing a sudden strange letdown. He saw and heard, for just a few seconds, the screeching arguments with Gaby; saw and heard Lisette forever trying to make peace between them. Why did he have to think of that now? he wondered, hanging away his trousers. "You'll be a fabulous set designer," he said, forcing back his enthusiasm, willing away the image. "Can't you just see it? I'll write the plays and you'll do all the sets. We'll be famous!"

"It's a very pretty picture." Eric smiled.

Dana pulled open the drawers of the chest and quickly laid his shirts, shorts and socks, the image of Lisette suddenly overlaid by an image of himself and Eric kissing. It all felt good, right, exciting. He was once more alive with expectation, anticipation. So much was happening.

They rounded up the half dozen other boys in their group, the ones who spent the majority of their time working on the various school productions and who all shared a common passion for the theater. The only one of the group who superficially might have seemed more appropriately placed on one of the playing fields was Jack Owen, who was big, the sporty-looking type. But Jack spent every free minute of his time writing, even during play rehearsals he sat in one of the orchestra seats with a notebook on his knee, writing. He was so uncomplicatedly good-natured and open-hearted, Dana instinctively sought Jack's company with almost, but not quite, the eagerness with which he yearned after Eric's attention. Eric was so aloof, so sophisticated.

As the group was making their way out to Jack's jalopy,

they received the usual share of ragging from the athletic types. The group smiled and ignored it.

Starting up the car—the boys all crowded in on top of each other, Eric on Dana's lap in the back—Jack said, "They've all got hockey pucks for brains, those guys. Where to?"

Unanimously, they voted down the roadhouse in favor of the restaurant on the highway. The food at the roadhouse stank for one thing and, for another, they were too likely to run into more of the hockey-puck types there.

Dana looked out the window, that image of Lisette sliding into focus. He studied it, fascinated, seeing very clearly her eyes—round and long-lashed, and her mouth—full, but not overfull, beautifully delineated. She's beautiful, he thought, realizing it for the first time. His reactions to this realization confused him. It was strange suddenly to see that he had a beautiful mother. He shook his head slightly, as if to clear it, becoming slowly aware of Eric's weight. A heated pleasure was building in his thighs. He laid his arm on top of Eric's knees and smiled up at him. Eric's hand surreptitiously squeezed Dana's shoulder. Dana suddenly wanted to kiss him again.

Over dinner, while Jack tried casually but without success to flirt with the waitress, the others questioned Dana about his play and his plans for the next one.

"We'll have to get old Bakey to let us put on one of Dana's plays," Eric said, holding Dana's hand under the table. "Get it polished up, Dana, and we'll start working on him."

"I'll get on it right away," Dana promised, giddy with success and the quiet pressure of Eric's hand.

It was all so easy. He sat this time on Eric's lap, riding back to the school, somewhat dizzily aware of Eric hard underneath him. Lazily he daydreamed about their futures, allowing them to intertwine as effortlessly as their concealed hands. Then, once locked behind their bedroom door—never questioning the spontaneity—they moved into each other's arms. Dana accepted it all as inevitable and received Eric's ardent words and experienced embraces feeling honored.

"Let me do this, Dana," Eric whispered. "I want to do this."

Dana closed his eyes and let the pleasure take him. Afterward, he thought how beautiful Eric was, how fair. Their skins complementing each other so well.

"You're beautiful," Dana whispered.

*"You're* beautiful," Eric whispered back. "I love you."

Dana was thrilled, his heart suddenly gone wild. It wasn't in the least difficult to whisper, "I love you, too. I'll *always* love you."

"We can't let what people think of us matter," Eric said passionately. *"You* and *I* know what matters. We're not like *ordinary* people."

How profound! Dana thought. Eric could put words to the feeling of specialness Dana had always had about himself, and now had about Eric as well. Inspired, he went to work with a fury. Old Bakey agreed to put on one and then another of Dana's plays. Life was glorious! The only bit of unpleasantness came via, of all people, Jack, who stopped Dana on his way out of the theater one afternoon to say, "Don't buy Eric's act all the way, Dana. He's the kind of guy who takes advantage."

Dana looked at him, hurt.

"How do you know that?" he asked.

"Listen, Dana, it's none of my business what you do, you know. I like you. We're friends. I hope we'll be friends for a long, long time. But Eric's nobody's friend. When he's finally got everything he wants, he'll drop you and go on to somebody else. I've seen him do it before. I don't care, you know, if you're that way. I mean, that's your business. But you're a friend of mine and Eric just isn't anybody's friend. Except his own."

Dana wanted to say, Eric loves me. Instead, he said, "If you're a friend of mine, you'll stop saying things like that about Eric. You don't know him. You don't understand."

"Okay," Jack said. "Just be careful. Guys like Eric can wreck guys like you."

"What does that mean?" Dana asked hotly.

"Take it easy," Jack said, seeming so implacable Dana wanted to hit him. "I don't think you really know who you are, Dana. And hanging around with Eric isn't going to help you find out. Just remember I'm your friend. I really mean it. That's all. I'll shut up about it now." He turned to walk away, then stopped and looked back. "It's great about your plays getting put on. No kidding! They're very good, Dana. I'll see you around."

Dana stood feeling very brought down. He had a strong

desire to run after Jack, talk to him, have Jack explain his
meanings more fully. He liked Jack. Jack was so open, so
honest. Was it possible he was right? No, Dana thought. He
was just one of the ones who didn't understand how things
were. Hadn't Eric warned him? He shoved it all away and
hurried off to meet Eric.

They agreed to apply to the same college, and were accepted. They did a minimal amount of subtle wheeling and
dealing, and succeeded in getting a room together. Dana continued to feel quite happy with his life, but from time to time,
remembering Jack's advice, was sufficiently uncertain about
his relationship with Eric to question it at those times when
they were apart.

He began to wonder if he was being completely fair to
himself. After all, he'd never really done much socializing with
girls and he'd never made love to one. He was curious about
that because certain girls and women drew at him, catching
his eye and attention.

He and Eric made love frequently. Making love with Eric
was somehow like making love to some extended part of himself, the finest part, the very best part, because Eric was so
wonderfully talented, so cleverly articulate and witty.

Dana couldn't resist giving him gifts, small things he thought
would look well on Eric or please him. He liked giving gifts,
and giving them to Eric, watching Eric's delighted expression
seemed the most marvelous thing Dana could do. Eric never
protested the giving of these gifts, never made a false show of
feeling unworthy. He simply said, time after time, "Dana, how
terrific!" Although Eric was older by seven months, Dana felt
infinitely the older, years and years older, as if the protection
and care of Eric were a privilege to be taken with complete
seriousness and devotion.

Still, he had certain doubts. Not about Eric, but about his
own preferences. It was possible, he thought, he might be the
sort of man attracted equally to members of both sexes. The
idea did hold a definite appeal; the possibility of nurturing
friendships in two such distinctly different directions offered a
potential widening of his perspectives.

So, upon arriving home for his midterm vacation, and re-

calling various of his childhood encounters with Julienne—
whom he still met occasionally around town—he called up
and invited her out to dinner, single-mindedly determined to
test both his sexuality and his preferences. After all, she'd
allowed him to examine her breasts in the schoolyard that time.
And once he'd gone home for lunch with her, she'd let him
watch her go to the toilet. Surely she hadn't changed all that
much.

She was not quite so pretty as he'd remembered her, he
thought, with a degree of disappointment. Seeing this, he began
to doubt the good sense behind the venture. For one thing, he
felt decidedly disloyal to Eric, going on a date with a girl behind
Eric's back, when he knew positively Eric was incapable of
doing anything like it. For another thing Julienne was so overtly
female, so blatantly sexual. At eighteen she admitted to several
"affairs" with a cleverly casual air, plainly stating her availability and frankly declaring, "I've always thought you were so
nice, Dana. I've been hoping and hoping you'd ask me out. I
just can't believe it's finally happening and we're actually here!
What're you studying at college? I'm taking everything easy
so I can get out and go into teaching. Teaching's really the
best thing and the fastest way to get right out and start earning
some real money."

Her nonstop conversation made him increasingly
uncomfortable, although he managed to conceal this with an
air as cleverly casual as hers. Meanwhile, he stored her words
and gestures in a mental side pocket for future use.

"A lot of the girls from the old school are in my classes,"
she went on. "D'you remember Susan? And Olga?" On and
on she went, bringing up names of people he couldn't remember, citing occasions when they'd supposedly done together
things it was his firm conviction were events only within the
environs of her fanciful imaginings. Surely he hadn't spent all
that time with her?

She ate with gusto, pushing the food into her mouth, swallowing it all down as quickly as possible in order to continue
her reminiscences almost without pause. This, too, bothered
him because he was particularly fond of Ginetta's and the food
here and wanted to take his time savoring the especially fine
salad dressing and the delicate sauce on the veal. But he couldn't,

because her incessant chattering and obvious lack of interest in the quality of the food wouldn't allow it. He wished she'd simply be silent so that, if nothing else, he might fully appreciate the meal. Even Glenn, he thought, would have displayed more enthusiasm for the pleasant setting, the superior food. Glenn might be only a child, but she had a certain intuitive understanding of the specialness of occasions and was gratifyingly appreciative of new tastes, new foods. Next time, he decided, he'd bring Glenn to Ginetta's. It was a complete waste of time, money and a fine meal bringing someone like Julienne to a place like this.

Most conveniently, Julienne's parents happened to be out for the evening. When he took her home, she said, "Come on in for a while." He went in with her, still determined to avail himself of this opportunity.

The house, small and spotless and unforgivably pedestrian—he hated himself for being such a snob, but couldn't help his feelings—made him claustrophobic. He couldn't stop thinking about Eric, and the feeling he was transgressing here, on the brink of indulgences that were surely self-destructive and not in the least enlightening.

After a minimum of small talk—Julienne's gushing compliments on several of his plays she'd heard on the radio—she insinuated herself closer to him on the sofa. He looked at her very red, lipsticked lips—they looked sticky, bloodied—feeling faintly repelled yet withal far too curious to stop at this juncture.

The curiosity propelled him past her unpleasantly wet, searching kisses—so unlike Eric's which were sweetly controlled—into a preliminary investigation of the contours of her body beneath her clothing. He was surprised at the immediacy of her responses and the breathless totality of her willingness to have him continue these investigations. She went so far as to assist him by reaching up in back of her and unfastening the catch of her brassiere before boldly placing her hand between his thighs, startling him into an assertive reaction.

"Let's go upstairs to my room," she said eagerly, taking him by the hand.

Shakily, he accompanied her up the stairs to her small, fussy bedroom—thoughts of nothing and everything swimming in his head—watching, fascinated, as she divested herself of her clothing, all the while keeping her eyes on him, urging him to hurry up.

Feeling his interest waning in direct proportion to the number of articles accumulating on the floor—a slithery heap of stockings, garter belt, brassiere, slip, pants—he nevertheless went ahead and undressed, taking care to fold his trousers and drape his jacket over the back of a chair. Thinking about touching her tiny breasts in the schoolyard, he was shocked to see the ripe opulence of those once-tiny breasts.

"Gee, you're gorgeous!" she said, running her hand over his chest, down his belly. "You really are gorgeous. I can't believe it! I mean, you're practically famous and everything and here you are, *with me!*" She pushed him down, knelt between his thighs and put her mouth on him. He thought of Eric, the somehow hard determination of Eric's mouth; comparing him to Julienne. This was so much more stimulating somehow, arousing him tremendously. Julienne had obviously done this quite a number of times before and had developed an impressive expertise, delivering a great deal of pleasure while, at the same time, appearing to work herself into a near-frenzied state simply by involving herself with his body.

What surprised him most was her softness, everywhere: her body, her mouth, her hands. Soft. After Eric's solid, muscled body, Julienne's softness was astonishing. He could, he thought, quite easily understand why so many of the boys—like Jack—were so keen to make love to girls. They were surprisingly nice to touch, touched surprisingly nicely.

At length, feeling it only fair to reciprocate, he stopped her and eased her down on her back, commencing a careful investigation of her body, driven by that curiosity he thought might one day do him in if he didn't learn to exercise a bit of caution. For the moment, he was certainly safe enough. She did smell good—for which he was very grateful—and the quality of her skin more than pleased him; it was so silken, soft, especially her breasts and nipples. He attempted to please her but was still really only satisfying his desire to know. Yet everything he said and did seemed to please her enormously. So, disregarding her already assured responses, he looked at her closely, venturing to touch her and found himself not so much bothered by her, to him, incomplete structural composition, as bewildered by how to go about reciprocating.

She, however, knew precisely what she wanted, and in an alarming gesture—one that almost completely shattered his tenuous pleasure—she widely spread her thighs and arched herself up, whispering. "Do me, Dana, do me!" He looked at her face, then down at the apex of her thighs and knew there was no way he could do what she was asking. She didn't have what he wanted or desired. She was doing things that upset his sense of decorum and propriety.

Suddenly, wanting this ended, he moved closer, aiming himself blindly into her. Having accomplished this penetration, he paused to examine his reactions, deciding he didn't like it. It felt all wrong, too soft altogether, too moistly elastic. She began to move, threatening to swallow him somehow, yet coercing him to respond to her unwanted attentions. Very quickly, he came, then withdrew; frightened, particularly when she groaned in disappointment at his precipitous withdrawal and began frantically stroking herself, writhing about while he watched. And he did watch, right to the end, feeling unexpectedly saddened by her leaping activity and final, shattering cries. How sad, he thought, how very sad and horribly wrong of him to have led her to expect more than he had to give.

Ashamed of himself for having led her along into a delusion, he got up, asked if he might use her bathroom and went off to cleanse himself, then quickly dressed. Upon returning to the bedroom, he bent to kiss her forehead, saying, "Thank you very much," and went directly home to telephone Eric just to hear the sound of his voice, for reassurance. He suffered with the unreasonable fear that Eric might somehow know, might suspect what Dana had done and be unable to forgive him. But Eric sounded like Eric and, of course, Dana would never tell him what he'd learned or how what he'd learned only made him love and value Eric all the more.

The call completed, he went down to the kitchen and stood for a moment looking at Lisette, thinking how extraordinary it was that he'd never actually seen or conceived of his mother as a female, someone soft and vulnerable like Julienne, someone who had opened her thighs and, in pleasure, accepted what had been the makings of him. Looking at her now, his image of her beauty and her reality superimposed upon one another, he felt for the first time very close to her, this tall, wide-eyed woman with her mass of graying hair and long, nervous hands, her lovely mouth.

He wanted more than anything else at that moment to tell her he loved her, but he'd allocated all the love he had to give, having placed it in Eric. For the second time that evening, he felt a truly terrible guilt in having taken what rightfully belonged to one person and given it to another. He'd made love to Julienne when it should, by rights, have been Eric. And he'd given his love to Eric when, it felt, he should have given it to Lisette. He felt torn apart by misgivings, but it was too late to alter events.

Looking directly into her eyes, in a quiet voice, he said, "I think you ought to know. I'm homosexual."

Her eyes stayed on his for a long time. Then she lit a cigarette, took a deep drag, exhaled slowly and said, *"Eh, bien. C'est ça.* It makes no change in my love for you. I hope you will find happiness with your life."

It killed him. He closed himself into the circle of her arms, unable to face the expression in her eyes. Choked, he murmured, "Thank you," then rushed off to his room before she had a chance to say anything further.

She continued to stand, the cigarette burning unnoticed between her fingers, feeling the blow in the pit of her stomach. She'd known. Hadn't she known? It shouldn't have hurt, but it did. She admired his courage, and was gladdened by his trust, but torn with sadness at the prospect of the lifetime of difficulties that was bound to be his destiny. He'd looked neither happy nor unhappy making his declaration, but simply aged, and resigned.

The cigarette was burning her fingers. She looked at it, put it out and lit another. She stood gazing out the rear kitchen window, until this second cigarette was almost burned out. She lit another. Then another.

The next afternoon Ray came in from a successful lunch with his producer to find Lisette sitting at the kitchen table, pencil in hand, staring down at a piece of paper. He went around in back of her chair to put his hands on her shoulders,

saying, "Things are really moving now. A very worthwhile
lunch, that. What are you doing, darling?"

"A list for the groceries. I will be finished in one or two
minutes more."

"Let it wait," he said, his hands pressing into her shoulders.
"Finish it later." He reached over to take the pencil from her
hand, and pulled her up out of the chair, turning her around
to align her body against his. "Come upstairs, darling." He
kissed her on the side of the neck.

"But Ray, just a few minutes more..."

"Now," he insisted, kissing her, holding her immobilized
inside his arms. "Come up now, darling."

She knew she'd go up with him. But she didn't want to.
She felt tired, having slept badly.

"I have some work..." she began.

"You'll do it later." His hands were on her hips now. "Come
on, darling." He took her hand and led her to the stairs and up
to the bedroom to throw off his clothes. He advanced on her,
stripping her with practiced efficiency. Sighing deeply, he bent
her back to the bed, his entire body luxuriating in at last gaining
access to hers.

She looked at him, watched his hands moving over her, felt
his fingers working to stir her and felt a terrible melancholy,
viewing what was happening with a distant, sympathetic sadness. She couldn't seem to respond. His mouth came up to
hers, and she stopped him, her hands on his face, searching
his eyes, seeing the hunger there. She had never refused him,
had never wished to. How could she now? She accepted the
descent of his mouth on hers, response creeping slowly into
her limbs. Slowly. So that he brought her to a point of willingness, then plunged ahead, finishing too soon, leaving her
caught on a peak, suspended. He rested for several minutes
with his head on her breast, then kissed her again saying, "I'd
better get a move on or I'll be late." Looking elated, he got
up to shower and dress, and went out, saying, "Love you. Meet
me at the station and we'll have a late dinner out."

"I have Glenn's parents' night tonight," she said.

"Come along after."

"I will try."

He left and she lay in a sodden, exhausted sprawl,

recovering, too enervated to finish for herself what he'd left uncompleted. She felt angry. It wasn't like him to show so little regard for her responses, her satisfaction. She got up and went into the bathroom to bathe. Then, having made up the bed, she decided she simply had to rest for a little while. Just a little while.

She was awakened several hours later by Glenn burrowing in close to her, whispering, "I'm home. Did you have a nice sleep?"

Lisette gathered her close, holding her, listening to Glenn's soft voice saying, "We decorated our whole room for tonight. Wait 'til you see it! We made flowers and alphabets and everybody's writing is up on the board."

Lisette continued to hold her, struggling to wake up, stroking Glenn's hair.

"I must telephone for a sitter," she said her voice still thick with sleep. "I should have done it hours ago."

"I'm going to go over to Joan's house for a while, okay?"

"All right. But not for too long, eh? We must do dinner early. Gaby dislikes eating so late."

"I won't be too long," Glenn promised, and went off.

She couldn't get a sitter, and asked Gaby, "Will you stay in this evening to look after Glenn while I go to her parents' night?"

"I have plans," Gaby said curtly.

"What plans?"

"I'm going out."

"Gaby, I cannot get a sitter and I have promised Glenn I will go to meet with her teacher. Only one hour."

"I'm sorry," she said, not in the least sorry. "I'm going out."

"It would not inconvenience you to delay your plans for an hour," Lisette said quietly. "I would like you to do this."

"I'm *sorry*," Gaby said again. "I don't ask you to change your plans for me. Why should I ruin my whole evening? She can stay here by herself."

"Eight-year-old children do not stay in a house alone."

"Well, that's too bad." She flounced out.

"You are detestable," Lisette said under her breath. "Selfish, unkind."

She went upstairs to Glenn's room to say, "I can't get a sitter and Gaby must go out. I will simply have to take you with me."

"Okay," Glenn said easily.

The two of them set off in a rush to the school and along to the classroom, to join in at the end of a long line of waiting parents. Lisette stood examining her anger with Gaby. She'd grown no more tractable, no less difficult with time. If anything, she was worse.

Standing there, holding her mother's hand, Glenn looked around at the other mothers and fathers, then up at Lisette, noticing for the first time how plainly the shape of Lisette's breasts showed under her blouse. She noticed also her mother's clothes. She looked back at the others.

A few late arrivals came to stand behind them in the line. The line slowly moved forward. It took a long time and Glenn couldn't stop looking at the other parents and then at Lisette, over and over, every time seeing something more about her mother that wasn't like the other mothers. When they were finally next in line, Glenn went to stand by the door, watching as Lisette shook Miss Baker's hand, then stood with her head slightly tilted, eyes on the floor, listening to what Miss Baker had to say.

All at once, standing watching, Glenn was convinced everybody there was looking at her mother's breasts, at her unusual clothes, at her long gray hair, and hastily condemning Lisette as strange, different. I love you so much, Glenn thought, deeply dismayed. Why don't you look the way the other mothers do? Why aren't you like them?

It was a shattering revelation. She actually felt as if she hurt inside with the pain of seeing, knowing her mother wasn't one bit like the mothers of her classmates. She was silent, thinking about it, as they made their way home. Lisette stopped on the pavement finally asking, "What is it? You are very quiet, *petite*. Something bothers you?"

Glenn couldn't answer. She didn't know how to put into words the feeling she'd had.

"What?" Lisette asked again, aware that something had happened. Glenn never refused to discuss her thoughts and feelings.

"I'm just tired," Glenn lied. Then she did suddenly feel tired. "That's all, mama. I'm tired."

Lisette studied her face a moment longer, then began walking again, Glenn's small hand damp inside hers.

"You did not wish me to meet with your teacher?" she asked.

"Oh, no, mama. I did want you to. I just . . ."

"What?"

"I don't know. Mama, how come you don't wear . . . ordinary things, clothes like the other mothers?"

"I wear what is comfortable for me," she answered, anguish gathering in the pit of her stomach. "You dislike how I appear?"

"I guess not. I don't know. Did you like Miss Baker?" she asked, rearranging her grip on Lisette's hand. "Did you think she was nice? I think she's so nice."

"She is very nice," Lisette agreed, waiting for more.

"I wish you were like the other mothers," Glenn said almost inaudibly, at once sorry for saying it.

"In what way?" Lisette asked, sensing the ways.

"Oh, nothing."

Lisette's mouth had gone dry. She wanted suddenly to kneel down on the pavement and hold Glenn very tightly. "I love *you* as you are, *petite*," she said softly. "Just as you are. And I am very proud of you."

"I know that," Glenn said, sensing she was making her mother very unhappy. She was making herself unhappy. "I love you too, mama," she smiled, thinking, I just wish you weren't so different.

They arrived at the house and Glenn went off to bed hoping to wake up in the morning with that awful feeling she'd had at the school gone. But it wasn't.

Lisette telephoned Ray at the station to say, "I am unable to get a sitter. We will have to change our arrangements."

"Damn! There's a group. We were all going to go."

"You go on your own," she suggested. "I am fatigued. I think I will go to bed."

"You know I hate going without you."

"I know that, *chéri*. But I cannot leave Glenn here alone."

"I know it," he said disappointedly. "I'll cancel out and come home," he said.

"You wish to go, Ray. You should go. You will enjoy it. Go and I will see you when you come home."

"You all right, darling? You sound a bit down."

"It is nothing. You have a good dinner. *Au 'voir.*"

"If you're sure," he said.

"I am quite sure."

"All right then. Get a good sleep."

The next morning, Mrs. Petrov announced, "Now I start to come only three days a week. I have much work to be doing at home. Is okay?"

"You must have this time for yourself?" Lisette asked, wondering how much work she could possibly have. She lived in a small cottage with her husband. She had no children. The baby she'd been hoping to make had never happened.

"Is so," Mrs. Petrov nodded.

"What days will you come?"

"Monday, Wednesday, Friday I come. Is okay?"

"Yes, all right."

"Good, good."

Mrs. Petrov went off to change the bed linens. Lisette went out to the kitchen to light a cigarette—her hands trembling—and stand looking out the window. She felt as if she were in the process of disintegrating. Too many things were going wrong all at once. The idea of having to tend the house on her own four days a week exhausted her. The house was so big.

Ray said, "Hire someone else."

"No, no. I like Mrs. Petrov. She is good. She doesn't require telling. And she is very much attached to us. Ray," she turned away from the window, "I feel so tired."

He finished the last of his toast and said, "You're doing far too much. Do a little less, darling. Then you'll not feel so tired."

"Not in that way. *Tired.*"

He looked at her, made suddenly apprehensive by the sound of her voice, the look of her eyes. "You're not ill, are you, darling?" His voice and manner at once softened with concern.

"Not ill," she said, gazing off into space. "Something. But not ill."

"We must do something about this," he said. "Perhaps a vacation. Yes. A vacation."

"But there is Glenn," she said, her eyes returning to him. "We would have to take her."

"Nonsense! Dana will be coming home shortly. And Gaby is here. Surely they're capable of seeing to Glenn for a week or ten days while you and I are away. Then there's Mrs. Petrov, to keep an eye on the lot of them."

"Gaby will not babysit."

"She'll bloody well do what she's *told!* She doesn't do a damned thing around here except pound hell out of that bloody piano. If she's not going to take a chair in some orchestra and she's not going to take a job, the least she can do is a bit of babysitting for her own sister."

It was decided they would go up north, to stay at the borrowed cottage of one of Ray's friends at the station. Once the decision was made, Lisette turned her focus entirely to the coming vacation, lightened and immeasurably eased at the prospect of being away from the house, the city, the children for the first time since Glenn's birth.

She had been working hard, as Ray had pointed out. Her poetry had been "rediscovered" and requests came in regularly from colleges and women's groups to have her come read her poetry and speak. Her publishers reissued her two books with a minor advertising campaign and all at once she was something of a celebrity. Her family planning work with Elizabeth had had to take a back seat to her speaking engagements, but she continued to go out with Elizabeth once or twice a week to speak with some small suburban group.

Elizabeth said, "It's about time you two had a vacation. You're driving yourself awfully hard. It'll be good for you."

"You will handle the groups on your own?"

Elizabeth laughed. "I could handle anything! Amazing what a good idea it was divorcing Roger. I feel quite as if I got rid of my old self along with him. You go and have a good time and don't worry about a thing. I'll see you when you get back."

Reassured, she began preparations. By the time she and Ray

were actually set to go—loading their bags into the trunk of the Packard, along with boxes of groceries—she felt considerably better than she had in months. Bestowing hugs and kisses on the children, she lightly admonished the elder two to take good care of Glenn and to telephone and leave a message at the lodge nearby should any problems arise.

The place was beautiful. The cabin was rustic with a hand-pump in the kitchen that provided ice-cold water—the only indoor water supply—and a privy at a discreet distance from the cabin. There was a huge stone fireplace in the living room, a Franklin stove in the kitchen and another in the bedroom, a vast, old, wood-fired range in the kitchen.

Ray at once set to splitting logs for the fire while Lisette unpacked the provisions.

"John said it gets good and cold here at night," he said. "I might as well lay in a good supply of wood."

Having stored the food and placed their clothing in the chest of drawers, she went outside to have a look around, finally settling on the step of the small porch to watch Ray finish stacking the wood. She felt an anxious stirring inside, a tension that held her limbs in its grip. She couldn't seem to relax and tried to force herself down into a calmer state by taking notice of how extraordinarily blue the sky was, how good and clean the air smelled. The lake drew at her so that when he'd finished with the wood, she said, "Come, go with me to the water. Perhaps we could swim. The air is still warm."

Very aware of her almost tangible anxiety, he offered her his hand and they went to the shore of the lake where he stood watching as she dropped down to test the water with her hand.

"It is warm," she smiled, rising, studying his eyes. The anxiety turned to a kind of panicky excitement as, her eyes still on him, she began quickly to undress, overcome by the temptation of the water, the luxurious prospect of immersing herself without benefit of clothes or spectators. She watched him watching her—refusing to be deterred by this voluntary broad-daylight unveiling of her aging body—thinking, Please let go of yourself and take pleasure in this with me. I need help, need you to help me. Somehow. Or perhaps I will drown here, quietly go under and not come up again.

She turned, took several steps into the water and dived under. Shocked by the cold, she came up for air gasping, pushing the wet hair out of her eyes. He was still standing in the same spot, watching her. "Come!" she called to him, fearful he was finding her ridiculous, an aging, naked woman cavorting like a fool. She beckoned to him, smiling tremulously, horribly afraid. Everything in her life seemed to be slipping away out of her control. She wanted him to forget his ambitions, his career, to forget himself.

With a smile taking form on his mouth, be began to remove his clothes; wondering what thoughts could possibly be in her mind. She seemed, at some moments, to be traveling off somewhere without him. And he couldn't cope with the uncertainty her solo journeys aroused in him.

"You're quite mad!" he laughed. "We'll both go home with pneumonia."

"No, no," she said seriously, willing him to enter into this with her, afraid to look and see that he'd changed his mind. She dived deep, keeping her eyes open, seeing the definition of the rocks below on the lake bed, the trunk of a fallen tree. Going out farther, the water became colder still. She surfaced at last to see him about to enter the water, his skin very white, startlingly white in this environment. He disappeared beneath the surface and came up near her, swam over close to her.

"It is wonderful!" she said, fearing her inability to smile; treading water, she watched him carefully.

"Bloody cold!" he complained, keeping his smile, his hands reaching out to her; their arms and legs tangled. "Lisette," his voice was soft, small in the vast openness, "I don't know what to do for you."

"Just this," she said, able all at once to smile. "Only this." She pressed her mouth to his for a moment before disentangling herself and swimming away, knowing he'd follow.

They stayed in the water until the cold became too much. Then, carrying their clothes, they ran dripping back to the cabin to towel dry. Laughing. Ray exclaimed, "We should've thought to bring the bloody towels down to the water!" Then a sudden silence, and their eyes met. The towels dropped to the floor. Their skins startlingly cold met and they lay down on the bed.

"I am so happy we came here," she whispered, her hands skimming lightly down his back. "You are happy, Ray?"

"You know whatever makes you happy makes me happy."

Nothing ever reached him more directly, pierced him so acutely as those moments when she whispered, "I love you, love you," and her body lifted closer, her mouth opening against his. Signals and caresses that had always activated inside him a consuming greed for her, a desperate hunger. Her body, her soft whispering voice, her skillful loving touches were everything he wanted, needed, had to have. The ravages of time were of no significance, no importance, because the sight of her face melted him. Her long legs and slender arms encircled him more perfectly, more satisfyingly than anyone else's ever had or could.

He put his mouth to her throat, then to her breasts and she held his head between her hands, alive to all the sensations. This place and the water, his mouth reawakened her to all the responses she'd feared she'd lost, dispelling the anxiety, and easing the terrible tension. She dismissed her separate self, the one who for far too many months had sat to one side of her, silently shaking her head at the antics of these two aging reprobates. He was good, sensitive and gentle and knowledgeable, respectful of her ways and needs. And that was all that mattered, nothing else, not the children or her fears for and of them, not that huge, energy-sapping house, or the work that had ceased satisfying more than the surface of her needs.

He could, with his dominant strength, convince her of the depth of his caring, the resiliency of their union. And while they bent and turned, stroking and tasting the twists and curves of each other's bodies, she committed herself to him finally and for all time. He was right, of course. Nothing else mattered, only their meaning to each other.

Her muscles flexed, going tight, strung to fine wires, she was convulsed with pleasure, at last made so softly compliant that his entrance into her body was peaceful, profoundly meaningful, catching her up in a bubble of breathless elation, a net of caring. He tied her slowly, steadily tighter into the net until she was irretrievably his, solely, totally his. And nothing ever again would come between them. She went with him, let him take her, abandoning forever her separate self. She was unable to provide, on her own, the nourishment needed to sustain that self. She released it, her eyes tightly closed at the last so that she never saw it go.

# Four

      Gaby met George Shea at a concert. She attended because Annette was giving her first important piano recital and had begged Gaby to come, saying, "You've *got* to be there! I'm going to need somebody to cry all over if it turns out to be a disaster. I'm so *scared!*" As an afterthought, she'd added, "Bring your family, too! Bring anybody!"

    Gaby agreed to go but didn't care to pass along the invitation to the family, even though she couldn't find anyone who'd go with her. She preferred to go alone rather than with the family, although going to places on her own always made her feel like a child again, uncertain and unsure of herself. But she'd go. She dressed in her favorite evening dress, threw back her head and made a solo entrance into the concert hall, working her way through the crowd to her fifth-row-center seat with all the dignified mystery she could muster. She tripped over George Shea's feet as she was attempting to get past him. She managed to save herself from falling and, miserably embarrassed and distraught, pushed on past to her seat while George Shea spilled out profuse apologies, following her all the way in to the center of the row, saying, "I'm so sorry. Really! Are you all right? You're all right?"

Finally, sufficiently restored to herself to risk facing him, she looked up to see a big, round-faced man with very white skin, carrot-colored hair, and beseeching brown eyes. Her anger began to seep away as she smiled and said, "I'm quite all right, thank you," noticing out of the corner of her eye that the woman with him was watching the proceedings with an irate expression, which made Gaby smile more widely, asking, "I hope I didn't hurt you. I honestly didn't see your foot."

He smiled at this, revealing white teeth and a pink tongue that moved fascinatingly over his lower lip before he spoke again. "As long as no harm's been done," he said, extending his hand. "I'm George Shea. My apologies."

"Gabrielle Burgess," she said, allowing him to take hold of her hand. He didn't shake it so much as apply a gentle pressure while gazing into her eyes. Then he released her hand, still smiling, to make his way back along the row to his aisle seat. He was at once engaged in an argument by the woman accompanying him. For some reason, this pleased Gaby, and her composure having returned in full measure, she arranged herself to await the start of the concert, thinking she'd been right to come alone.

In the intervals, she covertly glanced over, each time finding George Shea's eyes waiting to connect with hers. By the time the intermission came, she felt quite flushed and overheated. Something very exciting and romantic was happening and she was anxious to see where it would all go.

Waiting out the intermission, she smoked a cigarette, not enjoying it particularly, but of the opinion that a cigarette lent one a certain air of sophistication. It certainly didn't make Lisette appear any more sophisticated. If anything, Lisette's cigarette smoking was, in Gaby's view, like Lisette herself: overdone. The smoking, the endless wine drinking, she was just so damned French. And yet, without even trying to make the best of herself, she could take Ray away. She didn't even bother with lipstick, for heaven's sake. There were times when the sight of Lisette's beautifully shaped, unlipsticked mouth made Gaby want to strike her. The sight of Lisette's mouth did something awful inside Gaby, something for which she hadn't any words or definitions, just an awful, awful feeling. And seeing Ray sometimes pressing kisses on Lisette's mouth, Gaby wanted to start screaming, to tear the two of them away from each other and hit Lisette, kill her, beat her until her mouth was a bloodied pulp.

She didn't want to think about that now, so carefully smoked her cigarette and watched the continuing argument between George Shea and his lady friend. Every so often, his eyes roved about the lobby as if he was looking for her and she calmly waited for him to find her. He did, at last, and kept his eyes on her for several minutes, ignoring the angry gesticulations of the woman with him until she, too, turned, saw Gabrielle, exclaimed aloud and stalked off, leaving Mr. Shea on his own.

Excitement thudding in her chest, Gaby watched him decide. She could actually *see* him deciding. Then he made his way across the lobby to her side, saying, "I guess you saw that."

Gaby nodded, continuing to smoke her cigarette in what she was sure was mysterious silence. "She's leaving," George Shea said.

"She did seem awfully angry," Gaby said, as if she were well above that sort of behavior.

"We weren't having much of a time anyway," he said. "So, I guess that's that. I don't suppose you'd care to join me?"

"What do you do, Mr. Shea?" she asked, extinguishing her cigarette with care.

"Do? What do I do?" His eyes narrowed slightly, then widened and he laughed. "What do *you* do, Miss Gabrielle Burgess?"

"I compose, teach, conduct. Annette is a friend of mine."

"Well, you don't say!" His eyes moved up and down the length of her body: a big, red-headed man who'd assumed complete control of the situation so effortlessly Gaby felt suddenly less sure of herself. "Compose and teach and conduct. And a friend of Annette's. Isn't that interesting?"

"Is it?"

"How old are you? What do people call you?"

"Gaby. Almost twenty-one."

"I think we'll get married, you and I. Let's go, the intermission's over." He took her arm and directed her back to the seats, proprietarily taking claim of her hand and keeping hold of it throughout the entire second half of the concert, not even letting go to allow her to applaud. He leaned close to whisper in her ear, "I like your profile," and, "I'll take you out to dinner after the concert," and, "I'll see you home. My car's parked across the street." He distracted her so totally with all these attentions she had no idea how well or badly Annette performed or what selections she played. While George Shea stroked her hand and wrist and whispered in her ear, a little voice in her head was saying, You think you know what you're doing, Gaby. But you don't. You'd better be careful.

Oh, but why should I? she wondered, looking at the shape of his mouth, the awful yet compelling pink tongue that emerged every so often to moisten his lips. His thumb grazed her wrist, sending unexpected streamers of excitement lazily uncoiling inside her.

He took her to Ginetta's, bought her champagne and fresh asparagus and strawberries out of season. He took her for a ride around town in his black Cadillac and kept his arm around her while he drove and soft music drifted about their heads. He took her home to Remington Park and put his hand on her breast when he kissed her goodnight. She left him convinced all her dreams were about to come true.

Gaby was going to marry George Shea.

Glenn stood in the bedroom doorway watching Lisette get ready. Papa was sitting downstairs with Dana, both of them all set to go, waiting for Lisette. Glenn did a turn to make her dress float, the skirt lifting, whirling, and Lisette looked over and smiled. Glenn smiled back. It was exciting to be going to a wedding. Even if it was Gaby's.

Lisette couldn't seem to make herself move. They'd all be late if she didn't hurry. But her body wanted to go slowly, her eyes kept returning to Glenn in the doorway, watching her make her party dress flutter and fly. Glenn's preoccupation with the dress was entrancing.

Glenn straightened her skirt and leaned against the door watching Lisette put dots of perfume at the base of her throat and between her breasts, and then stand up to pull on her nylons and fasten the garters, twisting around to make sure her seams were straight. She thought her mother's legs were very nice and liked the way the seams divided her legs so neatly.

"Are you tired, mama?" Glenn asked.

Lisette looked over at her again, then smiled, picked up the perfume and dabbed some behind Glenn's ears.

"You look beautiful," Lisette said, standing with the stopper still in her hand.

"So do you," Glenn said, relishing her mother's closeness. She was so soft and her arms, her shoulders were so smooth-looking, the swell of her breasts inviting. Lisette moved away and Glenn felt disappointed, as if there'd been something that was supposed to happen but hadn't. She kept on watching as Lisette put on rouge and applied lipstick with the tip of her little finger.

"You should wear lipstick all the time," Glenn said. "It makes you look so pretty."

"I never remember," Lisette said, taking the dress Gaby had selected off its hanger and stepping into it. The close fit of it felt strange, unsettling. The color was one she'd never have chosen: deep blue. "You like this dress?" she asked Glenn, turning toward her.

"It's really nice," Glenn approved. "Don't you like it?"

Lisette looked down at herself, then at her reflection in the cheval-glass, forgetting to answer. Was it a trick, an illusion? Was Gaby trying to prove some point in selecting this dress, insisting, "You're going to look *right!*"

She lifted the long skirt to make a last, unnecessary check of her seams, then stepped into her shoes and, with a sigh, switched off the light. She paused in front of Glenn in the doorway to put her arms around her.

"Aren't you excited?" Glenn asked, leaning back to look at her. "I'm excited. I've never been to a wedding before, you know."

Again Lisette failed to answer and Glenn took hold of her hand as they went downstairs, wondering what was wrong. Sometimes, it was as if because she'd starting seeing all kinds of things wrong with the family, with her mother, she was being punished in some way for seeing. The punishment was the slow withdrawal of Lisette's attention. At the times when she managed to delay Lisette's rush—from the house, or up

the stairs, or into the kitchen—the entire time she had Lisette's
attention, she had the guilty feeling she was doing something
she wasn't supposed to be doing. Then she'd feel lonely and
want her mother back, wanting things to be the way they'd
been before.

Ever since they'd gone away on that vacation, Lisette had
been different somehow. And when Gaby had announced she
was going to marry George Shea, Lisette had started getting
more and more different. Glenn just couldn't understand what
was happening. Nobody in this house was like anybody else.
When she went to her friends' houses, she'd study their families
and see how different they were compared to her own.

Some of the kids got all excited, asking Glenn, "What's it
like to have a father on television?" and how it was having a
mother who was kind of a famous poet. It all made Glenn feel
funny and embarrassed because she didn't really know what it
was like.

For a while, she made believe she was an orphan they'd
adopted, or she was Lisette's little girl but not Ray's. She
wanted some kind of explanation for why she felt so separated,
so different from the rest of the family. Like Dana. He wore
velvet suits all the time now and had nicotine stains on his
fingers and went around always with a script tucked under his
arm. He seemed really old. Gaby did too.

"Mama," Glenn asked at the bottom of the stairs, "do you
love me?"

"Of course I love you," she answered, turning to look at
Glenn. "You think I don't love you?"

"No. I . . . You look really nice," Glenn said helplessly.

It was a very showy wedding with Gaby in antique white
satin and flowers artfully woven into her hair. After, there was
a large, noisy reception. Typical of Gaby, she'd insisted on
selecting what every member of the family would wear but
excluded everyone but Ray from the actual ceremony.

Mid-ceremony, Lisette whispered to Glenn, "I do not think
these two know whom they are marrying."

Intrigued, Glenn whispered back, "Why?"

Her eyes still on Gaby and George Shea, Lisette whispered,
"For Gaby, this is all a fantasy she has arranged. For him, as
well. They will both be disappointed in what they find." Then,

realizing to whom she was speaking, she turned to look at Glenn and smiled. "I speak my thoughts aloud," she whispered. "Don't take it seriously, *petite*."

She saw the mystification spread across Glenn's features and for a moment wondered what was happening—to all of them. Glenn was steadily growing away from her, just as Gaby and Dana had done. So many complications to life, she thought, sighing as she watched the ceremony. Decisions were made that in some way or another affected the ones we least wish to harm, or to lose. For dubious gains. But no, she told herself. She and Ray had made their marriage, kept it intact and that was all that mattered.

She turned to look at Dana. His expression was one of quiet amusement. He, too, it seemed, was seeing the farcical aspects of this marriage. He was so cynical. She worried about him.

He'd left college at the start of his third year. With the proceeds from the sale of a number of scripts, he had purchased a small house in which he now lived—quite happily, he claimed a bit too often—with Eric, who had also left school. His claims of happiness too often failed to match the disquiet that shadowed his features when, believing himself unobserved, he chanced to look across the room or the dining table at Eric. Their relationship was showing small signs of strain and she feared Dana would be badly hurt when Eric took himself off to someone else. It seemed obvious and inevitable that Eric would. His eyes, too, were shadowed, by what Lisette interpreted as an ambition to rise higher than Dana, to have more than Dana could offer him. Eric displayed a certain ruthlessness that chilled Lisette and made her wonder how Dana could be so blind to Eric's failings.

She thought of Dana telling her, "Really, I'm not a child. I'm twenty, close to twenty-one. And I *know* what I'm doing, what I want. I very much dislike having to explain myself, especially to you. I thought all this was understood ages ago."

"It is understood. But that does not mean to say it pleases me to have to see so much you try to hide. Come talk with me, Dana. *Talk*."

"I will. It's just that I'm so desperately busy right now getting this script finished. I just phoned to keep in touch because I haven't had a chance to stop by the house. But we'll have dinner. I'll take you out one night, just the two of us and we'll talk. I'll call you."

But he wouldn't.

Ray, with his continuing success, demanded more and more of her time, of her. He continued to make social commitments for them both without consulting her, simply writing in the times and places in her diary. They entertained, were entertained, went here, went there. What had started as an effort to save her own life was evolving into something rapidly going out of control. She was being moved not of her own volition but by Ray's perennial determination to have more success, and more. They went here and there, then she returned home and attempted to dig past what time and success were doing to them both in an effort to find the selves being slowly buried beneath the layers of social veneer and professionalism. She reached blindly toward the people they still were somewhere underneath all that. The result was she only felt fully reassured and at rest when she could lie at peace against Ray's chest, listening to the mellow murmur of his voice, feeling the proof of his love through her skin.

The ceremony ended, Ray returned, reaching for her hand, and whispered, "I daresay they'll lead each other a merry dance."

Unable to stop it happening, she dropped her head on his shoulder and gave in, for a few moments, to the ache inside. The tears stung her eyes.

Alarmed, Glenn put her arm around her mother's waist and tried hard to cry, too. She'd never seen Lisette cry. It unnerved her, frightened her badly.

Even Dana was rattled by this emotional display and in the rush of guests and noise asked, "Is there anything I can do?"

Ray calmly replied, "Not a thing, thank you, Dana. We'll be along directly. You might take Glenn with you, there's a good lad. Off you go now, the two of you."

The two children moved off up the aisle—Glenn craning to look back—and Ray pulled out his handkerchief to dry Lisette's face, searching her eyes for a reason.

"You're all right, darling?"

"I am sorry," she whispered, struggling for a smile. His arm was solid around her waist. Her body felt suddenly frail, insubstantial. "I was..." What was I? she wondered, looking into his eyes. What I was, I was young again and free. I had not given my life to you, to these children like a book you might each carry off and forget to return. "It is nothing, *chéri,*" she murmured, reluctant to leave his arms. "Come, we must go."

He continued to hold her.

"Gaby was right." He smiled, smoothing her hair. "You do look bloody marvelous in that dress. Beautiful."

"Oh, Ray," she smiled, "you are impossible."

"Most likely," he said, brushing his lips against hers. "But I love you."

"I love you," she whispered, looking into his eyes; his strength an infusion. "We will be late. Everyone has gone."

"Then we'll be late. This is more important. *Are* you all right?"

"With you, I am all right."

"That's what counts," he said. "Isn't it?"

She nodded, looking now at his mouth. She wanted him to kiss her, to make her feel safe.

"If it were a matter of my choice," he said with a smile, "I'd take you home to bed this minute instead of to the reception."

"If it were a choice," she sighed, "I would go with you. Kiss me, then we go."

Gabrielle felt so well, so happy, in her beautiful dress with everyone there to see her. George looked simply splendid in a black cutaway and silk shirt. He'd bought a house on the Shore and they were going to go there directly after the reception. Later they planned to take a long vacation in the late summer. It was all so perfect.

Midway through the reception, she and George exchanged signals—it was all such fun—and escaped out to his car to drive away laughing, picking bits of confetti and rice out of their hair. She was desperately nervous beneath the laughter but nonetheless sat close to George as he drove, trying to imagine what it was going to be like making love. She kept telling herself it would be glorious, romantic and exciting. But she was terrified. She'd held him off all this time, determined to keep their love affair as poetic and beautiful as it had been from the beginning.

George had sent her flowers, taken her out to expensive dinners, bought her gifts, spent lavishly on her. He was very wealthy. She was so happy about that. He'd tried to explain his business dealings to her but she found it all far too uninteresting and complicated to hold her attention. Satisfied he could provide her with the setting, as well as a gorgeous new ebony Steinway grand she'd longed for, she abandoned herself to perpetuating the romance, holding George off with both hands and frequent mention of her virginity.

There were moments when with his mouth on hers and his hands persuasively curving over her fully covered breasts, she felt overtaken by such pure, blinding lust it was all she could do to stop him when his hands sought to go beneath the skirts of her long dresses or down the necklines. But she did stop him, determined to keep everything right.

"It's too bad," George was saying, heading for the Old Shore Road, "you decided not to have your little sister in the wedding. She's an awfully cute kid. It would've been a nice touch, having her. And your folks, your mother especially, they looked wonderful. I like your family, Gaby."

"They are very unusual," she said, wishing he hadn't decided to talk about the family. "Wasn't it wonderful?" she laughed. "I hope the photographs turn out well. I can't wait to see them. I saw the most marvelous silver frame in Hamilton's last week, just perfect for on top of the piano."

"I can't wait to see *you*," he said, drawing her close against him. "It's been one hell of a long time between drinks, you know. I don't know another woman alive I'd have waited this long for. I plan to keep you in bed for days, weeks."

She laughed again and lit a cigarette in order to free herself of his arm, thinking, Days? Was he crazy? They weren't going to stay in bed for days. Surely it didn't take very long to get it all over and done with.

"We can stop for dinner if you're hungry," he said, reaching over to take a puff on her cigarette, then returning it to her.

"Oh, I ate tons at the reception," she lied. "I'm not hungry at all."

"Good!" He grinned and drove directly on to the house.

She floated through the living room to stand by the windows, admiring her favorite view in the entire world—the lake, with the trees in the foreground. Then she turned to admire her piano. George went out to the kitchen and returned carrying a bottle of champagne and two glasses. "Let's go up," he said, and took hold of her hand, drawing her in the direction of the stairs.

"Right now?" she asked, frightened, looking about the room.

He pulled her over and kissed her so that she flushed and, laughing giddily, went with him up the stairs, to stop cold at the sight of the bedroom with the shades drawn, and the bed. It was one thing to worry over the details with the decorator, quite another to be presented with the completed room. George busied himself pouring out the champagne, giving her a glass, clinking his glass against hers. She had the feeling she was staring, that her eyes had suddenly grown too large for their sockets.

"To us," he said, sipping from his glass. "Perfect! Crazy about champagne." He looked at her and set down his glass, once more taking hold of her hand. "You're not scared, are you, Gaby?"

"Oh, no," she lied again, dry-mouthed.

"Don't be scared. I'd never hurt you. I've been waiting a hell of a long time for right now to get here. Taste it." He urged the glass to her mouth. "It's the best."

Watching him over the top of her glass, she took a good swallow. She felt reduced in size, almost miniaturized by her fear, terrified he would, despite his protestations to the contrary, hurt her in some awful way. He was so big, overpowering. And God only knew what was under his clothes. Regardless of the fact that Lisette had, all Gaby's life, talked and talked about the sexual aspects of male-female relationships, her words had never had any basis in reality for Gaby. It was all something vaguely scientific, clinical and utterly repugnant, in no way specifically applying to her; something her mother talked about for its shock value, or perhaps for some perverted sense of emancipation. Like all that birth control and family planning business Lisette so adored to go on about. Now suddenly it was all real, about to happen, and the idea of having George put himself inside of her was singularly frightening and re-volting. She did like having him kiss her and the way he caressed her breasts. But that was romantic. To take off her clothes, be naked in front of him, have him naked, she couldn't bear the thought of being seen without her pretty dresses, having him see the breasts she'd never wanted, the carefully hidden, carefully ignored nether regions of her body. She quickly drank some more of the champagne, praying she might become very drunk very rapidly.

George took off his jacket and bow-tie, then refilled both glasses.

"It's customary," he said, sitting down with her on the end of the bed, smiling a smile that made her insides turn to lead, "for the groom to get the bride so shellacked she winds up the next morning with absolutely no idea what went on the night before." He kissed her lightly on the mouth. "But I didn't wait all this time to lay a corpse. Necrophilia doesn't appeal to me. I want you right here with your eyes open."

"I think I have to use the bathroom" she said, abruptly rising so that some of the champagne sloshed over the rim of her glass and down her hand.

In the bathroom she stood grinding her hands together, chilled, wishing she could stay in there forever, or go home. She'd go home and go to sleep in her old room, wake up to find she'd dreamed all this. But how could she stay in the bathroom? She washed her hands, took great care drying them, then opened the door and emerged to see George standing in his shorts drinking his champagne. Her heart tried to beat its way past her ribs, all the way out of her body as he set down his glass and put his arms around her, pressing her against his huge, naked chest.

"You really are scared of me," he said, looking a little angry. Was he angry?

"No," she whispered, fractionally eased by the light motion of his hand on her hair.

"This is it," he said, tightening his hold on her as his mouth swooped down on hers and his tongue darted into her mouth, capturing her attention. His kisses did please her, but in a way that made her hate herself. She suffered the kiss, very aware of his hand unfastening her dress, and stood rigid, determined

not to cry as he pulled the dress down off her, then her slip.
Her arms wanted to lift, cover herself. But he had her now,
had her trapped, was removing her brassiere and throwing it
aside, closing his hands over her exposed breasts with a pleased
sound as he dragged her against him, forcing her to feel him
jutting against her thighs.

"I'm going to eat you alive," he whispered, then peeled
away the last of her clothes and backed her over to the bed
where he lay down with her and lined her up against him, his
hands working. All over her, everywhere. She couldn't keep
track of where his hands were going, his kisses distracting her,
making it impossible for her to say, Stop or Don't or any of
the other things she wanted to say. His hands made her overheated, made her squirm—she wished she could beg him to
stop—as they traveled down her back, over her buttocks, up
the insides of her thighs. She tried to keep her legs together,
appalled at the idea of having him touch her there; there, where
everything was so awful.

"Loosen up," he whispered, caressing her clenched thighs,
insinuating his hand between them to find her dry, tense. He
was moved into tremendous excitement by her obvious fear
and inexperience. She hadn't lied. She'd been telling the truth.
He was glad. She jumped when he drew his fingers up and
touched her, her eyes startled, round. "Relax," he smiled,
knowing what he could do with her, anticipating what he'd do.
"I want you to enjoy this."

"I can't! I *can't!*"

"Oh, yes you can. You're going to love it." He put his
mouth on her breast, teasing her nipples with his tongue.

She strained away from him, her eyes closed, feeling as if
her neck would break, trying to fight off the awful pleasure.

"What are you *doing?*" she asked frantically as his mouth
went to her other breast, his sucking at her making her insides
feel peculiar.

"Enjoying you," he answered, moving down to her belly,
dipping his tongue into her navel so that she jumped again.
"I'm going to make you so happy you'll lose your mind." His
hand kneaded her breast as his mouth moved over her belly.
He rubbed his cheek against her hip, her thigh; he kissed her
kneecaps, her ankles, her feet. His wet mouth made her shiver.

She dared to look at him, overwhelmed by his size, his hard
muscular limbs. She was overwhelmed, too, by the reality of
his determined expression and terrible nakedness, and watched
with something close to horror as he wrenched open her thighs—
his strength making her legs feel no more substantial than thin
ropes—then pushed his head between them. She tried to twist
away when he put his wet mouth on her. There.

"George, I . . . George!"

What did she want to say? He was making her body dance,
flooding her with heat and creating an achy, twisting sensation
that was awful but inescapable. She didn't know what to do,
couldn't think; sickened by the sight of her legs draped over
his shoulders and his red head bobbing between her thighs.
Why hadn't Lisette told her about this? Or had she told her?

She kept waiting for it to hurt, but it didn't hurt. It was
good, awful, making her feel weak. She squirmed, victimized
by the monstrous pleasure that jolted her every time his tongue
hit just there, there.

Then he stopped and came up over her, kissing her breasts
again, her throat, her mouth; his fingers pushed up into her,
moving back and forth inside her, so that her eyes strained and
she was running away while lying absolutely still, pinned like
a butterfly to his hand.

He turned her over, ignoring her protests, so he could take
his hands and mouth down the length of her spine. Spreading
her legs, he buried his face between her buttocks, pleased by
her startled cry.

Not there, she thought, hiding her burning face in the pillow.
Oh, *please*, not there! She couldn't bear it. All her secrets, he
was taking them away, exposing them. Turning her again, he
returned to her breasts. She expected him to do that over again,
blood rushing into her face at the idea of wanting him to do it
but she did want him to because he'd pushed her past shame
and embarrassment into something that had no name, something that desperately needed completing. And he did it. He
kept on and on until her body was heaving and her head turned
from side to side, frantic. She felt was going mad; he'd driven
her mad. Shame and pleasure combined as he arranged her on
her hands and knees. She wanted to cry at his putting her on

her hands and knees like an animal, a dog or cow. He did it. He put himself all the way into her. She started to cry, sobbing; trapped by his arms holding her, his fingers playing her like a Bach cantata, all motion. She was going to break but no. Something extraordinary happened inside her. Everything seized, her monstrous body jerking, jolting, the sound of his satisfied grunts of pleasure hot in her ear, then subsiding like ripples closing over a stone. She was suddenly rendered quiescent, accepting his thrusting presence hopelessly, helplessly until it finally was ended and he laid her down, folding her into his arms. Holding her captive against his damp chest, he pressed now-tired kisses on her forehead, her eyes, her mouth. He kissed her into unconsciousness as a shuddering sigh escaped her. And at last, mercifully, she could fly away.

"We're going to start a family right away," he told her. "Three kids, at least. Christ, are you something! I knew you would be if I could just manage to get you down from up there."

"But my career..."

"Come on, Gaby!" He looked annoyed. "If, *if* something comes up in your career, we'll worry about it. But you damned well know nothing's about to happen. You've got your nice piano, the house, all the rest of it. You can sit down there and play to your heart's content, write your little pieces of music. And have a few kids while you're waiting for your big career to happen."

"But how can I? I mean, I have..." This wasn't the way it was supposed to be. He was hurrying her into having children, taking away her dreams, talking about her career as if it were something she'd made up. Children. She was even more terrified of having babies than she'd been of doing all this, and knew that while she might've been mistaken about making love, she knew, without any doubt whatsoever, that having babies was sheer agony.

"I'm hungry," he said, scratching his chest like some giant, satiated animal. "I think I'll go down and get some food together. I told the housekeeper we wouldn't be needing her until next week, so you'll have to take care of the place 'til then. I

laid in a lot of cold cuts, salads. Why don't you wash this,"
he put his hand between her legs, "while I make us something
to eat?"

Mortified, hating him, she watched him pull on his shorts
and then go out. Wash this. He was a pig. All those months
she'd believed he was the one who'd make all her dreams come
true. He wasn't going to let her do any of the things she wanted
to do. He wanted babies. Right away. A pig and he'd turned
her into one, too. For the first time since childhood, she wanted
her mother, wanted to call up and say, Mama, come get me!
I want to come home. I hate it here! For a few moments she
toyed with the image of herself racing into Lisette's arms.
Lisette would, of course, welcome her. Lisette would. You
could say or do anything to that woman and she'd take it.

Well, she thought, getting up off the bed, I'm certainly not
going to do that and have them all laugh at me, gloating. But
what would she do? She ran water into the tub, her nostrils
tightly closed against the stink of her body, her eyes carefully
averted from the slimy ooze on her upper thighs. God! She'd
trapped herself and she hated him.


Eric announced he was leaving.

"I hope you're not going to create a scene," he said loftily,
meticulously folding and packing the last of his clothes. "It's
been years, you know, Dana. These things happen. I've met
someone else."

"I'm not surprised," Dana said tiredly, seated on the side
of the bed with a cigarette, watching Eric pack. "Nothing very
much surprises me any more. Who is it? Anyone I know?"
You used me, he thought, grieved. Jack was right. I should
have listened. You used me to get a foot in the door, to get
yourself started in television. And I let you.

"No one you know," Eric paused, looking at the open bag.
"Say," he said cheerily, "you'll never guess who I ran into
yesterday!"

"Who?"

"Jack. Big Jack Owen. Remember?"

"I remember. I see Jack every now and then. We've stayed
in touch."

"Oh!" Eric looked disappointed. "I didn't realize you'd kept in touch with Jack."

"I have," Dana said quietly. "He's getting married. A dreary thing with massive breasts. I'll miss you, Eric."

"Look." Eric sat down on the bed beside him. "Let's end it without recriminations. We've had some marvelous times, but the truth is we've outgrown our need for each other."

"No. You've outgrown the need. I haven't."

Eric got up again. "Well, I'm sorry about that. But that's the way it is. I think I've got everything. I'll stop by in a day or two for the chest of drawers and the silverware. I don't think there's anything else."

"One other thing," Dana said, opening the drawer of the night table to remove a small gift-wrapped package. "This is for you."

Eyebrows lifted, Eric accepted the package. "Am I supposed to open it?"

"By all means." Dana's hand gestured in the air.

Eric removed the gift wrapping, then stood silent, examining the gold watch inside.

"You shouldn't have done this, Dana," he said thickly. "It only makes it all the more difficult."

"You don't seem to be experiencing all that much difficulty. And anyway, I wanted you to have something to remember me by."

"I'm going to remember you," Eric said, closing the box. "You know I will. I hope we'll always be friends."

"We won't be friends," Dana said evenly, stubbing out his cigarette before getting to his feet, feeling terribly tired. "Ex-lovers make dreadful friends. I'll help you with your bags."

He lifted one of the suitcases off the bed and carried it downstairs, setting it down by the front door, then turned to watch Eric coming down with the second bag. Outside, a car horn sounded three times.

"There he is," Eric said, the package bulging in his breast pocket. "This is it."

They embraced, then broke apart. Dana opened the door. Eric carried out one of the bags, came back for the second. Without another word, Dana closed the door and went to fix

himself a drink. Depressed, he sat down in the suddenly op-
pressive living room with his drink. He wouldn't cry, absolutely
would not. In fact, he thought, the worst possible thing for me
to do is sit here and indulge this depression. He got up, abandoning the drink, and went out, thinking he'd stop by the house.
If Glenn was there, he'd take her for a walk, or to a movie.
Something. He had to see someone who wouldn't abrade his
already raw nerves. And Glenn was the ideal one.

Lisette said, "Dana, what a good surprise! You will stay,
have dinner?"

"I thought I'd take Glenn out for dinner."

"Oh mama, can I?" Glenn danced from one foot to the other.

Lisette didn't seem to hear her, she was studying Dana's
face, his eyes.

"It is ended, eh?" she said softly.

"It doesn't matter." He tried to be offhanded.

"Why don't you stay, have dinner? We will talk."

"I'd really rather not."

"Mama, can I go?"

Lisette looked at her finally, then reached out to place her
hand on the top of Glenn's head.

"Go up and change your clothes. You will go."

Glenn threw her arms around Lisette's waist and hugged
her. "Thank you," she cried, then dashed off to change.

Dana, sensing some sort of interrogation pending, said,
"Please don't ask me. I honestly can't right now. I'm not up
to it."

Lisette lit a cigarette, then, on impulse, held her hand out
to him. He took it, kept hold of it for a moment, then let go
saying, "I think I'll just go up and help Glenn pick out a dress."

So many things happened all at once. First, Gaby got married. Then Eric went away and left Dana. Right after that, she
got her first period. She thought it was very exciting, until
Lisette sat her down to say, "When the time comes that you
find someone you will wish to make love with, you will make
an appointment to have yourself fitted with a diaphragm." Glenn
stared at her in disbelief.

"That's a million years away, mama. I don't have to worry about things like that *now.*"

"Of course it is not for now," Lisette said gently. "I only wish for you to be prepared for your future. You will find now sexual feelings come to you. So it will be good for you to masturbate. It is the very best way to know yourself."

*"Mama!"*

"One day," Lisette said, keeping her voice soft, "you will be grateful for the things I am telling you now. These are not matters for disappointment, *petite*. Facts of life. Important facts. Important for the woman you will be. To experience love fully, you must know yourself well. You find me terrible." She smiled, masking her dismay at Glenn's reaction. "But if you have a daughter one day, I hope you will tell all this to her. It will perhaps make her life easier."

"How's it going to make my life any easier? Sometimes, it's as if you think I'm twenty-five or something. And other times, it's as if I'm not even here at all. You and papa. I don't know," she said, bewildered. "It's not . . . right. I don't know."

"What is not right?"

"Oh, I don't know. I was so happy. And now it's all . . . spoiled."

Lisette drew Glenn to her and held her saying, "I wish to spoil nothing for you. I wish you could be glad you have someone who comes to be truthful with you. I love you. I care for the future you will have, Glenn. Nothing is spoiled. I tell you the things I do because I wish for your life to be the best it can be. Does that spoil everything for you?"

"No." Glenn sighed, comforted by her mother's closeness. "I guess not."

"Making love is a very great pleasure when you know your own self, your body. You will know and you will find pleasure."

"Okay, mama." Glenn gave in, made drowsy by the scent of Lisette's perfume, her softness. "I love you," she murmured, eyes half closing. She opened her eyes at the sudden intensity of her mother's embrace.

Lisette clung to her fiercely for several moments, thinking, Yes, love me, love me, I need you to have love for me, to forgive and love me.

\*     \*     \*

Glenn arrived home early from school one afternoon on one of Mrs. Petrov's days off. She'd cut a study class, feeling bored, and decided she'd go home, get her homework out of the way and then perhaps take her sketchpad and go over to the park to draw for a while. On the way to her room, she stopped, noticing the door to her parents' room ajar, hearing whispers. From where she stood in the hall she could see them reflected in the dressing table mirror. She stood, astonished by the sight of the two naked people on the bed, making love. She didn't want to watch, knew she shouldn't, but couldn't help herself. She was fascinated by this new, naked view of these two people, aesthetically drawn to the lines, the curves, the really wonderful correlation of entwining limbs. Breath-held, she watching their mirrored reflections, saw them kissing and caressing for a very long time, touching each other. Captivated by their involvement, she was rooted to the spot as she watched. Both of them wore expressions she'd never seen before: beatific, serene expressions. She saw them join and begin a lengthy, really very beautiful ride together that peaked in a series of cries emanating from Lisette as she sinuously wound herself around Ray, arching closer, her head straining back; the line of her throat compellingly vulnerable. He continued moving a minute or two longer before emitting a wild, strangled cry and collapsing on Lisette's breasts. Glenn blinked several times, then wet her lips.

She moved away, went on to her room to sit in a state of astounded gladness. That had been real. She'd seen it, heard it. Real. She could more readily understand now why her mother had so diligently urged her to be prepared. That was something it might be very nice indeed to do some day. She loved her parents—suddenly, fully—for having seen them in so private a performance; loved them for the way they'd looked at each other, touched each other; the expressions their faces had worn. She felt a certain piercing sadness too, wishing somehow that what they gave each other could have been what they gave to her. In an instant of purest clarity, she very completely understood that, in that way, her mother and father gave only to each other; completely giving, nothing withheld; their purest love.

As quickly as the insight had come to her, it evaporated, and she was left in a state close to awe at what she'd seen, and lonely for having seen it. All at once, she wanted someone in her life who could love her so unreservedly, with such tenderness.

Upon arriving downstairs, Lisette was surprised to find Glenn sitting curled up on the sofa, and further surprised by the quality of the smile Glenn offered her. She smiled back, saying, "You are home early, *petite*," to which Glenn answered, "I cut study hall."

Lisette continued on to the kitchen, to stand with her heart thudding, blood suffusing her face as she realized Glenn had seen them.

It was all very well to be open and frank about sex. But it was something else entirely to have one's young daughter witness a heated sexual performance. Her mind raced backward, trying to think of what they'd done, how they'd done it, and how long Glenn might have watched. Undoubtedly, she'd watched. That smile. Not a condescending one or an offended one, but a smile containing some understanding. It is all right, she told herself, closing her mind to the details. It is all right. Glenn does not make cruel judgments on us. Not Glenn. Not yet.

But, my God! she thought, her face on fire as she thought of Glenn standing outside watching her and Ray; seeing the two of them doing things never intended to be seen by a third. She recalled the afternoon she'd demonstrated to that group of women how to insert and remove a diaphragm, intent on finding a link. She couldn't. She shook her head, shook away the terribly naked feeling she had, standing fully dressed and ready to go out.

Impulsively, she kissed Glenn before going off to meet Elizabeth, stopped for a moment by Glenn's eyes raised to meet her own, the sight of Glenn's hand poised over her sketchbook. Then she smiled and went on her way, thinking, She sees. Eyes that transpose color, light, tone from here to there, lines and shadings made on paper. She is an artist with the eyes of an artist and not those of a child, or of someone who fails to understand.

Glenn, she thought, feeling lifted, will come to me. She alone will, in time, return to me.

"You seem a bit preoccupied," Elizabeth said. "Anything wrong?"

"I am not sure how I feel. I have a wish to talk about it."

"Something's happened?"

"Glenn. I am quite sure she saw what she was not meant to see."

"Oh?" Elizabeth turned to look at her, eyes wide. "Really? Good God! I've always had a horror of that happening to me."

"Yes?"

"Thanks to you, I've come a long way, Lisette. But that far I doubt I'll ever come. You didn't . . . I mean, did you know she was watching?"

"Not until after."

"How do you *feel?*"

"Strange," Lisette admitted. "I have tried to tell myself it is like that afternoon, with the diaphragm. But it is not the same. Not the same. I feel very . . . I have no word for it." She held her hand in the air and fluttered it. "Like that. Afraid. As if someone comes at me with a big knife. We have time," she said, inspired. "I have a need for a drink. Yes?"

"God, yes!" Elizabeth said soberly. "Just imagining it, I think I could do with one myself."

"I am very grateful for you, Elizabeth. Sometimes, I think I would go mad if I did not have you to speak with."

"You'll never go mad," Elizabeth smiled. "Not you."

You are wrong, Lisette thought. I feel very close to madness much of the time. Aloud, she said, "A large drink. A very large drink." And then she laughed, hearing the strangeness of it echoing inside her head for a long time afterward.

# Five

Gaby felt she'd hardly had time to acclimate herself to the house and to being called Mrs. Shea when he had her pregnant and sick with it for weeks, months. And when he wasn't hurrying off to do his business in town, he was hurrying her up to the bedroom to strip off her clothes, forcing her to do the things she hated, things that compounded her steadily growing hatred of him. Arranging her this way and that, he pushed himself at one end of her or the other, accusing her of, "... being a goddamned rag doll, Gaby. I thought once you knew what it was all about and started enjoying it, you'd get a little involved." He dragged her head down to his lap, to come spewing into her mouth so that she erupted into convulsive sobbing and ran off to the bathroom to vomit, wishing she'd never seen him, never married him. She began phoning Lisette in the mornings after George had left, to chat, for the first time in her life experiencing a measure of gratitude that Lisette was there at the other end to listen. Gaby tried to cover her misery with chatty comments about the house, the garden, the decorating, hiding it all for months until it refused to be contained any longer and, bursting into tears, she sobbed into the telephone, exclaiming, "I *hate* him! I don't *want* a baby! I don't even *like* babies."

Lisette, for her part, had been expecting this all along. But her expectation in no way equipped her to deal with Gaby's sudden attempts to render Lisette sympathetic to her plight and to offer advice. She did try, saying, "If you are so unhappy, don't stay with him. You must decide what it is you want," and tried to advise her as she might have advised one of the women in the groups she addressed: with logic and gentleness. But Gaby wasn't satisfied with Lisette's advice. She wanted something more, much more: to be told what to do, how to do it and where and when. Lisette couldn't do that, especially when Gaby—once past her hysterics—expressed her other feelings.

"I love the house," she said, a longing to her voice. "And my piano." Silently she added the money George gave her to the list.

"Gaby," Lisette said patiently, quietly, "you will have to decide and do what is the best for you."

Gaby, losing interest in what seemed to her to be motherly platitudes, said, "I'll think about it," and hung up to wander through the house, letting her hand trail over this piece and that piece, torn by her inability to make a decision.

Lisette began to dread the daily calls.

"She wishes to leave him but does not wish to leave his money," she told Ray. "She wants me to make the decision for her. But if I say to her, Come home. Leave him and come home, she will blame me later for destroying her marriage. What is it I am supposed to do?"

"I'd say just what you're doing," Ray said. "I can't say I'm surprised. At any of it."

"They will come to a bad end," Lisette said fearfully. "This will end badly. Why must she blame me?" she asked him, her voice rising. "I do *not* understand this! I cannot understand it! That she must blame me for her mistakes, her misfortunes. I did not say to her, Marry him, Do not marry him. It was her decision. But every morning, the telephone rings and she is there and I can hear the blame in her voice. Why? What is it that I did wrong with her?"

"Why do you insist on believing you've done something

'wrong' with her?" Ray exclaimed angrily. "I've said for years and years that Gaby is Gaby. She is the way she is. It's no fault of yours."

"But I am the one she telephones, the one she complains to. What am I to do?"

"She's going to have to decide for herself. You know it and I know it. There's no point to getting yourself so worked up about it."

"There *is* a point," she said. "There is very much a point. She must have someone to blame for her failures, her unhappiness, and she has delegated me. I cannot bear very much more of this!"

"Then tell her so! Bloody hell! She's done nothing but create problems since the day she was born. I can tell you I'm damned tired of it. Tell her and have done with it!"

"What," she asked quietly, "precisely is it you think I am to tell her?"

"Tell her to solve her own problems and let it go at that! Please," he said more softly. "*I* can't bear to see what it's doing to you. Write her off," he said abruptly. "Write her off as I've done. She's bound and determined to create hell no matter where she is or what she's doing. Accept that and treat her accordingly."

"I can't, Ray. She's my child. I can't do that."

"Then you'll have to go on putting up with all this nonsense."

"Yes," she said, looking down at her wrists, noticing how prominent her veins were.

George just wouldn't leave her alone, even when she was huge and could hardly move around and the doctor had said there was to be no more lovemaking until after the baby was born. George ignored all that.

"You'd say anything!" he shouted. "Anything to get out of it! And you know you love every single minute of it!"

He made love to her, disregarding her protestations, her cries of pain. Accusing her of lying, endlessly lying in order to avoid him. "You're driving me crazy with your evasions, all these idiotic complaints!" He grinned every time he succeeded in making her respond. She despised him a bit more for every orgasm he gave her, loathing his hands, his mouth, his hideous erections, despairing over her entrapment, the pregnancy. He interrupted meals in order to fondle her. She had to believe he was crazy, and wondered heartbrokenly how she could have made such an epic mistake, believing him to be romantic, ideal, the one she'd been waiting for.

She approached the baby's due date in a growing state of terror, convinced George would somehow injure her with his constant, ceaseless invasions of her body.

Her labor started late one afternoon and, in a panic, she ran to telephone her doctor who advised her, "Calm down. It'll be a good few hours before you need to come in."

"But how do you *know* that?" she asked him.

"I know it," he said, with tried patience. "Just relax!"

She couldn't. She wanted to be at the hospital that minute. Her bag was packed, ready; it had been for weeks. But she'd made almost no preparations for the baby, unable to bring herself to start outfitting the room George had designated would be the nursery. She'd bought a few things only because Lisette had made such a fuss, taking her downtown shopping, declaring, "You must let papa and me make you a gift of some things for the baby." To demonstrate her own nonexistent interest in the coming child, she had picked out a few sleeper suits. Everything else for the child had come from Lisette.

She was in the bedroom putting one or two last minute items into her bag when George arrived home.

"I've got to go to the hospital," she told him, hurrying as best she could to change into her one decent-looking dress. She'd die before she let anyone see her in the grotesque sacks she'd been wearing the past few months.

George stood watching her with an expression she'd come to recognize and fear and she couldn't believe that *that* could be on his mind when she was telling him she had to go to the hospital because the baby was coming. What followed was a nightmare. She simply couldn't make herself believe she'd actually gone ahead and married this man. He was, without question, a complete madman.

His eyes narrowing, his mouth spilling out the ritual string of accusations having to do with her lies and evasiveness, he came across the room saying, "You're trying to run away from me. Isn't that it? You're not fooling me. If you think you're running out after everything I've done for you, all the money I've spent on you and this house, think again!"

When she fought against him, he hit her hard in the face, whirled her around, bending her forward over the unyielding bulk of her belly and surged into her, clutching her thighs while she struggled to breathe, to maintain a grip on her sanity. The pain mounting to intolerable proportions, she fainted.

Suddenly shocked out of his activities by the realization that she'd become a dead weight he was supporting, he called for an ambulance, frantically rearranged her clothes and wiped the trickle of blood from her nose—the result of his blow to her face. The blood came away readily enough, but the bruises stayed. He was all at once convinced people would see her and know what he'd done. They'd never understand she'd goaded him into it, driven him almost out of his mind with her daily lies and fantasies and complaints. He was horrified by just how far she'd driven him.

Two hours later, their son Corey was born. A contrite George went along to the room to see Gaby, on the way framing his apologies, his explanations. He was prepared to reason with her, to try to make her see that half the responsibility for everything that had happened was hers. But Gaby became completely hysterical at the sight of him and started screaming, kept on screaming until two interns and Gaby's doctor came to escort him out of the hospital. Furious now, George stamped out. Gaby had to be sedated.

That night after Corey was born was the single worst night of Gaby's life. Sleeping, she dreamed she was back in the house with George and he was once more trying to kill her with his blows of one kind or another. Waking, she was in pain from the episiotomy, and grief-stricken by the sight of her still-bloated, wobbling belly and her horribly engorged breasts. She wept throughout her waking hours, moaned throughout the sleeping ones, and, finally, it was morning. Her head ached, her thighs ached. Her entire body hurt.

Lisette arrived very early, having had an almost incoherent call from George, to be met with a view of Gaby sitting sobbing on her bed, black and blue bruises marking half her face, frenziedly smoking a cigarette. Sinking into a chair, feeling somewhat nauseated, Lisette asked, "What has happened?" Gaby poured it all out, every last detail of what had happened the previous afternoon.

Horrified, Lisette said, "But he might have injured the baby. And you. How could he think of doing such things! Why have you not told me of these things, Gaby? You told me nothing of this."

Gaby looked at her with an expression of such intense misery combined with contempt, Lisette flinched.

"You never wanted to hear!" Gaby cried. "All these years, you've been hearing the things you want to hear, not the things I was trying to tell you. I *did* try to tell you. But for months, all you've talked about was making decisions, how it was up to me to make a decision. You wouldn't *help* me! I did try. I don't understand you." Her eyes were slitted, her mouth thin with hostility. "All you've done for years and years is push me away . . . take papa away from me. And when I wanted you, needed you to help me, all you wanted to do was take me shopping for this fucking baby. I don't *want* a baby!" she near-screamed. "I *never* wanted one. But I've got one now and I'm just going to have to make the best of it. I'm going to take Corey and I'm never going back to George! Never, never! He's going to pay for everything he's done to me. I'll make him sorry for every single hour of every single day of this last year. *He's going to pay!* And don't look so shocked. I can swear! George taught me. Along with a lot of other things. Fuck, fuck, *fuck!*" She took a deep breath, refusing to allow herself to feel anything for this woman sitting beside her looking so hurt, so confounded by the outburst. "I'm tired," she said, thrusting out her chin. "I don't feel like talking anymore. You let this happen to me."

Trembling, Lisette stood up. "I am sorry these things have happened to you," she said huskily. "I am sorry. But I am not responsible for any of it. You will not place the blame upon me. You are welcome to come home with the baby. You will always be welcome. You are my child and I love you. But I will not allow you to say or believe that it is my fault in any way for what has happened. I have taken nothing, no one from you. Ray was never yours to be taken away. And you will never speak to me in this fashion ever again. If you wish to come home, I will make a place for you. But you will not blame me and you will not try to come between me and your father."

"I don't *want* to come home!" Gaby snapped. "You think I'd want to come home after everything you've done to me? Go away! I'm tired!"

Stricken, Lisette left, and went home to pour herself a large drink despite the early hour and collapsed onto the sofa with her drink and a cigarette when the telephone rang. She got up, feeling exhausted, and went to answer it to hear George Shea say, "I know I haven't any right to call you or try to make you understand my side of things. But I know how it looks and I've got to talk to somebody or I'm going to go crazy. Please, will you just listen?"

"Go ahead," she said faintly. "I am listening."

"I didn't mind the money," he said frantically. "I didn't mind her spending all that money. Thousands and thousands of dollars. I didn't mind. I swear to God, I didn't. I *loved* her. She hated me. She lied and lied and lied until I couldn't tell when she was telling the truth anymore and when she was lying. I never meant to hurt her. I wanted the baby. I don't know what got into me. I just thought it was more of the same, more lies, more. She doesn't know what she *wants!*" he cried. "But I know what *I* want. I want out. If she comes back here and starts all over again, I'll wind up killing her."

"She will not come back," Lisette said, gripping her glass so hard her entire hand looked bleached. "For both of you, it is over."

"You've got to *understand,*" he pleaded. "Never. I've never done things like that in my *life!* I didn't mean to do . . . any of it. It was just . . . too much. Too much. Sixty thousand dollars. In one year. Sixty thousand. I swear to God I didn't mind. I'd have given her more. Anything. But the *lies*. All the lying."

"Mr. Shea," Lisette interrupted him, "I understand. I have no desire to mediate. I will not interfere. I understand. And I am sorry for the both of you. Please, I cannot speak with you more now. Let me be, Mr. Shea. I cannot forgive you. I cannot blame you. Enough now. Please." She set the receiver down gently, then, holding the glass with both hands, drained it in one long swallow. Shuddering violently, she set down the glass and went upstairs to lie down on the bed beside Ray, who was sleeping. Lying very still, unmoving, devastated, she thought, these children would blame me regardless of what I might have done.

Angry, guilty, yet relieved, George Shea settled a considerable alimony on Gabrielle, then quickly began pursuing a number of other women in an attempt to reconstruct his life as it had been before Gaby. Gaby started a new life, making a grand show publicly of her "proudest achievement," Corey, a red-haired, freckle-faced replica of his father. He was strikingly good-looking, but so strongly his father's son in appearance it was all she could do to tend the baby's minimal demands, barely able to tolerate the infant, turning him gladly over to the cooing ministrations of the young West Indian woman who came daily to tend to Corey and to the spacious apartment Gabrielle had taken downtown.

She tried to counter her intolerance of the child by devoting herself to her work. She wrote compositions for such boldly diverse instruments as piccolo and tympanum, and occasionally guest-conducted small orchestras in small towns to small success. She lived grandly and to the hilt on George Shea's money. The raging bitterness inside her was in no way eased by the regular arrival of the checks. She wished he'd die. Gradually she began to dream again of the perfect man, someone who'd arrive in her life and rescue her from the maddening demands of this baby that had been foisted on her without her consent, this baby who was holding her back in every way, this baby whose face and features and genitalia repelled her. She could scarcely bear to pick him up when he cried. So, most often, she simply closed the door and left him to cry, relieved when Coralee would go hurrying in to soothe and tend to him.

Initially, Glenn was thrilled by the idea of the baby. But when Gaby came to visit with Corey for the first time and deposited the baby in Glenn's lap before going off to have a long conversation with Lisette in the kitchen, Glenn's delight rapidly dissolved. Corey wet on her lap, then went into a screaming fit that scared Glenn witless. She was eleven years old. She had no idea what to do with the baby and couldn't get him to stop crying. Lisette finally came to her rescue, smiling as she picked up the baby, saying, "You must not be so easily frightened, *petite*. He is only a baby."

Only a baby, but he was an alarmingly angry one, one who, as he grew older, was part of the time sickeningly overindulged by Gaby, and the other part of the time screamed at by her for misbehaving. In time, no longer frightened by him, Glenn came to see Corey as a victim of his mother's frustrations. She sometimes volunteered to take him out for walks or up to her room just to give them both a break from Gaby's inconsistent behavior.

Once her fear of the little boy was gone, some of the delight returned. He was wonderful to look at, and she often sketched him while he played up in her room, climbing into everything, taking the charcoal from her fingers to add his own lines to her work.

Lisette loved Corey and forced herself to tolerate Gaby's visits, her complaining monologues, in order to have some time with Corey. Perhaps, she worried, she was indulging Gaby out of guilt. She no longer seemed to possess the ability to segregate fact from feeling, and rarely tried with Gaby. Her attention was available to Gaby, her affections were open to Corey, but her mind was elsewhere.

She was becoming preoccupied with time, oppressed by it. Frequently she wished she might—in some indirect way—hurry her own time along and have done with everything. Whatever energy she possessed went into her speaking engagements, the remainder into Ray. Often, when she lay in bed at night, she stared into the darkness wishing she could simply close her eyes and never again have to face morning, or her children, or the mirrors—distorting, carnival-glass reflectors—of her children's eyes. She felt numb, yet kept on going because there was nothing else left to do. She came alive in occasional conversations with Elizabeth or Glenn or Ray and was purposely deaf to Dana and Gaby. She was running on schedule, on demand.

"What is wrong with you?" Ray asked, deeply concerned by her frequent apathy. "If it's Gaby, I'm going to insist she stop coming here."

She put her hand on his arm, turning her head to look at

him. "I enjoy Corey," she said. "I have learned to tolerate Gaby. I simply do not hear her."

"But you don't seem to be hearing *me*," he complained, made helpless by his inability to put into words all his feelings. "I'd suggest we take a trip but I'm so damned busy at the studio."

"It doesn't matter," she said, staring at her hand on his arm. Claw-like, the veins on the back of her hand stood out. What an ugly hand, she thought.

"We'll go out to dinner tonight." He smiled. "Just the two of us."

"All right," she said distantly.

"Lisette!" he said sharply. "You're not listening."

"I am listening," she said, her eyes moving from her hand to his face. "You would like to make love to me, *chéri?*" She smiled a strange smile that came close to unnerving him.

"Is that what you want?" he asked, easing her over into the circle of his arm. "Tell me what you want, darling. Perhaps we should take a vacation. I'll see what I can arrange. Damn it! We will. I'll start working on it."

"Make love to me," she whispered, her hand gripping his arm. "I am cold."

He looked into her eyes for a long time, then kissed her. She actually felt cold. Her lips were cool. I'll warm you, he thought. Keep you warm, keep you here, keep you.

Her arm seemed terribly heavy as she lifted it around him, so heavy. And her eyelids were heavy too. It was easier to close them. Heavy. All of her. Make me lighter, she thought. Make me light and warm. Make me.

Gaby felt it was her right to make demands on both Lisette's time and energy because no matter what Lisette said, they both knew it was Lisette's fault that everything had gone so wrong with Gaby's life. So she came to the house at least once a week, bringing Corey. She was determined to have, at the very least, the time Lisette owed her. Her anger with her mother consumed her. She had to have someone to blame and Lisette was the logical candidate. Hadn't everything always been Lisette's fault? And since George Shea wouldn't even accept her

occasional telephone calls, who else was there? She was in-
furiated by his refusal to take her calls, as if she'd been the
one who'd tortured him and not the other way around. She
longed to get him on the other end of the line so she might tell
him precisely what she thought of him, but he wouldn't allow
it.

She was outraged when Glenn stopped her at the front door
one afternoon to say, "Why are you doing this? Why do you
have to come here and upset mama? That's the only reason
why you come. You do it on purpose. I know you do. You're
not happy unless you can come here one day a week and upset
her. If you can't come just to visit, why don't you leave us all
alone?"

"Get out of my way!" Gaby snarled, clutching Corey so
tightly he squealed and kicked her. "I'll do whatever I want.
This happens to be *my* home, too, in case you've forgotten."

"You're a sick *child!*" Glenn said, quivering with anger.
"Sick! If you don't stop all this, I swear I'll kill you. I'm not
surprised George wanted to kill you. You'd drive anyone to
murder! If you have to come here, act like a human being and
think about somebody else's feelings for a change instead of
your own. And give Corey to me! Put him down! You're
hurting him. God! You're making everybody a nervous wreck."

"You're the child! You don't know what you're talking
about!" she said, dropping Corey so that he landed on the floor
with a bang and picked himself up, howling. "You're just
jealous of the time I spend with her!" And with that, she swept
past Glenn, leaving her alone with Corey.

Still trembling, Glenn took Corey up to her room to play
while she sat on the side of the bed with her head in her hands,
wounded by Gaby's accidentally hitting upon the truth. She
was jealous, because Gaby was depriving Glenn of attention,
time that was rightfully hers. Gaby didn't love her, didn't care,
didn't even see Lisette as a person but as someone she could
say absolutely anything to—no matter how hurtful—without
any regard for the impact of the things she said.

Dana adamantly refused to involve himself, saying, "You're
not going to change Gaby. You're crazy if you think you can.
And don't worry about Lisette. While Gaby's going on and

on, Lisette's off somewhere, just filling in the blanks when Gaby leaves an opening. Don't be such a little worrier. You're not her mother, Glenn. I believe it's the other way around."

They didn't seem to see what she could see so plainly: Lisette wasn't with them *at all*. And Glenn didn't know, couldn't think of any way to get to wherever it was Lisette had gone. So, all she could do was refrain from further burdening her mother by leaving her alone. She coped with her own problems, taking whatever words or displays of affection Lisette offered with the avidity of someone dying of thirst in the desert. Lisette's occasional kisses and embraces were like drops of moisture on Glenn's parched lips. She hoarded these moments and forced herself to concentrate on the future because the present frustrated and defeated her.

When Lisette and Ray went off for a week's vacation, Glenn was hopeful the entire time they were gone that her mother would return restored, returned to herself. They returned and there was no change. Everything was the same. Lisette went out most afternoons to give poetry readings or to address some women's group with Elizabeth. Occasionally, when Glenn arrived home from school, she'd find her mother and Elizabeth deep in conversation, their heads close together, their words flowing urgently. Glenn wanted to say to Elizabeth, You know my mother. You can talk to her. Tell *me* how to talk to her, know her.

Elizabeth said, "It's the menopause. You know that. Why don't you go to your doctor and see to it?"

"I have not thought of that," Lisette said. "Why have I not thought of that? For so long, I have been feeling dreadful. You are so sensible, Elizabeth." She smiled, clasping Elizabeth's hand. "You must find me very scattered."

"Scatterbrained," Elizabeth corrected, squeezing her hand. "And you're not, never have been. See your doctor," she said gently. "I'm sure he'll give you some sort of medication."

"Do you know that I love you, Elizabeth? I love you. So many years we have been friends and never have I told you of your importance to me, my feelings for you."

"I'm equally guilty," Elizabeth said, flushing. "You're just as important to me. I love you, too. I'll go with you to the doctor, if you like."

"Please, I would like that. I am feeling the need...for a friend."

Pills and tonics made her feel much, much better, better than she had in years.

And Ray said, "Thank God! You can't imagine all the things I've been thinking."

"I can imagine." She smiled, embracing him. "I imagined all the same things."

"'Course that still doesn't solve the problem of Gaby," he said. "I wish she'd move to another bloody city or find some other man to drive out of his mind."

"She does not bother me so very much," she said. "Don't think of it."

"I rather like her little chap," he went on. "And Glenn's coming on nicely, she does jolly well with him."

"Glenn is a good girl. And Corey is a fine little boy. I feel so well," she said. "So well."

It didn't last. In a few months she was slipping again, so much so that Ray could scarcely get her to respond—either to his words or his embraces. She seemed so distracted so much of the time now he feared constantly for her well-being. But he was, to his surprise, finding in Corey some measure of what he feared he was losing in Lisette. Perhaps it was the boy's eagerness, or his insistence on hugging, being hugged. Whatever it was, Ray reacted positively to it, but he still watched Lisette constantly, trying to will her back into contact with their life together. He'd hold the boy in his arms, unable to comprehend the change taking place, refusing ultimately to believe these changes could be permanent. Lisette had always come back to him. She always would.

She was aware of everything, everything, but she no longer seemed to possess the ability to feel very much. She gave up worrying about it. Something was bound to happen. While she was waiting, she maintained the routines, the household, the family; she fulfilled her commitments, talked deeply and often with Elizabeth, who alone seemed to understand, and got through one day at a time.

# Six

At eighteen, finally finished with high school and eagerly preparing for her first year at the Art College, Glenn had given up her minimal attempts to bring the family together and to establish some measure of reasonableness in Gaby. It simply wasn't possible. So she silently—for the most part—observed Dana's frequent changes of partner, Gaby's once- or twice-weekly visits to the house with Corey, Lisette's perpetual motion, Ray's ever-upward climb to stardom. Sometimes, as she'd done as a child, she stood in the doorway of the master bedroom to watch Lisette readying herself for an evening out. She wanted simply to be near her for a few minutes, to be there to catch the few words Lisette might offer, to receive what had become the ritual dabs of perfume behind her ears. Anointed by her mother. Apprehensive about her mother, frightened for her. Lisette, although visibly tired much of the time, seemed even more beautiful. She kept on the go, out almost every afternoon to speak to some group or another, out most evenings of the week to be by Ray's side as she charmed and delighted some group or another. She was rarely home any more.

While the atmosphere in the house was disappointing, static, Glenn's life at the College was everything she'd anticipated. She loved it: woodcuts, batik, life models in the drawing and painting classes. She hurried eagerly to school every morning and was usually the first one setting up. Everything about it was perfect: the crisp edge to the September mornings, fresh-scented air, an exciting destination, projects to complete.

Friendships were easily made, casually maintained. Lunch hours were spent with three or four classmates at the local restaurant. Bottles of beer on the table; there were discussions of classes, instructors. She went out with her newly made friends to see exhibits or attend gallery openings, exchanging critical ideas, opinions.

She was concerned now with her abilities—what she could do, conceive of, achieve. She dressed simply—irritated by Gaby's ludicrous penchant for long dresses—without affectation, ignoring cosmetics altogether. She noticed some of the other girls whose eyes were elaborately decorated and whose clothes—like Gaby's—were forms of costumes. These girls made her sad with what she believed was their need to embellish—or was it disguise—their natural attributes. She wondered why they didn't or couldn't risk showing themselves as they were, and thought often of Gaby feeling the need to overstate her beauty.

When she thought of her own self, she thought of her brain, quite sure that what people saw when they looked at her was her essence or intelligence. She knew she wasn't beautiful or ever likely to be. She lacked Gaby's misty-eyed, tragic-heroine's pallor and aura of carefully fabricated mystery and suffering. Even Dana was better looking than she, she thought, with his tall, well-built body and graceful hands, his large eyes and finely-boned features. Both Dana and Gaby looked like Ray with his aristocratic features and hooded eyes. Glenn looked like Lisette with her too-long neck and too-pointed narrow nose, blue eyes and brown hair. All of those features which made Lisette beautiful, did not, Glenn felt, do the same for her. Glenn found herself too narrow in the hips, too thin in the thighs, too straight-leggedly tall altogether. It was her breasts that gave Lisette her lush, rounded appearance and actually redeemed her figure. Glenn merely looked long. She hadn't any redeeming attributes. She couldn't imagine anyone ever becoming interested in her because of the way she looked.

At school, for the first time, she received criticism on the too-tentative lines of her drawings and discovered that criticism both frightened and inhibited her, filled her with uncertainty.

"Look!" the instructor said at last one afternoon, removing the 5B pencil from Glenn's hand. "Don't be so timid, so anxious to reproduce exactly what you see. Get down how what you see *feels!*" He made half a dozen swift, bold lines over the many fine, tiny markings she'd done, then returned her the pencil, saying, "See! One or two good, strong definitive lines and you've got it!"

She could see he was right and looked at the pencil in her hand wondering how she could get herself to make those hard, clean lines. Beside the thick, sharp certainty of his half-dozen strokes, her own efforts appeared palely cautious.

"Stop *thinking* so much about it," the instructor added. "Just *do* it!"

Just do it! she told herself, looking up at the model. Do it! Her fingers fixed themselves around the pencil. She took a long, long look at the model's body, the curve of her buttocks, the cleft of her genitals, the slope of her breasts, and began another drawing. It worked. It was starting to come to her. She'd managed to establish a direct link between her eyes and her hand and the images suddenly began to flow onto the paper. She experienced a surging elation, all at once knowing she'd made contact with the very core of her talent.

"That's more like it!" the instructor said on his next and subsequent tours of the room, and she flushed with pleasure. She was learning, getting ever closer to transforming the mystical-feeling interior of her vision into reality.

By the end of that first year—disappointed at having received just an A-minus for her efforts, she decided to eliminate a number of extraneous courses in the next year and concentrate on her painting and drawing, to work harder, do better.

Ray secured a summer job for her at the station answering the telephones and acting as receptionist in the production offices. She went along to her first day's work convinced she was going to hate every minute of the job. She had no illusions about television people, having seen enough of her father and brother in action—not to mention Gaby on the lunatic fringe—to know that the backstage people were actually even more dramatic, more affected, more temperamental than the actors they so vehemently bad-mouthed.

The job turned out to be plain boring. The telephones seldom rang and the production people either spent their time tearing around screaming about the ineptitude of others, or took three-hour lunches scouting out new properties, commiserating with their associates, or wooing someone with talent or influence. She sat out the days drawing: little memory sketches of Corey, and very often, attempts to reproduce Lisette's likeness on paper. She was fixated, frustrated by her consistent failure to capture Lisette's essence. There must be some lack within her, something holding her back from her fullest artistic range as well as her emotional one. She often felt like weeping over her inability to fix Lisette on paper.

On weekends, she occasionally got together with some of the kids from the College. With the sole exception of Ralph who, everyone agreed, was definitely a little crazy—but unquestionably the most dedicated and talented of the group—none of them seemed more than superficially serious about their studies, their future, their art. Ralph, about to enter his fourth and final year at the College, was twenty-two, daringly long-haired and totally preoccupied with his efforts to translate his private visions into small water-color and India ink drawings. Sometimes he turned out something in oil with colors so subtle, so muted and ethereal it didn't seem possible someone like him could have executed them. He looked like a wild man, chain-smoked cigarettes, and drank an infrequent bottle of beer as he listened to the others, squint-eyed against the smoke from his cigarette. Then suddenly he'd declare, "You're all fulla shit!" or something similar, gulp down the last of his coffee or beer and depart, having managed to put an end to conversation every single time.

Glenn was intrigued by him because every time he made one of his scathing summary pronouncements, she had the guilty feeling he was absolutely right. Near the end of that summer, hoping to get to the roots of her fascination, she chased after him one evening as he made his usual exit.

"Wait up!" she called, grappling with the strap of her shoulder bag. "Wait a minute!"

He stopped, turned and looked at her—yellowy tiger's eyes, wild yellow tiger's mane—his expression one of severely tried patience.

"Why do you always do that?" she asked, falling into step with him as he turned without a word, and began walking again. "Come out with us and spend the whole evening sitting there not saying anything, then making an exit, telling us we're all full of it. If we are, why don't you contribute something to the conversation instead of just making those remarks and leaving?"

"What're you after?" he asked, flicking away the stub of his cigarette. "What're you trying to prove?" He walked very quickly, effortlessly, with a kind of fluid animal grace, taking long strides so that she had to hurry to keep up with him.

"I'm not trying to prove anything," she answered. "I'd only like to know what you think *you're* proving. If you disagree so totally with everything we say, why do you bother to come out with us at all?"

He gave her a long, slow, up-and-down look, then continued walking, his hands jammed into the back pockets of his jeans.

"Okay," she said, stopping. "Forget it!"

She watched him walk away, then crossed the road and headed for home feeling inexplicably disappointed and not knowing what to do about it. She'd hoped Ralph might have profound statements to make, interesting observations, perhaps even talk about his work. But he just seemed as crazy as everybody had always said he was.

She hadn't really expected much of him, maybe a chance at some insight into the strange, commanding qualities of his work. But, she thought, you couldn't force people to stop and explain why they were the way they were. Still, she'd so much wanted to hear what he'd say. He wasn't at all the way she'd hoped he'd be. She'd had this image of the two of them talking, and Ralph suddenly opening up, revealing himself.

Well, never mind, she told herself. If it came down to

making choices, she preferred people like her mother and father and Dana, Corey, too, to people like Ralph. There was something about them—her mother especially—endearingly human, even vulnerable.

Sometimes, her mother seemed so young that Glenn had trouble believing she was as old as she was. Fifty-seven. It *sounded* old, but it didn't sound like Lisette. Ray was sixty-six. He didn't seem that old, either. When the two of them were together, it was as if they were completely alive and utterly separated from everyone else in the world. And Glenn was acutely aware of not being a part of them, aware also that her mother was not as much a part of things as she used to be.

Glenn thought back to her childhood, to afternoons when she'd come home from school and gone racing up the stairs to climb into bed and rouse Lisette from her naps to hear and comment on what had happened to her all day. Now she could all too easily see that Lisette was no longer the same woman who moved through the house or her life, no longer the woman who had invited help with the evening meal but who now consistently refused assistance, claiming, "It only confuses me."

"Are you doing what you really want to do?" Glenn asked her on the evening before school was due to start up again.

"Which way?" Lisette asked, glancing around over her shoulder.

"I mean the family planning clinics, giving those talks. It's all been done, you know. Margaret Sanger, the others. You too."

"There are women everywhere who still do not know," Lisette said, turning back to the counter.

"That's not what I mean. I mean you've done a lot of really good things, things for other people. When do you do what's good for you, mama?"

"What I do is good for me," Lisette said softly, paying close attention to the vegetables she was dicing. She had a sudden, constricted feeling in her chest, a warning a confrontation was about to take place. She didn't think she had sufficient strength left to cope. "I do what is good for me," she said. "Now. Always."

"Do you? Do you really believe that?"

Lisette shrugged. "I ruined my breasts," she said. "I did *not* want to do that. It felt very much better without the brassieres. But what feels better is not always what *is* better."

Glenn blinked, failing to get the point of this tangential line. What did ruined breasts have to do with anything? And how were they ruined? In what way?

Lisette turned once more. "When I was your age," she said, "they were wonderful. It gave me so much pride, to make me put back my shoulders, hold myself—so." She straightened, thrusting out her chest, then exhaled and relaxed. "Freedom has many interpretations. I chose to begin interpreting my freedom through my body. In the process, I ruined my breasts." She paused, that familiar interior fluttering inside, a tightening preliminary to tears as she examined Glenn's bemused expression. "You do not understand," she said.

"I don't see what one thing has to do with the other," Glenn admitted. "We're talking about different things. And what's so ruined about them?" The fact that they were having a conversation—no matter how disseminated—was such an exceptional event that Glenn could scarcely think coherently. She was so excited at having inadvertently succeeded in capturing her mother's attention.

"They fell," Lisette said simply. "My pride was misplaced. I had to learn to separate the body from the mind. We are not speaking of different things, *petite*. It is only that you think we are."

This statement held Glenn in silence for several moments. She wasn't saying the things she wanted to say. But how could she say any of that when she couldn't help feeling it wasn't what Lisette wanted to hear, or even what she'd respond to?

"And what about the names?" she asked out of the blue, as if this was what they'd been discussing. "How could you give Dana a girl's name like Dana and me a boy's name like Glenn and then be upset when Dana has identity problems and can't be certain who he is? A name's very important to a child, you know." A mother is, too. Where are you? What happened to you?

Lisette put down the knife. "Dana's problem has not a thing to do with his identity," she said evenly, her throat pulsing.

"And his name has not a thing to do with his problems. How very foolish of you to say such things!"

"It's not any more foolish," Glenn said reasonably, "than telling me about your ruined breasts—I don't even know how you think they're ruined anyway—when that wasn't really what we were talking about."

"It was *exactly* what we were talking about! You are so limited in your comprehension, Glenn. You would wish everything to be so graphic, to be black and white, and precisely so, so that you may interpret it to your liking. But life is not like this. People are not like this. There are other shades, other considerations that must be observed."

"You think Dana's homosexual because of something *you* did!"

*"No!* You are wrong!" Lisette's voice was threatening to go out of control. "How is it you think you will do my thinking for me? Since when do you decide for me that I feel thus and so or such and such without ever *asking* what it is I am thinking or feeling? You make *tremendous* assumptions. Do you know that you do? Are you aware of this?" She was trembling now, her heart pounding. She hated this, was grieved by it.

"Well, what *do* you think, then? Tell me what you think," Glenn asked, her face very red.

"What I think. I think Dana leads a very sad life. And this makes me sad. I am his mother. I would wish for him to derive pleasure from his life. Just as I would wish it for Gabrielle, for you. You are my children. What sort of mother do you think I am that you believe I have no caring for your lives, your happiness?"

"Oh!" Glenn was stopped. Everything she was saying was coming out wrong; these were not even the things she wanted to be saying. They were hurting each other and that had never been her intention.

Lisette continued to lean against the counter studying Glenn's face.

"I see me when I look at you," she said softly, her throat aching. "A mirror that takes me back in time. But never was I so critical as you, as you are being of us. Or so disapproving. Nothing can be good enough, right enough to satisfy you. I watch you, see the things you do, how hard you work and it makes me feel good, makes me feel perhaps it will be you who makes the pieces fit for yourself as Gaby and Dana have not done, will perhaps never do. Dana might. But Gaby never. You, I think yes. I have thought this always. We give you freedom but instead of being glad of it, you make us small with your eyes. You narrow your eyes when you look at us and I can read on your face how little you think of us, of me, how little you think of what it is we have tried to give you. Or have you ever thought of it—what it is we try to give you?"

"I don't think that way of you," Glenn said weakly, stunned by her mother's passionate intensity. They hadn't ever spoken to each other in this fashion. "Maybe . . . I don't know."

"No." Lisette shook her head. "I don't think you have thought of it. You believe it is only you who have eyes to see, only you who are aware of others. Wrong. You are wrong. People do not always feel compelled to speak of what they see. People *cannot* always speak of these things. Of my children, it is for you I have had the most hope always. But nothing will ever be so easy or so graphic as you will expect. Nothing. Be more kind, *petite*. For us, because we do only the best we can. For me, because I do what must be done. And for you, because you have too many expectations of yourself. To expect so much is to never be satisfied. I know this well. You would not wish to believe, but to compromise is part of life. And you would not wish to believe, perhaps, but once, once I was you."

Glenn was flattened, shot down by Lisette's unsuspected insights. She sat staring wordlessly until Lisette moved to retrieve her knife. "You could set the table," she said, allowing Glenn an out, a chance for both of them to regain their composure. She heard Glenn push her chair back from the table and go out, and sighed deeply, fighting back the tears, staring down at the vegetables on the chopping board. This was the full price, finally: Glenn, too, would withdraw from her as the others had done. She sighed again, the tears sitting heavily in her throat, feeling too tired. A name's very important to a child, you know. An echo. Don't you think it's a little hypocritical . . . ? They would hate us for something, even if it is only the choice of names we give to them.

She despaired of children, having them, living through their seasons—one after the other—of discontent, displeasure, disapproval. For what? For a thirty-year-old woman with negligible talent and the stability of a firefly who hated her own child, a boy who might grow to be beautiful if given any sort of opportunity to grow. For a twenty-eight-year-old man of considerable talent, magnificent talent; who lacked the ability to recognize himself, to know himself. And this last. A nineteen-year-old almost-woman with undoubted talent and a worrying tendency toward self-doubt.

A pity, she thought, that Glenn had failed to see the point she had tried to make, because, oh, yes! there was a very real correlation between her dropped breasts and the question of doing what one wanted to do; that matter of freedom. Save yourself, she thought. Don't make the mistakes I have made and lose that freedom while thinking you are preserving it.

"I'm sorry," Glenn murmured, returning. "I didn't mean to be rude. I'm sorry if it came out sounding that way."

Lisette whirled around to embrace her, whispering, "Don't be sorry! Ah, yes, be sorry! But it was not rude. It is good that we speak together." Humility, Lisette thought, is worth everything. And you have this. This you do have. And the ability to love. "I love you," she whispered, "love you."

"Oh, mama," Glenn sighed, "you know I love you. I just want you to be happy, that's all."

It snapped the thread. Glenn realized with a terrible pang that Lisette was crying. She closed her eyes and held on hard, rattled.

"Don't, mama! I'm sorry if I said the wrong things, if I hurt you. Please, don't."

Lisette simply opened her arms and released her, left the kitchen and went upstairs.

Feeling awful now, Glenn stood and watched her go, then picked up the knife and took over completing the dinner.

Lisette lay down on the bed and lit a cigarette. The telephone rang. Someone will answer it, she thought. The ringing soon stopped.

Ray called out, "Glenn, go up and tell your mother to pick up the telephone. Tell her Elizabeth is on the line."

Glenn put down her knife and went upstairs to knock at the

door, open it and say, "Elizabeth is on the phone." She watched as Lisette reached over to pick up the receiver.

"Could you make lunch tomorrow, darling?" Elizabeth was saying. Lisette's eyes were on Glenn.

"Tomorrow?" Lisette said.

"There's something I really must talk to you about. I thought lunch out would be the best idea. Are you all right? You sound a bit distant."

"Fine," Lisette said, unable to take her eyes off Glenn who continued to stand with her hand on the door. "At what time?"

"Let's make it late, shall we? I've a doctor's appointment at eleven. I should be through by twelve-thirty. To stay on the safe side, let's say one."

"That will be fine. Where?"

"I have to be downtown. Hamilton's? Meet me at the Old Street entrance?"

"Good. At one o'clock."

"Lisette, are you sure you're all right? I'm not sure I care for the way you sound."

"No, no. I will see you tomorrow. One o'clock."

"All right," Elizabeth said uncertainly. "Tomorrow."

Lisette put down the telephone, stubbed out her cigarette, then held her hand out to Glenn. Glenn came over and sat down beside her.

"Dinner's almost ready," Glenn said. "You're going to come down, aren't you?"

"I will come down," Lisette said.

Glenn slowly leaned forward until her head was on Lisette's shoulder.

"Mama," she whispered, "don't be angry with me."

"I am not angry with you," Lisette said, stroking Glenn's hair, pleased by its thick softness and the warmth of Glenn's face in her neck. "I am a little bit angry with me," she said. "Nothing is so serious, *petite*. Don't think on it any further. But we must talk more, talk often, know each other." It can't be too late, she thought. There is still time.

"I want that," Glenn murmured, relishing the moment.

"Come," Lisette stirred. "Papa is alone downstairs."

Feeling oddly like a child, Glenn held her mother's hand as they went down the stairs.

*  *  *

They spotted each other. Elizabeth waved and moved to the edge of the sidewalk, smiling. Lisette stepped down off the curb, and in that instant, the merest fraction of a second, had to decide. She saw it all—the child and what was about to happen, and had to try to save the child, throwing herself towards him. As she did, she felt the impact everywhere: an explosion of pain. Falling, she thought, *One life for another. I will save this one.* Falling, falling into a yawning mouth of pain, she thought only to shield the child, save it.

Elizabeth screamed, *"NOOOOO!"* Too late. With the scream howling inside her head, she stood paralyzed.

Glenn was summoned out of her classroom by one of the school secretaries and told to go directly home. There was an emergency. She took a taxi and arrived at the house to find Gaby and Dana already there, standing ashen-faced and anxious-looking in the disordered living room.

"What happened?" she asked them. "What's going on?"

As typical as the room's disorder was Gabrielle's bursting into noisy tears and collapsing, atypically, into Dana's arms. Dana, looking distressed under the weight of his sister's raspy sobbing, eased Gaby away from him and into an armchair, then crossed the room to take Glenn's arm, propelling her back out to the hallway.

"Gaby and I've been waiting for you. Ray's at the Pavilion. We'll go in my car."

"What *happened* to him? What's wrong?" She wanted to hit both of them. Even now they couldn't stop play-acting long enough to acquaint her with the facts. She looked at Dana's blanched face, at Gaby draped across the armchair, filled with a sick dread.

"An awful accident from the sound of it," Dana said. "Not him. Lisette. Do you think we can get her to *stop* that so we can go?" he asked, looking back at Gaby with an expression of extreme distaste downturning the corners of his mouth. He despised Gaby at that moment for her synthetic grief-stricken display. He knew it wasn't real, knew it and wanted to strangle her for making the situation more difficult than it already was. "Do something with her, will you, please?" he begged Glenn.

"She's been doing that absurd lost-child act since I got here."

"Why here?" Glenn wanted to know. "Where's mama? What's happened? Why didn't you tell them at the school to tell me to go directly to wherever she is?" Something about Dana's face pierced her anger. "None of this makes *any sense!*" His face looked naked, stark. This is bad, so bad, she thought.

"I'll tell you on the way. God! *God!* Get her, will you? I just can't *stand* that *noise!*" He threw open the front door and went down the stairs to unlock the passenger door of his car, leaving it open as he went round the front and installed himself behind the wheel. Glenn watched for a moment, then tore into the living room, whipped up Gaby's bag, pushed it into her hand, shoved her out of the chair shouting, *"Let's go!"* and kept shoving at her until all three of them were in Dana's car on their way downtown to the Pavilion.

"Some damned fool of a blind old man who shouldn't have been driving in the first place!" Dana explained breathlessly as he tore along the streets. "Went right through the pedestrian crossing on Old Street. Hit her and two others. A small boy and his mother. The mother isn't too badly hurt, some broken bones. Lisette tried to push the boy out of the way. But he died right away. Elizabeth was there and saw it."

"Is she dead?" Glenn's voice was wispy with fear.

"They were rushing her into surgery when Ray called me," he answered hoarsely, then shuddered. The car swerved. He took a deep breath and righted the car.

"Oh God!" Gaby sobbed. "Oh, oh, it's so *terrible!*" She hadn't any feelings at all. None. She thought she might move herself into feeling something if she said all the things people were supposed to say when something like this happened. She felt completely clear-headed, removed, empty inside. And somewhere not too far from the surface was a stealthy satisfaction that contemplated with approval Lisette's having sustained possibly critical injuries.

Glenn sat with her shoulders hunched as if her body was sheltering a small nugget of calm and reason that sat squarely in the center of her chest. If she didn't move around too much or too suddenly, if she took time with her thoughts, she'd be able to maintain this calm, this reason. She tuned out her brother

and sister, not allowing herself to react until she had some facts
to react to. She refused to hear Gaby's artificial-sounding sobbing and Dana's angry voice insisting Gaby stop all that. Glenn
would say and do nothing until she knew all the details.

Ray was waiting for them. Elizabeth was standing at some
distance down the corridor, smoking a cigarette with mechan-
ical-looking movements. Ray's face—minus his usual profes-
sionally toothy smile and crinkly-eyed good humor—looked
very old, even elderly. It struck Glenn that her father really
was old. In four more years he'd be seventy. Her shoulders
turned in even more as her eyes moved to Elizabeth in the
distance. Hat in hand, puffing away on a cigarette, Ray said,
"We should know any minute," then resumed the pacing he'd
been doing prior to their arrival.

He walked up and down the corridor, too deeply fearful to
dare contemplate what might be happening behind that closed
door over there. A voice in his head repeated, She won't die,
she won't, won't. Over and over. She couldn't die. While his
blood seemed to have stopped circulating and his heart hurt
with every beat and if he dared stop moving, if he dared . . .

Elizabeth was torn apart by the monstrous irony, unable to
discontinue examining it. She was the one dying. Not Lisette.
This wasn't the way it was supposed to be at all. Another year
and she'd be counting—she saw now—on Lisette's support,
her friendship and understanding. Not this way. Not like this.
She looked over to see Glenn looking back at her and for a
moment was mesmerized by the illusion that it was Lisette
standing down there and not Lisette's daughter. But it was the
daughter. An awesome duplication.

She lit another cigarette and looked at her hands, seeing the
accident again. I'll see it for the rest of my life, she thought,
and was once more thrust up against the irony. This year the
rest of my life.

Lined up in a row on a hard bench, the three watched their
father walk back and forth, back and forth, his lips moving as
he smoked the cigarette, talking silently to himself. Then the
cigarette was crushed out under his heel and he stopped to stand
looking at the three of them, his mouth slightly open as if he

were about to say something important. They waited but he shook his head, took a step backward, his hat turning, turning in his hands, then he started pacing again.

Three strangers watching him, their faces unfamiliar. He had a stunning desire to stop and ask them to identify themselves. He saw them for a moment as intruders, obstacles in the course of his thoughts, these three who'd taken so much of Lisette's time, attention, and love. What right did they have to be here now?

Only an hour. But it was the longest of Glenn's life. She began the hour determined to remain in control of herself, not to fake reactions the way Gaby did or to become angry like Dana. But as minutes passed and her father went from one end of the corridor to the other, seeming to age with each completed lap, her calm slowly deserted her, leaving her devastated, positive Lisette was never going to emerge from this hospital. She got up stiffly and walked down the corridor, stopping in front of Elizabeth, examining Elizabeth's face. They stared at each other wordlessly, then Elizabeth touched Glenn's face and said, "You are so like her. So very much like her," then dropped her hand, her eyes shifting past Glenn, focusing on something distant. Glenn moved away and returned to the bench.

Gaby sat chewing on the side of her hand, wondering if there'd been blood. She hated the idea of that and tried to think of something else. If Lisette died, would there be inheritances? It was terrible of her to be thinking that way. She tried to think of something else, wishing it were George Shea in there, in an *ocean* of blood. Oh yes! A spurt of outrage set her heart to pumping wildly, sending renewed tears splashing from her eyes. That swine, sticking her with his awful child.

Dana was obsessed with the idea that he'd never told Lisette he loved her. He scoured the corners of his memory, trying to recall just one occasion when he'd spoken the words to her and was gripped by the most painful remorse at failing to be able to remember one single instance. He swore he would tell her the instant someone said they'd be allowed to see her. Surely he'd told her! He had to have done. He couldn't tolerate the idea that he hadn't. He kept on searching his memory, leafing through frantically, looking for an occasion.

With a broken back, shattered bones throughout her body,

perforated lungs, lacerations, contusions and an ultimately fatal concussion, Lisette failed to survive the preparations being made to move her into surgery.

Ray received the news of her death with a rigid spine and rapidly blinking eyes, not wanting to believe, refusing to believe. Rooted to the spot, his eyes fixed on some indefinite point in space, his hands kept turning the hat he held in his hands.

Elizabeth responded as if she'd been struck in the solar plexus. The air rushed out of her lungs, her entire body jerked forward and her eyes closed tightly. She bit so hard on her lower lip she drew blood, the taste of it salty on her tongue.

Gaby heard. Suddenly it was no longer a game, no longer something imagined. It was real and Lisette was dead. Dry-eyed, she slowly doubled over, aching with guilt and loss and a very real sorrow. She'd never wanted her to die, not really. I didn't want you to die, she thought, stricken. You were the only one who really cared. I knew that. I always knew that. She was able to straighten after a while, to look at Ray, realizing she'd have to look after him now. She would. She'd take care of him.

Dana got up, took several steps down the corridor then sank against the wall, sobbing, unable even to think of attempting to control the cries that ripped from his chest. His grief was immediate, consuming and total. He'd lost the one person he'd always loved utterly, and he had never bothered to tell her. He didn't feel he could withstand the blow.

Glenn looked at each of them, feeling it most in Dana. She saw the way he slid down the wall to sit crouched in the corridor like a small child, his head against the wall, his arm over his head. You did love her, she thought, looking past him to Elizabeth. And you, too. She looked back at Dana, thinking she'd comfort him later.

"I want to see her," she said, her hand iron on the doctor's arm.

The doctor, deciding she seemed the most rational and in-control of the family, nodded and held open the door so that Glenn might enter, to stand for several seconds absorbing the scene—blood-drenched sections of what had been Lisette's clothes in a pile on the floor—a nurse standing, her face masked, over by the sterilizer in the corner of the room, her eyes on Glenn.

She was on a table, draped with blood-stained sheets, all covered over, a long insubstantial form, narrow. Glenn couldn't breathe as she moved forward to uncover her mother's face with the irrational thought that the sheet would prevent Lisette from breathing. She did look dead, Glenn thought. Dead but not dead. But, yes, dead; completely still. It was one of the few times she'd ever seen her mother motionless. A smear of blood stained her forehead. Glenn took the edge of the sheet and wiped it away, noticing then the thick ooze of blood matting Lisette's hair, coming from her ear.

"You shouldn't," the nurse said softly, standing on the far side of the table, her face now unmasked and very young. "Really, you'll make it worse for yourself this way."

Glenn shook her head, then looked back at her mother, taking hold of the sheet and drawing it down, her eyes traveling over Lisette's body, seeing the numerous discolorations where blood had collected beneath the surface of the skin; seeing sometime embraces, hearing nighttime whispers. She dared to touch Lisette's shoulder, finding the skin still very warm, misleadingly warm. Her hand moved down Lisette's arm to her hand, cold and empty, the fingers slightly bent. She drew her hand back up slowly, over the curve of Lisette's shoulder, her eyes again meeting the nurse's.

"Was she awake?" Glenn asked, her voice small, vanishing.

"No," the nurse shook her head. "She didn't wake up."

Glenn looked down once more.

Mama, you're beautiful, beautiful, how fine your features, your eyelashes, your mouth. How did you see us? Were we beautiful to you ever, did you see us that way? Or did you only see us moving? The way I saw you, moving. I never thought you'd die, never. Maybe someday when we were old, all of us old. But not now, not like this.

Her hand of its own volition covered the side of her mother's face, the warmth so terribly confusing, as was the softness and the painfully beautiful definition of her features. Her face smoothed out, serene, pale. Oh God! Love I love you it hurts I love you let me close my eyes open them and have you here smiling at me not dead I never thought you'd die.

Back out in the corridor, caught up in a web of conflicting reactions, she stood staring as Elizabeth approached her, saying, "She was my dearest friend, one of the kindest people I've ever known." Elizabeth moistened her lips. "You're so like her, look so much like her. *Be* like her. And if you need to talk, come to me and we'll talk."

Glenn nodded woodenly. Elizabeth hurried away. Glenn's head turned to watch her go. Then she put her arm through her father's saying, "I'll take you home, papa." He stared at her, dazed.

Gaby was filled with resentment at Glenn's directing Ray away down the corridor, hurt by her younger sister's superior strength, superior understanding, superior self-control. She was jealous of the words Elizabeth had chosen to direct to Glenn and not to anyone else. For just an instant, standing there watching Glenn and Ray moving slowly to the exit, Gaby was a small child again, hurt and lost and alone.

Dana, pulling himself up from the floor, mopped his eyes, blew his nose and, without a word, took Gaby's arm to direct her out of there. Somebody, he thought, had to look after Gaby. She couldn't do it for herself. He paused at the door, looking back, knowing he'd never forget this place, that bench, the door of the emergency operating door. And the fact that of all of them, only Glenn had had sufficient courage, sufficient love to face their mother in death.

Desolated, Glenn upon arriving home willingly surrendered her father to Gaby's eager ministrations and went up to her room to weep throughout the remainder of that day, all of that night and all of the next morning. Then, the tears abruptly ceased, simply dried up.

She went into her parents' bedroom while Ray was out with Dana and Gaby making the funeral arrangements and stood for a long time looking at Lisette's dressing table. Aching inside, she stepped closer and, without thinking, picked up Lisette's perfume bottle, removed the stopper and carefully placed a dot of perfume behind each ear. Then, replacing the stopper, she left the room carrying the perfume bottle with her. The ache inside remained, feeling permanent.

# PART TWO

## *1958 - 1970*

A beam of light moves
   along the cobweb,
Now here, now there
At the whimsy of the
   wind
Just so my light
Comes now, comes then
At the whimsy of
   my mind.

*© 1978 Helen Wolfe Allen*

# Seven

Within a matter of weeks, Ray retired from the TV station. The house, as a direct result, became more littered, untidier, and possessed all at once of an unpleasant old man's smell. Glenn, when she encountered her father in her daily comings and goings, would smile, make inconsequential small talk and then escape, feeling increasingly guilty over her almost total inability to communicate with him. He wouldn't allow it.

Gaby, deciding she was needed by her father—and thinking, too, of all the money she'd save—packed up herself and Corey, put all her furniture into storage and moved back to Remington Park. Corey didn't mind. For one thing, he enjoyed the big old house, for another, he liked his grandfather.

Dana confided to Glenn that he could bear neither the atmosphere in the house nor the smell of decay, wished there were more he could do, but, "Frankly, this is all so depressing. Every time I come here, it puts me down for days after." Having explained himself, he then started staying away.

On returning to school, Glenn was surprised by the rush of sympathetic response from her classmates, and, most surprising, from the taciturn Ralph who, spotting her sitting in an empty classroom eating her lunch one afternoon in December, came to sit beside her and started to talk.

"I read about your mother," he said, gazing into the air in front of him. "I guess I was pretty disgusting that time you wanted to talk. But if you want to talk now, that'd be all right with me."

She stared at him, at a loss for words. She studied him with renewed fascination, seeing how pink and clean his skin was, noting the many different shadings to his long blond hair.

"They must," she said, giving voice to the thought as it occurred to her, "give you a rough time about your hair. Nobody else wears it long."

He smiled. She'd never seen him smile before. He had good teeth, fairly white despite his chain-smoking. His mouth had a nice definition, his lips smooth looking. Tiger's eyes and lion's mane. She smiled involuntarily, liking his face.

"My hair's just hair," he said, his eyes off in the distances again. "And I'm not crazy, not really crazy. Serious around here is defined as crazy. And the only reason," he turned and looked directly into her eyes, "nobody's calling *you* crazy yet is because you haven't found out how good you are and neither have they."

"What does that mean?" she asked, her sandwich forgotten, half-eaten on her lap.

"*I* think you're good," he said with authority, "I've seen some of your stuff. Look!" He picked up her sketchbook and turned the pages, showing her her own work. "There!" he pointed. "And there!" He turned more pages. "You've got such good eyes! Look at that! And right here!" He closed the book without having really explained himself, looked at her breasts, then at her mouth. He picked up her hand and turned it over, then released it. He leaned away to make a face at her dress, then leaned back to say, "Are you as square as the outfits or do you fuck?"

She was so staggered she laughed. "Are you *kidding?*" she asked, regarding him wide-eyed. "You come to offer sympathy or whatever and then you ask me something like that?"

"Okay," he said with equanimity. "So you don't. Don't make a big-deal fuss about it. You want to pose for me instead?"

"Why would I want to pose for you?" she asked, perplexed by him.

"Not why would *you* want to for me," he said. "But why *I'd* want you to for me." Again he leaned away from her, his eyes moving appraisingly down the length of her body. "You look right, but it's hard to tell. You'd probably be right."

"Right for what?"

"Some pieces I'd like to do. Never mind," he said, straightening. "You're right, I guess. I get thrown off by words. I start out to say something and then see something and forget about the talking part. You feel bad, eh?"

That sobered her. She looked into his eyes, seeing brown and black specks, dark irises, the pupils' fractional movements. Remarkable, his eyes. She nodded her head, entranced; her eyes moved down to his shoulders, across his chest. "She said I was being too critical," she said, her eyes stuck at the neckline of his shirt. "Of other people and myself, too. I hardly knew her. I wanted to." She saw his eyelashes. Golden, long, with white tips. "I know it's a pretty terrible thing to even think, never mind say it," she went on, "but my father's going to die without her. I just know it. I don't think I ever really realized they were keeping each other alive. That way. As if neither of them had a life without the other. That's frightening. I don't know if it should be that way."

"Sometimes it is," he said, looking at her throat, the length of her neck, wondering if she knew she was beautiful.

"Are your parents that way?" she asked, curious.

"*My* parents?" He laughed, passing his hand over his hair. "My parents," he said, as if he were about to read a story to a small child, saying, "My parents," instead of "Once upon a time."

"My parents, mother and father, are so fucking symbiotically attached you scratch one, the other says thank you. All negative. Her hand in his pocket. His hand up her cunt. You pay me, I'll fuck you. We make babies, you have to pay me more. Oh dear! Look at that, you made me two of them! You're gonna have to up your ante, fella. I only promised one baby. You gave me two. Vegetative hatred subtitled great love. Bad, very bad. Full of lies and dishonesty and a lot of retaliatory *getting*. You know getting?" he asked.

"I don't know what you're talking about."

"Getting," he explained. "You get laid, I get paid. You get a raise, I've got higher expenses. I get dinner, you get the dishes. Performance and reward. They scare the living shit out of me, the two of them. What're yours like?"

"I told you," she said.

"Well." His usual distracted look settled over him. "If you change your mind or anything, let me know. I've got the rest of the year."

"And after that?"

"Off. England first, then Spain. Maybe I'll see Dali. He takes a few students, you know. A few. I'd like to watch you masturbate," he said, not smiling, "see you when you're not in control. See ya." He shoved his hands into his back pockets and wandered off.

She sat a while longer, then picked up her sandwich, took a bite, thought of her mother—her mother and father stroking each other's faces, whispering, their bodies all one—and almost choked. She thought of Gaby and Corey, their voices echoing through the house and lost her appetite altogether. She dumped her lunch in the wire basket, got her coat and walked her way through the rest of the lunch break, her thighs aching from having held her legs so tightly together the entire time she and Ralph had been talking.

She did miss her mother, mourning most of all the lack of a more complete communication. It wasn't so much the actual woman she missed now as a series of habits and a presence. She refused to allow herself to go into the pain more deeply, knowing it would overwhelm and possibly immobilize her.

Funny, but until Lisette died, Glenn had actually harbored a small resentment at her parents for having shackled her with such an affected and pretentious name. Glenn Ellen Burgess. But with Lisette's death—and Elizabeth's haunting remarks— the resentment quietly disappeared and she accepted this name given her as a sort of memento. There was so little Lisette had actually given to her, Glenn found within herself a newly grown compulsion to hoard those few things she had been given, along with an intense craving to trace backward in as minute detail as possible her life, attempting to establish for herself a permanent, overall image of the woman. Her memories of Lisette, like the woman herself, seemed to want to rush bustling past her before Glenn had had sufficient time to fix any lasting impressions in her mind.

Again, she tried doing memory portraits, then destroyed them in frustrated and despairing anger. Not only could she not savor the total essence of the woman, she couldn't even accurately portray Lisette's physical specifics. It was sometimes as if her mother had been someone she'd imagined— possibly at the height of a feverish nightmare—and no amount of industrious backtracking would bring her into focus. At moments, she had the feeling she was mourning a ghost.

Had it not been for her father's continued grieving, she might have doubted what she'd seen with her own eyes. But she'd seen Lisette's corpse, the slow-seeping blood overflowing the rim of her ear, drip-dripping into the mass of thick gray hair. And she'd seen Lisette and her father, both of them naked in every way; a glimpse of their reality. So, there was no question that Lisette had been very real after all.

Her thoughts shunted back and forth like two lanes of traffic. One traveling on a bridge over a main road, the other in some tunnel beneath the road. And she was close to terrified of approaching the main road for fear of coming into collision with the nonstop traffic of her grief.

In just two or three months Ray became an old, old man. He made a few, brief-lived, rather pathetic attempts at playing his old, jovial self when some of his friends stopped by to say, "Come on there, Ray, let's go out for a few!" He'd pull himself upright and make a stab at one of those flashing grins that came across now as grimaces. Soon, all but two or three of the truly dedicated, old-days friends remained; the others melted away in an embarrassed, hearty series of promises to stop in again soon. It was too depressing, like seeing a clown at the circus take a really awful fall, then slowly realizing it hadn't been part of the act but for real and the man was in agony while the audience laughed and laughed.

The two or three friends who did come back regularly came with the mannerisms and quiet sobriety of people attending a long, ongoing wake. They sat with Ray in the disordered living room exchanging reminiscences and silences, staying an hour or so at a time before departing with solemn smiles and evident satisfaction at having done their duty by a friend. The house in Remington Park had become a funeral parlor. Glenn hated having to go home each day. She knew her father had lost all his desire to live, and witnessed his daily aging feeling sad and utterly helpless. She had no idea what to say or do for him, no idea what might induce him to abort his death trip, no idea even if it were her right to interfere. She couldn't determine if the failure were Ray's as a father, or her own, as a daughter. But the failure seemed to her to be unquestionable.

She telephoned, thinking she'd talk to Elizabeth, but no one answered. She tried several times, then gave up, wondering what they would have had to say to each other anyway. They'd just have talked about Lisette and Glenn didn't really think she could handle that.

Gaby fussed and hovered over Ray like a tall apparition, her long dresses making the dust rise, her bony musician's fingers pressing tentative caresses on her father's hands and shoulders. And while she wafted doubtfully through the rooms, lost to her fantasies of standing ovations and cries of ENCORE! and BRAVO! her son embarked on a process of what appeared to Glenn to be an attempt single-handedly to destroy the house and everything in it.

Around his bed, the wallpaper began magically to shred. Strips were missing. There were telltale fingernail marks where he'd picked at the paper to get under a seam so he could then peel off a goodly amount of the wallpaper all in one luxurious, satisfying go. Arriving at the plaster underneath, he then began to pick at the plaster until he'd managed to expose the lathing. Gaby clapped her hands together in an attitude of despair when Mrs. Petrov pointed out the damage, and stood in stunned silence paying homage to her son's talent for destruction.

Mrs. Petrov vacuumed up the mound of plaster dust, disliking the woman Gaby had grown to be even more than she'd disliked her as a child. She went to find Glenn to say, "Is unhappy boy, this one. Come, you see."

Glenn, suddenly furious with both mother and son, mixed up a batch of plaster of Paris and covered over the hole. Given any provocation whatsoever, she might have plastered Corey's hands to his sides, and Gaby's mouth. She was outraged, too,

with herself for being angry with Corey when it was so obvious
his manners and habits were a direct result of Gaby's inability
to discipline or even to talk rationally with him. And never
mind behaving consistently with the child. That was plainly,
impossibly beyond the range of Gaby's capabilities. Gaby hadn't
one consistent bone in her entire body. Corey was going to
grow up into some kind of monster if somebody didn't do
something. But Gaby wouldn't let Glenn near him. Glenn began
to long to escape the house, to run away before the entire thing
fell in on all of them.

Corey next succeeded, via something mysteriously flushed
down the toilet situated between his room and Gaby's, totally
to foul the plumbing—sinks and toilets backing up throughout
the house—with the result that it cost several hundred dollars
to locate the blockage and repair the water damage. The plumber
never did mention what it was Corey had put down the toilet.
Ray, looking confused and addled at being temporarily side-
tracked from his musings, wrote out the check for the plumber,
anxious only to get back to his chair in the living room and
his assortment of recollections: serene images of Lisette striding
across Saint Catherine Street, long brown hair sailing on the
wind, her breasts magnificent, her carriage so proud. Beautiful.
God, how beautiful! He heard her voice as she lay beside him
in the night, whispering lines of poetry; accented and sweet
her voice as the unanticipated scent of lilac brought by the
breeze on a spring evening; teaching him of love, loving; opening and closing herself around him like the languid swell of a
sea anemone, drifting, glorious. He longed to close his eyes
permanently and be carried away into the heart of his remem-
brances. Everything had ended, the joy gone. A great, giddy
game they'd played; running hand in hand laughing through a
lifetime. Ended. Her brightness, her softness, her caring. Gone.
He knew the children wanted him to get up and assume some
sort of control in the household but he couldn't and wished
they had the sensitivity, the understanding to leave him alone.
The only one of them all whose company he could tolerate was
Corey, whose insistence on hugging lifted Ray, at moments,
past his assorted dreamings and into active caring. He couldn't
bear to look at Glenn. He felt tricked every time. His heart
lifted eagerly, his eyes opened wider as if his vision were

deceiving him. Which, of course, it was. It was always Glenn, never Lisette.

Corey next started a kitchen fire by fooling around with the pop-up toaster, tried to put the fire out himself, realized he couldn't and went shouting through the house to lock himself safely in the upstairs linen closet while Gaby stood in the downstairs hallway wringing her hands. Glenn, after telephoning the fire department, threw flour all over the place in a partially successful attempt to stop the fire.

After the firemen departed—leaving an odd black and white path of outsized footprints from the kitchen to the front door—Glenn bolted up the stairs, yanked Corey out of the linen closet, threw him against the wall and smacked him as hard as she could across the face—tears springing from her eyes as she did it—before turning him round, bending him over and applying her shoe to his behind half a dozen times. Then, trembling and deeply, profoundly disturbed by what she'd just done, she flew downstairs to tell Gaby, "If you don't pay some attention to that child, if you don't start helping him, I'll have you *both* committed!"

At which Gaby decided, "You don't have the right to tell me or anyone what to do! And there's nothing at all wrong with Corey. He just happens to have a very healthy curiosity." Pulling herself up to her full six feet, she thrust out her chin defiantly, awaiting Glenn's response.

Feeling murderous, Glenn looked at her sister's preposterously haughty expression and laughed. "What Corey needs is a *mother!*" she said. "And what you need is about ten years with a good psychiatrist!" Then unable to risk saying anything more because the instinct to commit some further physical act of violence was overtaking her, she turned and marched up the stairs—still carrying her shoe—and down the hall to her room to collapse on the side of her bed and sit staring at the opposite wall, thinking, I've got to get out of here! Got to!

But she couldn't leave, unable to determine if it was guilt or continuing grief or an overdeveloped sense of responsibility that kept her from simply walking away from what was happening. As a result, her studies suffered. She couldn't keep her mind on her work and spent less and less time at her sketching, more and more time seeking an escape in reading. She read until her eyes burned and her vision blurred. Her year-end grade slipped down to a B-minus and she finished her second year at the College in a state of suffocating depression. She was failing, at everything. One thing happened causing the next thing to happen, failure after failure. She couldn't cope with Gaby or her father, wasn't allowed to communicate except briefly with Corey; she felt trapped and inhibited to such an extent she couldn't free herself for her work. So she was failing there too.

She had no summer job, and was obliged weekly to present herself to her father to ask for expense money. She felt as if her ribcage were slowly being collapsed by the tremendous pressures inside the house and by her inability to relieve them.

Corey, home all day for the summer holidays, was engaged wholeheartedly in his wrecking project. He somehow managed to smash one of the attic windows, didn't bother to tell anyone about it and within a week the house was being overrun by squirrels. There were birds nesting in the attic and an enter-prising swarm of bees had set up housekeeping inside under the eaves. The exterminators came trooping through the house, disposing of the bees, birds and squirrels. A glazier came to replace the window. And the bills came in to be paid. A few hundred dollars more. Ray, his eyes on other worlds, wrote out checks.

After that, Corey decided to run away from home, but not before lifting almost forty dollars from his mother's handbag—an art he'd learned watching Gaby rifle her mother's purse time after time—to cover his expenses. He was located almost twelve hours later by a patrolman at the amusement park where Corey had managed to spend every cent of the money Gaby had so cleverly obtained by slipping a check for signing beneath her father's nose. He had consumed four hotdogs, three hamburg-ers, two cones of French fries, five or six cotton candies, two boxes of popcorn, three hot-buttered ears of corn, two candy apples and seven or eight orange drinks. He began vomiting in the police station and had to be taken from there to the Children's Hospital where his stomach was pumped. Gaby, borrowing money from a grudging Dana—Glenn being without

funds and Ray in the habit of never carrying cash—taxied
down to the hospital to retrieve her child and returned home
with a blanched Corey who swore he'd be good from now on.

No amount of reasoning or commonsense conversation with
Gabrielle would induce her to see that Corey needed attention,
consistent, caring attention. Gaby considered Glenn's comments malevolent and repaid her with meaningful silence, refusing to speak to Glenn except when absolutely necessary.
Glenn didn't mind. She was beginning to believe that her sister
ought to be institutionalized or reported to some group or other
for being an incompetent, neglectful mother.

In any case, she preferred Gaby's silence to her senseless
attempts at rational conversation—those times when she'd get
a certain loose set to her mouth, her eyes growing large and
madly earnest as she went on and on. Glenn was positive there'd
be hope for Corey if he could get away from his mother. Often
he displayed a wonderful intelligence for a nine-year-old and
an interesting sense of humor far too mature for his years. His
destructiveness, Glenn was sure, was his way of trying to get
someone to take him seriously and offer some attention. But
anything she might try to do for him was successfully blocked
by Gaby.

Dana was no help when he came to visit bringing tales of
his unsuccessful affairs and successful career. Listening to him
speak quietly of his latest, most recently departed lover, Glenn
felt horribly sorry for him and horribly angry. She wanted to
take him and Gaby, Corey and her father, line the lot of them
up against the wall and bloodlessly, painlessly murder them.
Why couldn't they stop dreaming and playing and start attending to the very real crises in the house? The only one among
them who seemed even partially aware of what was going on
was Mrs. Petrov. But even she, after a few attempts to lure
Ray out of his dreamy lethargy with offers of borscht and potato
pancakes, gave up and performed her cleaning tasks in tight-
lipped silence, speaking only to advise Glenn that she was
raising her daily rate five dollars more and would they please,
please stop emptying the ashtrays into the wicker wastepaper
baskets because the ashes just went right through the wicker
onto the floor.

"I'll ask Gaby to stop it," Glenn promised.

Mrs. Petrov looked at her sadly, saying, "Your mama, she would not like for to see what happens here."

Glenn spent most of her free time that summer walking through the streets that bordered the Park or sitting in the Park trying to sketch or read. But her mind wandered and she'd visualize herself taking the small sum of money left her by Lisette and setting up some sort of new life for herself in a place of her own. It was impossible. One year's tuition at the College would take almost half her inheritance. And what would she live on? She found herself, to her horror, speculating on her father's death; imagining herself in possession of a decent sum of money, in a position finally to get away and live her own life. She was deeply ashamed of her thoughts. She didn't wish her father dead. She just wanted some way out.

She hadn't any real idea of the terms of her father's will. Even if there weren't any money, there was the house and that had to be worth quite a lot, unless Corey succeeded in destroying it first. People were very eager to own homes in the area. It was considered prestigious to live in the Park, have a Park key, Park privileges—the dog-watering trough, all that. She felt neither one way or another about it and, given an option, knew she'd sell the house in a minute and use the money to establish herself on her own. The house was just a house, didn't mean anything. She didn't think Gaby or Dana cared any more for the old place than she did.

Which was why when Ray died—quietly, of a coronary while sitting dreaming of Lisette—almost a year to the date of Lisette's death, Glenn was stupefied at the reactions of her brother and sister to the terms of their father's will.

For Glenn, his death brought sadness and relief. He hadn't wanted to live. She knew it and was glad to have it ended for him. Oddly, she reacted far more strongly to an obituary notice in the newspaper the day after Ray's death. Elizabeth had died. Glenn read it, studied Elizabeth's photograph and began grieving anew as if Lisette had died all over again. Somehow, as long as Elizabeth had remained alive in the world, Lisette wasn't completely dead. With Elizabeth now gone too, Glenn felt it really was all over.

Ray's death truly upset only one person—Corey. He wept

loudly, brokenly from the moment he learned of his grandfather's death, all the way through the services and funeral and for an entire week afterward. Glenn studied him, awed and moved by the depth of his feelings, certain now she'd been right all along about him and curious to know what other powerful emotions he contained. He was inconsolable. Gaby couldn't talk to him. He refused to sit near her and shrank from her touch, glaring at her with an expression bordering on hatred. He shrugged off Dana's hand and accepted Glenn's invitation to go for a walk with narrow-eyed quivering suspicion.

They walked for miles, bundled up against the cold December air, all the way down to the lakefront where, huddled on a bench, they gazed in silence at the green-gray waters crashing against the breakfronts. Eyeing Glenn, Corey brought out a package of cigarettes and a box of wooden matches and, just daring her to stop him, lit up, returned the cigarettes and matches to his pocket and inhaled with obvious pleasure. Glenn watched all this, greatly interested both in the performance and his apparent expertise. He could feel her watching and waited to hear what she'd say.

"Been doing that long?" she asked, her hands shoved deep into her pockets.

"About a year," he said around the cigarette, eyes on the horizon. "Don't give me any crap, either," he warned. "I've had enough of that from *her*."

Ten years old, she thought, studying his pinched profile. He held himself very tightly together, as though fearful of strong gusts of wind or emotion.

"Why shouldn't you smoke?" she said, thinking it made no difference. "You do everything else you want to do."

"How would *you* know?" he accused, flashing a hotly angry look at her before turning once more to the horizon. "All you care about is your own stuff, the things you do, the paintings, the books you read. You didn't care about grampa."

"But you did?"

"Sure," he said, keeping his voice easy, determined not to give himself away or to start acting like a baby again. "He was okay." He shrugged and switched the cigarette to the other hand. "He didn't bother anybody or anything. He had lots of really good stories to tell, too."

"What do you want, Corey? If you had your choice, what would you want?"

"What's that, some kind of game?" His eyes were suspicious. "You don't care."

"I might," she said. "What would you want? Tell me. I'd honestly like to know."

"Something," he said vaguely. "I don't know." I'd like to get about a thousand miles away from here, he thought. Maybe ten thousand miles.

"Do you like things the way they are?" She wanted to open him up, see if he'd talk about Gaby, if he had any objectivity about his mother and the life they were living.

He swiveled round on the bench to look at her with an expression of mingled disbelief and sardonic amusement. "Are you nuts?" he said, tossing away his half-finished cigarette. "You must be nuts!" he stated. "Do I *like* the way things are? Oh, sure," he said sarcastically. "I'm crazy about them. Just the way you are. What's that mean anyway, do I *like* the way things are?"

"Just what it means. Do you?"

He looked at her, leaning his arm on the back of the bench. "You *are* nuts!" he said. "I *hate* it! She's really nutty. D'you think I don't know about her? I know. Believe me! Uncle Dana's okay, when he wants to be. But he's so hung up about himself all he can do is make a big deal thing out of his boyfriends. And you. I don't know *what* you are. But you're really nutty asking me do I like the way things are. Next time I go, boy, I'll really go for sure. No more fooling around."

"You mean that wasn't for real? It was just fooling around?"

"Sure! Are you kidding? You don't think I've got the brains to know how to run for real? I just wanted to give *her* a headache. It made me so mad the way she was always bilking him out of money, sticking checks in front of his nose, getting him to sign them, spending his money because she didn't want to spend her own and thinking he didn't know what she was doing. Grampa knew. He knew all about her."

"She *did* that?" Glenn asked, disgusted.

"Sure she did. She used to do the same thing to gramma,

take money out of her bag when gramma wasn't looking, help herself to twenty or thirty dollars. She's got no goddamned *morals*, my mother."

"God! That is *disgusting!*"

"It is, isn't it? Let's go back. I'm freezing." He was starting to say too much. It was bad to start saying everything in your head.

They got up and started to walk back. On impulse, spotting an open restaurant with its front windows appealingly steamed-up, Glenn asked, "Want to have a coffee?"

"Okay, sure," he said offhandedly. He'd never had coffee in a restaurant. Cokes, hamburgers, hotdogs. But coffee was grownup stuff. Nobody'd ever offered him any. He glanced over at Glenn, saw she was serious and followed her into the restaurant and slid onto a stool beside her at the counter. She ordered two coffees, they came and he nearly burned the roof of his mouth off on the first sip but didn't let it show. He really felt pretty good sitting there with her and stole another look at her thinking she wasn't so bad really, and nice to look at. Better than his mom, that was for sure.

"I used to play hookey," he admitted, surprising himself. He hadn't known he was going to say that.

"What did you do when you did?" she asked, more and more interested in him.

"Aw, I'd just sneak back to the house and hang around with grampa. We'd talk about gramma a lot or watch TV, play cards, eat onion sandwiches."

"Where was Gaby while you were doing all this?"

"Sacked out upstairs. She's always sleeping," he said, wrinkling his pale forehead. "All she *ever* does is sleep. Like she's got to rest up for all that big important work she's got to do. Or maybe Prince Charming's going to come kiss her and she'll wake up in Wonderland or something."

Glenn laughed, saying, "I didn't know that."

"How *would* you know?" he said reasonably. "You're out first thing every morning, off to the College. So how would you know? Only time she's ever up at any kind of a decent hour is when Mrs. Petrov's coming and she knows she's gotta get up because the linens have to be changed. She's okay, Mrs. Petrov. You like her?"

"I've always liked her. She looked after me when I was a baby. Did you know that?"

"Yeah, she told me." He risked another sip of the coffee. Still too hot. How the hell did people drink this stuff?

"Would you rather have a Coke?" she offered, noticing his slight grimace.

"No, this is fine. Thank you," he added, his hand curved protectively around the thick white mug. "I like coffee."

He felt the coffee burning its way down to his stomach and thought, You're okay. He stole another peek at her. Really okay.

"Why're you such a little bastard?" she asked with a smile. "Doing the things you do, tearing the place apart."

"Why're you so perfect?" he countered. "Always fixing up because you're the only one who knows the right way to do things and everybody else is just screwing up."

"I happen to like things tidy. I'm good at . . . practical things," she defended herself, astonished by the depths of his comprehension.

"Okay. So what? Does that mean you've got to make everybody else feel like they're stupid?"

"Is that what I do, Corey?"

"You do," he said forgivingly. "But I guess you just can't help it."

She smiled. He smiled back at her. It was the first time in weeks, possibly the first time ever she'd seen him smile openheartedly. She felt something inside of her break in response to the rare sweetness and intelligence of his smile, as if he'd given her a priceless gift and she'd ignored it until almost too late to reciprocate.

He felt good all of a sudden, better than he had in a long, long time.

"I'm sorry," she said seriously, "if that's the way I make you feel. I don't like the idea of making anybody feel that way. But you're hard work."

"I know," he said with equal seriousness. "I guess," he switched subjects adeptly, "you'll be moving out now, huh?"

"I guess so," she answered. "I'll tell you something, Corey. I wish I could take you with me."

His eyes widened and he stared at her in disbelief, experiencing a shooting excitement. "What for?"

"It's going to be so quiet," she said glibly, hastily burying the notion. "It'll be hard getting used to. No repairs. No shouting."

"Oh! Yeah." He made a face and picked up his cup, holding it in both hands, his eyes scanning the Coca-Cola ads behind the counter. "Sure."

They returned to the house without further conversation. Typically, Corey dumped his coat and boots beside the front door and took off up the stairs to his room.

Annoyed, Glenn hung away his coat and her own, staring up the stairs trying to make sense of her feelings for the boy. There was something there, hidden away behind that angelic face and fiery hair, something she couldn't define. All those months he'd been sneaking home from school to spend his time with Ray. And no one had known. Or cared. And Gaby. Stealing from her parents. God! she thought, shivering. What kind of people are we? Am I?

She should have known, been somehow able to anticipate how Dana and Gaby would act. But afterward, she'd tell herself, I don't have a suspicious mind—which was true—and it simply wouldn't have occurred to her to expect any of that. But for years, the pain of this memory was a too-tender spot she couldn't bear to probe.

Ray left the house and its furnishings to the two older children. To Glenn, he left twenty-five hundred dollars and some stock in the station. The rest of his holdings were to be held in trust for Corey, Corey's father to execute the trust. Gaby turned purple upon learning the control of Corey's money would be in the hands of George Shea. She ranted and raved and stormed up and down the stairs slamming doors, smashing things, finally falling into tight-lipped silence.

Glenn was pleased for Corey, mildly disappointed for herself and horrified by the way Dana and Gaby proceeded to try to tear each other to pieces over the house, literally coming to blows over possession of a battered loveseat, shrieking at each other while dividing up the china and silverware. Like crazed animals. An arbitrator finally had to be called in and the decision was made to sell the house and split the proceeds between the two principals. The arbitrator would also make a fair split

of the furnishings. It was further agreed that Glenn would be
permitted to stay on in the house until she was able to find a
place of her own. But Gaby and Corey would have to move
out, to satisfy Dana.

With her limited funds, Glenn found it difficult. She spent
hours every day looking at flats, apartments, slowly growing
panicky because everything she saw was either too expensive,
too dark, or too something. And she was forced by her lack
of success to be there in the house nightly to witness the fighting
between Dana and Gaby—the arbitrator mediating—over every
single item contained within the walls. Things Glenn would
never have dreamed had any value were worthy of extensive
bickering. Lisette's mildewed, disintegrating Louis Vuitton
luggage. Dana traded off Ray's Gucci suitcase in order to gain
possession of Lisette's two bags, two chipped glass candle-
sticks, a yellowed linen tablecloth and a boxful of daguerreo-
types. He truly had no idea what he was doing. He simply
couldn't tolerate the idea of Gaby helping herself to anything
more that didn't belong to her. He despised himself for rising
to her bait, for haggling with her like some demented fishwife.
But he couldn't stop.

The sound of their arguing voices and that of the ineffectual
arbitrator rang inescapably through the rooms until in self-
defense and out of desperation, Glenn took to inviting Corey
out, to a movie, for a walk, a hamburger. Anything to get
away from the ugliness of their raw greed and lamentable lack
of family—or any other—feeling.

Corey called his mother a vulture. "I hate her!" he declared.
"Soon's I'm old enough, I'm getting away. A few more years,
that's all."

Glenn didn't know what to say to him, and wished more
and more she could have him with her. But Gaby would never
allow it. She kept thinking about it though and finally saw that
even if she couldn't actually do it, it might mean something
to Corey to hear her say it.

"If I could," she told him, "I would take you with me to
live."

She was rewarded by a look of such affection and gratitude,
she nearly destroyed the moment by sweeping him into her
arms as Lisette might have done. But she knew how dangerous

and misleading those gestures could be and held back from committing the error of allowing herself to be blindly led by her emotions. "I mean it, Corey," she said instead. "If there were any possible way, I'd do it."

He didn't say anything. He was a little disappointed because he'd thought she'd hug him. But at least she'd said it and that meant a lot. He knew she meant it.

The house was sold. Feeling panicky now, Glenn took a week off school to look for a place. No success and she felt outraged now at having been left so little, less than six thousand dollars altogether, not including those pretty worthless stock certificates. It was all she was ever going to receive that she wouldn't have to work for. Of that money, she'd need almost half to pay rent, eat, and clothe herself. It wasn't possible. She was going to have to leave the College at year's end, take a job and continue on toward her certification on a part-time basis. She felt cheated, betrayed, not at all prepared to find herself in the position she was in. Yes, she'd been wanting to get out, get away, but on her terms, in her own time, not this way, without alternatives. She was becoming quietly frantic when, by chance, she saw a Room To Rent sign on the school bulletin board and went along to have a look.

It was a large attic room with a skylight, a hotplate for cooking. The furniture was old and dilapidated, but the rent was low, the light excellent. She'd be able to add her own few bits and pieces to the existing furniture. Most important, she'd have ample room to spread out because the attic ran the entire length and width of the house. There was even a bathroom at the far end, sloppily enclosed—hastily framed-in, plasterboard nailed on—and left unfinished.

"You can do anything up here you like," the caretaker told her. "Just don't get no paint on the floors if you're gonna be painting. And no wallpaper. You put up wallpaper, you gotta take it down when you go."

"What about a refrigerator?"

"I think maybe I could find you one from somewhere, one of the other buildings the landlord has. Lemme see."

She paid the deposit and the first month's rent, then hurried back to the house to begin packing her belongings. She felt very much better, certain now that things would work out.

Corey knew the instant he came into the house and up the stairs that she'd found a place. When he arrived at her bedroom door and saw her hurrying back and forth packing her stuff, he was kind of scared for a minute that maybe this would be the end and they'd never see each other again.

"You want me to help you pack your stuff?" he offered.

She looked up and smiled, and he knew she wouldn't just go away and leave him. Not her. She wouldn't do that.

"Grab a carton," she said. "You can pack the books if you like."

"Sure."

Finally, when the room looked really empty, as if nobody had ever lived there, he said, "Okay if I ride with you in the taxi? Just for a look?"

She said, "Absolutely."

The two of them and the driver loaded her things into the cab and he rode with her to her new home on Wellington Road, to walk up and down the length of the attic before pronouncing the place, "Okay. I like it. It's really okay."

They got all the stuff up the stairs and she paid the driver. Corey could tell she didn't want him hanging around now because she wanted to get busy putting all her things away. He said, "I'll come visit," and hurried off. Back in the new apartment his mother had rented, he made himself a pot of stew from scratch. He watched television until the stew was ready, then more television while he ate his dinner. Then it was time to go to bed, all by himself in the big empty apartment with boxes and crates and cartons all over the place. His mother was out somewhere with her loony friends. It was too bad, he thought, Aunt Glenn didn't have a telephone. It would've been really great to phone her up—maybe even be the first one to call her—and say hi. Or something. But she didn't have a telephone, and he didn't feel like watching any more TV. So he took the wine bottle and replaced the cork, carried his plate out to the kitchen, cleaned everything up, and went to bed and lay in the dark wondering what would happen next.

# Eight

She used a small amount of her money to improve the attic. She taped and spackled the plasterboard enclosing the bathroom, then painted the cubicle yellow to brighten further the already bright room. The walls of the main portion of the room were finished with rough plaster applied between the beams—the ceiling left completely unfinished, which Glenn liked—and there was little she could do beyond a coat of fresh white paint. There was no need for curtains for the windows at each end of the attic because the neighboring buildings were not high enough to afford a view of the interior of her room. She tacked up some of her favorite drawings, stacked her paintings against one wall, rearranged the furniture so that the far half of the attic—away from the street—was the living area, and set up her easel and paints at the front end, designating that the work area. A table, two rickety chairs, the hotplate and an antique refrigerator minus its original crisper drawers completed the furnishing.

Since her tuition through to the end of that year had been paid prior to her father's death, she was able, to a degree, to continue her lifestyle fairly much as before. Except for the loneliness.

The silence of her room, of the whole house, oppressed her. She found herself listening for Dana and Gaby's hostile voices, Corey's footsteps. Finally, she took to playing her radio all the time, allowing it to underscore all her activities when she was home. It helped, but only a little. She had no telephone, couldn't afford one and expected no calls anyway, so it didn't make any difference.

She was, however, better able to concentrate on her work and her grades began improving, climbing. Dana occasionally left cryptic notes in her mailslot—she interpreted this as his way of apologizing for those weeks of shrieking madness— inviting her out to dinners that were never quite as successful and relaxed as either of them would have wished. He seemed in a state of permanent embarrassment about his behavior over the house and its contents and kept explaining his side of the issue, saying, "I simply couldn't allow her to take one more thing that didn't belong to her."

Glenn quietly said, "Why don't you just stop talking about it, Dana?"

"You are not," he told her, hurt, "as sympatico as you could be."

"You," she replied, "are not sympatico at all. You seem to have no ability to see yourself, or how you hurt people."

"How have I hurt you?" he asked, looking upset.

"It doesn't matter," she said. "Just forget about what happened. It's over. I understand why you did it. Let's not talk about it anymore."

He sat for a moment studying her, thinking he could see it more and more every time he saw her: how much like Lisette she was in so many ways. Not just her facial features, but certain mannerisms, and her intense dislike of unpleasantness.

"You don't like us much, do you?" he said, inspecting his fingernails.

"I like you a lot," she answered. "Sometimes." She smiled to cheer him up. "Gaby I like from a distance."

Gaby made no effort whatsoever at contact with Glenn or Dana. It was only through Corey that Glenn learned they'd moved into a modern new apartment building downtown and that Gaby was seeing a great deal of a wealthy, older man she'd recently encountered in the foyer of the building.

Corey's remarks about his mother and her new boyfriend were antagonistic, but nonetheless incisive.

"He's old, for Pete's sake!" Corey said dismissingly.

"How old?" Glenn asked.

"Boy, he must be at least forty-five."

"Corey, that's not so old. Your mother's almost thirty-three."

"He's *old*," Corey insisted. "You'd have to see him to really appreciate what I mean."

Glenn made tea and sat down on the floor with him, listening to him talk in his elliptical fashion about school and the other tenants he encountered in the apartment building and movies he'd seen on days he'd taken off from school.

"Don't you like school?" she asked him.

"I already know most of what I need to know," he responded.

That did seem to be true. She was amazed by his independence and capability. He got around the city either by foot or public transportation and seemed to know where everything was, including restaurants, which he'd grouped ethnically. She learned he had a passion for Greek and middle-Eastern food, and the two of them sometimes dined on pita and dolmas, making a meal out of appetizers, unable to afford more even if they pooled their resources.

In addition to a very small allowance from Gaby, Corey did periodically collect substantial sums of money from his father whom he visited solely for that purpose.

"It's interesting, you know," Corey told her. "He always has some woman around. But he's still got pictures of mom all over the place. I can tell the two of them hate each other, but all the two of them ever do is talk about how much they hate the other. They hardly ever talk about anything else. He's got to know everything she's doing, sits there pumping me every time I go. Interesting isn't it?"

Corey was so candid and open about his motives and feelings for people that Glenn found herself thinking of him less and less as a child and more and more as an equal. He was, obviously, never going to be a scholar, an academic. But he was going to be something, and whatever it was, it would be exciting. On the one side there was about him a quality that was old and knowing and weary. Yet, on the other side, his whimsical sense of humor and diminutive stature made him positively charming. She looked forward to his visits, encouraging him to come as often as he wished.

For his part, Corey couldn't stand his own apartment, the place was so noisy. Lying in bed at night, you could hear toilets flushing all over the place—above you, next door, across the hall—and it was so hot all the time. He was always turning the thermostats down and Gaby was always marching in and turning them back up again. And the place was small: two boxy bedrooms and a living room so draped and carpeted he got claustrophobic if he sat in it for more than half an hour. He hated it.

If it weren't bad enough, she'd latched on to this Lloyd guy who happened to hold open the lobby door for them one afternoon and now she was up in his penthouse night and day eating dinners old Lloyd had his "man" cook up, or going out to shows. She didn't even care what Corey did.

"I could burn the whole place down," he said aloud to himself, standing in the middle of the living room—with his shoes on, defiantly—one afternoon. "I could steal everything in the place or break all the furniture and nobody would even care. Might be days before she even noticed."

Fed up, he took off to see Aunt Glenn. At least she was always glad to see him and didn't mind trying new things. If it weren't for her, he thought, he'd probably just take off for good.

In the spring of that year, she was at the museum doing some sketches in the African room when she saw a familiar-looking figure go past the entrance, then return and peer in at her. Ralph. She smiled at his approach.

"I thought you'd be in Spain with Dali," she said, seeing he hadn't changed at all. The same tiger's eyes, lion's mane.

"Next year," he said, looking at the drawing in her lap. "Still at the College, eh?"

"Just until the end of this year," she said, wondering what it was about him that invariably made her feel compelled to explain herself. She disliked doing that.

He stood silently looking at her for some time, watching her complete her sketch before making an awkwardly offhanded gesture, saying, "Want to have a coffee?"

"All right," she agreed, and got up to begin putting her drawing materials away in her portfolio.

He carried the portfolio for her as they walked through the marble-floored echoey rooms on their way to the cafeteria downstairs.

"I've got a job here," he said at last, "with the curator. Working on restorations."

"Do you like it?"

"It's money. And I get a lot of off time. I saw in the paper where your father died." He looked at her—a flickering of his eyes—then looked away. "Not too lucky in that department, eh?"

"I suppose not. I only seem to see you after..." She stopped, realizing the thought progression was macabre.

"Yeah," he agreed. "That is kind of spooky, isn't it?"

They found a table, parked the portfolio, then went to get the coffee. "Still hanging out with that gang?" he asked her as they settled themselves at the table.

"Not so much. I see some of the kids once in a while. A lot of them dropped out last year, you know. There really aren't too many left of the group I started with."

"I could've told you that," he said. "I did tell you that, didn't I?"

"I don't remember."

"Sure. Most of them were just into the College because it gave them a kind of whippy prestige around the old home neighborhood. You know. Oh, look! Little so-and-so's going to art school! Isn't that nice, dear?"

"Are you still living at home?" she asked, remembering how he'd talked about his parents.

"Moved out last year. I guess you're out now too, eh?"

"I have an attic," she said. "I don't know how it's going to be in the winter, but it's good right now."

"Still scared to take your clothes off?" he asked with a small smile.

"What are we talking about?" she asked, gearing herself up for another invitation from him to fuck.

"Pose. Remember? I told you you'd look all right."

"You're really *very* complimentary," she said, color rising into her face. "I suppose your lines just knock girls off all over the place."

"No, I'm serious. I mean, just because I don't make speeches and do a whole lot of social shit . . . Words!" He made an angry face. "I'll tell you," he leaned closer to her. "I'll paint you or lay you. Whatever you like. Or both. No big deal. I'd like to do both."

"If it isn't any big deal, why do you keep asking me?"

"How d'you figure that?" He looked petulant. "Once before I asked you. It's not like every day, you know. A lot of girls, they'd be flattered."

"I'm not flattered," she lied, thinking she might go to his place just to see what it was like. She would if he could manage to ask her a little more nicely. She didn't feel like going home and spending another evening all alone.

"Yes, you are," he said slyly. "You just don't want to let on. You let a guy know you're interested, next thing anybody knows you've wrecked your reputation or some such shit. I know you're a virgin. I can tell. It's kind of why you get to me, sort of. I'd really like to see you get all worked up."

"Don't you think you're just a little vain?" she said, trying to maintain her composure. She was very rattled, on unfamiliar terrain. "What makes you think you could possibly excite me?"

"Won't find out until you try," he challenged.

She had to stop for a moment and think about that. No one had ever expressed such an overt interest in her, particularly a sexual one. Ralph's frankly stated desire was something new and puzzling. She'd given very little thought to her body, her sexuality. Having years before—hearing her mother's voice echoing in her ear—learned to masturbate to perfection, she occasionally satisfied herself and thought nothing more of it. She disliked thinking about it. Now, here was Ralph offering for a second time to enlighten her. He might not be around to make a third offer. And while she did find him a little difficult to talk to, she liked the shape of his face, his mouth. She pictured him without his clothes and felt suddenly overheated, moist. Ask me again, she thought. Be a little nicer and maybe. Sex might expand her awareness, enable her to see differently, work even better. All kinds of things.

"Thinking it over, eh?" he guessed, finishing off his coffee, then lighting a fresh cigarette. He decided she really had no idea she was beautiful. The fact that she seemed completely unaware of this turned him on hard. "Tell you what," he said, tipping back in his chair, the cigarette between his teeth. "We'll drop your stuff off at your place, grab some spaghetti downtown and then make it over to my place."

"Is that an invitation?" she asked, deciding she would go with him.

"You mean am I paying?"

"That's right."

"Sure," he said expansively. "I can handle that."

"All right," she agreed, not quite sure what she was doing in agreeing to go with him. She liked the way he looked well enough—he might be transposed rather beautifully into a painting—but she wasn't altogether certain she understood most of the things he said. His stunning self-assurance was somehow unattractive. He lacked modesty. But her curiosity far outweighed her qualms, so they set out to walk to her place.

He strolled from one end of the attic to the other with a proprietary air, pausing to examine the drawings and paintings she'd put up on the walls, then smiled at her disarmingly, saying, "It's not a bad place. And some of these are good." Satisfied with the way things were progressing, he waited for her to lock up before preceding her down the three flights of stairs and back out into the street. He didn't know what it was—aside from her looks—but there was something about her he liked. Maybe it was the fact that he knew she was nervous having him in her room, seeing her bed. Some girls were like that, he knew. They figured if you saw a bed it meant automatically you were going to put them down on it. He smiled. She'd be interesting to know. He liked the long rangy look of her, the silky-looking sway of her hair, the size of her hands, long, but with broad palms and a lot of strength. He'd enjoyed watching her sketching for those few minutes. You could get a definite feel for how good a person would be on paper by the look of her hand, her fingers around the pencil. She had that physical certainty in her hands.

She took deep breaths, realizing she'd scarcely been breathing the whole time they'd been inside. She'd been waiting for him to try something, to touch her, to make some move. He hadn't and she felt very relieved. They walked all the way downtown to an Italian restaurant that served excellent, inexpensive food. After two beers, Ralph grew more talkative, less abrasive, urging her to, "Drink up! Have another one," which she did, gladly. The beer made her feel less nerved-up, more relaxed, and she, too, was able to talk, and laugh with him, finding him less and less menacing with each swallow she took.

"You like the old ale, don't you?" he observed with a wide smile as she finished her fourth glass of lager. "Really smooths down the sharp corners and makes everything nice, eh?"

"It really does," she concurred, smiling back at him. She'd never had so much to drink in her life. She felt wonderful, loose and ready for anything. When she felt his hand on her arm, watched it travel up to her shoulder then down again to her wrist, she heard laughter inside her head and actually trembled at his touch. He was right. He could excite her. In one last lucid moment, she understood she was about to find out things about herself she hadn't known, and was anxious to get on with finding out. No longer nervous or even remotely frightened of him, she watched him pay for the dinner and tried to press two dollars on him for the tip.

"Take it!" she insisted. "I know you really can't afford all this."

He leaned over and pushed the two dollar bills down the front of her blouse, letting his hand brush across her breasts as he said, "When I invite, I pay." Then gave her another of those intense and meaningful smiles that seemed to be mocking her, stating, "I told you so, told you so!"

He lived not far from the restaurant and they went there, climbing the stairs in the dark because, he said, the light switch was broken, arriving at his flat a little out of breath both from overeating and the three-story climb.

"Let me at least make some sketches of you," he said, going around turning on lights. "Trade-off for the dinner?"

"Okay." She laughed, feeling wickedly uninhibited. "Where should I sit?"

"Without the blouse at least, okay?"

"I don't suppose you have anything to drink?" she asked, looking down at her blouse uncertainly. Now that it was happening, she wasn't sure again.

He had some red wine which he poured into a juice glass and gave to her. "Blouse off, okay?" he asked again, walking away from her.

She drank some of the wine, then unsteadily set down the glass and undid the buttons of her blouse. As she removed the blouse, she kept hearing him saying he wanted to watch her masturbate and she hoped that sort of thing wasn't part of what you did with a man because she didn't think she'd be able to. It was something so private, something to be done only when the night was too lonely, the house too quiet and getting to sleep was difficult. In her brassiere, she sat down in the only available chair, the glass of wine in her hand.

He was busy setting up, sharpening several pencils and didn't look up for a minute or two, then looked over at her and shook his head, agitated.

"The bra, the bra! I don't want to draw your *bra!*"

"Well," she said with drunken dignity, "I am not taking it off!"

"Shit!" He slammed down his pencils and charged across the room. "Just take the fucking thing off and stop assing around!" He reached in back of her with practiced hands, unhooked the bra, tugged it down over her arms and walked back to the easel leaving her clutching the glass and the brassiere, trying to cover her breasts with both.

"Come on!" he said, ready to begin. "Just come *on!*"

He was not going to defeat her, she thought, suddenly angry. She drained the last of the wine, plucked away the bra and sat boldly facing him, her cheeks on fire. She didn't dare look down and see herself.

"Turn a little more toward me," he said, not in the least interested in her discomfort. "Tuck your one leg under."

He made several rapid strokes on the paper before quietly saying, "I wish to Christ you weren't such a goddamned virgin. This'd be great if you'd stop playing around and take off your clothes. You're supposed to be an artist, for chrissake! What's the matter with you? You've done goddamned life models before. I've seen better than you, and worse, too."

You're just doing this so you can see me naked, she thought. I know what you're doing. But why am I fighting? Anyway, it wasn't as if he were touching her or anything, he was all the way over there. She stood up, keeping her eyes down, and took off her skirt, her half slip, her garter belt, her stockings and finally—not daring to look at him—her pants. Then she sat down again as he'd posed her, legs tucked under, a draft coming from somewhere as she asked for more wine.

"It's over there," he said. "Help yourself."

Bold, she felt so bold, walking stark naked across his room to pour herself some more wine, then walking dizzily back to the chair, settling into it once more.

She drank the wine more slowly this time, watching him as he worked. All at once she knew he wasn't seeing her, not her. He saw only the light and shade, the lines composing her. She knew that, because he was right: she was an artist. And that was the way she saw when she was working. There was nothing sexual here except in her mind and the wetness between her thighs that had been generated while he'd been urging her out of her clothes.

After an hour of sitting in the one position, she was beginning to sober up and starting to feel terribly cramped. "Are you almost finished?" she asked. "I've got to use your bathroom."

"In a minute," he said, his eyes opaque with concentration as he worked on for several more minutes before setting down his pencil with a loud sigh. "John's over there," he said, pointing over his shoulder to a pair of doors, the first of which turned out to be a closet, the second the bathroom.

After using the toilet, which was surprisingly clean—Why had she expected it to be dirty? He wasn't dirty—she washed between her legs, then inserted the diaphragm, feeling a terrible sense of shame to be squatting in this man's bathroom getting herself ready to be mounted. She wiped her fingers on a tissue, pushed the tissue into her handbag and returned to sit once more in the chair outside.

"Me too," he said, finishing refilling her glass and handing it to her before going into the bathroom. She got up and went to look at the easel, sucking in her breath at the sight of his drawing. It was incredibly good. She couldn't believe how real, how alive the drawing was, and how pretty he'd made her, how dreamy-looking and soft.

Guiltily, she returned to the chair and drank some more wine. Her fingertips were buzzing, she was wet again. Ralph might be just as crazy as people had always claimed but, my God, he was talented! It left her breathless again, thinking of how he'd drawn her, and less defensive about allowing him to see her without her clothes. If he could do that, maybe he wasn't just being arrogant, maybe she should feel flattered at his wanting to have her pose.

The bathroom door opened and he came out naked, startling her so that she sat up very straight, setting down her wineglass. She held her breath as he walked over, took her hand, pulled her up out of the chair and directed her to the bed hidden behind a curtain in the corner of the room. She wanted to say, No, wait a minute, but he effortlessly put her down on the bed—his hands pushing her shoulders down, down—then stretched out beside her, leaning on his elbow saying, "I was right. The body's definitely good. More breast than I'd figured, too."

She had no idea what to say or do so lay very still staring at him, waiting.

"You don't know one goddamned thing, do you?" he said, looking as if this insight gave him pleasure. "Scared, right?"

"I'm not scared of you," she lied.

He put his hand out to touch her arm and she jumped.

*"I'm not scared of you."* He laughed. "Take it easy. Want some more wine?"

She shook her head, her eyes round and alert as he spread his hand out over her breast, then took that hand down across her belly, around her hip. He said, "Relax," and eased his hand between her thighs, smiling self-satisfiedly when she jumped again. "Juicy," he murmured, his face closing in, his mouth getting closer and closer until it was on top of hers. "You really are . . ." He smiled into her face, then his expression became hungry and his mouth came down on hers again, his lips and tongue urging her mouth open, his tongue investigating her lips, making her dizzier, more breathless. His mouth went away and she opened her eyes to see him sitting up, kneeling beside her. She'd never felt the way she did now—eager, yet terrified. He bent over and bit her nipple just hard enough to make her

cry out in soft surprise, then he moved down the bed, pushing
her legs open, sliding both hands up the insides of her thighs
as he looked at her face before looking down between her legs.

"You want to show me how you do for yourself?" he asked
quietly, and she shook her head, No, no. Don't ask me to do
that, don't!

"Okay," he said, beginning to stroke her, looking from her
face back to what he was doing, watching; stroking until she
was lifting herself toward him, feeling the blood pounding in
her ears and the tremendous swelling, building pressure in her
groin. The same, but different, different. When his fingers
moved down, opening her, she helped. To fill the emptiness.
Frantically she wrapped her arms around him as he lowered
himself down on her, his fingers pushing into her, kissing him
with newly gained expertise. She felt she was going crazy,
splitting up into different selves in the heat of an excitement
she'd never dreamed could exist. Anything, she'd do anything
to keep the feeling, make it bigger, better, keep it longer. When
he sat up again, straddling her, pointing himself at her mouth—
his fingers touching her, touching—she understood and obeyed,
opening her mouth, making him sigh happily as she instinctively sucked at him. He said, *"Mother!"* from between clenched
teeth. "Wait a minute! I should've known you'd be good!" He
turned around, fitting himself into her mouth once more as he
held open her thighs, ducked his head and pushed his tongue
into her. Jolted, she closed her eyes and caressed him with her
hands and mouth until she was so violently, totally aroused
she could scarcely breathe at all and could only lift herself to
his mouth so that he'd touch her just there, once more it would
happen, there again, there there until she was gasping, a groan
breaking its way from her throat as he held her down, there
there there and her entire body leaped this way, that way,
shuddering, convulsed and he kept going on and on, making
her leap and dance until she had to cry out, *"Stop!"* in a ragged,
husky voice that was hers but not hers. Then he righted himself,
frenziedly biting on her nipples before putting his mouth to
hers again, his hips grinding against her, the hardness riding
between her thighs bringing her too quickly back to herself and
beyond into an awesome desire to have it all finally, know it
all, get it done. But she stiffened as he began pushing himself

inside of her and he whispered, "Take it! Take it! Don't go all tight now!" She couldn't understand him or her body's reluctance and hated the words, resisting his pushing until he stopped finally and began stroking her again with his fingers, trying to arouse her once more. But his fingers, his pushing hurt now and she didn't know where to go with the hurt, what to do about it, wanting but not wanting. He felt enormous, breaking his way into her. She looked up at his face feeling separated, seeing a surprising expression creasing his features.

"Are you in?" she asked in a whisper, ashamed of her ignorance.

In answer, he gave her an indescribable smile while at the same time seeming to expand inside of her. Then he gathered up the lower half of her body like an armload of kindling and proceeded to try to strike sparks, to create a fire. She closed her eyes to the indignity of her legs draped over his arms, accepting his plunging presence, observing him from some considerable distance. Once more she heard that distant, interior laughter, finding him and herself both too pathetic and ridiculous as he rode faster and deeper, hurting her in his urgency. There was none of the witnessed beauty in this, none of the exquisite tenderness she'd seen passing between her parents, none of any of it. She couldn't believe she'd come here, done all the things she'd done and was doing with this person she didn't even know—except for his talent. She wanted him to finish finally so she could get dressed and go home. She'd never wanted anything more. But it wasn't yet time and he danced between her thighs, lost to his own music, plunging hard, hard inside until the pleasure he'd given her before was remote and shameful to think of and all her thoughts were turned to an ending and the anticipated relief of being home alone in her suddenly valued attic.

Her legs were aching, and inside it seemed he was repeatedly hitting against some obstacle, over and over, hurtfully. An image came to her mind, a little drawing her mother had made one afternoon. The two of them had sat at the kitchen table and her mother had taken a pencil and made a little drawing, saying, "That is the cervix, there." Suddenly, now, all these years later, here in this place, with this man, she was aware of her cervix, its position inside her and its abuse. Please let it end, she thought. Please!

He seemed to go mad all at once. His face wet with sweat, his eyes narrowed to ecstatic slits, he quivered once, twice, wildly; then one, twice more, the last thrusts the most painful of all as if he was trying to push her cervix out of the way in order to get to something else he wanted inside her. Then, at last, he was still, a heavy, sweating heap lying on her, in her. Her thighs trembled with the strain of his weight and continued intrusion. Her hands lay curled at her sides—she couldn't bear to put her hands on him.

She hated his sweat, his breath hitting hard on her throat, his swollen body still high inside her. She willed him away. But when he finally moved, then withdrew, she moaned in shock and final pain, despising him, and herself. Sober now, she watched him roll over onto his back and light a cigarette, wondering how she could get herself out out of this place and away from this man.

"I . . . I'd better be going now," she said at last, unable to look at him, ashamed of her body, her brain, all of her. What *had* she seen as a little girl? She'd seen something, but it wasn't this. Not this.

He yawned, his forearm flung over his eyes, mumbling something she didn't hear.

She sat up, risked a look at him, then got off the bed, snatched up her clothes and hurried into the bathroom to dress, dismayed and depressed by the bloodied seepage down her thighs. She hurriedly cleaned herself as best she could with some tissues, dropped them into the toilet, flushed it, then, shaking, pulled on her clothes.

He'd fallen asleep, the cigarette still burning in the ashtray. Feeling like some kind of criminal, she carried her coat outside, waiting until she'd groped her way down the stairs in the inky blackness before donning her coat and dashing out into the cool night air.

Once outside, she felt somewhat calmer, and disturbingly new to herself. She began to walk home anxious to use this time to examine her feelings, her thoughts. She wondered what all the fuss was about. It was nothing, just nothing. Awful.

Stupid. Embarrassing. Muddled, the only fully formed thought circulating in her brain was her craving for a drink. She looked at her watch, surprised to see it wasn't yet ten, and stopped—something she'd never done before—at a liquor store she'd passed dozens, probably hundreds of times, to buy a bottle of wine before continuing on her way home. Holding the bottle secure in the bend of her arm, she already felt a bit better. What did it matter? she thought, anticipating a shower followed by a glass of wine. It didn't matter. It hadn't been what she'd thought it would be, but it didn't matter.

The attic welcomed her warmly and she was for the first time glad of its spaciousness, the rough-beamed ceiling and plastered walls. She was most especially glad it was hers alone.

Corey waited around for almost two hours. He sat on the steps outside her door, thinking any minute she'd be there, and they'd go out and have something to eat, talk. Finally, he'd decided she wasn't coming after all. He got up and went down the stairs, deciding on the way that he'd go downtown to the deli next to the bank on Old Street and have one of their kosher hotdogs and help himself to a whole bowl of those free pickles they always put on the tables and counter. After that, maybe he'd take in the triple feature at the Bellevue, a few doors up. It was too bad she wasn't home because he didn't like eating alone, and it seemed like that was all he ever did now: eat alone.

# Nine

In May there was a notice posted on the school bulletin board listing summer jobs and jobs for graduating students. Glenn went along to the secretary's office to have a look at the list of companies, noted that Hamilton's downtown was looking for someone in their advertising department and decided she'd go down and apply for the job.

She got all the way to the store—her sample portfolio tucked under her arm—when she was stricken by an attack of nerves that sent her trembling and perspiration-soaked into a nearby bar for a glass of wine to calm herself. She sat at a table just inside the door, grateful for the air-conditioned darkness of the place and drank her wine slowly, trying to think of some logical explanation for her sudden dread of the coming interview. It wasn't as if she'd never worked before. She had, at the station. And she wasn't overly shy about meeting new people. So what was it? Why?

She sat looking out the window at the street. It was the corner where her mother had died. Over there, Elizabeth had stood and watched it happen. She had a sudden vision of her mother being tossed by the car like a sack of old clothing and closed her eyes against it, then took another swallow of her wine, hearing Elizabeth telling her, "Be like her." No, no. She wouldn't think of that. She drank some more of the wine and glanced around guiltily, as if she were so suddenly transparent her feelings might be showing right through the surface of her skin. She recalled the overwhelming excitement of that evening with Ralph and knew she wanted to try again, but not with Ralph. She wouldn't see him again. He didn't like her. She couldn't go after someone who didn't even *like* her. She had that feeling again that the walls were closing in on her and the only relief from it came during her soon-to-end hours at the College, or when she was with Corey.

After a second glass of wine, fortified, she paid, tucked her portfolio back under her arm and made her way across Old Street into Hamilton's and on up to the personnel offices. She emerged just under two hours later as an employee, hired to work on their newspaper ads. She couldn't believe how easy it had been. They'd liked her samples and offered her ninety dollars a week with a salary review in three months if they found her work satisfactory. She was to begin in three weeks time, when school ended.

Her elation, however, was short-lived. By the time she was halfway back to Wellington Road, she was feeling lonely, in need of someone to share her success, to celebrate with her. Corey was still at school. It was only one-thirty. She put away her samples and paced up and down the attic until she had to get out or she'd go mad.

Ralph was sitting at a huge table, working with a very fine sable brush dipped in solvent and glanced up when she came in, dropped the brush into a jar, set down the canvas and lit a cigarette, tipping back in his chair, grinning at her.

"Long time no see," he said, the words grating on her ears, making her despise herself—remembering in too vivid detail that night and how she'd felt about herself then—for having come here. "I was getting ready to come see you," he said. "Been thinking about you." He had been, and feeling pretty bad about falling asleep on her that way so that she'd had to go home by herself when he'd have walked her home, would've laid her again too if she hadn't gone off so fast without saying anything. Looking at her now, he was again impressed by the fact that for a beautiful girl she didn't have even one of the standard beautiful-girl hangups, as if she thought she were ugly or something.

She let her eyes wander around the large room, seeing broken bits of statuary, canvases waiting for mending or restoration.

"I thought if you weren't busy," she said, "maybe you'd like to come out for a drink." *What am I doing here?* she asked herself. *This was all backward.*

"Great! I'm sick of it here anyway. Let's go!"

He didn't even try to pretend she'd come because of why she'd said she had. She decided it was one of the things that bothered her about him: that he wouldn't try to make her feel better or more relaxed by pretending, by making good the pretense and actually going out with her somewhere for a drink. He stopped to buy half a gallon of cheap wine, telling her, "I've got some food we can fix," and walked along at her side, swinging the bottle. "Kind of early yet to eat," he said, lifting her wrist to look at her watch. "You're not hungry, are you?" He let her wrist drop. The gesture irked her.

"No," she answered, thick-voiced, sliding into despondency. She trudged along heavy-legged, feeling miserably heavy. "Just thirsty. I got a job today." She tried to keep her tone light, and failed.

"No kidding! Where?"

"Hamilton's, art department. I'm going to be working on their advertising layouts."

His lack of response brought her all the way down to the bottom and she stopped walking.

"Let's forget it," she said. "This is a mistake."

"Come on," he said, his hand on her upper arm. "The second time's always better. Don't get cold feet now. Why d'you always have to make such a big deal out of everything? I don't get that about you. You want to get laid. I like laying you. What's the big deal?"

She stood stiffly unmoving, loathing him for putting into words why she'd come after him. She wished she could vanish like the smoke from his cigarette, just be gone away from him. He tugged at her arm and she went with him, wondering,

*What's wrong with me? I don't have to do this. I should turn around and go home.*

He opened the windows, then poured out two fruit-juice glasses of the wine. "Why *do* you make it such a big deal?" he asked, seeing the anxiety furrowing her brow.

*Because it is,* she silently answered. *It's just that it's not a big deal to* you.

"It's good, making out," he went on. "Relax!" He watched her pick up her glass and take a long, thirsty swallow of the wine. "Hey! I got a record player since I saw you," he said, crossing the room. "Some records, too."

She sat down in his one chair and watched him carefully remove several records from their jackets, setting them on the spindle of the portable record player. It cheered her somewhat to hear Beethoven emerge.

"Forgot how fast you can put the grape away," he said, refilling her glass before starting to undress. She sat rigid in the chair thinking he had monstrous vanity, preposterous vanity. Quickly she gulped down her second glass of wine, and got up to pour herself a third one. He came up behind her to slip his hands around under her arms and squeeze her breasts, causing something inside of her to go so completely out of control she nearly dropped the heavy wine bottle and began breathing so erratically she was on the verge of crying.

It had to be good, she wanted it to be good. She couldn't stand the thought of having come after him, come to this place, lowering herself somehow if it weren't going to be good and make her feel better. She watched him strip off her clothes with an impatience she was coming to recognize in him. Still standing there beside the table, he put his hand between her legs saying, "I figured out what went wrong last time. I should've made you come *after*." Very little he said made any sense to her but the wine and his investigating fingers and his tongue in her mouth took her past hesitation and had her bending eagerly to accommodate him. She felt positively depraved standing there with his fingers inside her, liking it.

He sat her in the armchair, dropped to his knees in front of her, pulled her legs over his shoulders and sent his tongue burrowing into her until she was moaning, her head lolling as her fingers dragged his head closer. He stopped and she couldn't believe he could stop, leaving her that way but he did stop, explaining, "That's where I blew it last time. And no way we're going to blow it this time. Come on. Over here, come on!" He took her to the bed, laid her down, offered her more wine which she drank quickly, feeling it hitting the expanding emptiness inside because she hadn't stopped for lunch, then relinquished the glass as he let his fingers trail down between her buttocks teasingly. Very confidently he told her, "I was thinking about it. Since that time, you know. Too bad you went off that way. But I've figured it."

"I don't know what you're talking about," she said very slowly, finding it nearly impossible to talk. She squirmed under the pressure of his broad fingers, vowed to herself she'd never come back after this, never.

"Never mind," he said. *"I* know."

Apparently, he did, because whatever it was he'd figured out, he'd done his figuring accurately. He played with her body, teased and probed and kissed and caressed her, taking her up and down, stopping every time she began to move too urgently. He let her cool down, offered her more wine, then started all over again. By the time he turned her over, held her open and came surging into her from underneath, she was already blindly moving into the vortex of a stunning orgasm that required only the merest touch to pitch her headlong into it.

Enormously pleased with himself, he took his time, savoring the prominence of her pelvic bones beneath his hands, intoxicated by the contracting elasticity surrounding him. He delighted in keeping her up there, caught up in a series of groaning climaxes that had her sobbing by the time he allowed himself the ultimate pleasure of violently clutching her thighs as he came pounding against the vulnerable cushion of her buttocks, her body secured to his by his powerful arm locked around her middle.

She'd never conceived of pleasure as torture, but she understood, in the final moments, that that was what she was experiencing. And she hated this, too, because there was such violence, such a lack of any but sexual feeling. She vowed, sinking, she'd never see him again.

Afterward, she fell into a drunken sleep from which he had quite a lot of trouble rousing her. When she finally did surface, she staggered off to the bathroom simultaneously stricken by attacks of vomiting and diarrhea and sat on the toilet with her head hanging over the sink, feeling sicker than she'd ever felt in her life.

When the worst of it had passed, she availed herself of his shower, threw open the bathroom window, then returned to the living room to dress herself with trembling hands, saying, "I don't feel well. I've got to go home." He looked at the greenish cast to her features, pulled on a shirt and his trousers and took her home in a taxi, put her to bed and made her a cup of hot tea.

"You really oughta lay off the grape," he said, looking sincerely concerned. "I never did know anybody could just chugalug the juice the way you do. It's no good for you, that stuff. Drinking it that way."

In spite of herself, she was touched by his gruff attempts at expressing his concern and, to her chagrin, she burst into unhappy tears. He lay down beside her on the narrow bed and stroked her hair, every so often wiping her eyes until her tears subsided.

"I know you thought it was just something I was saying but I really was getting ready to come see you," he said, touching her cheek. "You just couldn't believe that, could you?" He didn't wait for an answer but went right on. "I never did know anybody like you, you know, Glenn. You want to hate yourself because you like it. It doesn't make any sense. I mean, it can't hurt you getting laid."

"No, that isn't it," she said tiredly, too exhausted to try to explain her tangled feelings to him. "I'm going to go to sleep now. Thank you for bringing me home. I appreciate that very much."

"You get to me," he said. "But I sure don't *get* you. Want to do something Saturday night?"

"What's Saturday night?"

"My last weekend before I leave."

"Oh. For where?"

"I'm finally going. I told you I would. Next Tuesday. Sailing on the *Franconia* from New York to Southampton, going to Spain."

"You're really going." Once more she was fascinated by him.

"Yup. I know." He smiled. "Nobody ever thought old Crazy Ralph would go. But I got my bucks together and I'm going. So you want to do something Saturday night?"

"All right."

"Okay." He sat up. "Pick you up here at seven. Okay?"

"Okay."

He patted her a little clumsily on the top of her head then let himself out. She lay listening to his footsteps descending the stairs, wishing she hadn't started crying in front of him. She shouldn't have let that happen. Never mind. She turned off the light and went to sleep.

Corey had known Gaby was up to something. He'd been waiting for weeks, knowing she was planning to rope in the old guy. Then, in she waltzed with Lloyd on her arm, all smiles and ho-ho-ho. Corey knew the minute he saw her face she'd nailed the man. So he shot into the bedroom and called his dad and said, "I think you'd better get on over here, dad. She's about to pull something."

Old George said, "I have no intention of seeing your mother."

"Well, you'd better intend to if you want to keep me around. I have this feeling she's going to try to pull something smart."

"Goddamned woman!" George said. "All right. I'm on my way."

Corey went back out to the living room, almost laughing at the sight of his mother sitting on old Lloyd's lap, like some big kid. Absolutely ridiculous. She jumped right off, of course; hating getting caught. She went right into her plans. Her and Lloyd. On and on and on. The whole time Lloyd just sat there nodding away, his shiny silver-haired head bobbing back and forth like some nutty jack-in-the-box, eating the whole thing up.

Then George arrived, and she went right out of her skull. Everybody got into the act. Corey sat on the floor and smoked a cigarette—not one of them even noticed—heard them all out, then got up and said, "Okay," and headed for the door.

"And just where do you think you're going?" Gaby demanded.

"Out! To take care of things." He turned, challenging her to try to stop him.

"Well, just make sure you come straight back here."

"I'll be back when I get back," he said, and slammed the door. Hard. Just to show her.

Again he sat on the steps waiting, knowing Glenn had to be getting home from the College any minute. But she didn't come and didn't come and he was getting very hungry. He made up his mind to cut school and go wait for her the next day. He went down the stairs, deciding he'd make it to Chinatown just in time to beat the price changes, and loped along the sidewalk thinking about an egg roll and some won ton soup.


Corey was waiting for her when she emerged from the College the next afternoon. He was leaning against a telephone pole, smoking a cigarette. He looked like a miniaturized man, except that he wasn't so small these days. He seemed to be growing a little. Yet, he did seem old. In some ways, older than any of them.

"Guess what?" he said, falling into step beside her, swinging along with a bouncy, sneakered step.

"What?"

"She's getting married."

"No! Really?"

"Honest to God! And you know what else?"

"God! No, what?"

"This Lloyd, the one she's marrying, he can't stand me one little bit. So, she's gonna get in touch with you." Don't let me down, Aunt Glenn! You're my last chance here.

"I don't understand."

"She's gonna make you a deal."

She stopped and looked at him, sensing what he was about to tell her. "She doesn't want you to live with them?"

"That's right," he said, keeping his voice cool, casual. But his eyes were filled with his feeling of betrayal. "You gonna go for it?"

"There's not really enough room for you in the attic," she

said, trying to think where she could put him.

"Oh, wait!" he said, knowing everything was going to be okay. She wouldn't let him down. "There's all *kinds* of stuff going on," he said, starting to kind of enjoy it all now. "I got my dad into it and they had this wild screaming fight with Lloyd jumping around telling everybody to 'Keep calm! Just keep calm!' You should've seen it! It was wild!"

"And what happened?"

"I'm getting shipped over to my dad's."

"But I don't understand. What does that have to do with making a deal with me? Let's go over to the coffee shop and sit down. This is too confusing."

As they crossed the road, she was gripped by that same murderous rage that had overtaken her during those days and weeks when Gaby and Dana had fought over the furnishings of the house. Her entire body tensed with it now and she wanted to annihilate Gaby, kill her, beat her to death for doing this to Corey.

They took a booth, and when the waitress came, Corey ordered two coffees, crossed his arms on the tabletop and continued his explanation.

"Dad said he'd take me on weekdays during the school year. But she'd have to have me on weekends. That's because," he explained, "he has to be free for his big social life. Okay? But, see, everybody's already made all kinds of plans for the summer so they're going to try to talk you into letting me stay with you for the summer. They'll even buy a bed for me and pay you money, too." He stopped, searching her eyes. Then, quietly, he said, "Do it, will you, Aunt Glenn? They're tossing me around like a beachball. You're the only one I know will leave me alone. And I'll stay out of your way. I've got all kinds of stuff to do. I won't bother you or anything."

"You're sure you've got all this right?" she asked as the waitress set cups of coffee down in front of them.

"You know I don't screw up on details," he said, adding cream and sugar to his coffee. He'd been practicing, dropping into coffee shops every so often to sit at the counter, have a coffee and a doughnut. He could handle it straight from the urn now, hot as they could get it.

"I'd really like to have you," she said, visualizing the two of them doing all sorts of things together—movies, walks, picnics. "I really would. Nothing's the same anymore."

"It sure isn't," he quickly agreed. "Boy, would I love to be back at the old house with grampa, playing gin rummy for a quarter of a cent a point, eating onion sandwiches on pumpernickel bread with lots of salt and butter. And the way gramma would come rushing in like she was always in such a big hurry. And then she'd sort of change her mind and sit in the kitchen with me, talking about stuff." Telling me everything I'll ever need to know, he thought. Telling me anything I wanted to know about. Looking out for me. Like you're doing.

"When is all this supposed to start happening?" she asked, watching him light a fresh cigarette. "You're really smoking way too much, Corey."

"Nerves. They're all getting on my nerves."

"When?" she asked again.

"Tonight, tomorrow. They're planning to drop over, talk to you. You know, they're even going to offer to get you a telephone so everybody can check in and see how the kid's doing. They're all nuts, shitheads!"

"They expect you to move in with me *tonight* or *tomorrow?*"

"Probably. You know how she is." He shrugged, tipping off the ash from his cigarette with a smart little tap on the lip of the ashtray. "If she's gonna do it, whatever it is, it's gotta be right away this minute or forget it."

"When's your birthday?" she asked, unable to remember.

"July. I'll be eleven. When's yours?"

"February. I'll be twenty-two. I can't believe it. It seems so old all of a sudden and I'm not ready."

He looked at the remote focus of her eyes and picked up his coffee, enjoying the combined tastes of the coffee and cigarette. It was all going to work out. A damned good thing he'd thought of it. Otherwise, they'd have shipped him off to some goddamned boy scout camp, and there was no way they were getting him into any stinking uniform. He'd look out for her, he decided. She kind of needed somebody to look out for her. And she'd look out for him too.

"You know what gramma told me one time?" he said, remembering.

"No. What?"

"She said if anything ever happened I should go to you. 'She's my daughter,' she said. 'Glenn is *my* child.' I kind of didn't get it, you know. At the time. I was just a little kid then. But now I sort of see what she meant."

"She said that?"

"Yeah. Hey! You like baseball?"

"I don't know," she said, thinking about Lisette saying that. "Do you?"

"I'll take you to a game," he said expansively. "You'll like it. It's a good thing to do on a Sunday afternoon. Hotdogs and peanuts. Great sitting up there shouting, eating all that garbage. The sunshine. You'll like it."

"What else did she say to you, Corey?"

"Gramma? Oh, lots of stuff. Facts of life kind of stuff, you know. And what she thought about things."

"What things?"

"Oh, this and that. Like she one time told me she didn't really think Dana was actually queer. That's not what she said, you know. But that she didn't really think he was. It was just that he had this... compulsion... Yeah, that's the word. This compulsion to take notes about everything but his own true feelings."

"My God!" she said softly. "I think that's true. Go on! What did she say about Gaby?"

"Oh, wow!" he laughed. "I couldn't quite buy that one. But I always liked to listen, you know. And what she said, she said, 'Gaby is a hurt little girl. And she will always be a hurt little girl. Only Gaby knows why. And she has forgotten.'"

"That's true, too," Glenn said, staggered. "Corey, you're remarkable! How could you remember all those things?"

"Easy," he said. "I remembered because I wanted to hear. I kind of think people forget the stuff they never wanted to hear in the first place. But when it's stuff you really want to hear, you remember it."

"Well," she said, impressed. "I'm going to have to listen very carefully to you." She took a sip of her coffee, then said, "It'll have to be Sunday if you're coming. I've got a date Saturday night. I wouldn't want to leave you home all alone."

"That's okay." He smiled, knocked out by how she cared about things like that. "I'll come Sunday."

"I start work in three weeks," she said, looking a little bewildered. "Isn't it funny?" Her eyes were caught by the deep green of his. "I never thought I'd be doing any of this. Working, leaving the College, having. . .None of it's the way I thought it would be."

"It never is," he said wisely. "Nothing ever is. That's why you've always got to be looking ahead, watching to see what's coming. But you'll like baseball. You'll see."

She laughed, saying, "Give me one of those," and reached for his cigarettes. "Maybe I'll like these, too, if I try."

It was the happiest time she'd ever known. Corey liked to come downtown and wait for her outside the employees' entrance after work. Usually he effervesced with ideas. He'd have suggestions about where they should go for dinner and what they should eat, as well as several alternative plans for the balance of the evening. There were the triple features at the seedy Bellevue downtown—one of his favorite places because you could sneak a smoke and half the time the ushers were so boozed up they didn't even bother checking out the audience. Night games at the ballpark. Concerts at the bandshell. The amusement park. An evening at the planetarium. A fireworks display at the fairgrounds.

He spent his days poring over the newspapers, scouting out activities, interesting things to see and do. He liked surprising her by having everything planned out—what they'd eat and where they'd go and how they'd get there. She got such a charge out of it when he'd tell her what he'd come up with. Having decided on the evening's schedule, he'd go down to the big public pool at the shore and swim for a couple of hours, or bike around town on the new Raleigh five-speed he'd persuaded his father to buy for him. He really loved the bike. It was almost too easy to talk George Shea into doing stuff like buying a bike or doling out the dollars for some new jeans. He'd found this really good thrift shop where he could get nearly new levis and stuff for way less than in the stores and, with the leftover money, he'd pay his way into the public pool, have his lunches. He didn't consider it stealing. He got everything he said he was going to get. He just didn't get it where he'd said he'd get it. He really needed the money and his dad was so pleased not to have to pay the alimony anymore, he was glad to shell out a few extra bucks for clothes and stuff.

Glenn was fascinated by him. He was always moving, always thinking, always talking, brimming with ideas about almost anything, everything. He was able to remember almost verbatim conversations with Ray and Lisette and was happy to repeat them for her edification. Yet, surprisingly, he'd sit quietly for hours on their occasional evenings in, listening to the radio and reading—he favored how-to books on a wide variety of subjects ranging from investing in the stock market without a broker to containerized vegetable growing, and cookbooks in particular—while Glenn worked at something she'd brought home from the store or did still-life sketches or five-minute studies of Corey.

Their time together had a remarkable quality, she thought. It was compressed, crammed with exchanges of thoughts and ideas; active. His enthusiasm was contagious, delightful, and she was awed by the difference between the Corey now and the Corey then.

"Why," she finally asked him, "were you such an awful monster all that time?"

"I was just experimenting," he answered openly. "It wasn't my fault if a lot of things didn't work out."

"What kind of 'experimenting?'"

"Oh, just stuff. Things to do."

Bored, she thought. He'd been bored. And we were all so self-important and preoccupied, we didn't take the time to see him, hear him, help him. Except for Ray. Ray had—in spite of appearances—heard, listened, seen. And cared. She loved her father for being there to help Corey when no one else could or would.

Living with him, though, was definitely not boring. His natural eagerness made her see a great number of things very differently than she might have.

He thought her work at the store was very interesting and checked out Hamilton's ads in the daily papers, always on the lookout for work she'd done. When he'd find something of hers, he'd be lavish with his praise, saying, "This one's *really* terrific! Those shoes really look like shoes should, like you want to put them right on and wear them away." He meant the things he said. He wanted her to feel good.

He did. He had a way of making her feel clever, even special. And she thought perhaps his future might evolve directly from his enthusiasm and this ability, this wonderful talent, for making people feel better about themselves. He also had a well-developed sense of privacy and made himself understood without having to resort to words. His bed, his corner of the attic comprised his territory. He expected her to respect his area just as he respected her drawing board, her private property.

He liked the idea that he was looking out for her and promised himself she'd never be sorry for letting him be there, for wanting him to be there. He was always up, dressed and on his way out when she awakened in the morning, saying, "Check with you later, okay?" as he went off.

It wasn't until after he'd gone to live with his father that she understood he went out this way in order to allow her to get herself together and wide awake without having to feel embarrassed by his presence or obliged in some way to provide some kind of immediate entertainment for him.

The more she knew of him, the deeper into her feelings he grew until her thoughts automatically included him, as did her plans. Corey was real and alive and one of the few people she'd known who fit into this category. He was perceptive, bright and funny and she gave herself over entirely to his plans and ideas.

During the course of the summer, at his urging, the two of them sampled every kind of food the city had to offer. From Indonesian, to French, to Chinese, to German they ate their way through the different tastes and textures. They saw all the home-team ballgames that summer, swam every Saturday and Sunday unless it rained, took in every new art exhibit, concert and free show available. They went roller skating, bowling, and drove golf balls—doubling over with laughter—at the driving range; they played miniature golf, visited the zoo and even tried to teach each other tennis with two beat-up rackets Corey unearthed at the thrift shop.

He never seemed to run out of ideas and found things to do in the city she'd never imagined existed. He took her to the open-air markets—there were three of them and she'd never known about even one—to Chinatown, to the botanical gardens. He worked out a clever system of transfers so they were able to travel halfway around the city and back for just one fare each.

On those afternoons when they went swimming, he insisted on concocting lunch, busying himself at the hotplate, shooing her away when she became curious. Later, he would produce a huge bag of sandwiches—wonderful sandwiches—they'd devour before going back in to swim off their meal. He made Italian sandwiches of sausages, fried onions, green peppers and tomatoes. He made fried egg and salami sandwiches that were delicious, even cold. He bought long loaves of Italian bread, scooped out the squishy dough and piled his own homemade egg salad into the cavity. His homemade egg salad consisted of chopped eggs, imported mayonnaise, Bermuda onions, green peppers, celery, and black olives, with a sprinkling of paprika on top. "For color," he laughed. "You can't eat something that doesn't look good."

He created whole meals on the hotplate that were marvels of ingenuity, experimenting during the afternoons while she was at work, presenting her with a dinner of stew on a bed of rice that was superb.

"What's in here?" she asked, eating hungrily.

"I found this terrific store," he told her. "They sell all kinds of sausages from places you never even heard of. There are about six different kinds of sausages in there, some onions, Tabasco, a little of this and that."

"But the rice! It's perfect! How did you learn to cook this way?"

"Gramma taught me. Didn't she teach you?"

"I obviously didn't learn as well as you did. You're wonderful, Corey!" she laughed.

"I've got my eye on this Chinese grocery store," he said. "I've been thinking I'd try making some Oriental stuff."

*Gramma taught me. Grampa told me. Didn't they teach you? Didn't they tell you?* Where was I? she wondered. What was I seeing when I should have been seeing, listening, hearing?

"Corey, I'm so happy having you here."

"Mmmm." He nodded, his mouth full. "Me, too."

She brought him up to see where she worked and to meet a few of the people she worked with, noting not without pride

the way his eyes ranged over everything, everyone, missing
no detail. She loved him. And when, the first week in September, they packed up his things and he left with his father,
she was stricken by his absence like a physical blow. She sat
down in the depleted attic staring at the telephone and the
stripped-down bed, feeling a burning loneliness inside that made
her throat swell closed and her heart beat far too fast.

You'll be seeing him, she told herself, walking up and down
the length of the room. It's not as if he's gone forever. But he
might as well have been, because he was no longer there.
Without him—so quickly—she felt claustrophobic and too
alone. It did no good telling herself there were all kinds of
things she could now get done in peace without his distracting,
always-on-the-go presence, because she didn't feel like doing
anything. It did no good telling herself that much as she loved
him it was good to be on her own again, because it wasn't.
Before the downstairs door had even closed on him she was
so miserably lonely for him she felt she'd die. Why could she
never seem to keep what she wanted, want what she had?
Corey, by rights, was hers.

He intensely disliked his father. His mother traded him away
for a new husband who didn't like children. He felt like a
beachball, he said. She knew that, *knew* it, and wanted to keep
him. Yet she knew it could never be no matter how much she
and Corey might want it, because he had more parents than he
knew what to do with. Parents, she thought scornfully. *I'm* his
family. He's *my* family.

It wasn't fair to have to stand there and watch him go, his
red hair dark and flat from being watercombed. Looking too
clean, too much an old man inside a little boy's body, he'd
shaken her hand, saying, "Thanks a lot, Aunt Glenn," then
turned, got all the way to the door and came running back to
hug her, receive her hug and kisses, then ran away down the
stairs and out to the car where George Shea was waiting. She
couldn't bear it.

Pacing up and down, she thought for the first time since
he'd left of Ralph. He *had* liked her. She hadn't wanted to
believe it but in the end she had, because, in his blunted way,
he'd said, "If you want, you know, you could always come
with me." And she'd been so warmed, looking at his yellow

eyes, seeing the sincerity there, even knowing how impossible
the situation was—she could never just up and leave, having
promised to take care of Corey. She'd had the luxury of lying
skin to skin within Ralph's arms, dreaming for a time of how
nice it might be to take a canvas bag of books and clothes,
tuck her portfolio under her arm and go along with him to sail
away on the *Franconia*. He'd said he'd write. More than four
months and he hadn't written. Now Corey was gone too. What
was life for? What was she doing?

She was suddenly overcome by a terrible need for a drink
and an overwhelming sexual hunger. Walking up and down
with her arms wrapped around herself she tried to think, tried
to see some sort of destination in her future. She looked guiltily
at her drawing board and the small piece of work she'd brought
home to do for the store. What about my work, my painting,
my drawing? She'd done nothing, not a thing all summer long.

Tomorrow, she decided. Lunchtime, she'd go out, do some
sketching, start getting back into her own work. She had to
make a future. And what was wrong with having a drink?
Nothing. There was nothing wrong with it. She was old enough.
Corey's eleven and he smokes. Why shouldn't I keep some
wine, drink in my own home if I want to? Why not? I can if
I want to.

Grabbing up her handbag, she flew down the stairs. Her
head had filled with that thought: Why shouldn't I? If I want
to, I will. She walked the several blocks to the liquor store and
decided to lay in a proper supply of drinks. Supposing she had
guests and they wanted a drink. She hadn't anything to offer.

She bought red wine and white wine, gin and scotch and a
small bottle of vermouth. She'd set up a little bar. She'd cover
Corey's bed with some pretty fabric—some she'd seen on the
fourth floor at the store—buy a small table and make that part
of the room into a sitting area. She'd spend a little more money—
her babysitting salary for the summer—on her home. After
all, this was her home, she told herself, the place where she
lived.

The echoey emptiness of the attic wrapped itself around her
throat as she came through the door carrying all her bottles and
she felt half-suffocated, her head throbbing still from the impact
of this blow, this loss. She poured a glass of red wine, then,

glass in hand, spent at least half an hour lining the bottles up
this way, that way, trying to find the most attractive arrangement; finally digging up an old round lacquered tray—Lisette's
tray. Glenn's eyes filled with tears at the sight of it—and stood
all the bottles on the tray before stepping back to admire her
work, the red wine already easing the throbbing in her head
and cooling her throat. Thinking of Corey, she laughed aloud,
spoke aloud. "You're stupid, Glenn! Go call him up!"

She sat down, flipped through her address book, found
George Shea's number, picked up the telephone—the thump-
ing now in her chest along with a happy, so-optimistic feeling—
and dialed, all expectant, hopeful. She'd feel so much better
hearing his voice. His father answered and said, "Corey's already in bed for the night." She looked at her wristwatch and
said, "But it's not even his bedtime yet." Mr. Shea responded
in a cool, scornful voice. "Vacation's over. He has school in
the morning. A child has to keep regular hours."

Deflated, she said, "Yes, of course," and, "Will you tell
him I called?" and, "Goodbye."

Then she cried. She sat drinking her wine, every so often
stopping to wipe her eyes and nose, drinking until the room
had gone dark and there were night sounds outside in the street
and her mind sauntered back through thoughts of Ralph and
that Saturday night they'd seen each other for the last time.
Ralph. She saw him with his mouth on her breast, saw the
lion's mane moving between her thighs, saw him putting himself inside of her, saw those yellow eyes, heavy-lidded with
lust, and liking too. He *had* liked her. She knew it.

I wish I were with you in Spain, she thought, lurching across
the room to turn on the light. Her eye was caught by the work
she'd brought home and hadn't done. She sat down on the
stool, selected a pen, a nib, a sheet of good stock, dipped the
pen in the ink. Quickly, she did the drawing. Then, laughing
aloud, she added an embellishing series of stylized scrolled
loops. "That's better!" she announced to the room, recapping
the ink bottle and setting down the pen. "All done!" She turned
off the gooseneck lamp arched over the drawing board, went
in search of her wine, found the glass empty and refilled it.
The radio. A good classical station. Mustn't forget to set the
alarm.

While she was in the tiny stall shower, singing loudly, she realized she'd forgotten to eat. Without Corey she hadn't any appetite. She paid attention as best she could to the task at hand—getting herself cleansed of the day's grime, the day's disenchantments. Putting soap to her body, every area felt so sensitized it made her legs weak. She hurried through the shower, hastily dried off, carried the last of the red wine to bed with her.

In the dark she suddenly opened her eyes and looked down at herself, at what she was doing. What if Corey saw? Her heart pounded fearfully. No. Corey was gone, gone. She closed her eyes and kept on.

Corey leaned against the door and watched his father put down the telephone.

"Was that my Aunt Glenn?" Corey asked quietly.

Startled, George looked around. "What are you doing still up? I thought you'd gone to bed."

"I don't go to bed this early. Was that my aunt?"

"As a matter of fact it was. Hell of an hour to be telephoning, expecting to speak to a child."

"So that's what you told her," Corey said evenly.

"That's exactly what I told her. And what's this? Since when do you interrogate me?"

"Since right now," Corey said, keeping a lid on his temper. "Since you suddenly started deciding who I can talk to."

"Go up to your room!" George ordered.

"Don't try to push me around," Corey said. "I'm not my mother. I don't push."

"You're starting to get on my nerves," George warned.

"Don't you ever do that again!" Corey warned him. "I may be just a kid but I know a hell of a lot about a lot of things. Probably more than you'll ever know. And don't you ever tell my aunt she can't talk to me. You *ever* do that again, I'll kill you!"

"Watch your step, fella!"

"No," Corey said, "you'd better watch yours. I happen to love my Aunt Glenn. And she happens to care about me. Which you don't. You ever interfere that way between me and my aunt ever, ever again, I'll kill you. And you don't tell me what

to do. You don't tell me when to go to bed or when to get up
or when to go to the can. I tell myself, understand? I wouldn't
be here except I don't happen to have too much say in the
matter. Because if I did have any say in the matter, I'd be with
my aunt right this minute. And neither of us would be taking
any of this crap from you. So you just remember what I said
and everything'll be fine." He paused for a moment, then turned
and went up to his room.

George Shea smashed his fist into the wall then yelped with
pain. Furious, he went to fix himself a good, strong drink.

The next morning, Glenn was horribly hung over and reeled
her way through the attic downing aspirin with her morning
coffee, trying to get herself sufficiently pulled together to make
it in to work. After a second cup of coffee and a tepid shower,
she felt better; she pushed the work she'd done the night before
into her portfolio without stopping to look at it and hurried off
to the store.

Mrs. Swayze, her superior, came round to collect the copy
and Glenn turned it in, then sat back feeling panicked, trying
to remember what she'd done. Something with squiggles and
curls. She groaned softly and covered her face with her hands.
They'd fire her, ask her did she think they were paying her
every week to fool around, tell her to pack up her brushes and
pens and take herself out of there. She sighed and sat up,
looking at the new pieces she was to do for Thursday's ad. No
point to sitting waiting for the bad news. She might as well
get on with the job.

She felt far too queasy at lunchtime to eat or to do the
sketching outdoors she'd promised herself she'd do. So, after
downing a glass of Bromo in the women's restroom, she went
down to the fourth floor to have a look at the fabrics. At least
she'd keep *some* of those promises she'd made herself. She
bought four yards of good-looking hand-screened fabric with
her store discount, then wandered along to the furniture department just to look around and fell in love with a burnt
bamboo stand that would make a beautiful bar or plant-stand
and—What the hell! It cheered her up to spend some of Shea's
money—bought it.

By the time she returned to her cubicle her spirits had lifted and the nausea had ebbed. There was a note on her desk saying, Please see me. Signed, Mrs. Swayze. Everything sank again. She'd really done it after all. They were going to fire her. Two weeks' severance pay and good day to you, Miss Glenn Ellen Burgess.

With a knocking, rattling sensation in the pit of her stomach, she went—hands wet, mouth dry—along the corridor to Mrs. Swayze's office, which was actually only a larger cubicle than her own, but with a window, and stepped into view.

"You left a note," she said.

"Oh, Glenn!" Mrs. Swayze looked up from the copy she was proofing and smiled brightly. "Sit down a minute, will you, dear? Let me just finish this bit."

Confused, Glenn slid onto the wooden chair wedged between the outer edge of the cubicle and Mrs. Swayze's desk and watched the middle-aged woman blue-pencil her way through a block of copy. Then, finished, she poked the pencil into her hair, lit a cigarette and smiled again at Glenn.

"Everybody likes that little piece you submitted this morning," she said. "I took it around and it got some reaction."

"It did?"

"They're going to run it," Mrs. Swayze went on. "And we thought we'd give you a few larger pieces to try your hand at. Mr. Hamilton takes a very keen interest in everything that goes on in the store, you know, particularly the ads. And he liked your piece. I thought you'd like to know that."

"Thank you very much," Glenn said, wetting her lips. She couldn't believe she wasn't being ordered to the pay office and wished she could remember what she'd drawn.

"I'll drop you over the next layout item in a little while. Congratulations! Keep it up and you'll find yourself in one of those corner offices." She laughed, pleased with her little joke.

"Thank you," Glenn said again, thinking she'd have to buy the newspaper in the evening to see what she'd done. My God! What did I *do?*

She returned down the corridor to her cubicle feeling better, happier with every step, and sat down at her desk looking at the telephone, thinking of whom she could call to share her good news. The only person she could think of was Dana. He sounded bored, unimpressed, but invited her to dinner.

"I'm between 'friends' at the moment," he said, in the kind of prissy, put-on voice he didn't usually use with her. "So, let us dine. What's your fancy?"

"Dana, this is me," she said. "When you talk that way, I don't know who I'm talking to."

He sighed and his voice dropped at least an octave. "You're right," he said. "It's a goddamned game. Listen, come have dinner. We'll talk and you can tell me all about your successes in the marketplace."

"You know something, Dana?" she said softly. "When you put on that play-gay voice, it isn't real. You know? It's scary. To me, you're real when you tell me you're blue or you're in love or you talk about your newest script. But when you start tossing around those cute little euphemisms and being something else, it makes me so—edgy. As if there's nobody I know who's really real."

"Okay," he said. "Point made. It's a good thing you're my sister," he laughed. "Because I'd belt anybody else for remarks like that. Meet me, lovey, I'll wait for you here."

"Okay," she agreed and hung up to sit thinking about the dreary old station with its uneven wood floors and institutional-green paint on the walls and corridors. A depressing building. People at the TV station were always talking about expanding, getting into newer, larger facilities. For as long as she could remember, all the way back to 1948 when Ray had first started there, they'd been saying the same things. But no move ever got made. They did acquire two outside buildings they used for rehearsals and broadcasts. But the production offices, the business offices remained under the green-patinaed roof, inside the worn red-brick walls of the sprawling two-story, creaky-floored building in what had become one of the worst sections of town, with a Salvation Army hostel down the road, a Sea-man's Hostel two blocks up and, in between, a series of seedy restaurants, decrepit apartment houses and alarmingly dark al-leyways.

And that was where she'd meet Dana.

Oh, well! She cleared off her work area and sat back waiting to receive her new assignment.

A dress ad. They'd taken her off accessories and were giving her a chance at a quarter-page dress ad. She was excited and

terrified and strained to remember what she'd done in that other
ad that they'd liked so much. She simply could not remember.
Because she couldn't remember, she felt too intimidated and
insecure even to begin trying to do anything with the sample
dress. She went back along to Mrs. Swayze's cubicle.

"Would it be all right," she asked, "if I took this home to
work on tonight? I'll have more time . . ."

"Of course," Mrs. Swayze cut across her explanations. "Just
take care, won't you, dear?"

"Oh, I will," she promised.

"If this one's as good as that other," Mrs. Swayze said,
"you'll probably get to move up to fashions fulltime."

Glenn packed the dress carefully in tissue in a Hamilton's
bag, then sat down once more at her desk, finding herself with
almost three hours to kill. She had no other work to do. In her
absence at lunchtime, the two small drawings she'd been working on had been removed and the note from Mrs. Swayze push-
pinned to her board. Nothing to do. And no point to sitting for
three hours staring into space. She picked up her handbag, the
bag with the dress, and left.

Back at home she removed the dress from the bag and hung
it on a padded hanger—one of Lisette's, she stood for a moment touching the worn pink satin—laid out fresh paper on
her board, lined up her pens, inks, then backed away to look
around the room realizing there was something she'd forgotten
to do, trying to remember what. She saw Corey's denuded bed
and remembered. The fabric. She'd forgotten to claim it from
the employees' package room. The bamboo stand was going
to be delivered. She'd have to make a note to herself to pick
up the fabric. She was becoming absent-minded.

She looked at herself in the mirror, deciding Dana would
be caustic about the outfit she was wearing. She couldn't face
the prospect of an evening that commenced with some of the
poisonous remarks he was capable of making thoughtlessly.
So she changed into a shirt and pair of slacks, draped some
gold chains around her neck—cheap but effective, she was
picking up all kinds of useful ideas doing the ad layouts—
dabbed a little rouge on each cheek, picked up her handbag
and left. She'd be able to kill at least an hour by walking
downtown to the station.

As she was closing the door she looked over at Corey's bed. It felt like years since he'd left. Only one day and already everything was changing. Nothing ever stayed the way you wanted it to. While he'd been with her, she'd felt steady, secure. Now because of something she'd done when drunk she was headed in an entirely new direction. But her identity. What had happened to that? If there was no one to talk to you, no one to see you or the things you did, how could you know if you were still you after all? She closed the door and started down the stairs. Smiling suddenly, she wondered if she was going to have to get drunk in order to duplicate her efforts of the night before.

She had a flash thought of herself the night before, sprawled naked on her bed pretending, pretending. She shook her head, shook away the awful feeling the image brought with it; a demoralized, ugly feeling. Don't think of it! Forget it! A dinner with Dana would make up for some of what she'd spent on the fabric. A dinner she wouldn't have to provide for herself.

One day, she thought, descending the front steps to the street, one day I'll never have to think about how much things cost, free dinners, any of that. I'll have it. Nothing will matter.

He couldn't believe how he'd thought it might be kind of fun, living with his father. I must've been nuts! he thought now. George Shea was almost a worse nut than his mother. When he wasn't on the phone promoting some deal or other, he was calling up women, making dates. Putting on his smooth, ooky voice and sounding like an idiot. And the house was way the hell out on the lake. The housekeeper wasn't too bad. Nothing like as nice as Mrs. Petrov. He still dropped over to see her from time to time. She'd always get so excited when he did that. It really gave him a big charge. But getting around was a problem. He had to put the bike away in the garage, because it was pretty useless except for quick, boring trips around the neighborhood. When he wanted to get to town, it was either buses or hitching rides. So for the most part, he hitched. Women stopping for him most of the time, thinking he was a little kid or something. "Are you sure you know where you're going, dear? You're not running away from home, are you?" They'd give a little ha-ha laugh just to show how on top of life's situations they really were.

It was pretty rough getting time out. The whole gang of them had his *life* mapped out. He could hardly get away from them. Except for sometimes cutting classes, which wasn't really worth all the trouble because Aunt Glenn was working during school hours so he couldn't see her. And Mrs. Petrov was okay but he couldn't spend his whole life going to see her.

So, mostly, he hung around with Grace, the housekeeper. She didn't bother much. They'd share a beer and play gin in the kitchen for a tenth of a cent a point. While good old George was out making millions, or trying to score with another one of his women. Some life, he thought, bored out of his mind. I'd better get out of here soon or they'll ruin my head, he thought.

# Ten

       She remembered to buy the early edition of the paper, had a look at her ad and laughed out loud, refolded the newspaper and ran toward the bus stop—Dana had given her taxi fare but it was just as easy to take the bus—anxious now to get back to the attic and start on the dress ad. She couldn't quite believe the store people liked what she considered cartooning. But they'd said they did, so she'd try to capture the same feeling with the dress.

    She put the dress on and stood on a chair, studying herself in the mirror, turning this way, that way to get a feeling of the important lines. Then she removed the dress and sat down to make several pencil sketches. She did the completed piece in India and sepia inks—the sepia would emerge an interesting gray color in newsprint—with a light wash over the body of the dress, letting the wash indicate the volume of the garment; she gave the model an elongated, stylized figure with a minimum of lines and then enclosed the whole with those Beardsley-type swirls and elaborate connected coils she'd used on the other piece. She submitted it the next day and within a week found herself moved into a slightly larger cubicle, at work fulltime on fashions; her salary raised to one hundred dollars. She wasn't at all sure that what she'd done was that good or that original and felt a bit of a fraud accepting her new work space and small increase in salary.

The job was just a job, demanding, fatiguing, delineated by deadlines and constant, ceaseless pressure. The department was understaffed for one thing, and, for another, she quite soon became bored and mildly resentful as well because she wasn't doing any of what she really wanted to be doing—neither in her life or her job. But aside from nebulous ideas having to do with painting, drawing, she hadn't any definite idea of what it was she actually did want to be doing. All she did know was that this wasn't it.

The thought of spending the next five or ten years of her life in a cubicle at Hamilton's was sufficient to send her hurrying out on her lunch hour to the bar across the road for a glass or two of wine, for fortification, for a lift.

She rarely saw Corey now. He was transported directly from his father's house every Friday afternoon to his mother's apartment and returned to his father's on Sunday evenings. Occasionally, he simply took himself off on a Saturday morning before his mother or Lloyd was awake and let himself into the attic with the key Glenn had had made for him in the summer. He'd stop first to pick up a few things at the coffee shop, then wake her up with toast and coffee. They'd sit on the bed, eating the toast and drinking the coffee, bringing each other up to date.

He couldn't manage it as often as he would have liked, and phoned every so often just to say hi.

"What're you doing?"

"Oh, nothing very much. What are you doing?" she asked.

"Going nuts hanging around the House of Usher here. Or going nuts in town listening to Lloyd playing hero for my mom. Boy, she really eats it up. It's sickening. The two of them doing these performances all the time. 'My darling,' he says, 'anything you want. Nothing in the world is too good for my darling girl.' And she goes flitting around in something long and blowy, doing her *Gone With the Wind* act. All frail and soft and so sweet. It's just sickening."

"I know. Come see me. It's too quiet around here."

His visits were highlights, times of quietly intense pleasure. The sight of Corey, his presence, returned to her her sense of reality, a feeling for her own identity. And her love for him would awaken yawning, as she herself did, to sit within her smiling at the sight of his face, contented in his presence.

On Christmas Eve as she was preparing to go out for the evening to Dana's house—telling herself she was going to have to buy a space heater because the damned attic was too cold— Corey let himself in, sat down on the side of the bed and chatted to her through the bathroom door while she was dressing. He noticed, that she'd been really fixing the place up with a few new things: a nice silver-framed mirror on the wall and a tiny vase full of dried flowers.

"You're not going to believe the latest!" he said, lighting a cigarette, taking a long drag. He could hardly believe it himself, and was sure her reaction would be the same as his.

"What?"

"That moron, Lloyd? He's talked everybody into sending me away to a goddamned *boarding school!*"

"No!" Glenn came out of the bathroom in her bra and pants, a death-sentence feeling instantly upon her. *"Seriously?"* She stood in the doorway holding her hairbrush staring at him.

"And you know *where?"* he continued, thinking he'd been right. She was taking it just the way he had.

"Where, for God's sake?" She sat down heavily on the bed beside him, still staring at him.

"Way the hell in New goddamned Hampshire, that's where!"

"What's there?" she asked, thinking it was all meant to destroy her, removing him even further from her.

"Some stupid prep school Uncle Dana went to."

"St. Andrew's," she said. "It's too much, too much!" she exclaimed, wounded. "When?"

"After the New Year."

"I can't believe it!"

*"You* can't believe it!" He made a snorting sound in his nose. "Boy, I'll kill that moron Lloyd! This whole thing's his big, bright idea because they don't like having me around crapping up their big, romantic weekends. He probably gets embarrassed trying to put it to her with the kid in the next bedroom. He's a fool! So's she!"

"And your father agreed?"

"Oh sure! What d'you think? He doesn't want me around crapping up his *week!*"

"Oh, Corey, it's not *fair!* There must be something we can do. You don't *want* to go, do you?"

"Shit! Are you kidding?" He looked at her with disgust creasing his face. "My all-time dream," he said bitterly. "Boarding school. Jesus!"

"Maybe they'd let you come stay with me..." she began but he was shaking his head.

"I already tried that. First thing." His expression changed, becoming a mixture of angry and sad as he thought of how he'd tried and how his mother had gone screaming crazy at the suggestion, shouting and throwing her arms around. You're not going *there!* Over my dead body! And getting all suspicious then, she'd said, What exactly are the two of you up to anyway? Which made him mad so that he forgot himself and answered her, which he shouldn't have done, telling her, You're jealous of the whole goddamned world. Aunt Glenn and I happen to be friends. And you can't stand that, can you? He shouldn't have said it. It just frosted her cake, that's all.

"And?" Glenn asked.

"Bad influence," he said. "They're so goddamned dumb, all of them."

"*I'm* a bad influence?" she said, flabbergasted.

"You're too young. Let me stay up too late, let me run wild, all that kind of garbage. They don't know what the hell they're talking about."

"But we had fun. It was *good*. I loved having you here. *You* were happy here, weren't you?"

"Are you kidding? It was the best fun I *ever* had. You— and gramma and grampa—are about the only ones who've never bossed me around or told me a lot of kid-stuff crap, treating me as if I had some brains."

"I walloped you." She smiled, remembering.

"Oh, that was okay," he said, looking down at the ashtray on his knee. "I kind of had that coming. It was okay. I understood why you had to do that."

"*Corey!* I'm going to miss you so much. I can't believe they're doing this."

"If I had the money in my hand, boy, I'd run away right now, this minute. Just take off and that'd be the end of it."

"You couldn't," she said softly, tiredly, the defeat having somehow crept right into her bloodstream. "You know you couldn't." They were both caught, trapped, she thought.

"Knowing it doesn't mean I can't think about it. *Boarding school*," he groaned. "Creeps and weirdos go to boarding school."

"That's not true."

"How do you know? When did you ever go to boarding school?"

"Well, I didn't . . ."

"You don't *know!* You shouldn't talk about stuff you don't know about."

"It won't be that bad," she said feebly, having no idea how good or bad it could be. She tried to remember what she'd heard Dana say about his years at school. "I'll come visit you," she said, inspired.

"Sure! How? Walk?"

"I'll get a car, borrow Dana's or rent one or something. But I promise you. I swear it. I'll come down at least once a month and visit you."

He brightened, studying her eyes carefully. "You mean it? You really would?"

"If I said I would, I will."

"Well, okay." He said, stubbed out the cigarette and put the ashtray down on the floor. Maybe those moron types at the school would think she was his sister or something. "I could maybe stand it if I knew you were going to come see me. Boy, oh, boy! I feel like they're sending me to prison. Up the river. Sing Sing." He laughed suddenly. "San Quentin. The Big Rock. Alcatraz. They'll give me a nice striped uniform and a pick for breaking up the old rocks."

"It probably won't be so bad." She smiled. "I've heard New Hampshire's really beautiful. And I know Dana loved it there. He always said he did. You might even actually like it, you know."

"I'll hate it and you know it. I *hate* rules. Rules're for people with no brains of their own to figure out what's what by themselves. Anyway, I'd better get back over there before they start screaming some more. I wanted to let you know, you know? And give you this present. Did you get me something?"

She hit him playfully on the shoulder, laughing, as she got up to get his present. Then she stepped into her dress, watching as he tore open the wrappings and gaped at the wristwatch she'd bought for him. His mouth formed a surprised O and he looked at her wide-eyed, knowing she didn't have much in the way of money. And to spend it on something like this, for him. When his own moronic mother would hit up old Lloyd for gift money.

"It's fantastic!" he declared. "A for-real diver's watch with all the dials and everything. Boy oh boy!"

"I thought you might like it," she said, pleased by his excitement as he quickly wound the watch and strapped it on, telling her to, "Open yours! Hurry up!"

It was a heavy, bulkily-wrapped package. She pulled off the paper to see a cardboard-bound book with SCRAP-BOOK embossed in gold leaf on the front cover. Inside, on page after page, were all the Hamilton ads she'd done, neatly clipped, trimmed, mounted and dated underneath.

"You *did* this!" she said, amazed by him, by his ideas, his thoughtfulness. "I can't get over your *doing* this!"

"You should keep your stuff," he said seriously. "You're really good. And someday, when you're famous, that stuff'll be important. You like it, don't you?"

"It's the best present of my life," she said, meaning it.

"Good! I guess I'd better get going now before they go crazy over there. You know how she can be. You'll come see me?"

"I promise you I will."

"Okay," he said, looking once more at his new watch. "Just make sure you don't forget."

"I won't."

She hugged him, he hugged her back hard, then went running noisily down the stairs. She closed the door, still holding the scrapbook, and leaned against the wall thinking she'd have to take a loan, or borrow the money. Maybe Dana would lend her enough to buy a car. Or there was always the employees' credit union.

She'd simply have to have a car. New Hampshire was a long way away. But, she thought, putting the scrapbook down

on her drawing board, it would be someplace to go every
month, once a month. She'd leave on Friday after work, drive
there, spend Saturday and part of Sunday with Corey, then
drive back.

"God damn them!" she cried suddenly, tears flooding her
eyes. "Why couldn't they just leave him, leave us alone? Damn
them! Damn!"

She'd been looking forward to the evening at Dana's, knowing how he liked to fuss over preparations. Now she didn't feel
like going. His house would be magnificently decorated. And
he'd invited eight other people for dinner. "At least half of
them are straight," he'd told her, "for your benefit entirely."

"Are you sure," she'd asked him incisively, "they're not
for your benefit?"

Interestingly, he'd gone very serious, answering, "I'm not
sure. I'm really not sure."

She couldn't not go, but she didn't feel like going anywhere.
She poured herself a glass of wine. Things would work out,
she told herself. One way or another. She'd get a car, work
out her visits to Corey. She'd find a way.

As she was on her way out the front door, she realized she
hadn't checked her mail slot and went back down the hall to
lift the lid and pull out half a dozen envelopes, and a post card.
She couldn't read in the dim light of the hallway. The hand-
writing was small and tight, a lot of words crammed into the
small space of a card. She put all the mail into her bag and
ran out to the waiting taxi. She'd read the card when she got
to Dana's.

He wrote, "Painting hard, learning, learning. Afternoon
siestas for heat then more painting. Good wine and sign lan-
guage I can't learn Spanish but feet learned sandals, head learned
hat, hand learned wild perspectives. Come to Spain. Take a
vacation or something." He'd squeezed in his address and signed
it, Luv, Rulph. A tiny grinning face was penned into the very
corner of the card.

Luv, Rulph. He really did like her. She would write to him.
Suddenly, there were all sorts of things she'd do—visits to
Corey, letters to Ralph. She felt more in the mood for a party
now and turned to Dana, who'd been waiting, his elegantly

shod foot tapping a tattoo. In a burgundy velvet suit and open-throated raw-silk shirt, he was an Edwardian painting. Black hair, creamy skin with a hint of fresh color on his cheeks, long-lashed deep brown eyes and a wide, sensitive, full mouth.

"You look magnificent," she complimented him. "Really."

"Thank you. Now come *on*," he urged. "You're the last and they're all waiting to get the introductions done so they can sit down."

"But you do look wonderful," she persisted.

"So do you, if you insist. You look like Lisette, which should reassure you. You'll age well."

"Do I, Dana?" That pleased her.

"Try looking in a mirror sometime," he said, slipping his arm through hers. "You're the image of her." He propelled her into the middle of his exquisitely decorated living room—perfectly understated—and she experienced a mild twinge of envy for the money that allowed him to live up to the standards of his very good taste. He began making introductions, pausing along the way to provide her with a glass of Asti Spumante. "Cheaper than champagne and just as nice," he said, before making the last of the introductions and escaping to the kitchen before the hot canapes burned.

She stood in front of the fireplace with the crystal goblet of wine and looked over the faces of those assembled. Good-looking people, well-dressed people. Dana liked those around him to be what he called "well put-together." And everyone present was. With the exception of me, she thought, feeling definitely underdressed in the when-in-doubt black crepe dress. Her shoes were wet from the trips in and out of the taxi, her nose was beginning to run from the heat of the room. She conjured up an image of Lisette, trying to match her self-image to this other one. She could see certain general similarities, but the image of her? No, she couldn't see that. She moved slightly away from the fire, continuing her inspection of Dana's guests. Her eyes moved from one face to the next until, caught, she saw a pair of piercing gray eyes looking directly back at her, involved in a similar inspection. The color leaping into her cheeks, she raised her glass to her mouth and turned away, trying to regain herself, looking into the fire.

"Dana's little sister," he said, coming to stand beside her.

"I barely caught the name when he threw it. Glenn, isn't it?"

"That's right." She took another swallow of wine before risking a clearer, closer look at this man. "I didn't catch yours at all, I'm afraid." She smiled. He was unquestionably one of Dana's straight guests.

"John called Jack." He grinned.

"John called Jack what?"

"Jack Owen. Formally," he laughed at their nonsense, "John Elliot Owen."

"I will *never* forget it," she said solemnly, finishing the last of her wine.

"Thirsty," he observed. "Another?"

"Please." She surrendered her glass to him, watching closely as he moved gracefully through the crowd and out to the kitchen, returning with the glass once more filled.

"Glenn," he said, "are you a career-type woman?"

"I suppose so. I'm in the art department at Hamilton's. What do you do?"

"I write jet-propelled grabbage."

"Grabbage?" She smiled doubtfully.

"Gar-bage. A maudlin·nonending epic called 'Hand in Hand.'"

"The *soap opera?*"

"I am covered in shame." He bowed his head melodramatically, then rolled his eyes at her, adding, "And soap. Soap."

She laughed. "You know Dana from the station then," she said, unable to decide if he was a new variety of crazy or in mid-performance.

"I know Dana from our days at prep school," he said, dropping the act. "We've been friends fifteen, seventeen years. He won all the prizes. I flunked out. But here we both are at the same place at the same point in time. Are you married?"

"No." She shook her head. The question surprised her. She'd never thought about being married, but supposed she was now of an age when more and more people would start asking if she was. "Are you?" she asked him.

"Alas," he said, gesturing over his shoulder. "In the far corner, with the pearls and outsize, splendidly uplifted breasts."

She looked, saw, looked away and clapped her hand over her mouth to cover the laughter that exploded up from her throat; having seen only a white neck encircled by a strand of pearls and a swelling, thrusting, somehow ridiculous pair of breasts. She hadn't even looked at the woman's face.

"Strikes me the same way," he whispered into her ear. "Imagine! Eight years ago, at the advanced age of twenty-three, I thought the world's mysteries were encased within the cups of her lovely lacy bras. Only to gain privileged access and find out it wasn't the world's mysteries at all, but the poor creature's brains tucked up in there."

"You're terrible!" she said, half meaning it. "How can you talk that way? I mean, she's your wife."

"Only for about another eighty days or so. And I promise you the world has rarely known the disappointment I experienced trying to communicate with a pair of brains that size. Anyway, eighty-odd days and then, Glenn, my girl, stand well back! There will be celebrating and carrying on for days, weeks! You will, of course, come out celebrating with me?"

"Of course," she said easily, not taking him seriously. "Call me when the great day comes. I'm in the telephone book now."

"You didn't used to be?"

"I did not."

"You *are* thirsty," he said. "Another?"

"I think I will. It's so hot in here."

He was very tall, broad-shouldered and looked far more like a football player than a writer, especially a writer of soap operas. He had thinning brownish-black hair, a pointed, cleft chin, a smile of great appeal and those penetrating gray eyes. She laughed as he returned, thinking him bold and outrageous to embark on a flirtation right in front of his soon-to-be ex-wife. She didn't care too much, truthfully, about the wife. She was enjoying the attention being paid her, and delighting in Dana's visual questions and raised eyebrows as he circulated through the room carrying a silver tray of cold canapes.

She finished her third glass of wine before they sat down to dinner and by the time the meal had ended she was laughingly, happily high as the clouds, smiling into her coffee cup as John-called-Jack's hand moved lazily up and down the inside of her thigh, safely hidden beneath Dana's damask tablecloth; murmuring to her complimentary-sounding things. She found it hard to listen, pay attention. It was a lovely evening. They were all lovely people. She'd heard from Ralph—she laughed aloud thinking about that—and she was somehow going to get herself a car.

Jack couldn't stop looking at her, mesmerized by her mouth, her eyes, and her freshness. He hadn't any idea what he was doing but he couldn't leave her alone.

She smiled across the table at the wife, feeling sorry for her, thinking, Your husband John-called-Jack is very, very nice and he is making me very, very excited. I suppose you think I'm some kind of threat to you, she went on, feeling her eyes going out of focus. But I'm not. I'm really not. You've already lost him. And I'm not even twenty-two yet, not the "other woman" kind at all. "Other women" have bosoms more like yours. They're older and wear expensive lingerie and satin mules, that sort of thing. I would *love* expensive lingerie but I haven't got the money for it. I will, though, one day.

Jack kept his eyes on her face, watching the way her eyes directly reflected what she was thinking, feeling strangely elated by her responses.

She turned her head dreamily to look at him, gazing at his mouth as he smiled into her eyes. She wanted to speak, opened her mouth, couldn't speak, closed it. People were pushing their chairs back from the table, returning to the living room. Jack smiling, smiling at her, casually took hold of her hand, detaining her.

"Were you serious?" she asked him in an undertone. "Are you really getting divorced?"

"Check with Dana if you don't believe me. Are you always this suspicious?"

"I'm not suspicious at all," she said, her voice ranging out of control. "But how'm I to know if you're telling the truth? Are you still living together?"

"Uh-uh." He made a negative motion with his hand. "Not for years. You make me feel sad and happy both at the same time," he told her, not smiling now. "I could love a girl like you." He felt at that moment as if he did love her, as if they were isolated from everyone and everything. Just the two of them and the possibility of making sense out of life, being together.

"Oh!" She took a step away from him, in no way prepared for statements like this.

"Don't do that," he said quietly. "She's here with me tonight because I felt sorry for her. Which is a pretty sad summation of our whole marriage. But nobody should have to spend Christmas Eve all alone. And she would have had to because all her plans fell through. I'm not a liar. Or a seducer of young women." He smiled, thinking how very, very young she looked, and how sweet she was, how untouched by the real world pollution. A little ingenuous and so sweet. His senses had been becoming blunted because of a lack of reactions. She was making all his senses come alive again, making him feel something like happy. He wanted to hold her in his arms and sing softly into her ear, hold her for a long, long time. "Where do you live?" he asked, noticing her eyes were still slightly out of focus.

"Wellington Road. I have to go now," she said abruptly, looking around for Dana.

"I'll see you later," he said, reluctant to release her hand, let her go.

"Oh sure!" She laughed and tottered over to say goodnight to Dana.

"You're *smashed!*" Dana said accusingly under his breath, piloting her to the front hall and putting her into her coat. "Stand here and don't *move* until the taxi comes!"

"Is he really getting divorced?" she asked, her eyes narrowing as she looked back into the room trying to locate Jack. She wanted to see him once more, but her head felt too heavy for her neck to properly support it. She couldn't find him.

"Jack? It's in the works. She's such a dreary woman!" A horn sounded outside. "There's your cab! Here's your cab fare. You'll be here tomorrow at two. Right?"

"Of course," she said. "I'm not *that* drunk, you know!"

"You're that drunk and more!" he said peevishly. "The two of you carrying on, mooning over each other right at the table in front of everyone! It's a good thing no one else seemed to notice. Glenn, that's so damned *juvenile!* You're not like that. You go home, go straight to bed and sleep it off!" He softened, seeing he'd hurt her feelings by admitting to what he'd seen. Lord! She was so damnably hurtable. And that was Lisette in her, too. "Merry Christmas, little sister." He kissed her on the forehead.

"And to you, too, Dana," she said, looking as if she might begin to cry. "Sometimes I love you so much, Dana. When you're you and you're kind. You can be so kind. And when you are, I love you a lot."

"Goodnight," he said thickly, getting her out through the door and into the taxi.

"Don't play with her, Jack," Dana said quietly. "I wouldn't like to see that."

Jack looked affronted. "I don't make it a habit of playing with women. And I sure as hell wouldn't play with someone like your sister. She's a sweet woman."

"Well, explain to me then how you could carry on a flirtation so blatantly right at the dining table in front of your wife."

Jack stared at him for a moment, then smiled, a little embarrassed. "You don't miss a goddamned thing, do you?" he said.

"Very little," Dana conceded.

"I'm sorry you saw."

"So am I," Dana said. "She *is* my sister, Jack. And she's important to me. I don't like that sort of thing. It makes both of you . . . I don't know. It makes you both—*less,* somehow."

"You're putting a little too much stress on it," Jack said calmly. "The feeling there was mutual."

"Tell me something," Dana said, his expression becoming one of intense curiosity.

"What's that?"

"Does it feel right to you? Does it feel complete and satisfying? Or does it leave you with the feeling that there ought to be something more?"

"Are you telling me that that's your feeling with women?"

"No, actually." Dana lowered his eyes. "It's my feeling with just about everyone. How does it feel for you, Jack?"

"Complete. And satisfying. Maybe you ought to try women for a change," Jack suggested. "Or have you?"

"I have. I did. I don't know any more."

"Since we're getting into it," Jack said, "aren't there some women who appeal to you?"

"Some," Dana admitted.

"Pursue the appeal then," Jack advised. "Give yourself a chance. It seems to me you've never given yourself much of a chance, you know."

"Maybe. We'll see."


She went careering around the attic in the murk of the bedside light, giggling, shedding clothes as she went, humming what she was quite sure was a Christmas carol but unable to remember the lyrics something in Latin she could never remember the words couldn't even remember the words to the national anthem when they used to have to sing it in assembly she'd always just moved her lips while the words'd come out of other people's mouths.

A quiet tapping at the door stopped her. She tilted her head, listening, then began singing again. A louder tapping. Her heart skipped, lurched inside her. She tiptoed over, pressing her ear to the door.

"Glenn?" The tapping was right under her ear. She jerked her head away.

"Who is it?" She stepped away from the door.

"Jack. Open the door!"

She opened the door.

"Oh, you're perfect!" he exclaimed, and he laid her down right there after quickly closing the door. He put her right down on the floor while she blinked, thinking, I'm dreaming, dreaming. He chanted, "Oh, baby, baby, baby. My sweet sweet baby," in varying degrees of intensity and she closed her eyes to make it all go away because it had to be a bad dream. The floor tilted, the walls went round and round, making her stomach heave. She turned her head away feeling how round her eyes were.

"My God!" he cried, disengaging, leaping up frantically to pull up his shorts and his trousers as she sat up. Still heaving she sobbed, finally crying out at him, "You *hurt* me!" Getting to her feet she ran staggering down the attic to the bathroom sobbing, *"Hurt* me!"

He stood stock still for a solid minute before his thoughts cleared sufficiently to enable him to make sense of what had happened. He was anything but completely sober, but not so far from it that he was unaware of the dreadful assumption he'd made seeing her come to the door naked, believing she'd been waiting for him. He'd thought they'd made arrangements, but obviously she hadn't been waiting. And not only was she drunk drunk, but she was being sick again in there. The floor was a stinking mess and now he was very sober and ashamed as he'd never been in his life. First, because he'd never done anything like this and didn't quite know how or why. Second, because he'd believed she'd been extending an invitation. The truth was she'd simply been so bombed she hadn't known *what* she'd been extending.

He took off his overcoat, switched on some lights, found the hotplate and the coffee pot and got some coffee going before searching for and finding a roll of paper towels. He cleaned up the mess as best he could, leaving the sodden paper towels piled up in the corner beside the door. Then he walked around slowly, looking at everything, at her paintings and drawings, liking what he saw. He waited for her to come out, but she didn't. Finally, he went down the length of the room to knock at the yellow-painted bathroom door, asking, "Are you all right now, Glenn?"

Surprised he was still out there, she sobbed, *"Go away!"* then hung her head, squeezing her fists into her belly. The pain was terrible, and she was mortified by the sickness, by his still being out there, by all of it.

"I made some coffee and cleaned up," he said to her through the door. "Listen, I'm sorry. I was a little high. I misunderstood. Glenn?"

"Go away," she said less emphatically, turning on both faucets to drown out the sound of his voice. "Leave me alone!"

"No, I'll wait. We have to talk. I want to talk to you."

"Go talk to your wife! Go hurt somebody else!" she cried, her voice childishly high.

"Glenn, I'm *sorry.*" He felt worse by the minute. He liked her so much, wanted so badly to compensate for this, fix it up, correct it. "If you really want me to go," he said, "I will. But I'd really like a chance to explain."

He waited but she didn't answer. He tried again but still she wouldn't respond. She wasn't going to. He heard the faucets being turned off, then the sound of the toilet being flushed, the shower starting. Pointless. He'd totally fucked up. Totally.

Sober, depressed, and in need of a shower himself, he reached for his coat, pulled it on, stood waiting for a few more minutes hoping she'd come out, then finally, quietly let himself out.

"Goodnight," he said, knowing he couldn't be heard. "I'm really sorry."

She stayed under the shower until her skin was wrinkled and bright red from the heat and some of the drunkenness had been dissipated. Then, emerging from the bathroom, sniffing at the percolating coffee, she tiptoed down the length of the attic to see that he really had cleaned up, he really had made coffee, he really had gone away. She began to cry again. Lonely.

# Eleven

One thing the school had going for it, it sure was a good-looking place. Lots of trees, plenty of places to walk, places a guy could hang out on his own, do some thinking. But the rest of it wasn't so hot at all. Getting assigned to share a room with this guy Brady who was really pissed off and didn't fool around any trying to hide it because he'd thought he'd lucked out and wasn't going to have to share the room but would have it all to himself. And then, what do you know? Here came Corey and poor old Brady was going to have to share his room.

"Just don't get your stuff all over the place," Brady told him straight off. "I can't stand a messy guy."

"Worry about your own stuff," Corey said. "Let me worry about myself."

"You get dumped out or something?" Brady asked, easing off a little.

"Dumped out of the fucking house," Corey said, without inflection, not looking up from his unpacking. "Why?" He looked over finally at the other boy. "D'you get dumped out, too?"

"Sort of. My folks split up. He took off, she stuck me here."

"My mom remarried," Corey said. "How long you been here?"

"Since September."

"How is it?"

"Great if you're a jock. If you're into all that crap, it's terrific. Or if you're into the whole theater thing. Otherwise, it's a big zero."

"Oh." Corey kept on unpacking. "Your folks come to visit and all that?"

"My mom does." Brady shrugged. "She's okay, I guess."

"Got any sisters or brothers?"

"Nope. You?"

"Nope."

They looked at each other, trying out smiles, working at keeping their distance.

Between classes, Corey scouted out places where it was safe to cop a smoke. It wasn't easy. Every time he thought he had it all pegged, some gang would come racing past lugging all kinds of sports equipment, on their way to some game or another. Every time he turned around, it seemed, some gang of guys would come rushing by, off to one of their big-deal games.

On his third night there, unable to stand it any longer, he sneaked into the can before lights-out for a smoke. He was in there when Bobby Brady came in. Brady grinned. Corey offered him a cigarette. They started to talk, and things were suddenly a whole lot better.

"My mom's coming up this weekend," Brady said, taking a deep drag. "She'll take us out to dinner a coupla times. It'll be okay. You'll come with us."

"She won't mind?"

"Nah! She'll be so knocked out I finally found a friend she'll be tickled to death to take you, too. She gets all hot and worried that I've got 'antisocial tendencies.' Who wants to be 'social' with a bunch of zeros like they've got around here?"

"Okay," Corey said. "Great! Boy, the food here's really lousy. I'm going to have to do something about that."

"Something like what?"

"You want to starve to death?" Corey asked him. "Or d'you

want to help me get a little something organized here, so we
can eat some halfway decent food?"

"Like how organized?"

"I don't know. I've got to think about it. We're going to
need some working capital, though."

"Working capital? I think you're nuts."

"You won't think so . . ."

"Shit! Somebody's coming." Brady tossed his cigarette into
the toilet and flushed it, urging Corey to do the same.

"Take it easy," Corey advised, enjoying a last drag. "You'll
live longer."

Friday afternoon, after classes, he hitched a ride into town
and found a second-hand shop that had everything he was going
to need: a battered old single-unit hotplate, a couple of second-
hand dented saucepans and a frying pan in reasonably good
condition but minus a handle.

"Gimme five bucks," the store owner told him, "you can
have the whole mess and I'll throw in that boxacrap over there."

"I'll have to come back. But I'll take it. So don't sell any
of this stuff to anybody else 'til I get back. Okay?"

"Lissen, kid! First come, first served."

"I said I'll take it," Corey said firmly. "I'll be back later or
in the morning. Just hang on to it all."

He hitched another ride back to the school and tore upstairs
to the room where Brady was busily tidying himself up prior
to his mother's arrival.

"You can't come out with us looking that way," Brady said.
"At least wash up or something."

"Keep your shirt on! Listen, we've got to get five bucks
together. I've got two eighty-five. How much've you got?"

"I don't know." Brady pulled some change out of his pocket
and counted it. "Ninety-three cents."

"Shit! We need another dollar and a quarter."

"My mom'll give me that," Brady said, shoving his money
back into his pocket. "She gives me five a week pocket money.
We'll go halfers. Just what're we buying?"

"A hotplate, some cooking stuff."

"Are you *insane?* We'll get bounced. There's no cooking
allowed in the rooms."

"You let me worry about it. I've got the whole thing figured out."

"It's your funeral. Just do me a favor and get cleaned up, willya? My mom's going to be here any minute and she can't stand waiting. It's her one thing, you know? She just can't stand waiting."

"Okay, okay. You keep on this way, boy, you'll wind up really neurotic. You've gotta take it easy if you want to survive in this world."

Brady's mother was a big surprise. Brady didn't look one bit like her, so he had to look like his father. She was about the best-looking woman Corey had ever seen. He couldn't stop staring at her. Not too tall, but not too short either, with short, curly dark hair, big brown eyes, and an unbelievable body! He checked Brady out to see if Brady knew what an incredible mother he had but Brady was busy doing his good-son act and Corey could tell anyway Brady didn't have a clue what kind of mother he had. She wasn't all phony or cute, but just nice. She picked them up at the dorm and drove them out to this restaurant on the highway, asking Brady all kinds of really-interested questions about school and how he was liking it. She really cared if Brady was liking it. Then she leaned forward over the steering wheel to smile at Corey with a nice mouthful of teeth, asking, "How are you liking it, Corey?"

"Oh, fine." Corey smiled back, something wild happening inside his stomach every time he looked at her. "It's gonna be okay, I think."

"Well, good. I'm glad. I'm so pleased Bobby's sharing a room with someone he likes."

"Come on, mom!" Bobby blushed and nudged Corey in the ribs. Corey took it, thinking he really was going to have to clue Brady in about a few things.

He was able to study her more closely in the restaurant, noticing how tiny her wrists were. He liked that. Her hands were nice, too. She wore this one ring with a kind of milky stone, and a wristwatch. No other jewelry, except for tiny little pierced earrings with the same milky stones. Her throat was very white and her ears nice and small, peeking out from the curls. Her mouth was very pretty. He liked her mouth a lot and thought it would probably be very good kissing her. He thought about kissing her, shouldn't have thought about kissing her and concentrated heavily on the food, which wasn't too bad. The hollandaise was thin and watery but the asparagus was all right. The roast beef was on the dry side but the baked potato was excellent. He liked the fact that along with the chives and sour cream the management provided little bacon bits sprinkled on top of the whole thing. It was a nice touch. He'd have to remember that.

After the meal, Mrs. Brady drove them back to the school, saying, "I'll pick you boys up in the morning. We'll have breakfast. Then I thought I'd let you have a look around town while I get my hair done. How's that?"

"Sure!" Corey said quickly, thinking that would be the perfect time to pick up what was going to be his portable kitchen. "We'll be ready, won't we, Bobby?"

"Oh, sure," Bobby agreed, looking at Corey as if he'd suddenly lost track of what was going on and needed an explanation. He kissed his mother's cheek then went hurrying inside after Corey.

As they were getting undressed for bed, Corey said, "Ever jack off, Brady?"

Bobby simply stared at him.

"You haven't," Corey said. "It figures. Anybody told you the facts of life?"

Bobby continued to stare.

"Oh boy!" Corey sighed. "I can see I'm going to have to tell you a few things. You'd better get yourself together or the next thing you know those guys from the theater are gonna be climbing all over you."

"Hey! I'm no queer!"

"Well, then start getting in shape. Otherwise, when opportunity presents itself, you're not going to know what in hell to do with it."

"How come you know it all?" Bobby asked hotly. "What makes you so smart?"

"I just know, that's all. Your mom's really nice, you know, Brady, really a great-looking lady."

"She's okay."

"How long've your folks been divorced?" Corey asked casually, reaching under his pillow for the pajamas he'd shoved under there that morning.

"Coupla years."

"Oh."

"What d'you want to know for?"

"Just interested, that's all. You wanna use the john first or should I?"

"You go on. I'm not even ready yet."

"Okay. Listen, I'll tell you all about it. Okay? I mean boy! Somebody should've told you a long time ago. You know? It's about time you knew. Don't worry," he said gently. "I'll look out for you."

Corey picked up his toothbrush, toothpaste, soap and towel and went along down the hall. Luckily, he was alone. He closed himself into a cubicle, shut his eyes, and thought about Brady's mother. Her throat, and the shape of her breasts, imagining what she'd look like without her clothes. He was already flushing the toilet when Bobby pushed into the john a couple of minutes later. Corey thought a woman like Brady's mother was about as high as you could go. If you had aspirations. And he'd just discovered that he had some. It didn't matter if you never got there, but it was something very, very nice to think about.

He kept all the cooking things in a suitcase. After using the hotplate, he'd stick it outside on the window sill until it had cooled sufficiently to go into the bag. Washing up was easy. He just carried the pots down to the john and right in front of everybody cleaned them out. He was so casually matter-of-fact about it, nobody even bothered asking what he was doing. They ate off paper plates and Bobby said, "Wow! You know you're some kind of genius. I never met a guy in my life could cook like this. What is this stuff anyway?"

"Just some beef, pinto beans, a bit of this and that, garlic. If I had some real money, boy could I cook us up some food! Wait 'til my dad sends my next month's pocket money. Then we'll have a feast."

"I can hardly wait," Bobby said earnestly.

They kept up appearances at mealtimes in the dining room, but only picked at their food, saving their appetites for the concoctions Corey whipped up in their room. Their only problem was the smell of the food when it was cooking. Bobby kept the window open and stood by the door waving a towel around until it was time to eat. Then the two of them huddled by the open window, bundled in sweaters against the cold, gobbling up the food as fast as they could.

All their pocket money went into Corey's cooking projects.

"Just don't start blabbing it around," Corey warned him. "That'd really wreck the whole thing. Okay?"

"Okay!"

"I've been thinking maybe we could pick up a good, cheap, second-hand fan in town. That'd take care of blowing the cooking smells out the window."

"Boy, you're a genius!" Bobby enthused.

"Sure. Now, listen. I want to tell you a few things about life."

The incident with Jack triggered Glenn's thinking in a number of new areas. The first and most obvious had to do with wine. Without fail, if she drank more than two glasses she became very drunk and very ill. So, she'd give it up since it plainly disagreed with her system. Experimenting with the bottles of gin and scotch she'd purchased months before, she decided finally that, of the two, she preferred gin. It did have a decidedly medicinal flavor she at first found hard to take. But it went down far more easily than the scotch—which activated her gag mechanism when she tried to swallow it. Gin, when mixed with tonic, made what she considered a pleasantly refreshing drink, giving her a nice lift without making her sick. So, from now on, she'd drink gin. She was less tempted to gulp it down the way she did wine and since the taste was not nearly so misleadingly attractive, she'd likely drink less of it.

As she worked her way through her thoughts and experiments with the scotch and gin, trying to decide on her preferences, she began to feel worse and worse about what had happened Christmas Eve.

She'd never really given too much thought to herself as a person. She hadn't thought at all of herself in terms of being someone with rights, options, choices. She had, for most of her childhood, been preoccupied with trying to make sense of her family and attempting to determine her position within it. But Jack's forcing himself inside of her, coming at her that way, propelled her into a confrontation with herself from which she emerged angry and armed with justified vexation. She had, she knew, encouraged him to believe she was attracted to him. She had been, it was true. He'd seemed extraordinary to her, the things he'd said and done unlike the things other people she knew said and did. But what made him think he could just push himself inside someone else? Had the situations been reversed, she'd certainly never have forced herself on him. What, then, gave him the right, the supposed superiority to inflict himself on her the way he had?

Drinking her gin and tonic, she paced the length of the attic trying to get to the roots of her feelings, curious and eager to take stock and learn exactly what her feelings were. It was an exercise she'd never before done with complete attention and she found herself without answers to a considerable number of the questions about herself she posed.

Why, for example, had she encouraged Jack to caress her that way during dinner? She'd done it because she'd wanted him. She still wanted him. But she'd never have him now because she'd done all the wrong things, hadn't displayed any sense of herself as a person. She'd just gone through that whole evening wide-eyed and unaware, like a little girl, allowing herself to be led this way and that without ever stopping to ask herself what she wanted or how she felt. She was not entirely blameless in what took place later. She could see that quite clearly. So she was going to have to think more about what she was doing and not merely allow things to happen without exercising awareness and control. After all, her life was *her* life, under *her* control. If there were things she didn't want to have happen, it was within her ability to prevent those things happening.

She sat down, turning her glass around and around in her fingers, examining the widening implications of this concept. *My life.* I can make it what I want, take it where I want, have it the way I want it. But what do I want? Where do I want to go?

There were any number of things she might do if she had the money. But money was a large minus factor in her life and she was feeling it more each week. She was doing a great deal of hard work for very little salary, a lot of praise, a lot of ads printed, but not much money.

So, if she were going to begin doing anything, top of the list was money. Fine. How? She'd been at the store less than a year. If she left, the first question she'd be asked at the next place was why she'd left Hamilton's. If she said it was because she wanted more money, they'd ask why hadn't she stuck it out a little longer until the money came to her. Because, she answered herself, I don't want to waste my whole life sticking it out at a job I don't like all that much. She sat back, surprised, and pleased, too. She was learning quite a bit about herself.

I really don't like that job. Okay. What *do* I want? What would I like to do?

I wish Jack would call me, talk to me. No.

She wanted something requiring more imagination, more talent, more effort, something different. She couldn't make it come any clearer. Just something to give her more money, money to provide increased mobility, a nicer place to live, small luxuries. She wanted an apartment with a proper kitchen and a separate bedroom. God! A separate bedroom. I could make love to him properly. No. A decent-size bathroom, a refrigerator with all its parts intact. An elevator. Walking up all those flights of stairs at the end of an exhausting day was sometimes more than she could face. So, she'd delay returning home and go take in a movie, treat herself to a cheap meal out, a drink or two.

I want. She tried to put things in order. I want.

Number one: Why doesn't he call me?

No. Number one: More money.

Number two: A decent place to live.

Number three: No. Number One-A: A job. Something to work at that I enjoy. I would so enjoy seeing him. No, a job. After that, everything else will come. No, it won't, because I don't want to spend the rest of my life doing a job-job. I want to do what I want to do but I don't know what I want to do except that I will be successful, with a lot of money. Money is freedom. And making a lot of money doesn't happen in an art department or a *department* of any kind. It happens because of something you can do better or differently, more perfectly or more cleverly than anybody else. I can do good fashion ads, smart little line drawings. But so can hundreds, thousands of people. It doesn't make me unique. I'm not a good enough artist. I know I've got *something,* something I can do that other people can't. I know it. If I could just touch it or see it, know what it is. If I could *just* . . . He didn't really like me. He would have called.

She felt frustrated, hamstrung by her inability to see and know what it was she had that might lift her out of her present mode of existence and set her on the road to her luminous future. She knew with absolute certainty, complete conviction that she was going to have everything she wanted in precisely the way she wanted it while she was still young enough to enjoy it all. If she could only find her way down to that something inside of her that was different, special, unique. It was there. She knew it was. She was going to make it. People would know her name one day.

Dana, his mouth pursed unattractively, said, "If you can find a used car, I'll lend you the down payment. I'll even cosign for you. But I honestly don't have too much cash to spare at the moment. So I'm afraid you're going to have to see what you can get for two or three hundred down."

"That's not very much," she said, disappointed.

"It would have been more last week. The truth is, my last 'friend,' if you'll forgive the euphemism, took off with most of my cash, Ray's diamond studs and the toaster."

"The toaster?" She couldn't help herself. She laughed.

He laughed with her. "Too much, isn't it?" he said. "It really is too goddamned much! Taking the toaster." He mopped his eyes, then smiled at her. "I'm sorry, lovey. Last week, I could've given you six or seven hundred. The most I can swing now is three."

"I understand. Anyway, three should help a lot."

She went away trying to think of what to do. She still had a few thousand left of her inheritances. But she was drawing against that money regularly, using her savings to pay the rent. Her salary, after taxes and various withheld sums, was less than eighty dollars a week. Out of that she had to pay for transportation, food, clothing, everything. The situation was impossible. Without her savings, she'd be sinking further and further into debt weekly. As it was, every month depleted her account by another hundred and a bit, and she wasn't buying anything for herself beyond the absolute necessities. If she withdrew several hundred dollars to put toward a car, she'd be subtracting a number of months from her solvency. She couldn't risk it, terrified at the prospect of having to live on her tiny salary alone. To do it, she'd have to give up public transportation altogether, as well as the telephone, her personal art supplies and lunches in the employees' cafeteria. And even then, she'd be paying only the ninety dollars monthly rent, her minimal laundry and cleaning expenses, and personal needs like toothpaste and tampons. There'd be no point to life that way, no pleasure whatsoever. She'd rather not live if it meant living a life so totally devoid of even the smallest pleasures. God! One day, she promised herself. One day.

Mrs. Swayze, upon hearing Glenn was trying to buy a car, said she'd heard that the telephone company sold off the Volkswagens they used for service vehicles and perhaps that might be worth investigating. Glenn called the telephone company, was referred to the dealership that handled these cars and went along to have a look at the one bug they happened to have on the lot.

Its mileage meter had been turned back so many times it was no longer operational, so the mileage could only be guessed at. But she could have it for two hundred down, financing the three-fifty balance. Assured the car was mechanically sound— it seemed to be but she could only take the salesman's word for it—she haggled over the price, got him down fifty dollars, then made arrangements with Dana for the down payment, got a note from the bank for the balance and drove back to Wellington Road in the fender-dented bug. There was an available parking slot at the rear of the house Glenn could have for an additional eight dollars a month, and she took it. Then she sat down with pencil and paper and figured out that for the next year her expenses had just risen forty-five dollars a month, not counting gasoline and whatever additional costs would come along with owning the car.

She couldn't get to sleep that night worrying about how she

was going to handle her increased expenses. For hours she
turned first one way then the other, trying to think up ideas
that might improve her financial situation, and get her out of
the depressing trough of her life. She was beginning to hate
her life, to hate being an employee, someone with no status,
one of hundreds of faceless people filing in and out of Hamilton's every morning and every evening, punching in their
cards. A cow in a herd. She lay thinking up possible solutions.
But every time she thought she'd come up with an answer, the
negative side would present itself, causing her anxiously to turn
yet again, as if the physical act of moving her body might shift
the balance of thoughts in her mind, and flip up an answer.

By two A.M., desperate for some sleep, she sat up, switched
on the light and poured herself a drink. The gin would calm
her down, let her relax and get to sleep. She returned to bed
with her drink and sat in the dark sipping at the crisply tart gin
and tonic, hoping this might even help her marshal her thoughts.
Her stomach gurgled noisily as the level in the glass dropped.
Yet, with the last swallow—the ice cubes hitting against her
teeth—she was dismayed to find herself no calmer, no sleepier
than she'd been to begin with. She lay down nevertheless and
closed her eyes, telling herself, In a few minutes it'll start
working and I'll fall asleep.

In a few minutes she was thinking about Jack. She turned
onto her right side and lay there for what seemed like hours,
her eyes wide open in the dark, thoughts tearing through her
brain at breakneck speed. She couldn't shut down, turn off.
She turned to her left side again. He'd never called. She'd
never see him again. Or Ralph. Gone. Both of them. She wasn't
very good with men, obviously, or she'd be keeping them.

Making an angry-disgusted noise, she sat up once more,
again turned on the light, snatched up the glass—it was almost
three now, she saw—and fixed another drink, this time with
slightly more gin, slightly less tonic. She went back to bed to
turn off the light, make sure the alarm was set. Then, sitting
with her eyes well-accustomed to the dark, she made a face at
the first taste of this new, stronger drink; feeling it hit and
spread, she smiled because this time it was going to do its job.
Anxious for it all to get going, she gulped down the drink,

returned the glass to the bedside table, settled her head on the pillow and plummeted into sleep with the speed and weight of a dropped rock. Her lips curved into a smile and she was gone.

She made the long drive to New Hampshire to see Corey fully expecting him to greet her with a lengthy list of grievances. But he was more than usually philosophical, telling her very seriously, "You know, I've been figuring things out."

"Like what?" she asked, admiring the beauty of the school buildings, the grounds; a little dizzy from all the hours spent driving over the snowy, ice-patched roads.

"I guess I kind of knew it before, but I've been really proving it out here. The thing is, you've got to learn to make the best of what happens and give people what they want." He directed her down a path off the main walk. "I mean it," he said, looking into her eyes. "Give them what they want and you'll get what you want from them. It's no good trying to fight everybody. You just can't get anywhere that way."

"Go on," she said, intrigued by his logic.

"Okay," he said, warming to his subject, glad to have his favorite audience. "Like this guy, Brady, who shares with me. I get here and he's all hot and bugged because he figured he was going to get away with a room all to himself for the rest of the year. But, no. I come along and he's got to share. I don't like it any better than he does. He puts down his rules and I give him back mine. And a couple of days go by and there we are, the two of us watching each other." He laughed, enjoying his story. "Anyway. So, one night, when I can't stand it, I sneak a cigarette in the can. And in comes Brady, gets a whiff and the next thing there we are each having a cigarette, talking like crazy and he's inviting me to come out with him and his mom on the weekend. Just like that."

"What does that have to do with giving people what they want?" she asked, losing his point, not sure he'd made one.

"Well, maybe I didn't say it right," he said. "I mean you've got to give yourself and other people a chance. You know? If you can wait and make up your mind maybe later, the thing is you might find out things're really okay. I've got a portable kitchen all worked out. So me and Brady are eating good stuff."

"You like it here," she said.

"Oh, it's okay." He shrugged. "It's not as bad as I thought it'd be. It's not great either," he added quickly. "But I can handle it. I mean I don't have much choice, do I? I've got to be here, so I might as well make out the best way I can."

"Corey', I still don't get what you're saying. It sounds to me as if you're only being . . . fair. That's it. Fair."

"That's not the whole thing," he said, annoyed with himself for not expressing his thoughts more clearly. "I mean, for one thing you can make people like you and still be you without going all phony. You like different people for different things. Like one guy you like because he's really smart. And another guy because he's really funny. Or somebody else just because he's an okay kind of guy. And it makes that guy feel really okay about himself."

"And that makes you feel better, superior because you've got the whole thing worked out to a formula?"

"No," he said, surprised they were having so much trouble understanding each other. "It just makes you feel better because you've done something to make things better for yourself. I'm still working it out, you know," he said defensively. "I haven't got it all straight yet."

They walked along quietly for a bit and Glenn felt inexplicably let down, even saddened by what she thought Corey had been trying to say. To her, it sounded somehow as if he were teaching himself the fine art of compromise. If that were the case, she did feel sad because what she'd always liked most about him was his refusal to compromise, his adamant insistence on being himself no matter what the circumstances. If he were compromising now, then Gabrielle and Lloyd and George Shea were succeeding in what they'd set out to do: domesticating Corey, taming him. She hated the idea of that, the idea of coming back month after month to see him slowly losing his uniqueness, his originality and individuality.

He was thinking maybe it was because she was tired. It was a long drive from the city to the school and she'd worked all day. She did look kind of worn out, he thought, glancing over at her. Older, sort of.

"You're special," she said, giving voice to her disturbed thoughts. "You're very special, Corey. I'd hate to think that being here, having to be here is going to make you change."

"I know I'm special," he said without cuteness. "That's why I'm trying to tell you all this. Don't you get it? Half the guys around here don't think much. About anything. They don't know what they want or even what they're here for. So they're just mad, bugged with everything. *I* know why I'm here. I have to be here. So what I'm doing is making it the best I can for myself. You have to do that, Aunt Glenn. Otherwise, you'll go crazy. You can't get stuck in a place like this and spend all your time wishing you were somewhere else. You'll just waste a whole lot of time being mad and complaining instead of finding things to do that take your mind off it, things that keep you feeling good until the whole thing's over and you can start doing the things you really want to do."

"Biding your time," she said.

"Sort of. But not really. I mean, boy! If I took all the school spirit and that crap seriously, I'd just be another one of *them*. And what good would that do me? I don't want to be one of those guys who spend the rest of their lives being mad about everything because they've never been able to figure things out for themselves. So, what I do, I find the stuff I like and put my other things away for a while."

"What things?"

"The stuff I really want to do. Don't you have stuff you want to do?"

"Let's sit down for a minute," she said, spotting a relatively snow-free bench. "Tell me about the stuff you want to do."

"Lots of things," he said, gazing into space. "Make a lot of money. Be for myself. Maybe," he shifted his eyes to her, "we could go into business or something together someday. I've got all kinds of ideas."

She smiled. "What business would we go into?" she asked, wishing she had more of whatever it was that made him so certain, so quietly determined.

"Something," he said, sensing she really wasn't in the right mood for a discussion of his ideas. "I'm starving," he said. "And you've got to be pretty hungry too. There's a place out on the highway that's not too bad."

"I just don't want to see you change," she said soberly. "I love you the way you are, Corey."

"I'm not gonna change," he said. "And I love you, too, you know."

She thought about his philosophy all the way home, in higher spirits for having seen him. She felt recharged, energized, determined to begin making changes, getting herself headed into her future. After all, if Corey could have such positive, well-defined ideas on how to get on, the least she ought to be able to do was learn from him.

The first thing she did upon arriving home was to map out a plan for a calculated risk. She had to have more money to live on. She wasn't willing to go out looking for a new job just yet. It made bad sense. But why shouldn't she risk applying a little pressure, seeing if Hamilton's couldn't be made to put up dollars along with their accolades?

Monday morning, she went along to see Mrs. Swayze, asking, "I'd like to speak to somebody about a raise. Whom do I ask?"

Mrs. Swayze said, "I'll call upstairs for you."

Having been dismissed for the moment, Glenn returned to her cubicle and tried to get on with her work, but her mind kept wandering apprehensively. She was risking the job, risking finding herself out on the street, unemployed altogether. That would be disastrous at this point with her increased expenses due to the car. But if they valued her work as much as they claimed, then they ought to be willing to pay for it, willing to keep her happily producing for them. She was determined to bluff it through. But she wished she had enough time to go over to the bar for a drink. A drink would make her feel so much better.

Minutes later, Mrs. Swayze came along to say, "Mr. Hamilton will see you in fifteen minutes. Do you know where his office is?"

Glenn nodded, wiped her hands down the sides of her skirt and went along to the elevator to ride two floors up to the executive offices. She gave her name to the secretary who said, "He's expecting you. Go right in," and stood to open the door.

"Miss Burgess." Mr. Hamilton got to his feet, extending

his hand. "Come in, sit down. I've been intending for quite some time to have a chat with you and tell you how pleased we've been with your work."

"Thank you." She returned his handshake, then lowered herself into the chair. He was younger than she'd expected and better looking too, with green eyes. Lighter than Corey's, but green like his. She could easily project Corey twenty-five years or so into the future and see him in an office like this one, calmly in control, exuding an aura of success and wealth.

"We've been talking just this morning about letting you try your hand at several projects we have in mind," he said with a smile. She smiled back, caught by his green eyes, wondering why she was talking to the president of the company instead of to the personnel people.

"Mr. Hamilton," she said, not wanting to waste any more time—either his or her own. "I've been offered another job, at much more money."

"I see," he said, pushing his chair back a little from the desk, his features assuming a serious set. "We'd be sorry to lose you."

In the brief silence following this remark he looked at her eyes, seeing there something that made him think of his daughter. She was only eleven but she had the same determined yet fearful look to her from time to time. And when he saw it in Lisa, he had the impression she was both seeing and not seeing, a part of her concentrating hard on the moment while another part of her was staring into something so immense and of such compelling importance it simply couldn't be ignored. A vision, a personal vision, fiercely private, zealously guarded. It dismayed and bewildered him, this passionate intensity. He wondered if Miss Burgess might also have been an adopted child and whether that fact might have something to do with this visual expression common to them both.

She had the feeling that his eyes were capable of drilling minute little holes all over the surface of her skin, holes that would let all her resolve and good intentions leak right out of her. She was a little frightened of this man.

"How much," he asked at last, "are you being offered in this new job?"

"One hundred and seventy-five dollars a week," she said

carefully, having at the last moment upped the figure by twenty-five dollars. She might just as well go all the way and get as much or as little as she was going to get.

"I see," he stated, steepling manicured fingers on the desk. His eyes bore into hers, burning tiny holes into the surface of her skin, searing her eyes. "And if we were to offer to match this figure, you'd consider remaining with the store?"

"Yes, sir."

"Is there really another job offer, Miss Burgess?" he asked cannily, cutting through all her carefully-prepared answers. She hadn't expected the question.

"Yes, sir," she lied, keeping her eyes on his.

He smiled and reached for a cigarette but didn't light it, holding the open box out to her. She shook her head and he put the box down.

"Might I ask with whom?"

"No, sir," she said evenly, "you might not."

She was so like Lisa, he thought, recalling a conversation he'd had with her recently. The tone had been so tensely similar. He'd not enjoyed it. This was not quite such a struggle, but difficult nonetheless. Glenn's blue eyes were opaque with determination. She was lying, he was certain. But he could see she'd stick to her guns. And he admired her for it. He allowed his mind to drift for a moment, his eyes taking in her shoulders, the tidy mounds of her breasts. Small breasts. They'd be round with dainty nipples. Soft. A tall girl with a lovely face and a certain appealing frailty. He found himself very aroused and was surprised by it. His wife was dying and he'd been involved with Jeanette for close to a year, the only other woman, outside Letty, he'd ever loved. But this girl drew at him. She was unquestionably gifted, valuable to the store. He wished suddenly he wasn't obliged to make a sensible decision, to be sensible at all. What he wanted to do was find himself magically alone somewhere with her, their bodies pressed closely together, with his mouth in the curve of her neck.

"Very well," he said. "I'll telephone downstairs now and put in a request for your salary increase."

"Thank you very much," she said, feeling as if he'd managed to strip her both of her clothes and her fabrications, leaving her there completely naked in the chair, and defenseless.

Neither of them were as smiling or as easy as they'd been to begin with. Wanting a drink now, she stood up to go.

"One thing, Miss Burgess."

"Yes, sir?"

"Stay with us for a time," he said. "In future, I can assure you you will not be forgotten or without reward."

"Thank you," she said again, surprising him by extending her hand across the desk to him. "Thank you very much, sir."

They shook hands. She smiled, stepped away and went out. He'd not risen to his feet. He remained seated and lit his cigarette finally, waiting for his body to subside, thinking how strange it was to find himself so avidly wanting this girl he didn't know. There had been any number of other women he'd found attractive in passing but hadn't responded to, except aesthetically. She wasn't exceptional. Oh, but she was. Beautiful. Not as Jeanette was beautiful. Jeanette was beautiful. Jeanette was exquisite, lush. But this girl. Beautiful, fragile. Yet with a core of steel. He felt tired all at once, as if he'd just raced up several flights of stairs.

She wouldn't stay with the company long, he thought, not with that combination of talent and restlessness.

Glenn maintained her composure until she got into the elevator. Finding herself the sole passenger, she let go and threw her arms into the air, laughing loudly, exultantly. She'd done it! God! She'd actually done it! And she'd do more, keep going now. It would all come to her, everything she wanted. Hadn't it already started?

# Twelve

At least twice a month, Brady's mother came up to the school to spend the weekend, taking the boys out to dinner, to the movies, or sitting in her motel room talking. A pattern evolved and Corey let himself go with it, glad of the regularity of the visits both from Glenn and Brady's mother. Three out of four weekends were taken care of. And usually he and Brady found things to do on the odd, unplanned weekend. In this way, he got through his time at the school without feeling totally abandoned.

He spent a lot of time preparing his and Brady's dinners, experimenting with recipes of his own concocting, storing the more successful ones away in his mind, discarding the rare failures. Throughout most of his days and nights, he daydreamed about Brady's mother, liking everything about her, particularly her name. Alyssa. Over and over, her name whispered inside his head. Alyssa, Alyssa.

His third year at the school, Brady said, "My mom says if you want to, you can come home over Christmas with me. You want to?"

Corey at once said, "Sure!" then felt guilty, thinking about

Glenn. But they hadn't made any definite plans and he'd make it up to her some other time. Just then he wanted more than anything else to see how Alyssa Brady looked and acted and sounded inside her own home, to be there with her for ten days, close enough to study her, to smell her perfume, to hear her laughing.

He phoned his mother, and Gaby said, "Well, if you're sure that's what you want to do, I suppose Lloyd and I will go away for the holidays. There's no point to staying here if you're not going to be coming."

"You and Lloyd go have a swell holiday," he said lightly. "I'll be home for mid-winter recess."

He phoned Glenn. She said, "I'm disappointed that I'm not going to be seeing you. But I'm glad you'll be with friends. You have a good time. I'll send you something."

"Have you got things lined up to do?" he asked, thinking maybe he really was letting her down, hating the idea of her spending the holidays alone.

"The usual dinner with Dana. Don't worry, I've got things to do. You have a good time, Corey. I know you will. And I'll come down to see you after the New Year."

"Okay," he said. They talked for a few minutes of other things, then said goodbye. He couldn't help feeling she hadn't been telling the truth, that she'd probably spend most of the holidays alone. It bothered him. He decided he'd make it up to her when she came down. Over the mid-winter recess he'd spend all his time with her.

Having satisfied himself about all this, he turned his attention to the coming visit with Brady and his mother. They were going to take the train down to Connecticut.

"Mom gets done in if she has to drive for more than a couple of hours," Brady said. They were standing on the platform in the freezing cold, waiting for the train. "It's more fun this way, anyway. I'm crazy about trains, aren't you?"

"They don't excite me much," Corey said, wondering what sort of kitchen they'd have. If it were a big house, the kitchen would probably be one of those huge old ones like the kitchen in gramma and grampa's old house. He thought about how gramma used to let him sit on the counter and watch, talking to him, while she made dinner. He didn't think of her all that often anymore but when he did, Aunt Glenn would get all mixed up in his head with gramma. It'd be Aunt Glenn he'd see, but it would be gramma talking to him. He couldn't figure that out.

"How long does it take to get there?" he asked Brady.

"We'll be there in time for dinner. It's a good ride."

Corey thought Brady had come a long way, but he was still such a kid about so many things. He was taller, older—we both are, he thought—but Brady was still a kid. Corey, when he looked at himself in the mirror, couldn't seem to see the kid there anymore. He knew he'd crossed the line, moved ahead. He felt an awful lot older than Bobby now.

Mrs. Brady was there at the station, waiting for them when they got in. She hugged and kissed both boys, laughing, asking, "How was your trip? Did you eat anything on the train? I suppose you're both starved as always."

Brady started answering all her questions while Corey busied himself with the luggage. He thought about her soft cheek and the now-familiar scent of her perfume and how it had felt for those few seconds being that close to her. Her fur coat, the coolness of her cheek, the feel of her mouth on his cheek, the shine to her eyes. Boy, she really got to him!

"I haven't made a lot of plans," she told them in the car. "I thought you boys would rather decide for yourselves what you want to do, so I've tried to keep it pretty loose. A few people are coming over for drinks Christmas Eve. I'm out for three evenings but I didn't think you'd mind that. I'm sure you'll find things to do. Netta's got dinner waiting for us. I knew you'd be starved." She laughed, keeping up a light stream of words that flowed over Corey so that he didn't really hear what she was saying but rather absorbed the tone of her voice and the airy musicality of her laughter. He smiled back at her when she leaned forward to look past Bobby and smiled at Corey.

"Your parents weren't disappointed at your not coming home?" she asked him.

"They were tickled to death," he said, smiling.

"Are you liking S.A. any better this year?"

"It's all right," he answered, studying her mouth. "I'm never going to be in love with the place. It's okay. It's just a school."

Her smile dimmed and her eyes stayed on him for a moment until she noticed that the light had changed and she eased her foot down on the accelerator. Her profile was thoughtful.

It was a big house. A cook-housekeeper came bustling out to greet the boys, saying, "Nice to have you home, Bobby."

Bobby said, "This is my friend Corey. This is Netta."

Corey shook Netta's strong, hard hand as Mrs. Brady said, "Let's get you boys organized with your rooms and then we'll eat. I thought the two of you would probably enjoy a change of scenery. So, Bobby, you're in your room and I've put Corey down the hall here, in the guest room. All right?"

Both boys said, "Fine."

Bobby went to his room and Corey followed Mrs. Brady down the hall to the guest room. "I'm sure you'll be comfortable in here," she said, switching on the light, then stepping to one side to allow Corey a view of the room. Twin beds, soft carpeting, swagged draperies, an adjoining bathroom.

"It's a great room," he said, allowing himself to look at her. She was standing by the door, studying him with an unreadable expression on her face.

She shook her head slightly and smiled saying, "Come down as soon as you're ready. We'll have an early night, I think. You're probably eager to get a good night's sleep after that long train ride."

"I think Bobby probably is," he said quietly, feeling suddenly in control of the situation, but unsure precisely what the situation was. "I'm not tired at all."

"Are you the same age as Bobby?" she asked, her hand on the door. "I can't remember."

"About the same," he said. "I like your house. And," he looked around, "this room. It's really very nice of you to invite me."

"We're happy you could come." She stopped in the doorway. "I'll leave you to get settled in now."

She closed the door and went toward the stairs examining her thoughts and reactions, finding both strange. She found herself reacting to a fourteen-year-old boy as if he were not a boy at all but a grown man. There was something about Corey not in the least boyish. It had always been there. She'd seen it the very first time she'd met him. He was so self-possessed.

And his eyes. Behind those deep green eyes was someone almost too aware. Every time he looked at her, her reaction was almost exactly what it would have been to someone two or three times his age. There was something mature and in control and very, very aware in his eyes. She chided herself, telling herself she'd been spending too much time on her own, overindulging in fantasies. Now she was reading too much into the words and gestures and eyes of a fourteen-year-old boy, a boy the same age as her own son. But one who, in contrast, seemed infinitely older than Bobby. She felt overheated, and angry with herself for responding so strongly to Corey. Yet her mind kept spinning out fanciful images, sexual images. She wasn't at all sure how to handle this, or how to stop.

After a very good dinner, Bobby said, "Hey! Come on down to the playroom! I'll show you my trains. I've got a whole set of Lionels. My grandad sends me some new ones every Christmas. I can't wait to see what it'll be this year."

Corey wasn't interested and couldn't think of any way to refuse without offending Bobby and hurting his feelings. He looked over at Mrs. Brady who said, "Perhaps Corey would prefer to see the trains tomorrow, Bobby. It's been a long day."

Disappointed, Bobby said, "You don't want to see them now?"

"Sure," Corey said. "I'll have a look."

"Great!" Bobby smiled eagerly. "Come on. We don't have to play with them tonight. I'll just show you the set-up."

Intrigued by Corey's very apparent change of mind and his touching concern for Bobby's feelings, Mrs. Brady went along downstairs with them, carrying her glass of wine. She stood in the playroom door and watched Bobby excitedly run around the room switching on the lights, chattering about the trains while Corey politely made appropriate noises and turned for a moment to look at her before returning his attention to Bobby.

His eyes. Was she going crazy? she wondered, taking a sip of the wine. Standing in the playroom of her own home she was having a very sexual response to this boy, a tremendously sexual response. It made her very aware of just how long it had been since she'd made love. Over two years. Not because there hadn't been opportunity, but because she'd lacked interest. There hadn't been anyone who'd done to her what this boy was managing to do: firing her imagination, arousing her dormant sexuality. She'd have to take care of it, she thought. She hated the idea of lying alone in her bed in the night, attending to herself. For as long as it lasted it was fine, she could close her eyes to the demoralizing aspects of the performance, but later, invariably, she felt depressed.

After a few minutes, she said, "I think that's enough for this evening, Bobby. You'll have all day tomorrow to show Corey the trains."

"Okay, mom." Bobby went around the room turning off the lights. Corey went up the stairs with Mrs. Brady.

"That was very kind of you," she said in an undertone. "You really weren't interested, were you?"

"No. But Bobby's a good kid."

A good kid. She glanced over at him, then continued on up the stairs to refill her wine glass before proceeding to the living room where Netta had got the fire started.

Corey settled himself in the armchair by the fire while Bobby started fiddling with the radio, trying to find a good station.

"We used to have fires in the winter all the time before my grandparents died and the house was sold," Corey said. "I like a fire. When I have my own home, I'll definitely have at least one fireplace. Probably two. It's a nice idea having a fireplace in the bedroom."

"There are fireplaces in two of the bedrooms," Alyssa said, crossing her legs, noticing how Corey's eyes followed her movements. "In Bobby's room and in the master suite."

"Is it a very old house?"

"Oh, not very. About thirty years. Tell me about your grandparents," she said. "You speak of them very affectionately."

"They were good," he said, smiling. "My grandfather was English. My grandmother was French, Canadian French. He started out as a bandleader, then got into radio and finally ended up as a host on a local TV talk show. She started out as a poet. But her big thing was family planning, birth control. She used to go all over the place talking to people, giving lectures, that sort of thing."

"They sound very interesting," Alyssa said, smiling.

"They were terrific. I still think about them a lot."

Bobby bounced over to sit on the end of the sofa opposite his mother, complaining, "I'm still hungry. You hungry, Corey?"

Corey shook his head.

"Okay. I'm gonna go get Netta to make me a sandwich with some of that roast beef. You don't want one?"

"No, thanks," Corey declined. "I'll have a Coke or something, though. If you're having one."

"Okay. I'll bring you one back."

In the silence following Bobby's noisy departure to the kitchen, Corey said, "I'd really prefer wine. But I don't want to throw Bobby off altogether. D'you mind if I smoke?"

Feeling pleasantly relaxed now by the wine, her eyes playing deceptive tricks on her, Alyssa smiled and said, "By all means. I know Bobby's been smoking for ages. I suppose the two of you have a fine time at school, sneaking off to have a smoke."

Corey laughed. "I wouldn't call it fine. We have a good time."

He lit a cigarette and looked at her legs, then back at her face. His eyes kept wanting to look at her breasts and he forced himself to stay focused on her face, concentrating on his cigarette. "It must be great," he said, "to have a fireplace in your bedroom. I really like the idea of that. When the old house was sold, my mom moved us into a ratty apartment. Not ratty really. Just modern. With those thin walls and noisy plumbing. Then, when she married good old Lloyd, she moved up to the penthouse and I moved out to my dad's place on the lake. Dad's house isn't too bad. I don't spend much time either place so it really doesn't much matter. But the idea of a fireplace in my bedroom, that's really good."

"It is," she said. "It's one of the reasons why I've kept the house. Really, it's far too big for just me and Bobby and Netta. But I love this house," she looked up at the ceiling, then around at the walls, thinking they were having a very ambiguous conversation. How subtle you are, she thought. Not a boy at all. Not in any way.

"How long've you lived here?" Corey asked.

"Fifteen years. We lived here from the beginning and I'll probably live here to the end."

Bobby returned with his sandwich and the Cokes and Mrs.

Brady got up saying, "I have a few things to do so I'll leave you two on your own. Don't stay up too late. We've got kind of a big day tomorrow. And, Bobby, put the lights off when you come up, all right?"

"Okay, mom." Bobby smiled over at her around a mouthful of sandwich.

"Goodnight," Corey said.

She stood for a moment looking in at them, then set down her wine glass on the hall table and walked away. Corey watched her legs disappearing up the stairs, experiencing what felt like a pain in his groin. Bobby was saying something but Corey was thinking about the shape of her mouth and how she'd looked sitting on the sofa in her pale blue dress, with her legs crossed. If he closed his eyes, he could see her naked. And that hurt even more. He was really going to have to get upstairs and into that bathroom. Ten whole days here looking at her, talking to her, watching her mouth when she talked and he'd probably destroy himself.

"You almost finished?" he asked Bobby, faking a yawn. "I'm really beat."

"You didn't drink your Coke."

"I'll take it with me. I'm ready to hit the sack. What about you?"

"You go on up. I've got to get the lights. I'll see you in the morning."

"Okay." Corey tossed his cigarette into the fire, picked up the bottle of Coke and went up the stairs and down the hall to his room, to find that somebody—the housekeeper probably— had unpacked his bag, put all his things away and turned down the bed. A small bedside light made the room look very homey.

"I asked Netta to unpack for you," she said from the doorway.

"Thank you," he said, turning. She was still in the blue dress. He'd thought perhaps she might be wearing something like a robe or a nightgown. "Thank you very much."

"You'll find soap and towels in the bathroom. If there's anything you need, let me know."

"Okay. I will."

What am I doing? she asked herself. Go away and leave

this boy alone. He's not a boy. No boy ever looked at me that way.

She smiled suddenly. "Would you like to see the master bedroom?" she asked. "With the fireplace."

"I'd love to," he said. "If it's not a big bother."

"Come along." She stepped out into the hall. "It's no bother at all."

At the end of the hall, she pushed open the door and he went inside with her to see a vast room with a fireplace at the far end. The walls were painted pale gray, the moldings white, the carpeting an even paler gray. There was a huge bed, an armchair, a desk by the windows. A fire was going in the fireplace and the lamp on the desk was lit.

"It's beautiful," he said. "I wouldn't want to move either if this were my house."

She was standing quite close to him. Her hand now moved through the air between them to fall lightly on his hair.

"Who has red hair," she asked, "your mother or your father?" His hair was so soft, so thick.

"My father," he said, suddenly feeling he was suffocating.

"It's soft, very soft."

"Are you playing some kind of game with me?" he asked, looking into her eyes. They were the same height. But without her high heels, she'd be smaller.

"I don't know," she said dreamily. "I don't think so." She withdrew her hand, almost hypnotized by the beauty of his face, the deep green of his eyes.

All at once, he knew what was going to happen. It would happen if he wanted it to. All he had to do was make it happen. But how? What needed saying and doing?

"I only came because I wanted to see you," he said. "I really should've gone home for the holidays. But I wanted to see you."

"I knew that," she said without thinking, realizing she had known. She'd invited him because she'd been wanting to see him. "I'm going to have to do something about you, Corey," she said, holding her hand over her mouth, her eyes on the fire. No one would understand this, she thought. How could they? "Go say goodnight to Bobby and get ready for bed," she said, gazing into the fire as if hypnotized. "Then," she wet her lips, trying to see the logical progression, "come back here. Quietly," she cautioned.

He didn't say another word, just left the room, closed the door carefully and retraced his steps down the hall to the guest room. He took a quick shower, pulled on his pajamas, then went to knock at Bobby's door to say goodnight. Seeing the glazed, sleepy look to Bobby's eyes, he knew Bobby would be asleep within minutes. He returned to the guest room to have a cigarette, pouring the untasted Coke down the bathroom sink. He finished the cigarette, put it out, turned out the light, closed the guest room door and tiptoed—unnecessarily, the hall was thickly carpeted—back to the master suite. He thought about knocking, decided it would make too much noise in the dark stillness of the sleeping house and opened the door.

The lamp on the desk was off now, the only light coming from the fire. He closed the door quietly, his eyes adjusting to the dimness and looked over to see her in bed, under the blankets, her head turning slowly.

"Lock the door and come here," she whispered.

He locked the door, then went across the room to sit down on the side of the bed. His heart was beating so fast, so hard he thought he might actually have a heart attack. "Here," she whispered, indicating he should come closer to her. He kicked off his slippers and sat down on top of the blankets beside her, startled when her hand touched his chin, turning his face to her.

"This is outrageous," she said softly. "Positively outrageous. If I stop to think about it, I'll . . . I'm not going to think about it. Are you frightened? I'm frightened."

She looked it, he thought. She looked suddenly smaller, too, in the big bed; her hand was cold, her eyes very wide. She'd taken off her makeup and brushed out her hair. He looked at her arms, at her bare shoulders, experiencing a thrill of excitement realizing she hadn't anything on. He put his hand on her cheek, looking at her mouth.

"I think you're so beautiful," he whispered.

She made a strange sound and held his face between her hands, looking deep into his eyes for several seconds before drawing his mouth down to hers. He was overwhelmed by the softness of her mouth, so much so, he found it close to impossible to think at all. Her mouth opened, her tongue touched against his lips. He opened his mouth, met her tongue, reveling in the softness of her lips. She made another sound and wound her arms around his neck, her tongue moving into his mouth as she sank back against the pillows, taking him with her. She was suddenly very much warmer. And he felt as if he were drowning under his robe and pajamas, especially when she put her hand on his throat and kissed him again before hoarsely whispering, "Take off your pajamas, Corey. Come under the blankets."

He climbed off the bed and removed his robe, then his pajama top. Color flooded into his face. He was embarrassed at the idea of having her see him naked, of having her see him in the condition he was in.

In one frantic motion, he stepped out of the bottoms, yanked up the blankets and slid beneath them. If she touched him, he'd explode. She sat up, the blankets slipping away, and he stared at her breasts feeling as if he were going to die. He couldn't believe this was actually happening, that the two of them were naked, in her bed. He sat stiffly against the pillows, wanting desperately to touch her, but afraid to.

She took hold of his hand, her eyes closing, and placed his hand on her breast. He could feel her heart beating fast, and he knew she'd really meant it. She was scared, just as scared as he was. It made him feel a bit better, seeing this, a little bolder. He closed his hand over her breast thinking nothing had ever been softer or more beautiful or felt better. It was absolutely the most beautiful, fantastic thing that had ever happened to him: this beautiful, naked woman, with his hand on her breast. He could touch her. Anywhere. But he didn't dare. He didn't want to do anything wrong, anything that might spoil what was happening.

She leaned over and kissed him again, then, with her cheek against his, whispered, "I don't know what I'm doing. This is impossible. Don't be afraid of me, Corey. It won't work if we're both afraid. Touch me. It's all right to touch me. I want you to."

She lay back and extended her arms and, very carefully, he lay across her, not wanting her to feel or know but she shifted, murmuring, "I want to feel you, see you," and he was completely on top of her and her hands were moving down his back, around over his buttocks as her mouth brushed back and forth against his.

"You're not a little boy," she whispered, putting her hand on him. "My God! I knew you weren't." Then she kissed him, so eagerly, so deeply he couldn't control himself, felt it happening and groaned. He wanted to die. He was screwing up the whole thing. But she was whispering, "It's all right, all right. It doesn't matter. It happens to everyone, Corey. It doesn't matter. Touch me. Please, I want you to. Do whatever feels right to you, whatever you want. It's all right."

She kicked away the bedclothes and held him, whispering, her hands gliding over him, determined now to make this right, make it good. Having gone this far, it was ridiculous not to see it through. He sat up and she lay still as he looked at her, his hands tentatively curving over her breasts, then moved down to her waist, her hips.

"You've got good hands," she whispered, smiling at him. "Don't be afraid to touch me. I won't break. It feels good."

"Does it?"

"Better than good." She smiled, caressing his arm. "Do whatever you feel like. Anything. It's all good."

She opened her thighs slightly and watched as his head turned and he looked down at her. He was getting hard again. Her belly was so soft under his hand. He wanted to do it all right, do it properly. But everything gramma had ever told him had gone flying away out of his head and he couldn't remember, couldn't think, couldn't do more than lightly touch her breasts, her waist, her hips, not daring to touch her below the waist. But kissing her was wonderful. And her hands, the way she touched him. He had the feeling he was dreaming, that he'd wake up and none of this would have happened. But it was happening. He lowered his head to her breast, then looked up at her asking, "Is it all right?" and she put her hands on the sides of his face again and directed his mouth down to her breast, sighing, shifting again. He loved it, loved her, and was stunned by her response to what he was doing, encouraged to continue on until she was raising him, directing his mouth back to hers as she drew him down on top of her, directing him with her hand, opening all around him, urging him forward, whispering all the while he couldn't hear could only feel the most astonishing feeling of his life so much softness and her mouth on his. I'm inside her, he thought, I'm actually inside her. It was too much, too potent. He came again and thought she'd throw him out. He was lousy at this, rotten, but she kept on holding him, keeping him there touching him so intimately, so importantly, whispering, "Don't move, don't! Just stay there!"

He sank down into her, all softness, dizzy with her kisses and the movements inside she seemed to be closing in all around him in melting warmth, her thighs closing him in so that he was coming back again and she knew it felt it, began to move slowly underneath him, rearranging them so that her legs were between his. She shifted again, and this time he promised himself he'd do it right keep himself under control. Except that it was hard to exercise any control when her body, her mouth were mesmerizing him, drugging him. She was sliding back and forth under him, the motion giddying, the pleasure extraordinary. He'd never felt anything better. He wanted to push into her, pushed and she made a soft sound, encouraging him to push more, keep pushing harder. He didn't think he'd be able to keep going very much longer the feeling was so good. She whispered, "Lift just a little, now there, there," all of her moving. He was holding off, astounded by what was happening to her. Her body suddenly went rigid, her legs steel around him. He pushed harder and she went completely stiff for a moment then clutched him with both hands, pulling at him inside. She shuddered, against him. What was happening inside her was tremendous, dragging him into a need to keep moving without thinking. It was the best, the best; nothing in the whole world was better ever. He fell; far miles and miles of falling into the welcoming circle of her arms. He fell, happier than he'd ever been in his life.

She rested beside him, shared a cigarette with him. Then they started again and he stroked and kissed her breasts, gratified when she made the sounds she did, her fingers weaving through his hair. Then she showed him, telling him, "Here, touch me here. It's all here, my God! Yes! Your hands God your hands, yes!" He could tell when it was right, feel it was

right by the way her body moved to him, came up to him.
Giving her pleasure was such a wonderful thing to do; if he
put his mouth on her breast, his hand there, his other hand
there and kept doing that, she went wild, half-sobbing, shuddering. Wrapping her arms around him she held him hard on
top of her, telling him, "You're beautiful! No one has ever
been you; no one will ever be you. Are you tired? Do you
want to stop?"

"No, no."

"I don't want to stop. I can't. You're sure?"

"Yes. Tell me what you want, show me I want to make you
happy. You make me happy. You're the most beautiful woman
I've ever seen; this is the best thing that's ever happened to
me. I want to know how; I want to know all the best ways,
the right ways. Show me; tell me. Do you like it when I do
this?"

You're going to be a lover of women, she thought, surren-
dering; all of it, everything had gone far beyond her control.
She'd unleashed him. He'd gone racing ahead, finding it all
out in just one night. Her fourteen-year-old lover. He liked it
all, liked the feel, the taste, the tremendous feeling he got
realizing he'd lost all his fear and regained his curiosity, his
instincts. He gauged her responses, measured them carefully,
wanting this never to end but to go on and on forever. He'd
never dreamed from conversations at the kitchen table with his
grandmother that this was a gift she was giving him, a knowledge and an understanding.

Alyssa cried. Softly, quietly. Tears rolled from her eyes as
she lay against his chest and he stroked her soft, soft breast,
loving her. She whispered, "No one has ever made love to me
more perfectly, Corey. Or satisfied me so totally. I think I
knew. I think I did."

Then she was whispering, "Corey, wake up, dear. You have
to go back to the guest room." He woke up slowly, aware that
their legs seemed stuck together, as if he'd grown into her,
into her body. She was disengaging herself gently, smiling,
caressing his face, whispering, "You've got to go back. I wish
you could stay here, but you can't. Tomorrow. Tomorrow
night. All right? Go on now, darling. Just put your robe on,

don't bother with your pajamas. Kiss me before you go. My God! You're so sweet. I wish to God I weren't too old. Go on now. Sleep well. Tomorrow night."

It was all so dreamlike, he didn't even remember making the trip back down the hall to his room and awakened in the morning feeling happy, eager for the night and for the rest of his life. He'd stepped over another line and there'd never be a returning.

While Bobby was bringing the last of his bags from the car to the platform, Alyssa took advantage of these few moments to say, "I'll see you in a few weeks, when I come up. Just remember what I told you, Corey. All right? No love, no falling in love. If you can keep your perspective, I can keep mine. Because if I think about this, really think about it, I'm going to be very bothered. So I'm not going to think about it. And you're not going to, either. But you make me happy, Corey. I want you to know that. It's just that we both know it's a completely impossible situation and there's no future. All right?"

"Yes, all right." He felt a little sad, because he'd wanted to tell her he loved her. But, of course, she was right.

True to his word, Mr. Hamilton saw to it that a number of interesting and challenging projects came her way. There was an inter-department contest held for redesigning the store's logo and packaging. Glenn, with two gins under her belt, sat down one evening and dashed off a logo design just for the hell of it and received the five-hundred-dollar prize and the assignment to carry her design through to every area from the Hamilton's stationery to their shopping bags. This effort earned her another twenty-five-dollar raise and one of those coveted corner offices. Mrs. Swayze treated her with fawning deference, pointing Glenn out to departmental newcomers as the epitome of success. Occasionally, Mr. Hamilton descended from the executive level to stop by Glenn's office. He never said very much, just asked how she was getting along, studying her with those light green eyes that always left her feeling stripped naked and too defenseless. Had he come in, closed the door and put her down on the floor, she wouldn't have been able to resist him. She wouldn't have wanted to. He was too handsome, too intense to resist. She quite often dreamed of him, dreamed he actually did come into her office and make love to her: a strangely silent, very violent communion.

When his wife died, she wrote him a brief note expressing her sadness—she did feel very sad about that—and, on impulse, attended the funeral; watching him and his daughter and a very beautiful dark-haired woman throughout the services. Then she went home and concentrated on forgetting the incident.

Several weeks later, he came into her office, closed the door and sat down on the chair beside her desk. He lit a cigarette and looked at her for some time before speaking. Her heart was beating irregularly and she sat watching him, waiting.

"It was very kind of you," he said. "Your note."

"Yes," she said, moistening her lips.

"Everything is all right?" he asked, finally breaking his gaze, looking around her office.

"Fine, thank you."

"Good, good." He sat a few seconds longer smoking his cigarette, then got up and went out.

After the door closed, she put her head down on her drawing board, trying to catch her breath.

Once a month she drove to New Hampshire to visit Corey. Once a month, sometimes twice, she dined with Dana. Gaby had begun telephoning every so often just to say hello. Their conversations were stilted, broken by lengthy pauses. Glenn had no idea why she called, but never asked.

Her social life, beyond the family contact, was nearly nonexistent. For a time, she dated Mr. Hamilton's junior assistant. But after having a little too much to drink at the staff Christmas party and somehow allowing herself to be made love to by standing up inside somebody's locked, darkened office by this same junior assistant, she stopped seeing him. The wordless confrontation—a teeth-clenching interlocking of bodies—alarmed her to such a degree she blocked it completely from her mind. In order to keep it successfully blocked, it was necessary to discontinue seeing him.

She often thought about Jack but forced herself to stop the instant she began. She did the same thing when she found herself idly speculating about Mr. Hamilton.

She really didn't have much time for a social life. She had more work than could be done in store hours and took projects home at least three nights a week, usually oftener; more work than any one person ought to have been expected to do, but she was being paid a lot of money and felt obligated to earn it, particularly since she'd fraudulently gained the money in the first place.

There was rarely ever enough time for her to leave her office for lunch, so she'd hurry through the line in the employees' cafeteria, grab a sandwich or a bowl of salad and carry it back upstairs to her board to eat along with an uniced gin and tonic made from the supplies housed in the bottom drawer of her filing cabinet. The drink was far more important than the food because it gave her a boost, a shot of energy to carry her through the afternoon, see her home. Once home, her first automatic move was to prepare a small pitcher of martinis, pour one, store the pitcher in the refrigerator and then begin laying out the evening's work.

She ate on the go, or standing up, anxious to be done with the food so she could get back to her board and finish working finally. Once finished, she'd switch off the lamp, pour the last of the martinis into her glass and collapse for a few minutes' breathing space before a shower and bed.

This routine was broken occasionally when, due to the pressure of catalogue and newspaper deadlines, some of the work had to be farmed out to freelancers. Then she'd have an evening or two to herself. She'd use this time to write to Ralph, answering his infrequent rambling letters; to write to Corey, responding to his chatty, humorous postcards; or to go out to dinner with a friend or two from her College days. She'd almost always have too much to drink, ending up the next day hung over, but absolved herself of guilt by telling herself it was her privilege to relax once in a while and enjoy herself without having to worry about some problem having to do with the store.

The store was like some demanding, nagging child, always pulling at her arm for attention. There was always something the store needed done. And whatever it was, it somehow managed to find its way to her desk. She didn't mind being asked to do the ad layouts and the catalogue art work as well. But having jobs dumped on her desk that could've gone to any number of other people was infuriating. She'd clamp her teeth together, unobtrusively fix herself a drink from the bottom drawer of the filing cabinet and set to work.

Dana continued to introduce her to his straight men friends. She'd sometimes go out for an evening with one of them. But every time, without fail, she'd find herself thinking about Jack, making comparisons, wondering what had become of him and why he'd never called after that disastrous night.

It was strange, she thought, how often she'd sit in the attic daydreaming about how marvelous it would be to get involved, really involved with some man; having someone she could go out to dinner with regularly, make love with regularly. She'd fantasize about evenings spent over sumptuous dinners, or at the theater, evenings culminating in bed. She'd go about preoccupied for days, embellishing these fantasies. Jack starred in every one of them, except when Mr. Hamilton made one of his surprising drop-in visits to her office. Then it would be Mr. Hamilton in her fantasies for a few days, until her attention gradually shifted back to Jack.

But when presented with an available male, she'd tighten up, finding reality in no way as appealing or as satisfying as her imaginings. She hated feeling as pressured in her free time as she did during her working hours. One way or another, her dates all managed to apply pressure. They did it either verbally, through allusions to sex or sex-oriented stories, or they did it physically, taking hold of her arm, or her hand, or sliding an arm around her waist when she'd have preferred them not to. She wished they'd stop, wished she understood why they thought it was their option to make gestures of this nature when she gave no sign, nor the slightest indication she was interested. Jack had done it, too. He was probably just as agressive and assuming as all the others. She wished she could stop thinking about him.

It seemed that despite her initial uncertainty about Ralph, he was, nevertheless, the only man she'd known who'd treated her openly. And because of that, she'd found it impossible to stay away from him. He'd done none of the standard, formal things—opening doors, holding chairs, calling her up. But each time they'd been together they'd both known why they were there—even though she'd been unwilling to admit to that fact at the time. She could see it all so clearly now. And no one else she'd met made her feel quite as Ralph had.

Well, Corey did. But that was different, having nothing to do with romance. He'd changed so much, was still changing. By the middle of his third year at St. Andrew's he'd given up smoking, grown very tall, lost his babyishly rounded cheeks and formed still more definite opinions on any number of subjects.

"Those things are really bad," he said of cigarettes. "They wreck your air. And, if you think about it, you ought to give up drinking." He pointed at her gin and tonic. "That's even worse stuff than cigarettes."

"What makes you think that?"

"Anyone could figure it out. It's crazy to do things like smoking and drinking, things that interfere with your body, your thinking. I've been thinking about getting off meat, too."

"You're going to become a vegetarian?"

"Probably not. But meat's pretty disgusting, if you think about it. Did you ever think about it?"

"I can't say that I have," she answered, self-consciously taking a swallow of her drink. "If you do do it, let me know how it is. It might be interesting."

That remark earned her one of his rare disapproving looks. She flushed, temporarily at a loss for words. He saw and said, "It's okay. I guess there's not much else you could say if someone tells you he's thinking about giving up meat." He smiled, and she was again struck by how very adult he was. His face and body were finally catching up with him. Perhaps that was why, she reasoned, he seemed so formidable to her. She knew nothing of Alyssa. That was a secret Corey never shared.

He still spent at least one night of Alyssa's regular two-night stay with her when she came up to visit Bobby. She'd fallen into the habit of taking both boys out to dinner, ostensibly returning both to the school but in reality taking Corey back with her to her motel room to indulge in night-long lovemaking sessions that were mutually very satisfying and kept both of them looking forward to her next visit. They both knew it couldn't last very much longer, but for as long as it lasted, he was very happy being with her. And she expressed considerable fondness for him.

On each of her visits, Glenn now felt as if she'd embarked on a lengthy course of learning how to get along, make do, advance in the world with a boy almost eleven years her junior as instructor and coach. Unfailingly, after her monthly visits with Corey, she'd head home enlightened in some way, her enthusiasms and optimism rekindled.

When he asked about her life—her job, her social activities, her interests—he displayed such heartfelt interest and such an almost palpable disappointment when she confessed to an all but nonexistent social life, she felt he'd managed in his short lifetime to isolate and equate essential values in a way she could not. She tried to benefit from his philosophical conversations, all the while wondering where he'd go and what he'd do with his beyond-his-years knowledge and insights. He was, as she'd said years before, special. And his specialness enhanced her life, enriched her spirit and helped her through a time she was finding daily more difficult, less meaningful.

"You don't have much of a life," he said, "from the sound of it. You've got to *make* it what you want it to be." He sometimes worried about her because she seemed so frail and so in need of looking after. But what could he do? He wanted her to be happy and wondered why it seemed as if she lacked the capability to *be* happy. He wanted to say, What's missing, Aunt Glenn? Something's missing but I can't put my finger on what it is. Are you aware that there's something missing? She seemed so dissatisfied and distant often, her eyes examining the space just somewhere over there, seeing something he couldn't begin to imagine.

"I'm trying to make it into something," she responded, struggling to comprehend what was happening to her. Something was happening. It was just that she couldn't seem to determine what, precisely, it was.

She was getting what she'd wanted from the store—more money for certain luxuries—but the satisfaction of these achievements never lasted more than a day or two at most. As soon as she'd started receiving a larger salary, her expenses had risen proportionately, leaving her no further ahead. The car fell apart within days of her final payment. The repair estimates were more than the car's value, so she'd traded it in on a newer car and was still making monthly payments years after she'd anticipated an end to them.

She was becoming disenchanted altogether with her attic and dreamed now not just of an apartment but a house of her own, a place with a room to work in, a spare bedroom for Corey when he visited, a proper kitchen and a bathroom with a tub. She couldn't remember when she'd last enjoyed a bath. She never had time enough to avail herself of the tub in the motel when she drove down to visit Corey, so it might as well have not been there.

Enough simply wasn't enough. Every time she latched onto something, telling herself, When I get that I'll be happy; when she did get whatever it was, she wasn't. Along with everything else, there was something gnawing away inside her, constantly urging her to hurry up and get rich, get famous, because she was getting older. This made her insides roll because she couldn't see any distinct road leading her toward wealth and fame. So that that interior something was never at rest, always agitating, prodding her; and to appease it, she'd have another drink or two—in order to sleep, to work, to simply make it through one day to the next.

There were so many things she wanted. Yet she couldn't help feeling that most of her desires would be satisfied if she could just take a few significant steps into success. Not just bigger and more arduous tasks to perform at the store, but something outside all that, something independent, something done by her alone that perfectly illustrated her special talent.

She wanted her success to fall within the area of her painting and drawing abilities but was convinced she'd somehow misdirected herself. Her design talent wasn't original so much as openly derivative. People didn't reap fame as a reward for second-hand, newly packaged ideas. Well, Andy Warhol. But he didn't count.

She also wanted someone to arrive into her life with the gift of vision to see her specialness, someone who would take note of all her supposedly attractive externals but who would, more importantly, be smitten by what could be seen through the windows of her eyes if only this someone would find her, stop, and take the time to look in and see. She wanted either to be

rescued from her constant hunger for success or to have the
hunger satisfied once and for all. If she were to be rescued,
she wanted a man of good looks, talent, intelligence, imagination and sensitivity to do the rescuing. When she faced herself
in the mirror and considered that long list of preferred qualities
in a lover, she became depressed and frightened. She still
wasn't beautiful to her own eyes, nor was she aging well, as
Dana had prophesied. Time seemed to be plainly telling her
she never would be beautiful. There seemed to be small, if
any, market for angular, slightly underweight women with
straight brown hair, unspecial features and fairly good eyes,
too-small breasts, no noticeable hips and a scary tendency to
put on weight around the middle on those rare occasions when
she remembered to eat with regularity. She had straight legs
with, mercifully, decent ankles. With the right clothes, she
actully felt she looked good, but she couldn't afford to dress
the way she wanted, so that was going to have to wait too.

"What's the matter with you, lovey?" Dana asked. "You
don't seem on top of things at all. And frankly I think you've
got a little bit of a self-image problem."

"I don't think you should talk to me about self-images,
Dana. Perhaps it's a problem that runs in the family."

"Stop worrying so much," he said gently.

"I can't."

She worried about all sorts of things, wondering if her being
unable to afford to dress herself as she wanted could conceiv-
ably prevent that special man from noticing and finding her.
But if he were special, she argued with herself, it wouldn't be
her designer clothes but herself he'd be bound to notice. She
told herself all sorts of things along this vein but believed none
of them. She was well into the long-term project of finding
and putting to use the gift within her that would one day make
her visible to the world.

She had nightmares that had her up at two or three in the
morning sitting in the dark drinking just one more gin and tonic
to help her get back to sleep, but succeeding only in sending
herself into the depths of deeper, more horrifying nightmares.
She'd awaken in the morning with a headache and a growing
hatred of this job she had to do five days and most evenings
of every week of her life; her life was draining away while she

remained not one bit closer to any kind of satisfaction in any area of her life. But her options were so limited, she was so in debt to the store and the bank for the little she did have, she was committed to continue on, sustaining herself on the shrinking hope she'd locate her special talent, or be found by a lover she could love, someone who'd love her at a time when she was willing to love him.

There were moments when she hated herself for all kinds of sins and omissions, adding to that list as she exercised her memory. She'd never really properly valued her parents, particularly her mother, while she'd had them. She believed now that she'd been vain, condescending and shockingly superior toward her family, utterly lacking in understanding. She had to have been. Why else had Corey received such a legacy of compassion and tolerance from them, such an outstanding ability to deal with life's situations and its people, while she fared so poorly in those areas? She again and again relived that puzzling conversation she'd had with Lisette in the kitchen and at last saw what it was Lisette had meant about freedom beginning with the body. So she stopped wearing brassieres out of memory and love of her mother. At first, she walked around with a perpetual flush of color along her cheekbones and the perimeters of her ears, positive everyone was noticing the jiggle of her newly freed breasts, gradually losing the flush and even the scant pleasure as she realized that people did indeed notice, but didn't particularly care. Occasionally, men would ogle her breasts if she was wearing something fairly form-fitting. And once, as she sat in a restaurant having dinner, a very pretty, somewhat older woman than she sat at a table nearby with her eyes riveted to Glenn's breasts the entire time Glenn was in the restaurant. Glenn couldn't decide if the woman was sexually interested, curious to try going brassiereless herself, or simply enamored of Glenn's breasts. Whatever it was, she was embarrassed and hurried through her meal, unable to breathe properly until she was safely back at the attic with a good, strong drink in her hand. Despite these sometime puzzling experiences, she was slowly, she thought, coming to some understanding of what Lisette had tried to tell her.

Other times, she hated herself just because, because of her face or her hands or her cuticles, because of her straight up-

and-down body, or straight up-and-down hair. Because. Because. She hated herself, and could hardly bear bathing herself, so filled was she with hating herself yet having to be responsible for the maintenance of herself. For what? For whom? Why have her hair done regularly at the store salon? Why go to the humiliation and expense of dispensing with the diaphragm and having herself outfitted with an I.U.D. when her body went untouched and seemed likely to remain so? She'd given up letting herself get drunk enough to be easily made love to by someone she didn't even want. No, she was all wrong. Her life was wrong. Nothing seemed right. Corey seemed right. More often than before, Dana seemed right, too, when he'd refrain from displaying his unattractive, put-on bitchy side and exhibit a warmly gratifying awareness of her, her life, her career.

"You're wasted there, you know," he stated one winter evening in her fourth year at the store. "They'll work you to death and you'll let them, because for some unknown reason you don't think you're any good. You really should pick up and move on to greener fields while you're still young enough and in a position to bargain."

"Where should I pick up and go *to?*" she countered. "I'm not going to work for another department store, that's certain. Advertising agencies are exactly the same except for the decor, and I'm not honestly sure I even want to do any more ad work. I want to do something, but this isn't it."

"Then get out," he said.

"How *can* I get out? I don't know what else to do. Don't throw things like that at me, Dana. It doesn't help. Be constructive, but don't tell me to 'get out.'"

"I'm sure I could help you find something at the station," he said, thinking about it. "They're always moaning about being short on good people for sets, costume design. You took all that at the College, didn't you?"

"I did. But I don't know if I'd want to be another Burgess at the station. I don't know."

"It can't hurt to try."

"It might hurt," she said. "For one thing, I'm getting over two hundred a week now at the store. Would the station pay me as much as that?"

"Probably more," he said glibly, having no idea what salaries were. "But, lovey, you can't lose anything just by asking."

"Yes, I can," she argued. "If word got back I was out looking, I could lose my job. And I *need* that money." I made a promise, she thought. I promised Mr. Hamilton I'd stay.

He decided to ignore the rebuke in her tone of voice.

"They're finally going to start construction on the new station building," he said, switching subjects somewhat. "They're talking merger. If it goes through, there'll be all kinds of excitement. What I wouldn't give to have some of that old stock right now. I'll bet you're going to wish you'd kept yours if this deal goes through. Those shares'll double and split and double again and heaven only knows what else. They've already split twice."

"Papa's shares?"

"That's right."

"But, Dana, I've still got them. I never thought they were any good. So, I just kept the certificates for, I don't know, sentimental value, I guess. I almost threw them out a while back."

*"Oh God!"* he exclaimed, paling at the thought. "My darling Glenn, get yourself a broker and take those certificates to him right away. You're going to get a great, great deal of money."

"Are you serious?" she asked, feeling the spreading heat of his excitement.

"Am I serious?" His face was alive with it now, glowing. "I'll tell you how serious I am. I'll personally take you to *my* broker. We'll get him to set you up a portfolio. Those shares'll be worth an absolute stinking fortune. Isn't it lucky you saved them! My God, think if you'd thrown them away! I can't bear to think of it."

"How much, do you think?"

"Who knows? It could be as much as a quarter of a million or more. Maybe more. It depends some on the merger."

"Dana," she said slowly, trying to keep a firm grip on her sense of reality, "what happens if that merger doesn't go through? What would the stocks be worth then?"

He stopped for a moment considering that, "At rock bottom," he said thoughtfully, "right now, probably forty or fifty thousand. Most likely more."

*"Dana!"* she cried. "Why didn't you ever *tell* me? All these years, halfway starving to death. How could you let that happen to me? I'm your *sister*. Doesn't my life mean anything to you?"

"You mean a great deal to me," he said. "More than you could probably ever imagine. But how was I to know you hadn't cashed those stocks in when Ray died? How was I to know what you'd done with them?"

"You're right," she said, taking hold of his hand. "I'm sorry. I didn't mean that. Of course you couldn't have known. Oh my God!" she half-whispered. "All this time, I thought they hadn't really cared. I was happy for Corey because he gave both of them so much and I gave them such a little. Really, very little. Dana. He did leave me something important and I never knew it. I feel so guilty."

"Now, why on earth would you feel guilty?" he asked, bemused.

"Because I didn't think they loved me. I didn't think I was important to them...I don't know what I really thought."

"Let me tell you something," he said, covering her hand with his. "Lisette loved all of us. God only knows how she did! We weren't lovable children. But she loved you best, I think. I was never jealous of that. I mean that from the bottom of my heart. I was never jealous. Gaby has all the jealous bones in the family. And Ray, in his vague, busy-busy fashion was a good father, a responsible man. He'd never have left so much to Gaby and me without making sure you were left equally well provided for. Strange family," he said. "We were. We are. If you'd asked me, I'd have told you, Glenn. But you never asked. I care. I've always cared. You know, when you were born, I used to sneak upstairs in the afternoons when Lisette was out giving her talks and play with you, for hours, give you your bottles, make you laugh."

"I didn't know that." She smiled.

"Well, now you do." He smiled back.

"Dana, are you happy?"

"Oh, Jesus! What *is* happy?"

"I don't know," she said softly, clutching his hands.

"Neither do I, lovey. Isn't that hell?"

"Well." She cleared her throat and smiled again. "We have to have a drink to celebrate my new-found wealth."

"Definitely!" He summoned over the waiter.

They drank to her future, then drank again. Dana kissed her goodnight, put her into a taxi and sent her home.

She couldn't come down. Her entire body was pulsing with excitement. It was only by having one final bedtime drink, only by closing her eyes and pretending, picturing Jack—of course, of course—could she bring her body down, ease and quiet herself sufficiently to sleep, to get through to the next day when the big changes would begin.

She was advised by Dana's broker she could use her stocks as collateral, borrow against them. So she did. She wrote out a letter of resignation, effective at once, then sat back to wait.

Mrs. Swayze looked genuinely sad and said, "I've sent your letter upstairs. I'm sorry you're leaving, Glenn, but you're remarkably talented and you deserve the best."

Touched, Glenn impulsively hugged her, finding herself on the verge of tears as she said, "Thank you. You've always been very kind to me."

"You're the sort of person it's easy to be kind to. Good luck, Glenn," she said, and went away, leaving Glenn a little mystified as to her meaning, wondering, What sort of person am I?

She finished the last of her work, handed it in, then started clearing out her office. At five o'clock, people filtered past the doorway saying goodbye and good luck, wishing her well, people she thought had never noticed her existence. She brought her bottles of gin and tonic out of the bottom drawer of the filing cabinet and fixed herself a drink while she went about placing her personal belongings—far more than she'd realized she had—in a Hamilton's bag. She took her time, smoking a cigarette, drinking her drink; methodically emptying drawers, clearing the top of her drawing board and the window-sill.

It was almost six when he appeared in the doorway and stood looking in at her, lighting a cigarette, silent as always.

"May I?" he asked, indicating the gin bottle.

"Of course," she answered, handing him a paper cup, then standing back, watching him mix himself a drink.

"Cheers!" he said, holding the paper cup up in the air before taking a swallow.

"Cheers!" she said inaudibly, her throat hurting.

"You stayed longer than I thought you would," he said, stepping inside and closing the door. The outer offices were completely silent, deserted. The store was closed, empty. "I expected you to leave much sooner."

"I told you I'd stay," she said.

"Yes," he said. "You did." He drank some more of the gin, tapped his ash off into the ashtray, then continued looking at her.

"I was just gathering my things together," she explained needlessly.

He moved closer to her, stopping to extinguish his cigarette, draining the drink in one swallow.

"I'll help you take your things down," he offered quietly, his eyes burning into her. Always they burned. Little holes his eyes could make in the surface of her skin.

"Thank you," she said helplessly, unable to move.

"Do you know you're beautiful?" he said, closer still to her. She shook her head.

"You are," he said, his hand reaching out to touch her hair. "Beautiful. How could you not know?"

"I don't know," she whispered, about to cry.

"I will miss you," he said, whispering now, too. "I will miss you very much. Seeing you."

"I...I..." His other hand was on her cheek now, his face coming closer, the green eyes glowing, intense. He was going to kiss her, he'd kiss her and she'd disintegrate.

"I have never done this before," he whispered. "I will never do this again. But I have to."

She nodded, knowing, and felt the tears start up as he came closer still and kissed her gently, slowly, causing that certain something inside of her to go totally out of control so that she'd have fallen if he hadn't held onto her, hadn't held her very close, kissing her so caringly.

She opened her clothes, stroking the back of his neck tenderly as he pressed his mouth to her breast, bending her back, caressing her lovingly, meaningfully. The tears streamed unnoticed down her cheeks. She hadn't any thoughts, none at all; captured by his mouth on her nipple, his hand on her inner thigh, the scent of him all fresh and clean, crisp. She reached out and turned off the light, baring herself, volunteering herself into his hands, his mouth as he bent her back, back, down on the drawing board, and lifted her to his mouth. She closed her eyes, held his face between her hands and arched closer to the inhuman pleasure. His hair was soft, soft, her fingers moving in his hair holding him there to her, there and so slowly, so gently he kissed her into a frenzy. Then he rested his cheek on her belly, shaping her breasts with his hand until she whispered, "Please, go home now, Mr. Hamilton. Please go home now."

Silhouetted in the light from the windows she saw him straighten up at last. His hand drifted down over her lips, pressed against her cheek. He said, "Goodbye, Glenn. Have a good life, a happy life. Forgive me for this."

"I do," she whispered. "There isn't anything to forgive. Just please go home now."

"Yes," he said, understanding. He moved away, swallowed by the shadows. The door opened, closed. His footsteps receded down the corridor. She sat up and pressed both her hands between her thighs, rocking back and forth, sitting on the edge of the drawing board, crying, thinking, I don't even know your first name.

# PART THREE

## *1970-1977*

All that I wanted to do
All that I wanted to be
All that I wanted to have
All that is left is me.

*© 1978 Helen Wolfe Allen*

# *Thirteen*

The merger did go through. Her stock certificates
were turned over to Dana's broker—now hers—her job at
Hamilton's was no more and she was finally the owner of a
new small car, a three-bedroom house downtown in one of the
older, charming sections of the city, and an income-producing
portfolio.

She also owned a retroactive guilt for believing her father
hadn't cared about her. He had. She simply hadn't known what
to do with what he'd left her. She felt guilty, too, for her
thoughts through the years about Dana and Gaby and their
enviable lives of relative comfort so nicely enhanced by their
inheritances. She'd gone through five years of near-poverty
unnecessarily and felt like the fool of all time for not having
had the sense to ask about the stock certificates. The self-anger
was tempered by a "better late than never" refrain that sang
with regularity in her ears. What did any of it matter now? She
had freedom, mobility, all the time she needed in which to
start working seriously toward the success she'd always wanted.

Once the workmen were gone from the house, she went
upstairs to stand in the studio doorway looking in at her drawing

board, the skylight above, her easel, and art supplies all nicely lined up and displayed in rows on the stripped cedar shelving, unable to decide where to begin. She toyed with the idea of a children's book, something she'd write and illustrate herself, but though she hadn't any doubt she could easily do something of the sort, she just didn't happen to have an idea for a children's book.

She did feel an extraordinary compulsion to sit down and write something, put words to paper. But she put this notion aside convinced she was succumbing to some sort of mania endemic to the Burgess family. They all had to be writers in one way or another: Lisette with her early iambic pentameter and later on, blank verse; Ray with his ironic, carefully created monologues, witty and wry. Tapes of his show-openers were now fought over as collector's items. People compared him to Fred Allen and bartered tapes like—Glenn thought—crazed Indians in the old movies with mirrors and beads; then Dana, the most truly talented, grinding out oddly erotic dramas, understated and suspenseful, that lingered for days in the mind like the faint aftermath of incense. Even Gaby still slaved, or so she claimed, at her compositions. Music, true. But compositions nonetheless. For triangle and harmonium, for humming voices and eleven oboes. Her efforts had been all but abandoned now that she'd managed to find and secure a second husband who raved about Gaby's unrecognized genius.

Lloyd might be boringly repetitious and several hundred years out of date with his live-in "man" who fetched and carried, cooked and cleaned, but he certainly loved Gaby. Glenn was, as far as she was able, sincerely happy for her sister, because under Lloyd's influence and consistent lavish praise, Gaby was beginning to emerge as someone recognizably human. She was no longer as suspicious, acquisitive or hostile as she'd been in her twenties. And she was stunningly beautiful. Whenever Glenn saw her she had to stop for several moments— deaf to Gaby's nonstop conversation—simply to absorb the perfection of Gaby's features, her extraordinary beauty.

Dana, too, for that matter was spectacularly good looking. Women literally stopped in the street to look at him. What, to Glenn, seemed most interesting about Dana was that, so often, he looked back. He exuded an aura of very male sexuality that was terribly enticing. When she asked him about it, he said, "Some women, certain women almost make my heart stop. But there's something, I don't know what it is, but it frightens me."

"Maybe," she offered, "it's in you and not in the women."

"I'm beginning to think you might be right," he said. "It's just that I've never come across a woman I *knew*. Do you follow that? Someone I'm able to recognize at once. It's different with other men. Oh," he said impatiently, "this is all so pointless!"

She let the matter drop, having learned from his signals where not to proceed further.

If she were to take up writing, surely it would have to be construed as hereditary. She did very much want to write, but the family and her ongoing dread of finding herself trapped inside something unreal, something synthetic held her away from committing herself to making an effort. It might only prove to be delusion and that was dangerous.

So everything changed. Yet nothing was changed. She had the money at last and the attendant freedom, but there was nothing further she wished to buy and nowhere she wanted to go. She couldn't dig up sufficient motivation so start working at anything in any concrete direction, so, as a kind of last resort measure, she began taking accredited evening classes at the Art College, hoping to complete her certification. With that in hand, she might at least instruct, and teaching art classes would be infinitely preferable to frustrating herself endlessly trying to find and isolate the one special talent she had that would sky-rocket her to fame.

Corey, having arrived at his full height of six-two, with what had at last evolved into a mellow bass voice and a face finally thinned down to a pleasing oval, turned sixteen and quit school just as he'd always threatened to. He said goodbye to Bobby, who got very choked up and said, "Any time, anything I can ever do for you, just let me know. You're the best friend I ever had. And I won't forget that."

He took the train down to Connecticut to see Alyssa. She was waiting at the station and smiled, waving when she saw him. They walked to her car and the parking lot and got in.

"I thought we'd have lunch," she said, sliding behind the

wheel. "I know a very nice restaurant in Greenwich. All right?"

"Sounds great."

"Are you going to go right home?" she asked.

"From here," he said. "I'll fly back."

"Tell me," she said, "what will you do? I've missed you." She glanced over at him, a surprised expression on her face. "I didn't think I would. I never think I will. Two or three weeks go by and I find myself missing you."

"I always think about you," he said. It was true. He thought often of her bedroom that first night, of the firelight, and his nervousness.

They chatted throughout the ride, Alyssa turning every so often to look at him. Although she'd been gearing herself up to it for months, she was shocked to realize how truly unprepared she was to have it end.

Settled at a table in the French restaurant, Corey said, "I'm going to go into business."

"Tell me about it," she said, interested, her eyes fixed on his. She wanted him one last time, she thought.

He quickly outlined his plans and she listened all the way through, then beckoned the waiter, saying, "I think we should order now. I reserved a room." She lowered her eyes. "At the Sheraton."

"Good," he smiled. "I'm glad."

"I'm actually relieved," she admitted with a little laugh. "I had the idea you might not want to."

"I'll always want to," he said quietly.

"I'm being a bit stupid," she said, playing with the stir-stick from her drink. "I lied," she said in a low voice, looking into his eyes. "I do love you, Corey. God knows, I could never explain it to anyone without sounding depraved somehow. But I do. All these months, you've made me so happy. You've never abused the situation or our relationship. God! Am I talking coherently? Corey, what I want to say . . ."

"I know it," he interrupted. "You don't have to do this to yourself. It's why I came. So we could say goodbye."

"Why," she said in a strangled voice, "did you have to be twenty years younger? Why couldn't you have been just ten years younger?"

He held her hand and smiled. "Just because," he said. "Because. Now why don't we stop all this and enjoy the lunch? Okay?"

In the darkened motel room, she held him silently in her arms for a long time. Finally releasing him, she said, "No one could ever accuse me of indulgences with a child. Not if they knew you. You're more of a man than anyone I've met or probably ever will meet. Don't lose touch altogether, will you? I'd like to know how you're getting on."

"I won't," he promised.

And that was the end.

A week after his return from St. Andrew's, feeling stifled and bored half out of his mind at his father's house, he hitched into town, planning to stop for a meal downtown before heading over to see Glenn. For old time's sake, he went to the deli on Old Street, slid onto a stool at the counter and ordered a lean corned beef on rye with mustard and a side order of their home-made coleslaw. Then, while waiting for his food, he looked around. His interest was caught by a very pretty girl sitting in one of the booths, smiling as she fed what looked like apple-sauce to a baby trussed into an infant seat.

He sat watching as the girl one-handedly ate a sandwich, all the while smiling and chatting away to the baby. He noticed her hands were ringless and very attractive, long-fingered and slender. He spontaneously got up and walked over to say, "Hi! If I'm out of line, say so right away and I'll leave you alone. But I was sitting over there watching you and the baby, getting a kick out of it. I'm on my own and it looks like you are, too. It's no fun eating alone and I thought, if you didn't mind, I'd bring my food over and eat with you."

She looked up at him, a tiny blonde with round brown eyes and a wide smile. "I guess so," she said. "Sure. Come on over."

Delighted, Corey returned to the counter, told the waiter he was moving to the booth and went back to slide in on the opposite side of the booth, at once picking up a napkin to dab at a stray bit of applesauce on the baby's chin.

She watched him do it, smiling involuntarily.

"Is it a boy?" he asked, watching her spoon the last of the dessert into the baby's mouth.

"He sure is," she smiled. "Isn't he terrific? He's got the most incredible appetite."

"I'm Corey Shea," he said, holding his hand out to her. "I'm really happy to meet you."

Her eyes widening, she allowed him to take hold of her hand.

"Dawn," she said. "Are you cutting classes or something?"

"Nope. I'm out of school."

"Oh!" She nodded. He looked old enough, she thought, to be out of school. He looked to be about twenty, maybe twenty-one.

"How about you?" he asked.

"I'm still going part-time. I was full-time until the baby."

"What about your husband?" he asked casually, picking up half his sandwich.

"Don't have one," she said easily, a little defiantly. "I only wanted the baby, not his old man."

"Every kid should have an old man," he said seriously, examining her eyes.

"Depends on who it is."

"True. A lousy old man's no good to anybody. D'you live around here?"

"You ask an awful lot of questions," she said.

"That's right." He bit into the sandwich, then took a long swallow of his Coke. "But only when something really interests me. If you don't ask questions, you never find anything out. I'm sixteen. How old are you?"

"Sixteen? You're kidding! You sure don't come on like sixteen."

"I know that. It's because I know what I'm doing. How old're you?" he asked again.

"Twenty."

"That's a good age," he smiled. "You know what?"

"What?" She smiled back at him, unable to help herself. She liked him.

"I'm going to be his old man and you're going to be my lady. I think you're beautiful. I really mean that. It's not some kind of line I say to be flattering. I don't go around telling women they're beautiful. But you are."

She stared at him, then laughed, feeling something very positive happening inside her.

"Corey Shea," she said. "Sixteen years old, out of school What do you do?"

"I've only been out a week," he corrected her. "And I'm going to go into business. I'm still working the whole thing out in my head. But I'm definitely going into business. D'you live in a house or an apartment or what?"

"An apartment in a house."

"What part of town?"

She told him.

"Hey!" he laughed. "That's great! My Aunt Glenn lives three blocks from there. Great! You'll like my aunt. She's very special."

So are you, she thought, unable to stop smiling at him.

"D'you have to be somewhere when you leave here?" he asked her.

"The sitter," she said. "I've got to work this evening."

"Hey! Don't pay a sitter! I'll take care of him."

"Are you sure you know what you're doing?" she asked.

"I always know what I'm doing. When you get to know me better, you'll find that out. I always tell the truth. And I always know what I'm doing. I'll look after the baby and you'll go to work and when you come home I'll have a great meal cooked and then we'll talk. Okay!"

"Okay."

The entire time she was working she wondered about him, wondered if she wasn't out of her mind going off leaving the baby with some kid who'd picked her up in a delicatessen. But she couldn't help feeling he was everything he said and showed himself to be. And, most of all, trustworthy. She'd never met anyone she trusted so completely, so immediately.

She hurried home to find he had cooked a fantastic meal. They sat on the floor and ate by candlelight and he told her all about his mother, his stepfather, his father, his aunt and uncle, his grandparents. "That was your *grandmother?*" she said. "That's incredible! Her poetry is practically my bible! Your grandmother! That is too absolutely fantastic!" She finished eating quickly, then said, "Tell me what she was like! Tell me all about her! I *love* her. I absolutely *love* her!"

He stretched out and told her as much as he remembered about Lisette and Ray and the old house in Remington Park. She listened and listened and suddenly realized she was happy, and said, "I'm really happy you're here. I mean it."

He said, "So am I," and reached for her. She went willingly, and believed, afterward, she'd been given something priceless, something undreamed-of.

"Who *taught* you?" she asked, curled happily against his side.

"A very beautiful lady," he answered, contentedly stroking her arm.

"She must have loved you," Dawn said. "A lot."

"We loved each other a lot. But I'm going to love you more."

By the end of that week, he'd moved in with Dawn and the baby and started scouting out financing for his business. He wasn't ready yet to tell anybody what the business was going to be.

Glenn automatically raised her eyebrows upon hearing all this, but met Corey's new family and knew he had, again, done something that would prove beneficial to everyone involved.

"This is my lady," he said, introducing Dawn to Glenn. He said it with such meaning, so much caring, Glenn was overwhelmed with affection for both of them, as well as for the baby. Dawn had misleadingly childlike features, a babyish face. But it was purely in appearance that she seemed childlike. She was studying pharmacy, she explained, taking courses three afternoons a week and working three evenings and two full days a week at a nearby drugstore to finance her courses. She and Corey were taking turns caring for Zane, the baby, and working out living arrangements that sounded very sensible.

Corey assumed full responsibility for Dawn and Zane, saying, "Soon as I'm twenty-one, we're going to get married." Glenn hadn't any doubt that that's exactly what would happen. She felt deeply happy for him. He'd managed to create for himself an ideal family.

Gaby was outraged; on the telephone at every available

opportunity, telling anyone who'd listen how Dawn had trapped
Corey into a disgusting mess and was shackling her poor little
boy with somebody else's bastard.

Dana, arriving finally at the outermost limits of his patience,
told her to, "Stop calling, stop bitching and leave the kids
alone! You just can't *stand* to see other people happy! Go write
a symphony for garage door and garbage can lids and get off
everybody's necks!" Her telephone calls were simply more than
he could bear and, without fail, after every one of her calls,
he just had to get out of the house for a while to cool off. No
one on earth made him angrier more easily than Gaby.

After this particular exchange, he changed his clothes and
went downtown to The Inkwell, a club that had come into
being a few years earlier and catered to the writers and artists
in town. The food was very good, the bar woodsy, dim and
well-stocked, and there were usually interesting people around
no matter what time of day or night one happened to go there.

He was heading for a group of regulars he spotted in the
corner of the bar when he heard his name called and he turned
to see Jack Owen at a table in the far corner, with a woman,
a woman who at once captured Dana's attention.

"Come join us!" Jack insisted. "God! It's great to see you!"
He got up and the two men threw their arms around each other,
then Jack said, "Meet Cassy. A new friend. She's been imported to work on a series. You two ought to have a lot to talk
about."

She smiled—a dazzling, utterly transforming smile—shook
hands with Dana, then retrieved her cigarette and sat back,
looking slowly around the room while Jack and Dana began
bringing each other up to date. Dana tried to pay attention to
what Jack was telling him but he couldn't stop looking at Cassy.
Something about her piqued his curiosity, and something more
in her careful scrutiny of the faces around them, keeping her
eyes away from Dana. It was as if she were purposely forcing
herself not to look at him. She was wearing an exquisitely
simple dress of raw silk, long-sleeved, with a mandarin collar,
slashed down the front and secured with an antique gold pin,
tied at the waist, full skirted. She sat with her legs crossed.
Slim ankles, brown suede shoes. She gave the impression of
being tall, but it was the combination of small bones and long

legs that created the impression because, Dana thought, she
wasn't more than five-four or -five. She had large, very clear
hazel eyes; perceptive, intelligent eyes, and a very sensual
mouth. She wore a deep pink-brown lipstick. High cheekbones,
a small pointed chin. Fox-face, he thought. You have a fox
face. He looked at the definition of her shoulders and breasts
under the creamy-colored silk and experienced, for the first
time since Julienne, a positive stirring. He had a tremendous
desire to touch her, to touch her thick coil of ash-blonde hair;
to take her hair down, smooth it out. Despite the angularity of
her features, there was something hard-soft about her that was
very exciting. He kept hoping she'd say something—he longed
to hear her say something more than the hello with which she'd
greeted him; he wanted to hear the quality of her voice and
how she'd speak; to see her smile again. But she kept out of
the conversation, obviously reluctant to interrupt his and Jack's
catching-up. She seemed to have no desire to redirect the conversation toward herself. And that, too, intrigued him.

She sat, feeling his eyes on her, knowing he was staring,
taking her apart inch by inch and found she could tolerate it
as long as she kept her eyes averted. If she looked at him and
found some other response there than the one she wanted to
see, she'd be desolated. She'd heard about him—it was almost
impossible to avoid hearing about him at the station—but she
hadn't, in any way, been prepared for his height or his magnificent build or his remarkable good looks. Having heard about
him and having him sitting here now staring at her, she threw
everything she'd heard out of her head and tried to tolerate
graciously his visual inspection. She drank her drink, smoked
another cigarette, then another, and carefully kept out of the
conversation. But his continuing study of her was doing something very upsetting to her insides and if he didn't soon stop,
she'd have to invent some reason for leaving. She wanted him,
but she couldn't entirely disregard everything she'd heard. Not
everything. It simply didn't seem possible that all of it could
be true, not when he was sitting there, devouring her with his
eyes, silently urging her to join into the conversation.

He and Jack were winding down and still she'd said nothing.
Determined now to arrange a second meeting, Dana said, "I

thought I might have a few people over to dinner Saturday. Why don't you both come?"

"Well, I don't know about Cassy," Jack said, leaving the field wide open to Dana, having watched with interest the electricity between these two, "but I'd love it. I don't suppose your sister's still around?"

"Glenn? She's very much around. I'll ask her, shall I?"

"I wouldn't mind seeing her again," Jack admitted.

"Cassy?" Dana finally addressed her directly. "Have you plans?"

She turned, fixed those clear hazel eyes on him and smiled again.

"Where do you live and what time?" she asked in a low voice with a soft raspy edge to it that sent a shiver down Dana's spine as he responded to that remarkable smile, met her eyes and mechanically told her where, how to get there, and what time.

"Fine," she said, dropping her cigarettes, and lighter into her bag. "I'll be there. With pleasure." She stood up and extended her hand to Jack, saying, "Lovely meeting you," and then to Dana said, "I am looking forward to Saturday evening." Then she left.

Dana watched her go. "She's a writer?" he asked, his eyes on Cassy's narrow, retreating back.

"Costume designer. I get the feeling you're interested, Dana."

"I don't know," he said quietly. "It feels as if I am. How can that be?" he wondered aloud, at last looking at Jack.

"Anything's possible," Jack said. "She's certainly different."

"English, isn't she?"

"That's right."

"Isn't that interesting," Dana said. "And she's not with you?"

"Nope."

"Very interesting," Dana repeated. "Why not come back to the house," he suggested on the spur of the moment. "I'll give you dinner. Unless you have other plans."

"No plans at all."

"Good," Dana said distractedly. "Good."

* * *

With far too much free time on her hands these days, Glenn began offering to babysit Zane and soon found herself spending hours pushing the baby carriage up and down the streets, smiling as women occasionally poked their heads into the carriage to have a look at Zane and pronounce him beautiful. She accepted the compliments and continued on her way.

During those hours the baby was in her charge, she actually felt she was accomplishing something. Not only was she helping out Corey and Dawn, but in some indefinable way she felt she was helping herself. She'd walk the carriage the three blocks over to her house, turn up the thermostat in the living room, set the baby down on the rug—to nap, or play, or try to sit up—and make dozens of quick sketches in pencil or charcoal, feeling the knowledge returning to her hand as she accumulated more and more completed drawings.

Between caring for Zane and her classes at the College, she hadn't the inclination or the available time to sit brooding about her future, worrying about where her life was going and when, if ever, she'd finally find fame. She'd take the baby back, then hurry home to have a quick drink while she changed clothes in preparation for her evening class. Usually, she'd eat after class, either stop at one of the restaurants near the College or fix herself something quick at home. Food was a secondary stop in any case, because the day was programmed according to when she could start thinking about having a drink. Once the baby was safely home, it was time for a martini, time to push off her shoes, stretch out her legs, rest her head against the back of the sofa and savor her drink. After class, another drink or two, then some brandy or cognac after dinner, a nightcap, then bed.

It was so nice to meet Dana for drinks downtown or to stop by his house for dinner to meet some more of his eternally new friends, everyone casually drink-in-hand while the introductions were being made.

When Dana called to say, "It's short notice, I know, but come for dinner Saturday," she automatically said, "I'd love it," and without any expectations, went along. To again meet John-called-Jack.

He looked very uncertain, as if he feared she might start

battering him at any moment with accusations, recriminations and held out his hand to her with an expression that seemed to say he was fully prepared to accept the consequences of his actions even now, almost five years after the fact.

She took his hand thinking he was bigger, older than she'd remembered, better looking, too, although he'd lost more of his hair. The warmth of his hand and the contact with his eyes sent a tingle of pleasure—or was it alarm?—down the back of her neck and caused a quick clutch of anticipation in her belly.

"Did you get divorced finally?" she asked, finding it fairly easy to smile.

"Oh, finally," he smiled back. "Did you ever finally get married?"

"Nobody ever asked me."

"Not as many bright guys in circulation as there used to be," he said, releasing her hand, his smile more assured. It was exactly the same. The feeling hadn't changed at all. Just the sight of her and he was filled with longing for her, with pleasure at the look of her.

"Still writing the soap opera?" She took her newly warmed hand and cooled it on the damp glass of gin and tonic she was drinking to good effect.

"Graduated up to screenplays. And one so-so novel. I'm working. I was out in California for over four years. Are you still at Hamilton's?"

"I'm not anywhere," she said, satisfied now at knowing why he hadn't called, and wondered why she'd remembered his eyes as being blue when they were gray, clear and gray, reminding her of a mountain stream; his pupils might be round stones lying beneath the surface of running water. She blinked, catching his question as it was slipping away from her mind.

"I'm taking evening courses, working to get my certification. Other than that, I've been babysitting my nephew's baby, doing a lot of sketching."

"You look different," he said, his eyes narrowing slightly, as if his memories of her were as imperfect as hers were of him. "Beautiful," he said. "Beautiful woman." His tone of voice was so praising she hastily took a large gulp of her drink.

"Are you back in the city now for good?" she asked.

He nodded slowly. "Any chance of starting from scratch?" he asked. "First meeting, that sort of thing."

"I think so," she answered, confounded at his calling her beautiful.

She was beautiful, he thought, as they studied each other in the ensuing silence. He liked the shine of her hair, the way it fell precisely to her shoulders; liked the whiteness of her skin and the faint blush of color in her cheeks, the deep blue of her eyes. Of what had happened that night he had only incomplete recollections. He remembered lowering her to the floor, her being sick, her little girl's cry of "You hurt me!" He remembered her long, slender body and the flexed curve of her spine as she'd run staggering the length of the attic. He felt not so much embarrassed as terribly saddened by the memory because, for months after, he'd thought of her and would have called had she had a reason in the world to be willing to speak to him. Which he'd believed she hadn't. He hadn't been able to face an in-person apology, couldn't have risked it actually because he'd felt so guilty for the *tone* of what had happened. What had bothered him most at the time and still carped at the edge of his conscience was how very young she'd been, how unequal to a situation she'd greatly contributed to creating. He hadn't ever been able actually to blame her to any degree. Not for any specific reason. He just simply couldn't blame her. Maybe because he had almost ten years on her and quite an acquaintanceship with guilt in its numerous guises. Whatever the reasons, she'd stayed in his mind as someone he'd happened into one night with nearly ruinous results. He had often wished for a chance to rectify or make amends for what had taken place.

Now it seemed she was willing to give them both another chance and he couldn't help wondering how her life had been in the past years, whom she'd known, her involvements. Surely she must have had involvements, someone like her who'd so eagerly accepted his hand beneath the table. She must have had affairs. God knows, after the divorce he'd gone from one situation to the next driven by some terrible compulsion to keep his emotions entirely apart from his various drives, both sexual and mental. Maybe, he thought, he'd been doing some peculiar kind of penance for that night with Glenn. He couldn't say

what, but there was something about her—and it hadn't changed
from then to now—that prompted him to make funny remarks
he inwardly groaned over; prompted him to cloak his real desires and immediate, total response to her in quips and self-
deprecating comments about his work. Was it her frailty? Or
the disbelief ringing her eyes when he called her beautiful? He
had a sudden powerful desire to know her well enough and
intimately enough to be able to talk to her truthfully, openly,
as he'd never done with anyone else, except Dana.

Dana was the exception. Their varying sexual preferences
aside, their communication had always been profoundly successful. When Dana spoke of his affairs, his feelings, his be-
wilderment, Jack could easily relate and respond to what Dana
put forth because Jack had always responded to Dana's truth-
fulness and to his inability to recognize himself.

Dana's response to Cassy was an encouraging sign, Jack
thought. It was small proof of what Jack had always believed
about Dana: that Dana had probably, at some point in his life,
had one bad male/female encounter and he'd allowed this one
bad experience to set a precedent; to direct the course of his
life. Wrongly. There were quite a number of homosexuals Jack
had met and known and been friends with. Dana seemed utterly
unlike any of them in one essential area: Dana liked women.
He just didn't seem to realize that he did.

Perhaps, Jack thought, seeing the color deepening in Glenn's
cheeks as their eyes continued to converse, he'd never tried to
make the reconciliatory effort he should have with her because
he'd been a little afraid of somehow alienating Dana as a result
of his involvement with Dana's sister. It was all so damned
complicated, and stupid, too. He could only view his prior
behavior as childish and contemptible.

"I'd like to take you out," he said, on impulse once more
taking hold of her hand, finding himself completely without a
quip to dispense. "Would you consider dinner?"

She nodded, tranquilized by the warmth and pressure of his
hand. How had she managed to forget how attractive he was,
how physically appealing, commanding. "When?" she asked,
already filled with anticipation at the thought of spending an
evening with him.

"Friday?" he suggested.

"Fine," she agreed, not sure if she should withdraw her hand. "What time?"

"I'll pick you up at seven." ·

He didn't offer to take her home when she announced she was leaving, shortly after dinner, and she was relieved. She wanted a little time to acclimate herself to the many ideas all at once feverishly circulating in her brain.

With a nightcap between her hands in the cool darkness of her bedroom, she sat leaning against the headboard, thinking about Corey and Dawn and the peaceful harmony of the life the three of them were living together. She was happy for them, yet envious. She wished, as she had for months and years, that she could find a similar contentment. She wanted the well-remembered pleasure of being touched, loved. She'd been so preoccupied with survival these past years, she'd all but completely turned off her feelings, her instincts. Except for that one brief, somehow hurtful, encounter with Mr. Hamilton.

Now, in the course of one casual evening, she'd managed to get herself turned back on. Eagerness and wanting were pushing through her veins and she told herself it was reasonable, even mature of her to be willing to give Jack a fair chance all these years later. After all, he'd been willing to start fresh. Shouldn't she give both of them a chance?

Of course she should, she thought, drawing her lips in against the aftertaste of the gin—she'd forgotten to add tonic—feeling the barely diluted gin detonating in her stomach. And wasn't it nice to look forward to a date with someone she actually wanted to see again? A date. The formality of it appealed to her. I'm romantic, she thought, smiling to herself. I really am romantic. I didn't know I was.

She drained the glass, unsteadily set it down on the night table and slid lower in the bed, her arms folded under her head; giddying visions cast themselves on the screen of the ceiling, images of an undilutedly romantic nature. She loved the images both for themselves and for their inherent possibilities, too. After all, she asked herself, what experiences have I really had? Three times Ralph and I made love. That once with Jack. Four or five times, once each, with others I don't even remember. And that one encounter with Mr. Hamilton. I don't know anything about love, being in love. And if I don't let myself fall in love, if I never find out, I might grow old and bitter and jaded with never knowing.

She closed her eyes, already in love with the gloriously romantic images of herself and Jack she conjured up; the two of them beautifully dressed, dancing somewhere to slow sentimental music; Jack saying wonderful things, saying how beautiful she was, seeing into her through her eyes and telling her she was beautiful all the way through, inside and out. I might be beautiful, she thought, turning onto her side; curling slightly inward as if holding a parcel of good wishes protectively close to her body. I could be so good with someone who loved me. I could have the time, the quiet to do the things I've always wanted to do, to learn how I am, who I am, what it is I'm all about. To live without the pressures of ambition, secured by love, that might be the ultimately revealing state. The key to finding that special substance inside her that would inevitably set her aside, elevate her to her natural level.

Love, love. Sex, too, yes. To lie open, taking, taking in, being loved from the skin in, with whispered endearments and persuasive caresses leading away from the realms of imagination and beyond into the heat of bodily satisfaction. Afterward, to find both. Love and sex. Words, touching. I want want. Yes.

Dana kept hurrying to the door every time the bell rang, each time expecting it to be her, disappointed every time it wasn't. In between times—noticing it was getting late—he observed Jack and Glenn, nodding to himself approvingly. Then rushing to the kitchen to check on the dinner, he wondered if she'd changed her mind and wasn't going to come after all.

He paused a moment, alone in the kitchen, asking himself why he was so concerned, so up in the air waiting for her to get there. He had no answer. He only knew the disappointment would be crushing if she didn't come. And he couldn't ever remember feeling that way about anyone—male or female.

When, an hour and a half late, Cassy arrived, apologizing, saying, "I *am* sorry, darling. My car broke down and the automobile club took bloody ages to get there. I hope I haven't disarranged your evening." Dana smiled happily—she called him "darling"—He took her coat, then her hand—What was he doing?—to lead her inside and make the introductions. He was gratified by the look and sound of her, even pleased by the raindrops caught in her hair.

"What will you have to drink?" he asked.

"Let me come along with you and I'll concoct something of my own choosing. I'm not quite certain what I'm in the mood for." She was out of breath, her insides tight as a drum, her breathing constricted.

In the kitchen, she looked over the bottles on the counter, then reached for the bourbon, saying, "I've always fancied trying this. I'm very blunt, you know. Well-known for it, actually." She poured neat bourbon into a glass, then set down the bottle and leaned against the counter, looking at him. "I'm dreadful at social games and lovely little nuances. I had heard about you, Dana. I'd heard you were gay. It's not the feeling I had the other afternoon. Nor is it the one I'm getting from you now. What exactly is the feeling I'm getting?"

"I don't know," he said truthfully. "I honestly don't know."

"Are you bisexual?" she asked, her eyes steadily on his.

"I don't know that either."

"I'm embarrassing you."

"No."

"Good. I'd dislike that. Actually, it's just that I don't want to throw myself into something that's going to wind up being rather depressing for us both. I'm sure you understand. What I mean is, if you have some idea you're going to experiment on me, you'd best forget it straightaway. But, if there is some real feeling, it's quite, quite mutual. All right?"

"You *are* blunt," he said, admiring her ability to be so candid.

"You're wonderfully attractive. I don't like making a game out of relationships. Are you attracted to me?"

"It feels that way."

"Good." She smiled and took a sip of the bourbon, feeling it at once begin easing the tightness inside. She held her hand out to him, saying, "I'll stay and help you clear up, shall I?"

"Yes."

They stood a moment longer, holding hands, eyes locked. Her hand was soft and smooth. Then she said, "Right! Time to join the party. I never offer to help whoever's doing the cooking because I simply cannot bear having people around offering to help me when I'm the one doing the cooking." Still she continued to hold his hand, examining his eyes. "All right?"

"I feel the same way," he said.

His mind was so much on her—watching her circulate, talking to people—the party seemed to be taking place without him. Every time he looked at her, he felt an inner lifting and found it close to impossible to look away. He wanted to be beside her, touching her, seeing her smile. He couldn't think clearly. He moved back and forth among the guests, his eyes searching her out, watching, watching. Thick coil of ash-blonde hair and hazel eyes. Pointed fox-face. Sudden brilliant smiles and laughter that seemed to penetrate his skin. How subtle she is, he thought, seeing that she made no display of the fact that she was there to be with him. She made none of the proprietary gestures so many others he'd known had made.

At some moments, she was very plain, then, seconds later, very beautiful. Her facial expressions, her face itself was always changing, so that she appeared different to him each time he caught sight of her. He wanted more than anything else to hold her down, hold her still and study her closely, intensely; learn the qualities and characteristics of her face so that he might, more permanently, fix her image in his mind.

She talked to people, only partially aware of the conversational direction; totally aware of Dana's eyes following her, totally aware of him, and acutely aware of her body. There was a certain slight weakness in her knees and an insistent throbbing in her groin, so that she almost wished he'd stop looking at her. His eyes were as potent, from the distance, as his hands would have been had he been standing directly beside her, slowly, assertively caressing her. She longed for the dinner party to end, for the people to go so that she might remain alone here with him in his lovely house.

Finally, when the last of the guests had gone, she refilled her glass while he went about collecting up the ashtrays and empties, asking, "That was your sister, Dana?"

"That's right."

"She's very beautiful. I quite enjoyed watching her."

"Glenn's a good girl," he said abstractedly, making a face as he picked a mashed hors d'oeuvre out of the carpet.

"Woman," she corrected quietly. "She is not a girl."

"Whatever she is," he said straightening, "she's good. It's amazing how she's more like Lisette every year. Our mother," he explained, heading out to the kitchen, then at once returning with the emptied tray to collect up more things.

"Where is your bedroom?" she asked, stopping him.

"Upstairs."

"Why don't we go upstairs?" she suggested. "I'll help you clear this lot up later."

Was she cold-blooded? he wondered. Or simply direct? He was having a lot of trouble reading her meanings.

"I'll come up in a minute," he said, wanting that minute to compose himself. "It's the one on the left."

"I'd like to use your loo, if I may."

"Help yourself."

Carrying her glass, pausing to pick up her evening bag on the way, she went up the stairs. Dana stood watching her go, his heartbeat too fast. Perhaps this was a terrible mistake. What would he do if, when he got up there, she was in his bed? He wasn't ready.

He quickly gathered up the last of the glasses, set them down on the kitchen counter, then returned the liquor bottles to the cabinet under the counter, killing time.

Cassy, minus only her shoes, was sitting on his bed, the pillows propped up behind her, smoking a cigarette, and finishing her drink.

"I feel very at home in bedrooms," she smiled, crossing her ankles. "You do have marvelous taste, Dana. This is a smashing room."

Nervously, he stretched out across the foot of the bed, leaning on his elbow looking at her. She did seem very much at home, relaxed and comfortable.

"I have all my favorite bits and pieces in my bedroom," she said. "So I can look at it all, enjoy it when I'm relaxed." She stretched her legs so that her feet were just touching his chest. "It was a good party. I take it Jack and your sister have met before?"

"A few years ago, four or five."

"Mmmm, he seems quite taken with her. And she with him. Rather a nice match, don't you think?"

"I hadn't thought about it," he said, looking at her small,

and narrow feet. She'd taken off her stockings, he now saw. He put his hand around her foot, holding it against his chest. "You have very pretty feet," he said. "Beautiful, perfect feet."

"Thank you, I'm older than you are, Dana. Were you aware of that?"

"Are you?" He looked up at her.

"Five or six years," she said.

"You don't look it."

"So I've been told. But I am nonetheless."

"Have you been married?" he asked, moving his hand to her other foot, smoothing it.

"I have been. A bloody mess. He was a bit of a juggler. Me on his one hand and a lady or two on the other. I don't care for being part-time business. I like complete attention. Rather selfish, I suppose. But there you are. I know what I want and if I can't have it, I prefer to have nothing at all, do without."

"I see." He looked again at her feet, letting his hand venture some distance up her calf. "You've just shaved your legs."

She laughed. "For me, darling. I've always 'just shaved my legs.' I like myself. I like taking care of myself. Don't you like taking care of yourself?"

"I do," he admitted.

"Well, there you are then!" She leaned over and put out her cigarette. "I've also," she smiled widely at him, " 'just' shaved under my arms, oiled myself up like a channel swimmer and had my hair trimmed. I do all that sort of thing with frightful regularity. I enjoy it. Men have a simpler time of it. There's less to fuss with."

"That's true," he smiled, rounding her kneecap, delighting in the texture of her skin. "Tell me what else you fuss with," he prompted.

"Oh, this and that. Eyebrows, a bit of night cream every now and then to keep the crow's feet at bay. Regular dental checkups, gynecological checkups, all that lot." She slid down fractionally so that the soles of her feet were resting flat against his chest. "Are you comfortable, darling?" she asked, taking a last swallow of her drink.

"So-so," he answered. Every time she called him darling he had the feeling he'd just received a small electric shock.

"We must have you comfortable," she said, handing him a pillow. He tucked it under his arm, then leaned on it.

"That's better," he said, his hand on the underside of her knee where the skin was even softer still, warmer. "You have lovely legs."

"Thank you. You have a lovely face, a wonderful face. Wouldn't you like to take off your jacket? Surely you would."

He sat up, removed his jacket, leaned across to drop it over the chair, then returned to his former position across the foot of the bed. His hand returned to the underside of her leg, slowly stroking. He was beginning to feel more at ease, very natural; he felt an increasing desire to take off her clothes. She seemed prepared for anything, everything. Yet there was utterly no pressure, as if she were also prepared to accept the possibility of nothing at all happening. She lit another cigarette asking, "Would you like one?"

"Not right now," he said. "Thank you."

She dropped the match into the ashtray, smiling again. His hand was now between her knees. She was very wet, and finding it extremely difficult to remain calm. She uncrossed her ankles.

"That's very nice," she said softly. "Skin, you know, is perhaps the most erogenous area of all."

"I agree," he smiled back. "You do have perfect skin." His hand moved down again and, cupping her heel, he raised her foot to kiss her instep.

The breath caught in her throat and her eyelids fluttered but she didn't move. This was exquisite agony, wanting but knowing any sudden move on her part might destroy the tentative mood.

"How long were you married?" he asked, his hand once more between her knees.

"Four years. Although we actually lived together only two and a half. The other year and a half got used up on legalities."

"How long have you been divorced?"

"Eleven years."

He looked up at her briefly, then down again at her feet, lifting her long skirt to kiss her on the knee. She sighed and stubbed out the cigarette, then sat up, bringing her legs around under her. Following suit, he also sat up, watching her every move.

"Would you like to undress me?" she said softly. "Or would you prefer me to do it?"

"I'd like to," he said, his throat feeling suddenly swollen.

"And shall I return the favor?" she asked, her fingertips tracing his jawline.

"If you'd like to."

Her hands went to his tie. She unknotted it, dropped it over the side of the bed, then undid the top two buttons of his shirt, coming forward to place her mouth on his throat. Her touch was light, persuasive. She straightened, once more looking into his eyes as he reached out and began unbuttoning her blouse. The silk too was weightless with mother of pearl buttons. He took each of her hands, holding them in turn to unfasten the buttons at her wrists. She sat perfectly still, watching as he drew the shirt back over her shoulders and off.

Why had he thought her angular? he wondered, his hands going to her shoulders, sliding across to her neck, up over the sides of her face, into her hair. Thick hair closed over his fingers, tumbling down. There was so much more of it, it was much longer than he'd imagined. It spilled down past her shoulders. Bringing her face closer, he wanted to kiss her. Her mouth was softly moist, receptive. She sighed again, still unmoving, as he ended the kiss and she continued with his shirt buttons, bared his chest, then laid her hands flat over his breast. He kissed her again, both hands going in back of her to unfasten her brassiere. Then he sat away to look at her. The wisp of lacy brassiere dangled from her arms. He removed it.

"You're surprised," she said, another smile shaping her mouth.

"I am," he admitted. Her breasts were much fuller than he'd expected. They seemed almost too much for her slender torso. Full and perfectly round and beautiful, too. His hands closed over her breasts. He drew in his breath with the pleasure. My God! he thought, elation surging through him. My God my God! This was too much! He couldn't move for several moments, his hands circling her breasts, his fingertips astonished at the softness of her nipples. He released her at last so that

she could remove his shirt. Then she got off the bed and stood
waiting, looking up at him expectantly as he unzipped the velvet
skirt, laughing softly at his surprise at finding her nude.

"I took everything else off when I came up," she said, her
hands on his waistband.

"I'll do it," he said, quickly divesting himself of his trousers,
draping them over the chair, unable to look away from her.

"I approve of your shorts," she laughed. "Men who wear
those dreadful tight jockey things have a bit of a problem, I
think." She sat down on the side of the bed and swung her
legs up as he stepped out of his shorts then removed his socks.

She lay back telling herself, Go slowly, go slow. But it was
so difficult. All the elements were so right, so absolutely right.
He stretched out beside her, admiring her small hips and long
legs.

"A boy with breasts," she said huskily. "I've been told it
before."

"I wouldn't say so," he said, lining himself up against her,
the pleasure heightening. "I'd say you're very much a woman.
With breasts," he smiled and eased over on top of her. "You're
beautiful, Cassy." He opened his mouth on her nipple and she
shivered, her fingers in his hair.

"Have you ever?" she asked in a whisper. "With a woman?"

"Once," he whispered back. "Years ago."

"And you didn't like it," she guessed.

"I didn't like or dislike it. It wasn't anything."

"Do you like it now?"

"So far, I do. Tremendously."

"Would it make you feel good to know you're making me
terribly excited?"

"Am I?" He kissed the side of her neck.

"Yes, terribly. That doesn't happen to me very often these
days. I sometimes feel I've grown calluses over all the sensitive
spots, so there's no longer any feeling."

"I've felt that way," he said, his mouth against her ear, then
on her cheek, finally her mouth. He was aroused by her lips
moving over his, her tongue searching the interior of his mouth,
lazily, maddeningly, as her hands went gliding down his sides,
across his back.

He felt her thighs opening and slipped his hand between

them, seeing her eyes flicker, her pupils dilating as his fingers probed uncertainly. She opened more and gently took hold of his hand to direct him. Her wetness was oddly stirring, that he'd generated this response in her. He shifted and watched his hand, looking at her. He wanted to look at her, to touch her. She seemed very complete. Her increasing heat was compelling. He kissed her again, as her body moved under his hand, her breathing irregular.

"Would you like me to do this?" he asked, shifting down.

"Yes!" she whispered, bending her legs open. "I'd adore you to do that, if you'll come round up here and let me do the same for you."

Again, she gently directed him until they were side by side. She put her hand and then her mouth on him and the pleasure was piercing, tremendous. He lowered his head tentatively. She smelled sweet, tasted sweet. He had no idea where, but her hand went to his cheek, then down around his chin, raising his head slightly as her thighs arched open. He let her lead him, allowed instinct and her responses then to guide him. And the more she responded—quiveringly, immediately—the more he wanted her to respond. He kept on, dizzy with feeling and caring until she was suddenly pulling away from him, urging him down on his back, whispering, "This one time let me," has she straddled his lap. Her eyes glazed, her features somehow blurred, she slid down over him. Placing one of his hands over her breast, she led his other hand down. She lifted and fell once, slowly, whispering, "Do that, darling, please. I'm going to come."

She leaned far back, her thigh muscles taut, one hand bracing herself, the other, behind her, stroking between his thighs. He was overwhelmed by all of it, by all of her, and rubbed her gently, finding her more and more beautiful as she quiveringly rose and fell, rose and fell faster and then faster, then suddenly removed his hand to replace it with her own. Her breasts were very hot under his hands, her entire body burning. Her head thrown back, her hand was suddenly still as she cried out and her fingers gripped his thigh. Outside she was utterly motionless, frozen, her mouth open, eyes tightly closed. Inside was all motion, pulsing, elastic. He felt happy, purely, completely happy. He moved inside her, began rubbing her again to keep her contracting; to finish inside her. He wanted to come inside of her, and did, marveling at her knowing, at the way she came forward on his chest and kissed him slowly, hungrily, until the panic at last subsided.

Then, her face against his neck, she whispered, "If you're gay, darling, I'm completely crazy. But no matter," she sighed. "Are you pleased?"

"Oh, yes, very. The only problem with me, you see, is the more I get, the more I want. And I want more. Will you give me more, darling? Of the other?"

"Was it all right?"

"Marvelous. Did you like it?"

"I actually did. You taste sweet."

"So do you." She smiled into his neck. "Fancy another go?"

He laughed. "How old are you?" he asked. "Or am I not supposed to ask?"

"Oh, you may ask," she said. "I haven't any feelings one way or another about age. I've told you. I'm close to six years older than you."

"But how do you know how old I am?"

"Darling," she laughed. "Don't be thick! I *asked*."

"Jack?"

"That's right. Do you know I could barely sit still the other afternoon, just looking at you? A case of complete and immediate lust the likes of which I've rarely experienced. Couldn't you feel it?"

"I felt something."

"Feel *me*," she whispered. "You send me wild. Anything at all, darling. Anything. Whatever you like. I like it all. Only one thing, I'm afraid."

"What's that?"

"I'm not a boy, darling. I can't take it that way. It hurts."

"I wouldn't hurt you," he said, holding her tightly. "I know how much it hurts."

"Oh, Dana," she whispered. "Darling, loving isn't hurtful. It's healing. Here, I'll show you. I'll show you."

# Fourteen

The bank manager sat listening to Corey's plans with a good-natured but patronizing expression on his face. Corey saw it, knew what it meant and grew increasingly angry as his logically planned presentation failed to alter that benevolently superior gaze. There wasn't even an outside chance that this guy was going to do more than give out pats on the shoulder and some "fatherly" advice. Corey stopped mid-sentence to sit for several seconds staring at the man's face, at the practiced, kindly expression, the arching eyebrows over blue eyes that had seen brighter, more truthful times.

"Don't stop!" the manager said, thinking Corey nervous. "It's all right. Now you just keep right on going."

"I don't think so." Corey stood up, angry with himself now. He'd known from the start this was going to be an exercise in futility. So why the hell had he started? Well, okay! He'd started all right but there was no law that said he had to compound the damage by wasting any more of his breath in finishing. "We're wasting time," he said, moving around in back of his chair, looking at the man, thinking there'd come a time

273

when he'd have the kind of power this man had right now. And he'd use it a lot more intelligently, more importantly.

"Don't be nervous," the manager said, exercising even more of his benevolence. "Take your time and tell me all about it."

"I haven't got any more time to waste on you," Corey said, realigning the chair. "You'd sit there and hear me out down to the last detail. Then you'd look good and thoughtful for a while. And then you'd sing me a song I know backward. How do guys like you get to be bank managers anyway? You haven't got any *vision*." Without giving the man any chance to respond, he picked up his various papers, tucked them into the folder and walked out of the bank.

Dawn said, "I don't understand why you're so angry. I really don't. I've never seen you this way."

"That guy was perfectly willing to sit there and waste *hours!* His time, my time. For nothing! Just to prove what an okay, open-minded guy he is. But there wasn't a chance he'd give me the money. It bugs me that there's somebody who could be doing some good things and all he's really doing is wasting time. Well, I don't have that kind of time to waste even if he does. It makes me so mad seeing a guy like that who could do some good things and all he does is waste time trying to make himself look good. He wasn't even *listening*."

"Are you sure about that?"

"Oh, I'm sure. I've seen guys like that all my life. All they can see is what looks like a kid sitting there and they're not going to give any credibility to anything a kid has to say."

"What about your mother?" she offered. "Or Lloyd. Wouldn't it be worth a try?"

"Lloyd," he said, sounding wearied. "Lloyd. If I had the bread and he had the peanut butter, he'd die before the two of us could get together and make a sandwich."

"Maybe not. Maybe he's not the way you think he is. And he's got lots of money. It couldn't hurt to try, could it? You're so close to getting everything started. It's crazy to be stuck at this point when there are people in your own family who might be interested, given a chance."

"I want to do this on my own."

"Corey, it's not working out. What difference does it make,

as long as you get it done? What about your Aunt Glenn? She'd
help you in a minute. You know that."

"I know," he said distractedly. "Okay. Maybe I'll give Lloyd
a shot." He won't do it, he thought. There's no way he'll do
it.

"Why not Glenn?" she asked.

"I'm still thinking about it," he said vaguely. "I don't know."
He looked at her, and smiled. "I'm sorry," he said, touching
her hair. "It's just that that guy made me so mad. It's stupid
to get that mad."

"That's right," she smiled back. "It is."


If they set it all up, choosing a specific evening and all that,
the chances were that Gaby would get herself so worked up
she'd wreck any chance he might have with Lloyd. Not because
she'd *want* to wreck it, he reasoned, but just because she couldn't
seem to do things any other way. So the best thing was just to
casually phone up, make sure they were both home and say,
"If you're going to be there for a while, I thought I'd come on
over." She was so surprised, she couldn't even begin to say
anything. Corey's visits were so rare. "I'll be over in half an
hour," he said and hung up.

"Don't bulldoze them," Dawn advised. "They're not bad
people. She's just scared of a lot of things. And he's out to
take care of her."

"Red Riding Hood and Grannie," he said.

"Listen, if it works, great! Don't knock it! It isn't all that
easy to keep a thing going, you know. It might not be your
kind of thing but it works for them."

"Okay, okay!" he grinned. "Point made. Over and out."

"You've got all your papers?"

"I've got it all."

"I'll keep my fingers crossed," she said. "But even if they
don't go for it, you'll still get this off the ground. You know
you will. And I know you will. And don't get *angry*. Okay?"

"Okay, chief!"

He left and she made herself a cup of tea, then sat cross-
legged on the floor, hoping she wasn't crazy and that Gaby
really did have some kind of feeling for him. Because it'd be
terrible to have him go over there and get a lot of grief he really

didn't need. What he was trying to do really was a very good thing. She could see how those bank managers had to see him, as an outspoken kid; but she knew how he really was and that he'd do this if it took him forever.

Lloyd's manservant, Peter, opened the door, then vanished. Gaby came to greet Corey looking as if she fully expected him to march right in and destroy the penthouse, Lloyd, her marriage, her entire life. He was stopped for an instant by her fearful expression, realizing Dawn was right. His mother was scared. Now that he thought about it, he could see she'd probably been scared for as long as he could remember and had covered the whole thing over with shouting and a lot of noisy piano playing. He wondered why.

Lloyd came out, extending his hand with a smile, saying, "Good to see you, son! How are you? Come in, come on in!" Corey looked at him, wanting to laugh at the affectation of the Oriental robe Lloyd wore over his shirt and trousers and the embroidered Oriental-looking slippers on his feet. Gaby was in one of her typically long, floaty dresses. The two of them looked ready to go to a masquerade. Two kids playing dress-up in a penthouse.

Amazing, he thought, shaking Lloyd's hand. The three of them went into the vast living room. Gaby's treasured grand piano was positioned in front of the window that went from floor to ceiling, wall to wall. There was the piano, four very big potted plants and nothing else. It looked good. At the near end of the room were two facing sofas in crimson velvet. He and Lloyd sat on one of the sofas, Gaby settled tentatively on the other, at once lighting a cigarette. She never took her eyes off Corey, as if she expected him to steal something or perhaps to physically attack either of them.

Lloyd, smiling, said, "Gaby, darling, why don't you have Peter make us some coffee and a few sandwiches. I wouldn't mind and I think Corey might like a cup of coffee."

"Yes, all right," she said uncertainly, getting to her feet. She looked very tall, yet somehow insubstantial. She cast a last wary look at Corey and went out.

"Okay," Lloyd said, suddenly business-like. "Let's hear it!"

Corey looked at him for a moment, then reached for his

folder. Everything inside him insisted this was perhaps the most colossal waste of time yet.

Lloyd listened intently, asking questions every so often; he asked to look at Corey's projections and figures, then sat silently for several minutes having yet another look at the paperwork. In the interim, Gaby wafted back to the other sofa, lit another cigarette and tried to look composed.

"Why ask me?" Lloyd said at last. "You've never especially liked me. I can't say you haven't had your reasons. But this is quite something to put in front of me."

"Why not you?" Corey countered. "Or don't you invest?"

"We're talking about a hell of a lot of money here. It's a first-rate proposition, I grant you. But why should I sink that kind of money into it?"

Corey both tensed and relaxed simultaneously so that his muscles seemed to be pulling against each other in opposing directions. He wanted to get up and walk out, but forced himself to remain where he was.

"It's a great idea," he said. "You admit that. Anybody who invests stands to make big returns. I need a few investors I can work with. I think I might be able to work with you." I'll never be able to work with you, he thought. This is another idiotic game.

"What brings you to that conclusion?" Lloyd asked interestedly.

"Who knows? Maybe because you like to take on the unusual, the not-so-easy." Both men turned to look at Gaby, then back at each other.

Lloyd lit a cigarette and crossed his knees.

"What about it?" Corey asked.

"You're a hard driver," Lloyd said. "Straight ahead, right to the point. Let's do a little more talking here."

"Let's just forget it." Corey reached for his file.

"Take it easy!" Lloyd said. "I may be all kinds of things but I'm not stupid and I won't be stampeded. If you weren't Gaby's boy, we wouldn't even be talking. So just slow down and give me a chance to assimilate all this."

"This is turning into some Mickey Mouse game you think you're going to play because of my mother. I'm not going to hang around here and have you give me a whole routine on how I'm 'Gaby's boy,' so you're going to play nice. Shove it, Lloyd!"

He picked up his file and got up.

"Why don't you give him the money, Lloyd?" Gaby said softly, so that Corey looked at her, astonished; unable to figure out what was going on here. First she'd seemed terrified of him, now she was telling Lloyd to get involved in the financing.

"How come?" Corey asked her, puzzled, as Peter came in and set down a tray on the coffee table. Lloyd at once busied himself pouring out the coffee while Corey stared at Gaby, waiting for her to say something.

"You look so much like George Shea," she said. "Sometimes it bothers me."

"Have a sandwich," Lloyd offered, picking up one of the cups of coffee.

"What's going on here?" Corey asked, flummoxed.

"I think Lloyd should invest," Gaby said. "Just as long as *that girl* isn't going to be getting any part of it."

"Oh, Jesus!" Corey got a stranglehold on his temper. *"That girl,"* he said, "happens to be my lady. And she's not interested in *anybody's* money. You started to do kind of a nice thing here," he said to his mother. "And then you had to start in on Dawn."

"I want you to have . . ." Gaby began.

"Now, just a minute," Lloyd said.

"Hey!" Corey raised his voice. "Nobody ever asked *me* whether or not I ever liked old Lloyd here or whether I enjoyed getting bounced around all over town. Nobody ever bothered to ask. Well, I don't happen to think it's any of your business about me and Dawn. We've got something good going and it's none of your concern."

"It concerns me," Gaby said. "After all, you're my son . . ."

"Oh, *please!* That's too much. Let's just forget the whole thing! It was a bad mistake on my part coming here, thinking maybe we could get together." He moved toward the door.

"But we want to help you," Gaby said. "It's just that you don't know, you can't be sure she isn't taking advantage . . ."

"Don't you worry about it," Corey said evenly. "Don't even *think* about it." He arrived at the door.

Gaby came hurrying out. "You're not giving me a chance," she said, looking childishly unhappy.

"You're not giving me much of a chance, either," he said, less angrily. "So that makes us even. Thanks for your time."

"But I . . ."

"It's okay," Corey said, suddenly feeling sorry for her and hating the feeling. "We'll just forget it. You go on, have your coffee. I'll talk to you soon."

He arrived home so confused he could scarcely separate his thoughts.

"They're like something out of Charles Addams," he told Dawn. "Good old Lloyd running up one track and down another, sideways, backward. While good old mom's telling him to give her 'son' the money but just make sure the money doesn't get into the *wrong* hands. I could hardly keep up with the changes."

"So that's that," she said. "I'm sorry."

"Am I crazy or was I there?" He shook his head and put his arm around her shoulders. "Telling me I look so much like George Shea it bothers her. Then telling Lloyd to give me the money. The two of them all dressed up in their weird outfits in that big empty place with Peter going around in his white serving jacket, with slippers so he won't make any noise."

"I'm sorry," she said again.

"And she looked so *confused,* as if she were reading the lines they gave her to read but none of it was making any sense. And how come I was being so ungrateful and angry when she was trying to be so nice? The whole thing was pathetic. You're right," he said. "She's scared. She's scared of me. Maybe she thinks I'm going to be old George all over again. What the hell did the guy *do* to her?"

"I thought it might work," she said.

"I knew it wouldn't," he said, massaging his scalp. "Shit!"

"I'm really sorry, Corey."

"It wasn't your fault. I'll get the financing," he said, more determined than ever. "Boy! They're both nuts. That was the nuttiest hour I ever spent in my life. You know that? I wish you'd been there so you'd know what I'm talking about. Anyway, that's that."

"She did try," she said, "in her way."

"I know it. I think she really wanted me to have the money. The problem is everything she does has all kinds of glue. You get stuck if you don't watch out where you put your hands. I can't get over how scared she was of me."

"Let's go to bed."

"Yeah," he sighed. "I think so."

"You'll get it done," she said, getting up. "I know you will."

Zane woke up in the middle of the night, crying. Corey got up and went to get Zane, to walk up and down in the dark, holding him, soothing him; thinking of his approach to his father, determining the best way to convince George, to get him to allow either an invasion of the trust body or to float loans against it. Walking back and forth as Zane fell asleep again, he envisioned the whole thing.

He thought about his mother, unable to sustain any anger. Dawn had changed his perspectives, on many things, but about Gaby mainly.

My mother, beautiful and scared out of her head, wanting to do things but afraid somebody else might benefit from her once-removed generosity. Still, she did try. That's something. What a family! Uncle Dana, Aunt Glenn, my mother. People all kind of screwy in one way or another, but kind of lovable, too. No, really okay. "Why don't you give him the money, Lloyd?" It was a step. It actually was a step. The first time she'd ever done anything like that. Maybe someday she'd get out of all that and just be. Just be.

He returned Zane to the crib, went out to the kitchen for a glass of grapefruit juice, then back to the bedroom to sit drinking the juice watching Dawn sleep. Small and silent, her breathing was so soundless the absence of any sound woke him up sometimes. He'd lie in the dark and watch the fractional movements of her body in sleep then, reassured, sleep again himself.

The thing would go. Of course he'd ask Glenn. Wasn't she the one, the only one he'd always known would be for him? Now there was Dawn. But that wasn't the same. Glenn wouldn't even ask why or what for but just do or give whatever needed doing, or giving. Everything would work out. Things were already working out. He put the glass down on the floor and climbed under the blankets. Look at the way things were working out! With his lady and his boy.

He folded his arms under his head, gazing at the ceiling, thinking about Alyssa, remembering, as if all that had happened between them had been twenty or thirty years before. When he was young.

"I'm going to call good old George," Corey said to Dawn next morning. "And just watch! I'll call and he'll make an *appointment* to see me. Some more running around in circles."

"They're your circles," she laughed.

"Yeah," he agreed, wrinkling his nose. "Lucky old me."

George said, "I'm awfully busy right now, Corey. Could we make it for lunch one day next week?"

"Oh, sure," Corey made a face at Dawn. Mouthing, I told you so. "Which day is good for you?"

They agreed on a day and Corey hung up saying, "At least there are no big surprises with old George. He runs straight down the old track like a racehorse."

George, after a lot of talking, agreed to allow Corey to invade the trust for twenty-five percent of his financing and promised to arrange an additional loan using the corpus of the trust as collateral.

"It makes good sense," George said, eyeing his watch. "Just don't go wild. Take your time and make sure of your associates. How's—what's her name?—Dawn? And the boy?"

"Fine. Thanks a lot."

"See!" Dawn said happily. "Didn't I tell you? You just can't ever be sure which way people are going to go."

"Only some people," he smiled. "Listen, I've got this great idea for veal and noodles I thought I'd do up. So don't eat a lot of garbage at the store tonight. And we'll eat when you get home. Okay?"

"Veal's kind of expensive."

"No problem," he said. "I borrowed on my allowance. Old

George just gave me one of those looks and went rushing off to his big meeting."

Dawn laughed. "I've got to rush off to my big job. Oh, Zane's got a kind of a red bottom. Let him play around in the tub for a while, okay? And then a lot of that ointment."

"Okay, chief!"

"Even if you never do get to be a tycoon," she said, "you're the best sitter I've ever had. Not to mention a couple of other things."

"I love you, lady."

"I know it. I love you, too. You won't forget about Zane's ointment?"

"I'll use whatever's left over on the veal."

# *Fifteen*

Jack arrived on time Friday evening with a bottle of rum in one hand and a plastic sack of limes in the other. When she opened the door, he gave her a quick kiss on the lips, stepped inside and said, "Very nice house. Do you like rum?"

"I don't know," she said, still reacting to the kiss and wondering if she hadn't overdone the set-dressing. The lights were off, the entire first floor was candlelit by huge, fat, scented candles that cast a dim orange glow over everything. She'd even gone shopping and bought an expensive black dress that buttoned down the front. Easy to take off. She watched him set the rum and limes in the kitchen, thinking, I'm too obvious, too easy. He has to know I've set all this up. She reached for the glasses, but he said, "I'll bartend, okay? You just relax and enjoy. You'll like this."

She hung back near the door watching him deftly slice twists off one of the limes, then wring them into the rum and tonic drinks he prepared. He looked and smelled good, in a cream-colored turtleneck sweater of some silky-looking fabric, with a brown tweed sports jacket and dark brown trousers. She liked

the fact that he was going bald but didn't try to comb his hair
way over from the side or try to disguise the fact in any way.

"You look very nice," she said, thinking he'd find her juvenile and hopelessly inept. She was so foolishly nervous—
as if she'd never had a date, never had a man in her home
before. Well, she hadn't. Not in this house. This was different.
This time it was important. She wanted this night to be the
beginning of something, not just an experience whose duration
would be, at most, only a matter of hours. She wanted the two
of them to be starting something that might range off into
infinity.

"So do you," he said, the candlelight contriving to make
him look softened, aglow. "You look radiant. Cheers!" he said,
handing her a drink, taking a swallow of his own, then studying
her over the rim of his glass.

"Let's go into the living room," she invited, carrying her
untasted drink ahead of her as she led the way back through
the house. She even had a fire going. He had to know she'd
done a great deal of staging. But he seemed not to notice or
to think the candlelit atmosphere and crackling fire out of the
ordinary. He sat down on the sofa stretching his legs out in
front of him, looking very contented as he lit a cigarette, then
offered her one which she declined.

"Great room." He smiled at her as she sat down beside him
on the sofa.

She felt she was transparently conveying her desires with
every move and gesture. Sitting beside him had to state her
intentions, her availability, and she wanted to stop everything,
just stop; go back upstairs to her bedroom and put on a less
accessible dress, then come down again and sit in her favorite
chair by the fire. She wasn't being real. None of this felt real.
It had a staged flavor to it and she couldn't help feeling she'd
overdone everything from the candles to her own expectations.
She took a sip of her drink, surprised to find the taste agreeable,
saying, "This is very good! Really, it is!"

"Rum's nice for a change," he said, turning slightly in order
to look at her while they talked. Tonight, he thought, she
actually looked more beautiful than ever before, with an excited
look to her eyes and a bright flush of color in her cheeks. He
breathed in her perfume, pleasantly stirred by the look and

smell and sound of her, taking his time to appreciate the length of her legs and the whiteness of her skin in contrast to the black dress. He very much liked the dress, too, and had a sudden powerful desire to slip his hand down the neckline and feel her breast against the palm of his hand. He hadn't expected to feel quite as he did, but the firelight and the candles and her perfume had achieved what she'd hoped they would and his senses were pleasantly sharpened.

"So," he said, taking her hand and smiling at her, "tell me what you've been doing for the last five years."

She laughed, telling herself to calm down, get in control. "Really, very little," she said, glad at least her voice was steady. "I'd love to hear about your screenplays. And your novel. Where can I buy it? I'd love to read it."

"I'm not so sure about that. But I'll give you a copy. Even autograph it if you like. I'm working on a new one now. It's coming out a little more cohesively. I'm finding the more I write, the easier it becomes to get it all down the way I want it. Hell," he said, squeezing her hand, "I don't want to talk about that. It feels like that's all I ever talk about. Do you know how glad I am to be here, to see you?"

"Are you?" She took another longer drink of the rum.

"It probably sounds like a line," he said, releasing her hand to retrieve his cigarette from the ashtray, "but I've been thinking about you the last few days. I thought a lot about you after what happened."

"You did?"

"I thought about calling. I wanted to. But I think the truth is I was too much of a coward, or too embarrassed or something. But," his expression was suddenly very serious, "I felt bad as hell about what happened that night. I want you to know that. I just didn't know what to do. But I didn't simply walk away and never think about it again. I thought about it for what felt like every hour, every day for months."

"It doesn't matter now," she said. "Let's forget it." Actually, when she thought about that night, remembering what she could of it, she derived a satisfying twinge from the memory. It had long since lost whatever unpleasant overtones it had once held. She took another sip. The drink was very mild, going down easily. She hadn't eaten, except for a piece of toast in the

afternoon, so she felt the effects of the rum almost immediately.
She drained the glass and set it down on the coffee table. He
was holding her hand again, staring into the fire. She looked
down at their two hands, then at his knees, his legs, his groin.
It seemed strange that he was here, that the two of them were
together. She had a sudden impulse to talk about love, about
feelings, and pushed the impulse away, then brought it back
to inspect it more closely, wondering if he mightn't like to hear
about how she thought she'd fallen in love with him. Ridiculous.

He turned, noticing her eyes had gone distant, preoccupied.

"What're you thinking?" he asked, tugging gently at her
hand. "You're away off out there somewhere."

She turned her head slowly, wetting her lips as she tried to
think of what to say. The sight of his face mystified and elated
her to such a degree she couldn't say anything for several
seconds. She examined his features carefully, deciding a lot
of women might not find him attractive, but she did. Oh, yes,
she did. She could see all sorts of qualities in his face, good,
appealing qualities. The shape of his mouth was very nice. She
watched the way he drank from his glass and liked the way he
did that, too, and the freshly shaven pinkness of his cheeks,
the amused curiosity in his clear gray eyes.

"I've always thought I'd be famous," she said. Hearing
herself, she decided she was speaking primarily for her own
benefit, actually to hear herself air these thoughts. "Always,"
she said, her eyes on his. "No matter what happened, I'd tell
myself it didn't matter because I was going to get what I wanted
someday." She stopped, wondering if he'd think she was crazy.

"Go on," he encouraged, his hand still closed around hers.

"Yes," she said, again wetting her lips. "It sounds crazy, I
think. It must, telling it to someone else. I don't know. It's
just the way I've felt. Different. Not the same as other people.
Knowing there's something I can do that other people can't.
But I haven't been able to settle down to it, get started doing
it. I had a feeling the other night, when we talked."

"What feeling?"

"It's hard to describe. When we started talking, I suddenly
felt as if I've been living all these years with a kind of—
identity, another person who's really me but who hasn't come

out of me yet. I sound crazy." She smiled, flustered and embarrassed.

"No, not at all." He shook his head. "Finish. Tell me."

"I don't know. I've always tried to think about how I want things to be, off there, in the future somewhere. Talking to you, I realized I haven't ever really done very much thinking about how I want things to be right now. *Now*. Not how I'd like it to be *if*. I've always done that. *If* I had this, *if* I did that. You know?" She paused. He nodded. She went on. "When I was a little girl, it seemed as if my mother one day just stopped loving me. I could amost feel her going away from me. And I wanted her back, wanted things to be the way they'd been before. I loved her so much, she was so beautiful to me and it felt terrible not being able to be with her in the same way. I'd sit downstairs in the living room and think, If I do this, or if I do that, maybe she'll start to love me again. I think that perhaps I was so concerned with all the 'ifs' I stopped being aware that she did love me. It was just that I wasn't the only one. There were the others . . . There's that," she said. "And how I am. I don't know how I am. It gave me the strangest feeling thinking about that. After dinner the other night, I came home and I couldn't stop thinking about it; thinking that if I didn't become involved . . . if I didn't start *using* my feelings I might end up old and bitter, not *ever* knowing about myself, who I am, what I am. Because I'd never really cared about anyone, been in love. It sounds so . . . But once I started thinking along that line, I simply couldn't stop. Now, I have this feeling that if I could just have a chance to stand still, to just *be*, then I'll be able to find out about me. And once I do that, everything else will come. I'm sure that's it. If I don't know me, how can I know what it is I'm to do?"

"Painting?" he asked. "Is that what you want to do?"

She shook her head. "I don't know. When I start a piece, I get very involved, very emotionally involved. I'll work hours, all night at something. I'm in love with the form, the colors, the shadows and shadings and blendings, one color into another. All of it. It's so emotional. Every line, every stroke, every little bit of color, it all *means* something. When I'm working, I know it's right, it's good, that what I'm doing is extraordinary, the best. I finish and feel fantastically satisfied.

"Then, the next day or the next week, I go to look at what I've done and it looks all wrong to me. And I begin to feel terrible, awful. The perspective is wrong. Or other people could do far, far better and it isn't at all as wonderfully unique as I'd thought. Then I feel so doubtful, about myself, everything. No," she said, thinking hard about it. "I don't think it could be painting. I don't know. I just do *not* know. I've wanted to write," she admitted, returning her eyes to his.

Christ! he thought, hoping to hell she wasn't going to spring a bagful of her efforts on him for his approval. He hated that. Tell people you're a writer and they've either got the greatest story of all time for you or they've written something and maybe you could help them get it published. Please, he thought, don't ask me to read something you've written.

"Have you written anything?" he asked, braving it out.

"No." She shook her head again, the gesture unexpectedly touching. "I've only thought about it."

"How about a refill?" he suggested, finishing the last of his drink.

"Thank you," she said, turning to look at her empty glass sitting on the coffee table, feeling herself coming down. She'd said too much and all the wrong things. He got up, picked up both glasses, walked around the coffee table, stopped, stood looking at her, then bent down and kissed her on the mouth. She returned the kiss, enjoying the coolness of his mouth, the taste of lime on his tongue. He kissed as nicely as she'd thought he would and she opened her eyes as he set the two glasses down on the coffee table, dropped down on his knees in front of her, wrapped his arms around her and kissed her again, sweetly but with intensity, so that she felt ignited and pressed her palms to the sides of his face as she closed her eyes again and tasted the warm interior of his mouth, sparred tongue to tongue, dizzily, slowly falling back with him. It was so beautifully romantic. Music emanated quietly, discreetly from the speakers in the corners; there was the scent of wax and perfume, his aftershave, woodsmoke. She'd created the mood, the setting, lured him into wanting her. Everything was going just as she'd pictured it.

Their mouths separated and he pressed his head against her breast, listening to the accelerated beating of her heart, feeling satisfied, deeply delighted and moved by her. She was different, completely unlike other women he'd known, naive in the nicest way and gentle. There was nothing grating or harsh about her. And when she'd talked about being a little girl, he'd been able to see her—actually had seen her once when the family came down to visit Dana at the school. But the memory was fuzzy, indistinct, an image of a long-legged little girl in a very short dress. He sighed, enjoying holding her slight body against him for a minute before releasing her with a smile, saying, "I'd better get those drinks."

His face was flushed too, she saw. "I'm hungry," she said, not wanting it all to happen too quickly, anxious to enjoy the evening and a dinner out; anxious to savor being in his presence before it came time to show themselves; before it came time to find out if they would fit together.

"What are you in the mood for?" he asked, crouched in front of her, his smile captivating.

"Anything at all."

"Okay," he said. "Anything coming up. I hate to break the spell but could I borrow your men's room?"

"Top of the stairs," she laughed.

He stood and went out of the room, up the stairs. She moved to pick up the two glasses, then decided against it and continued to sit where she was until she felt cooler, less feverish. Then she placed the firescreen in front of the fire and stood waiting for him to come back, smiling to herself, thinking, I like you. I love you. You could make me me if you wanted to love me.

She decided, standing there, that the reason she hadn't yet been able to make any inroads to her success was that she'd never been in love, never really loved. If she could fall, begin caring, she'd be completing herself and therefore she'd be able to exercise the full range of her capabilities and potential. And she wanted very much to know the feeling, too, how it was to *be* in love.

Cassy had said she'd make dinner. "But prepare yourself, darling. It's a borrowed flat and absolutely hideous. I'll do my best with bits and bobs and lighting, but you must promise you'll not be bothered."

"I'm not going to be bothered. I know I'm an awful snob.
But I am not *that* bad. Am I?"

"You're not bad at all," she said. "In fact—and I'm sure I
shouldn't tell you this—you're quite wonderful. Come at six.
We'll make it a long, lazy evening."

He didn't know what to do with himself. He'd never lived
with so much bursting energy, such high-wire elation. He wanted
to go in sixteen directions at once, feeling as if parts of him
actually were charging off in different directions; leaving him
with a decidedly scattered sensation. But he was happy, eu-
phoric, and hungry for more of her, more, as much as he could
get of her body, her voice, her memories; all of her, any of
her. Being separated from her for a day, a night was almost
more than he could bear. But he bore it and worked with a
fury in order to get through time until he could be with her,
see her and touch her again.

She came to the door barefoot with her hair down, in a
long, pale pink dress, with a string of pink glass beads around
her neck. He laughed and threw his arms around her and held
her, happy.

"It feels like months between visits," he said, his hands in
her hair, tipping her head back to look at her. "Months, years!"

"We've seen each other every night for a week." She smiled
up at him. "Surely that's enough for anyone."

No, it's not! It's not enough! I want you around all the time
where I can see you.

"At least come inside and let me shut the door," she laughed,
disengaging herself as he walked into the living room, looking
around visibly dismayed.

"You're right," he said. "It's hideous."

"A drink, darling?" she asked from the doorway, looking
amused.

"No, listen!" he said, going over to her, taking her by the
hand and sitting down with her on the decrepit sofa. "Come
stay at the house! Work in one of the bedrooms. You can't
live in a place like this."

Her smile faded. *"You* listen," she said, her voice quiet in
the aftermath of his exuberance. "I will not move in on you,
Dana. It isn't the way I do things. Not because I wouldn't like
to, because I would, very much. I can't help feeling you've

had far too many people leap at your generous invitations, too many who've availed themselves of you and your generosity and then gone on their way. Isn't that the truth?"

"It is," he said, brought down to earth. "That's the truth. But this is different."

"No," she said. "It's different because I insist that it be different. I will spend every night with you if it's what you want. All night, every night. But every morning, I must be here. How do I explain this to you?" She looked past him, then returned her eyes to his face. "When it's really right, when it's a certainty and not simply the elation of the moment, ask me again. I do wish to be asked, Dana. But only when you're quite, quite certain, all your thoughts very clear, your needs all decided. I think you'd despise me in short order, darling, if I joyfully came taxiing over bag and baggage. I rather suspect I'd despise myself. You do know what I'm saying, don't you?"

"You're telling me to break the pattern. I know. I know."

"That is precisely what I'm telling you. I am not someone who will quietly acquiesce to your whims of the moment. I don't dare. There's too much at stake here, too much emotional content."

"All right," he sighed. "You're right. I hate it, but you're right."

"Don't be brought down," she said softly. "Just sitting here on your lap has almost succeeded in making me lose my train of thought altogether."

"Is that true?" He brightened.

"Oh, yes," she smiled. "You may see for yourself."

He slipped his hand up under her dress, then closed his eyes for a moment. Opening them, he whispered, "My God, Cassy! You'll stay with me nights?"

"I will stay with you nights. But I will not leave anything belonging to me in your house."

"All right, all right. Whatever you say."

"It isn't a game, darling. Not a game at all. This is for you. So you can know and be very sure what it is you want."

Jack took Glenn to an Italian restaurant and they sat on opposite sides in an old-fashioned booth. "Are you cold?" he asked, noticing her shiver once, as if stricken by a brief tremor.

"A little. I should've worn my boots. My feet got wet."

"Take off your shoes," he said with a wicked-looking smile. "Then give me your feet."

She looked at him wide-eyed but did as he suggested and experienced a stunning shock of pleasure as she felt his warm hands direct her feet up onto the banquette and between his thighs. They smiled at each other like conspirators as he ordered two rum and tonics from the waiter. Then he leaned toward her across the table, took hold of both her hands and chafed them.

"Warmer now?" he asked, enjoying her wide-eyed reaction. For a moment he was seeing the little girl in her. Then the little girl was gone and she was very much grown up and lovely to look at.

She nodded, silenced by building anticipation. It was all going to happen and now that they were here in the restaurant to eat she didn't want to be eating. Yet she was very pleased to be out in a public place with him and took her eyes away from his to look around the restaurant at the other diners, thinking people had to know the two of them were together and happy. She was out with an attractive man. People had to notice. She felt, for a rare change, that she looked well put-together and was glad of her black dress and freshly done hair, the eyeshadow, mascara and rouge she'd ventured to use. She thought of the ludicrously expensive silk underwear—like the dress—she'd bought solely for this occasion, and wondered if he were somone who noticed things like that and appreciated them.

"Do you like to dance?" she asked.

"I'm probably the world's worst dancer," he said. "But if you want to go dancing, I'll take you."

"No, no," she said quickly, unwilling to believe he could be bad at anything. He'd do everything splendidly, beautifully. She knew that, knew it. "I was just curious. I don't really know anything about you."

"You'll find out," he said, shocking her yet again with pleasure because he was making an oblique reference to the future and including her in it.

"Will I?" she asked, suddenly coquettish in keeping with

the mood and the fresh rum drink spreading fire through her mid-region.

"Let's order," he said, accepting a menu from the waiter, undergoing another change of facial expression.

She read the menu over and over, unable to think about food, thinking of how he'd kissed her, then held her with his face pressed to her breast. His doing that had made her feel somehow protective of him, capable of offering him comfort. She closed her eyes behind the cover of the menu, for a moment seeing him removing her from her front-buttoned dress, complimenting her on her silk chemise as his hands replaced the silk, his mouth...

She ordered, then promptly forgot what she'd ordered, utterly distracted by the placement of her now overly warm feet resting between his thighs. It was such an intimate thing for him to have done. She felt distraught, halfway suspicious of their evidently mutual willingness to pitch themselves headlong into this romance.

The waiter left with their orders and Jack's hand slipped beneath the table and closed around her ankle, his thumb moving rhythmically up and down the side of her foot. His eyes were unreadable in the dull restaurant lighting.

"How do you want it to be?" he asked.

"What?"

"Your famous future," he smiled. "How do you see it?"

"Oh!" She relaxed against the back of the booth feeling wonderfully secure, held down by his hand circling her ankle, her feet pressing into his groin. "It's a little vague," she said dreamily. "But a great deal of money and people behaving a certain way. Deferential, I suppose. My fame preceding me, that sort of thing. I'm not really sure." She laughed. "Prestige. It's a fairy tale."

"No, it isn't. I can see you there."

"You can, Jack?"

"When you started talking about it before I could see it. There's something about you." He tilted his head slightly as if to gain a better perspective. "You're going to do something. I can feel it. Maybe," he said cautiously, some instinct telling him it just might be so, "you're going to write. Just, please, don't ever ask me to read anything you do write."

"Why not?"

"First of all," he said, "I'm a lousy critic of my friends' work. And secondly," he smiled, "it'd probably be good and I'd be jealous."

"Why do you say that?" she asked, starting to withdraw her feet.

"Don't do that," he said softly, holding her feet where they were. "It feels good. I say it because I have a hunch you could do all kinds of things if you set your mind to it, and do them well. Nobody likes that kind of competition. Or maybe it's just that I don't."

"But even if I did write, would I be competing with you? We're different people. We'd be writing different things. Even if we wrote about the same things, we wouldn't write them in the same way. *Because* we're different. So how could I be competing with you? Or anyone?"

"You probably wouldn't be," he said reasonably. "But I'd probably still be jealous. Maybe I wouldn't. I'm trying to be honest with you, Glenn. It's not something I've had all that much practice at: being honest. But I owe you that much."

"You don't owe me anything."

"You're wrong," he said. "I owe us both. I should've come back and to hell with being scared of making more of a fool of myself than I'd already done. I wasted five years. Of both our lives."

She opened her mouth, then closed it again, shook her head as if to clear it, then picked up her glass and drank half her drink in one swallow. He was making declarations. She was becoming a little frightened of what she'd started. None of this had been part of any of the dreams. Why were the dreams never the same as reality?

"I'm not going to . . . Don't get scared," he said even more softly. "We'll have dinner. Then we'll go home and go to bed."

Her insides were jolted. She stared at him, astounded at his putting into words his plans for the remainder of the evening. A dissolving sensation had been created inside her upon hearing him say, Go to bed. At least in this one instance she needn't fantasize, drumming up romantic images. He'd just promised to make this particular fantasy real.

* * *

"Tell me about you, your family. Where were you born?"

"In London."

*"Tell* me," Dana smiled, lifting the hair back over her shoulder. "I want to know. And I like the sound of your voice."

"I was born in Queen Charlotte Hospital in London," Cassy said. "My father was a barrister, my mother was a barrister. They were both terribly bright, terribly rich, terribly boring. Deadly boring. God forgive me, obnoxiously boring! I couldn't abide their endless conversations having to do with the bloody, involuted, convoluting, pettifogging niceties of their boring, bloody cases. Nice, bright, boring mummy and daddy. I have an older sister and a younger sister. My older sister is a living replica of my mother. My younger sister, thank God, is a rebel. She and I are very close, always have been. I had an aunt who was not boring. My father's sister, actually. And I think she took pity on me. Whatever." She made an "it-doesn't-matter" gesture with her hand in the air. "In any event, she left me rather a large sum of money when she died. I was seventeen. The money came to me when I was eighteen. I left home, took a flat and began my art studies. Dana, this is so bloody *boring!*"

"No, it isn't! It's interesting. Go on!"

"There simply isn't much to it. I indulged in a wildly bohemian sort of existence—defying one's parents sort of thing— had any number of sexual encounters with any number of young men. All very standard defiance techniques. A great deal of hearty laughter with a bit of studying thrown in to illustrate my seriousness. Managed to pass in and out of the Royal College of Art and then found I hadn't any idea what to do with myself." She stopped and leaned across him for a cigarette, lit it, then lay back.

"My mother died," she said, her tone altogether altered. "She felt ill one evening after dinner, said she felt she must rest for a bit. My father rang me in London at two that morning to say would I come, please, something was terribly wrong. I went. By the time I arrived, she was dead. Actually she had been dead for the better part of an hour. She'd been dead when he rang me.

"Things changed quite drastically after that. Perhaps because it made me aware of how suddenly one could lose one's life.

Without warning. And my mother was only fifty-three when she died. It frightened me, sobered me up considerably. I decided it was time I took charge of my life, did something with it." She cleared her throat and turned her head to look at him. "So I did. I made a career. I married. Quite wisely, I thought. Very badly as it turned out. I was divorced. Then I was involved for quite some time with someone very nice. Dana, I'm not sure I should tell you this. I'm rather frightened of telling you this."

"Tell me. I want you to tell me. Anything."

"It was another woman," she said very quietly, watching the reaction affect his features. "You see, I know all about it. *All* about it."

"What happened?"

"I felt safe, you see, and convinced for a time that this was my natural milieu. I have quite a talent for self-justification, rationalization. The truth is I was frightened. Not of anything specifically, but of everything generally. And it *was* safe. So safe my work slowly began to grow stale. I began growing frighteningly lethargic. Until finally I arrived at a point where I was obliged to see that being safe sometimes means slowly dying. It wasn't love. It was safety, and compromise. I found I couldn't continue. So I extricated myself. All very painful and unpleasant, but it got done. For the last eight years I've worked very hard at me, at knowing me, my needs, my priorities. I know them now. It's why I know what needs doing here. Because I've *been* you, darling. And no one but you can decide your priorities, your needs."

"Are you bisexual?" he asked, a little shocked and unable to understand why.

"No. I never was. I simply ceased functioning for a time, lay back and allowed things to happen. It was so effortless, don't you see. So terribly easy. Infinitely easier than groping my way up through all the layers of me in order to find daylight and fresh air to breathe."

"My God!" he said, taking the cigarette from her, holding it to his mouth.

"You're shocked," she said, watching him closely. "Why are you shocked?"

"I don't know why. I shouldn't be."

"You're right, darling. You shouldn't be. Had I not had the experience, I doubt very much I'd understand you, understand the point you're at in your life. I think," she said incisively, "what shocks you is not so much that, for a time, I lived with another woman, as the idea that another woman made love to me. Isn't that the truth?"

"You're telling me I'm jealous," he said.

"Are you?" she countered.

"What happened between then and now?"

"Some men," she said openly. "Quite a lot initially. Very few in recent years. I told you. I felt rather desensitized. There was so little caring, you see. It's the caring that elevates everything beyond routine."

"You're saying you care about me?"

She laughed. "Of course I care about you! I thought I'd made that quite clear."

"Why do you care about me?" he asked, putting out the cigarette, then rolling over on his side, facing her.

"Why?" she smiled. "Because you're wonderfully built, wonderful to look at, extraordinarily talented. You're gentle and sensitive and generous. You're also rather bitchy at times and caustic and unintentionally hurtful. I care about you." She shrugged. "When I'm with you, I'm glad I am."

"Will you stay all night tonight?" he asked, letting his hand trail down across her hip.

"Yes."

"Will you stay for breakfast?"

She smiled and kissed him lightly on the mouth. "I think not. It's too soon."

"It's not a game?"

"You have my promise. It is *not* a game. I am caring for you in the very best way I know how. And the best way I know how is to allow you more room to move about in than you think you require just now."

Jack ordered second drinks before dinner. Then they had wine during, and brandy after. They were both high—she a good deal higher—by the time they arrived back at her house. Her nervousness had long since departed—left with the ice at the bottom of one of those empty glasses. She went with him upstairs to her bedroom. Here, too, were scented candles, music, perfumed sheets. It was all beautiful, perfect. He began unbuttoning her dress and she smiled thinking she'd been very clever about the dress. She kept on smiling as his hands traveled over her silk underwear-clad body, and he made pleased, complimentary sounds. She didn't feel so much involved as deeply gratified and laid her hand tenderly over the top of his head as he lowered the chemise to uncover her breasts and put his tongue to her nipple, his hand spread over her silk-covered buttocks, lifting her closer. For just a moment, her eyes closed, it was Mr. Hamilton and she felt a kind of despair seizing her by the throat. Then she opened her eyes and it was Jack. Everything was all right again.

His eyes were eager as he set her down on the bed, then removed his clothes, sighing as he came down on top of her finally, caressing her for quite some time through the silk before drawing her pants down over her hips, pushing the chemise up over her breasts, taking both away. She lifted her arms, her legs, like a child, helping.

She couldn't remember all that happened. She was too drunk. But she did remember finding herself lying reversed on top of him, her hand idly stroking the inside of his thigh as she lazily but greedily lapped at him like sweet candy she craved and his lips and tongue created a very nice heaviness, a languid pleasure that burned its way through her gradually. It seemed they lay this way for a very long time, playing each other like delightful, pliant toys until she was somehow underneath and he was on top of her, grinning into her mouth, whispering, "It's as if we've made love dozens of times before. We know each other so well." She smiled drunkenly, happily, taking hold of him to direct him into her, stiffening involuntarily as he pushed inward. He was big, capable of hurting her. He had hurt her once upon a time. She told herself to relax. You want him, relax! She did, and found herself suddenly willing to accommodate him, eager to have him deep and hard inside her, to soothe something empty that lived there. It was a feeling unlike any other she'd ever had. But he was whispering again, saying, "Sorry . . . sorry . . . too drunk . . ." And then they were both asleep.

She awakened just after three with a start, surprised to find him soundly asleep beside her, then glad of his being there. She looked at him for a while before easing out of bed and going into the bathroom to sit for ages, it seemed, her head pounding miserably. She tiptoed downstairs to the kitchen to stand leaning on her elbow on the counter beside the sink waiting for the two Alka-Seltzer tablets to begin fizzing. They wouldn't. She took a knife and tried breaking them up. One of the tablets wasn't a tablet at all but the foam disk from inside the bottle. She lifted it out of the water, threw it into the sink, took up the knife and tried once more to break the other tablet. The pieces refused to fizz. She drank the water, leaving the still-solid chunks of Alka Seltzer sitting on the bottom of the glass. She rinsed the glass, refilled it with water, took four aspirin tablets, drank the water, then returned upstairs to crawl into bed beside Jack, curving herself against his warmth, feeling tearful, grateful. She hugged herself closer to him before plunging once more into a heavy, dreamless sleep.

He awakened just past seven with a painful erection and a terrific need to take a leak. He got up, went to the bathroom, then went downstairs and, on his way to the kitchen, stopped off to extinguish the burnt-down candles in the living room, collect up their glasses from the night before, switch off the outside lights and then get her automatic percolator going in the kitchen. He rinsed his mouth at the sink, checked the refrigerator to see what he could cook up for breakfast later on, then went back upstairs to lie there watching her, telling himself to let her sleep. Watching, he derived so much satisfaction from being there with her, enchanted by her sleep-flushed cheeks, her long, narrow body and small, round breasts, her delicate profile.

He heard an echo of his own voice, years before, saying, I could love a girl like you, and smiled, thinking, I *could* love you.

She came awake with her heart pounding, her hips rolling with a life entirely their own as his head moved between her thighs and his tongue drove into her, over her, all around, decimating pleasure. She didn't care about anything, anything at all. Vaguely she remembered nothing really significant had happened the night before as she spread her legs more, covered his ears with her hands and moaned, her eyes frantically raking the ceiling as he abruptly stopped, climbed up over her avid-eyed and determined and slid effortlessly, solidly deep inside of her.

Ignoring her own faintly salty taste on his mouth, she returned his hard, probing kisses, her legs straining down as her hips lifted into his rhythm, blindly arching to take him harder, deeper, whispering, "I can't feel you as much as I need to feel you. I'm so close. I need to feel more."

He grabbed a pillow, thrust it under the small of her back, then returned his mouth to hers as his hands went under her, over her buttocks, raising her more, holding her secure, as piston-like he shot in and out of her. She felt her eyes rolling back, closing. He was forcing her up to him, forcing her into him out of herself. Her fingers sank into the flesh of his back as she moaned again, her breath catching in her throat; her body held weightlessly locked to him as he sent her leaping into a cataclysmic orgasm that removed her from herself, from him, from reality. Don't let it end! she prayed. Don't! He held her harder still, driving, driving; keeping her convulsed until he tore his mouth from hers, buried his face in her shoulder and shuddered violently, crying out jaggedly into her ear, "Glenn!" and again, *Glenn!*" and finally, "My God, God! *Beautiful!*" as his hands came up, his arms encircled her; gasping into the curve of her shoulder, "You're good, so good. God, Glenn, you're so *good!*"

Exhausted, she sank—once more weighted—deep into the mattress, his body molded to hers, both of them damp, panting.

"Stay," she sighed, her eyes dropping closed. "Don't go home."

She shivered once, very violently, then descended again into sleep.

# Sixteen

In the beginning, they were wild with each other; meeting constantly to fall upon each other in a frenzy of lust, throwing off their clothes to make love there and then—wherever they happened to be when the fit overtook them. Jack sat her on the counter in her kitchen and sucked at her until she was pulling the hair out of his head, then with a manic laugh, he lifted her, shoved everything off the kitchen table, laid her down and made love to her there amid the salt and sugar spills; turning her over afterward to lick off the grains of salt and sugar.

They made love standing up in the shower at his wonderful apartment. Walls had been knocked down. A great expanse of openness, it overlooked the lake; there were dozens of enormous plants, sandy-colored carpeting, track-lighting, glass and chrome tables, deep down sofa and chairs. Wonderful. Once they did it right inside his front door, on the sandy carpeting. She didn't understand what was happening to her, had to believe it was love, she was in love. She couldn't leave him alone, couldn't bear to be apart from him.

One night as he was driving them out to dinner, she lowered

her head to his lap, exciting him to such a degree he had to pull over and stop the car, anxiously surveying the street for observers, until she'd finished and was sitting grinning at him as she wiped her mouth with his handkerchief. Anywhere. Except in-plain-view public places. But beyond this, she found herself unable to draw any limits. All she could think of day and night was him, his mouth, his hands, his thighs, his body joined to hers in some way; his arms holding her, his voice whispering in her ear. She'd think of him and tremble, instantly wet, distracted. She walked around in a state of arousal, always rawly sensitized from the session before.

He'd say he was going home to work. He'd leave, telephone two hours later to say, "I'm not doing one worthwhile god-damned thing. Will you come here or do you want me to come back?"

"I'll come to you." She'd go flying to him wearing as little as possible, to pounce upon him the minute his door opened; obsessed, starved. He taught her every variation he could conceive of, turning her sideways, backward, nearly upside-down; penetrating as much of her as he possibly could, but carefully, cautiously, fearful of hurting her.

The sound of his voice could turn her limp-legged. He could say something like, "I like to watch you when you come," and she would. His laughter was erotic. She'd lie awake listening for the sound of his breathing in the night, terrified he might have stopped. And she said, "I love you," to which he responded, "I love you, too."

They went in the spring, with Dana and Cassy, to a sea-food restaurant at the foot of a pier on the lake. They drank and ate and laughed and drank some more. As the four of them were walking back up the pier to the car, Glenn raised her arms and danced, turning, turning, her laughter drifting out over the water.

Cassy clutched Dana's hand, alarmed, yet entranced, whispering, "Look at her! Do you see?" Dana whispered back, "My God! She's exquisite." "She's out of control, Dana." She said nothing more, but her hand was very hard around his and Dana felt the message rather than saw or heard it. All he could see was his sister's exceptional grace, her exquisite beauty in the moonlight.

Jack leaned against the pier railing and watched her, smiling; watched her move, graceful; he felt so happy with the soft air and the sea-salt smell and the sight of her hair lifting, drifting as she turned, moving closer, oblivious to everything, everyone but Jack. Coming to rest against him finally, she looked into his eyes with sudden cascading emotion, whispering, "Jack, you make me happy." Tears slid down her cheeks, the taste of them salted raindrops. "Jack, I love you. Do you love me? Do you? Tell me that you love me, Jack." Before he could answer she was gone, turning, swaying, making music for the dance. He thought she was too beautiful.

Cassy turned inside Dana's arm, dropped her head on his shoulder and cried silently.

"What is it?" Dana whispered, bewildered by all of this.

"I love your sister," she whispered back, choked. "And no one seems to see what I see."

"What do you see, for God's sake? Please, don't do that."

"You must see it for yourself. Let me go, darling. I'll get her."

The two men stood side by side leaning on the railing, watching as Cassy went walking down the pier, the skirt of her dress billowing in the light breeze, strands of her hair coming free, blowing about her face. She walked slowly toward Glenn thinking, Little sister. Everyone's little sister. Always there, so they never see. She took hold of Glenn's hand, bringing her to a stop. Glenn's eyes grew round, tears streaming down her cheek. She floated close to Cassy, whispering, "I'm happy for my brother. He has you. Do you love him? I love him. Dana can be so kind when he wants to be. Kind. I want to hold you, hold everyone. Hold everyone. Hold me?"

I can't tell you, Cassy thought, holding her. They won't see. What will happen to you?

"Do you love him?" Glenn asked, touching Cassy's face, holding her. "You're making him so happy. Your face, Cassy. Who are you, Cassy? Who am I?"

"I'll help you if you'll let me," Cassy said softly. "I care because of you, not because of Dana. Someone must." I'm starting to talk like her, she thought, aware of Glenn's tremendous potency and moved by the wondering expression on Glenn's face as her investigating fingers traced across her face.

"I'd like to paint you," Glenn said. "Your face. You're so soft, Cassy. Soft here." She touched Cassy's breasts, then cried out. "You feel like my mama. I miss her!"

"You're drunk, Glenn," Cassy whispered. "You're so drunk."

"I know." Glenn's head bobbed, nodding. "I know, I know, I know. You feel soft like mama. She killed herself I know she did threw herself in front of a car because we couldn't love her back killed herself it was my fault our fault I never wanted her to die never."

Cassy shuddered, her arms closing hard around Glenn, whispering, "You love everyone too much, too much. It's time to go home, Glenn. Come with me. We'll take you home."

"Do you love me?" Glenn asked, raising her eyes to Cassy's beseechingly. "Do you love me? Did she love me?"

"We all love you. All of us. Why do you torture yourself? We love you. I love you. Jack loves you. You're lovable, darling. You're so bloody lovable. Let us take you home now. You're tired and you've had much too much to drink."

"I know," Glenn whispered, sagging suddenly, resting against Cassy, holding on. "I love *you*, Cassy. You make my brother happy. You make me happy."

Dawn said, "Glenn seems kind of too busy for babysitting lately." She smiled, mussing Corey's hair.

"She never says no if we ask her."

"I know that. But I really don't like to ask her. I mean, I know she would and I know she's crazy about Zane. It's just that she and Jack are so wrapped up in each other. I get this big guilty feeling even thinking about asking her to do something that doesn't include him."

"Is there something you're trying to tell me that I'm not getting?" he asked, putting aside his papers for a moment.

"Not really, Corey. It's just that sometimes I get this feeling about her. It's hard to describe. Just a feeling, that's all. Have you ever noticed how much she drinks?"

"She drinks," he said. "I know it."

"Corey, I think she's got a problem."

"You want to talk to her about it," he guessed.

"Do you think I should?"

"If *you* think you should."

"You're not going to get involved?" she asked quietly.

"Dawn, I can't say or do something that's going to hurt her. No matter *what* I think. But that doesn't mean you can't talk to her. It's just that *I* can't."

"You're a good person, Corey. You really are. Tell me what you think I should do."

"I think you have to do whatever you make up your mind to do. You always do. It's why I love you."

"Maybe we'll have them over, test the ground."

"Okay. I was going to do it anyway. I'm ready to do some serious talking, with both of them. Just one thing," he said.

"What?"

"Go easy. If you do decide you're going to say something, take it very, very easy."

"Oh, Corey! You know I would. I'm crazy about her. I'd *never* hurt Glenn."


"What I'm going to do," Corey told Jack and Glenn, smiling happily at Dawn before letting his eyes fix on Glenn's, "I'm going to create a five-in-one restaurant. In the new shopping mall they're building out at Forkwoods. It has to be a mall setup to work. That's why Forkwoods is going to be so perfect. There'll be five separate booths in a semicircle. Each one franchised from me. Kosher deli, Chinese, Italian, fish and chips, and Greek. Tables and chairs out in the middle. You decide what you're going to have, go to whichever counter you want, pick up your food and eat it at the tables. I'm going to call it the International Eatery. And if this one works the way I know it will, we've already got plans going for four other malls that'll be under construction starting next year. I pay for the space, the architect, the equipment. All of it. Then, each guy comes along and buys the franchise and the recipes from me for one of the booths. What d'you think?"

"I always knew you'd wind up a millionaire," Glenn said. "That's a wonderful idea."

"Not an *idea*," he corrected her. "It's more than halfway there."

"Seventeen," she said wistfully, "and more than halfway to your first million."

"He's going to put the income right back into the corporation," Dawn added, "to finance the other restaurants."

"We'll have dozens of them," he said. "Just one in every fourth indoor shopping mall and we've got a good fifty Eaterys nationwide."

"I think I might be interested in putting some money up for that," Jack said thoughtfully.

"I was hoping you would. I'd like to get together with you, take some time and really lay everything out, show it to you on paper. So far, everything I've raised has been on loan with my trusts as collateral. But I'd really like to get somebody I can trust to go into partnership with me in this."

"Let's do some talking about it," Jack said. "Maybe we both," he turned to look at Glenn questioningly, "would be interested."

"I'll give you my money," she told Jack. "The two of you make me a silent partner. What," she asked Corey, "will you do after you've done this?"

"Oh," he said, unruffled, "after that, we've got this idea for a boutique."

"What kind of boutique?" Jack asked, captivated more by Corey each time he talked with him, fascinated by the way his mind worked, and his limitless imagination.

"Dawn and I are going to run it together. She's going to prepare all-natural cosmetics, lotions, oils, that sort of thing. To order. She'll check your skin-type and make up stuff for you right there on the spot. Of course, we'll have a regular line of soaps and bath-oils, that kind of stuff, and eventually we'll probably get some distribution and franchising on that line too. It'll work like crazy. Everybody's going to get into natural stuff. We'll just get into it before it starts."

"You're too much," Glenn said, awed by their energy, their ambition; feeling guilty for the totally nonproductive state of her life at the moment.

"If you're interested," Dawn said, in her soft little-girl's voice, "we thought we'd ask you to design our logo and the packaging for our all-natural line."

"Just let me know when," Glenn promised. "I'd love to do it. I really must get to work, start doing something."

Dawn smiled at her, knowing it was the wrong place, the wrong time. But one of these times, she would.

* * *

"Dana, how do you feel?"

"About what?"

"About *me*," darling?" She felt on edge, very uncertain. She'd set down the rules and he seemed to have taken them far too literally. "I'm proposing," she said, "we make a declaration of feelings here."

He didn't say anything for a moment, but lay stroking her breasts, eternally entranced with her body.

"Are you afraid to say?" she asked gently, turning on her side to look at him. "Shall I be the one to say it?"

He closed his eyes briefly, then opened them. Her knowing, her understanding were constantly an amazement.

"I love you, Dana. I haven't any fear of committing myself. But now you have, haven't you, darling?" I gave you too much rope, she thought. Have I hanged myself with it?

"I'm not sure," he answered.

*Talk* to me! I'm not without sympathy, or doubts of my own, you know. It isn't a habit of mine to go about making conversions. I didn't even plan any of this, Dana. It simply happened. Had you not displayed the considerable interest you did, I'd have let it pass. But the way you looked at me that very first afternoon, I couldn't quite make myself believe it was an entirely hopeless situation. Now, I need to hear you tell me if we're to continue or you've some inclination to resume your former lifestyle."

"Why?" he asked, sensing she was about to tell him something very important.

"Because, darling, my work on the series is close to finished. I'm due to return home in another fortnight or so."

"And you want me to ask you to stay."

"I want you to ask me to come back. I haven't any choice in the matter of going. I must go back, for a few weeks at least. What are your *feelings*, Dana? I despise begging. I will not beg *anyone* for anything! If you're unable to declare yourself, I'll have to take it we've arrived at an impasse and I'll proceed accordingly."

"What would you do?"

She sighed and lay back, bending her arm over her forehead.

"You're testing me," she said wearily, feeling she was gam-

bling everything—perhaps too much—on having given him
sufficient growing and breathing space. "Dana, I'm almost
forty-two. You're not a child. You're already thirty-six, thirty-
seven soon. I cannot think or make your decisions for you. I
wouldn't, in any case. I've been on my own for a long, long
time. I expect I'll manage to continue along on my own. For
God's sake!" Her voice rose. She at once brought it back down.
"Can't you see, I'm in need of some *input?* I didn't think you'd
take everything quite so literally. But you have done. Perhaps
too literally. I'm trying to tell you I *want* to come back. I'm
willing to take the risk of starting fresh over here, breaking up
a very good career to start all over again. I am willing. If you
can't or won't say, that's it then." She reached for her cigarettes
and lit one. Her fingers were trembling. She wanted very much,
all at once, to get up and go back to her own flat. She'd made
mistakes, too many of them. She wanted to get up and go, but
was unable, unsure of just how to get up and go.

Dana noticed her hands trembling and felt scared. A voice
inside his head shouted, TELL HER! TELL HER! He opened
his mouth but no words would come out. Why? He couldn't
understand why. What was happening? As the silence began
to lengthen, she turned her head away; a tear slowly making
its way down the side of her face. It hurt him in the most
piercing way, seeing it. The hurt was somehow larger than the
fear, overpowering it. He reached out to catch the tear with
his fingers, brush it away; he took the jiggling cigarette from
between her fingers and dropped it into the ashtray.

"I want you to come back," he said, the words lacerating
his throat, like razor blades being pulled up out of his stomach.
"I love you, Cassy. Don't cry. I hate it. It hurts."

"Don't ever," she sobbed, "put me through anything like
this ever again! *Please!* It's the worst sort of deprivation, Dana;
withholding your thoughts and feelings. All the things I've
tried to tell you in the past months, the things I've tried to
make you see, it was all for you, because I've known so well
what you've needed. But you haven't made yourself aware of
my needs beyond the obviously sexual ones. I can live with a
great deal, but I cannot live with silence. Say anything, say
everything, but, please, please, don't make love to my body
and leave my mind out of it. My mind is very much present.

I'm too old for games-playing. If I'm willing to risk such a lot for you, the very least you can do for me is admit that you love me when I know—*I know!*—that you do."

"I do love you! I do!"

"Then *show* me, *tell* me!" This is no good, she thought. I *am* begging. I will not do this! I will speak my piece and go home, go away from you, I can't bear any more of this. "You can't be in love by yourself! It's something that must be shared. Must! I *love* you and it's frightening, so frightening. I'm terrified I'll commit myself to you and you'll one day see some young man who takes your fancy and I'll find myself left with nothing. I told you at the start I won't be part of a juggling act. If you want me, you want *me* and not half a dozen others. Evidently, you do not want me."

She jumped off the bed and began frantically gathering up her clothes, desperate to get out of there, away from him and away from this self of hers who could beg.

He got up and took hold of her arm, asking, "What are you doing? Where are you going?"

*"I will not beg!"* she cried. "No one. Not for anything. This . . . I won't!" She was holding herself stiffly away from him, her fists clenched. He put out his other hand to touch her face and she jerked away from him, looking agonized, crying, *"If you don't want me, let me go!"*

All these months, he thought. How long does it take to know? I know. I do know. He took hold of her by the upper arms, turning her forcibly.

She had no idea for a moment what she was doing. Everything had gone out of focus and she felt a fool, ridiculous, begging this man this younger man, this man! She threw out her arm and struck him. Her hand stung from the impact.

"God!" he whispered. "Don't do that!" He kept his hands fastened firmly around her upper arms and backed her toward the bed. "Don't do that, Cassy! Don't do any of this! I didn't see." He forced her down and held her still with his body.

"I want you," he said. "I'm going to go with you and bring you back, bring your things back here. We'll get married. I love you. There's never going to be anyone else I'll want or need, not as much as I want and need you here. I don't know what I am any more, Cassy. I don't know. But I do know you

have to be here. It's the *only* thing I know. Give me more time.
I need more time. But you have to be here with me."

She untensed all in a rush and closed her eyes, still shaking.
"You needn't marry me," she said. "All I need is that you
know what you want, and that you say so. Frequently. I need
to *hear* it. Do you understand?" She opened her eyes. "Dana,
no one of us is so secure we can live—not this way—without
knowing, hearing. I love you. I loved you the first time I saw
you. I'll love you next month, next year, twenty years from
now. I'll keep on loving you as long as you keep telling me
that I'm important to you, that you do care, do need me. You've
moved into my brain. I think of you every bloody minute of
the day. Don't you think I wanted to be here, that everything
in me wanted to say, Yes yes, when you said, 'Come stay at
the house?'" Her hands gripped his shoulders. "I gambled on
you, on your feelings. I've never really loved anyone but you,
Dana. But I will not, *will not* be a substitute for something
else you'd prefer to have but can't get. That's all, Dana. That's
all."

"I wasn't ever all that happy with the others," he said,
feeling as if he were slowly, steadily pulling the lid off the
storage area for all his emotions. "Except for Eric. But we
were so young. And there was so much idealism attached to
everything we said and did. When I'm with you, I know that
it's right and that it couldn't ever be any other way. So, we're
both going to go to England. And we're both going to come
back here. And we're getting married. Because you have to be
here."

"Yes, all right," she said softly. "All right. I'm terribly,
terribly sorry I struck you."

"Don't be. I think I deserved it. I've got to stop taking notes
and start involving myself in the dialogue. I love you, Cassy.
Nothing else matters."


Glenn and Jack went out a lot—on their own for dinner,
or to the homes of Jack's friends for an evening. They went
to parties, to movies, to the theater, or just out for drives.
Always, it seemed, they were on their way to somewhere. It
was a treat to stay in for an evening—either at his place or
hers—to eat quietly, have a few drinks, watch television, talk;

go to bed finally, a nightcap in bed, then—having managed to restrain themselves for four or five hours—go flying at each other. They frequently made love most of the night and slept well into the late morning, only to get up, eat something, and return to bed to make love some more.

Jack said, "I've never been so turned on, so all-the-time turned on for anyone in my life. And it's not just this," he said, caressing her between the thighs, "but *you*. If you're late, I go half crazy worrying something's happened to you."

She knew what he was saying. Under the words lay his proposal that they begin living together. She wanted to, but she wanted Jack to be the one to suggest the move. For months, he'd hint around the subject without ever directly suggesting it. She continued to hang on, waiting. And he kept thinking about it.

On one of the rare evenings when Corey was off somewhere promoting his business ventures and Jack had insisted that he simply had to stay in for an evening and do some work, Glenn accepted Dawn's invitation to come for dinner; she was taken aback when Dawn suddenly asked, "Are you happy, Glenn?"

"Happy?" Glenn couldn't think for a moment. "I don't know how to answer that."

"Are you happy?" Dawn persisted. "You always seem very high but high isn't the same as happy. I don't want to mix in or offend you or anything but I know Corey's kind of a little worried and so am I."

"About what?"

"Well, you drink kind of a lot," Dawn said, looking pained. "I sort of wonder sometimes if you know how much you drink."

Confounded, Glenn looked down at her drink on the table, then back at Dawn. "Do I?" she asked. "Do you think I do?"

"Listen," Dawn placed her hand over Glenn's. "Please, don't get upset, okay? I mean Corey really loves you. You're the only family he has, next to Dana, that he cares anything about. You've always been so good to him. And now, putting your money into the business. That means such a lot to him. And I'm not just talking about the money, either. That's a kind of faith that doesn't come with money. You're important to me, too. You've been good to us. I mean it. You're good to *everybody*. Sometimes, I can hardly believe you. I mean, when everybody else came at us screaming, warning Corey he was being taken, that I was just trying to get some kind of free ride for Zane and myself, you didn't. You came to have a look and decided for yourself what kind of thing it was Corey and I had going for us. I know you know that what we have is something real. I love him. He loves me. He takes care of me, I take care of him. My being four years older doesn't mean a thing, not anything. Not to him and not to me. Oh, at first it kind of threw me. I thought maybe he was trying to get his rocks off proving something, or like that. But an hour with Corey and anybody with half a brain knows he's not that kind of person. You know that, too. He's for real. Everything he says and does is real. Like with Zane. He's going to adopt Zane," she said thickly, "because he loves him. So," she cleared her throat and straightened her shoulders, "if I tell you Corey's kind of concerned about you and that I am too, because I love you, too, it's because maybe you do drink quite a lot of the hard stuff."

Glenn's throat was constricted with embarrassment and humiliation. They thought she was a drunk. "I'm not a drunk," she said hoarsely, again looking down at her glass.

"Oh, hey!" Dawn said, upset. "Nobody's saying you *are!* That's not it. Just that . . . Okay, like we buy a couple of bottles of gin every month. For you. Because we drink wine or beer, maybe some vodka once in a while for bloody marys. But . . . Oh, *shit!* Everything I'm saying now is making it worse. Look!" she took a deep breath. "All I wanted to say is we're concerned about you. We *care!* That's all. Please forget I brought up that business about the gin. We buy it because we want you to feel comfortable when you come here. I could kill myself for ever even mentioning it. I was trying to make a point and I shouldn't have said anything about it."

"I understand," Glenn lied, deeply hurt.

"No, it was tactless and awful and unkind," Dawn argued. "I'm sorry I said it. Please don't hate me for saying that."

"Oh, no," Glenn said. "I wouldn't."

She went home feeling blackly depressed, looked at the bamboo bar and purposely stayed away from it, thinking, I'm *not* a drunk. But, oh dear God! how humiliating! She felt so crushed she had to fix herself just one more drink to get a little lift, to make herself feel a bit better. And for once, she really didn't want to see Jack, didn't want to inflict her depression on him. Yet, when he telephoned just after eleven to say, "In the mood for company?" she couldn't say no.

He came to the house, let himself in with the key she'd given him after they'd been seeing each other six weeks, and stopped, to stand very still at the sight of her sitting on the sofa gazing off into space with a half-empty glass in her hand and only one candle lit for light.

"What's the matter, Glenn?" He sat down beside her on the sofa, draping his arm around her shoulders. "What is it?"

She had had, by this time, three more drinks to get herself picked up and had managed to forget altogether her original reason for being so depressed. She now focused instead on her nonproductive life and looked at him, a little bleary-eyed, saying, "Jack, I'm not *doing* anything."

"Fair enough," he said equably. *"Do* something!"

"Do you love me, Jack?" she asked him, carefully taking in his features, her forehead creased. *"Do* you?"

"Let me fix myself a drink and we'll talk about that, okay?"

"Sure," she said, her speech slurred. "We'll talk about that."

He fixed himself a scotch and water, taking his time, trying to think of reassuring things to say to her; trying to get to the bottom of his feelings. He asked himself, Do I love you? Christ, yes! I love you. But sometimes I have this feeling loving you will smother me. He picked up his glass and looked at her. It always surprised him how appealingly loose and easygoing she was after she'd had a few drinks, and how very beautiful she was, too. More beautiful—Isn't it funny? he thought, realizing this—than when cold sober. It had something to do with the way her hair fell less severely around her face and the way her features softened, and the way, the absolutely unbelievable way she'd make love to him after several drinks, or first thing in the morning. During the day it was never as good, never quite as—primitive. But after a couple of drinks, when she lost some of her doubtfulness and her smiles began to come more readily, he wanted to obliterate her with his lovemaking; he wanted to go on and on in that perfect state, riding until they were both crazed by the pleasure and fell into each other's arms exhausted, clinging.

Do I love you? There's never been anyone I could talk to

the way I talk to you; no one who's held me the way you do.
She held him with such gentle caring, lay with her arms around
him; the two of them talking quietly in the night and he felt
secure and loved as he never had, made important, too, by the
quality of their sharing.

He resumed his seat beside her on the sofa, set down his
glass, took hers from her and set it down, too; then turned her
around so they were facing, her hands cool inside his.

"I *love* you, Glenn. I do love you. All the women I write
now are turning into you. Nobody looks as beautiful to me as
you do. There's no one I want the way I want you. In every
way. If it's what you want, I'd like to move in here with you.
Would you want that?"

She nodded her head slowly, that puzzling expression still
on her face. "Dawn and Corey think I'm a drunk," she said,
chin quivering, eyes filling with tears. "I'm not a drunk, Jack.
It's just that I'm not doing anything. I've got to *do* something."

"Okay," he said, cradling her against his chest. "You'll do
something. Start back at your classes, for openers. Okay?"

"Okay." She sniffed, huddled against him.

"Then," he said, having long since moved past feeling
threatened by the idea, "why don't you give writing a try?
You've been talking about it for months and months. Sit down
now and try it on. I'll even give you my old portable electric
to work with. I don't need it now that I've got the new one."

"Okay," she said again, thinking about making love to him,
wanting to unzip his trousers, put her mouth on him. Just
thinking about it made her heart start thudding heavily.

"When, do you think?"

"When what?" she asked, rubbing her head along the inside
of his thigh. I love you, Jack. I love you so much. Am I sick,
loving you this much? Maybe I don't love you. Maybe I just
love this.

"Jesus!" he laughed, responding. *"Move in.* When?"

"Tonight, tomorrow, whenever you like. I...Jack... All
right?" She looked up at him questioningly as her fingers moved
over him.

In answer, he shifted to make them both more comfortable,
utterly unable to resist her.

He closed his eyes and stroked her hair, holding back because . . . he didn't know why. He held back and let her go on and on until she stood up, lurched, then laughed, pulled off her pants, threw them aside and then, changing her mind, took off all her clothes before climbing on to his lap. Lowering herself onto him, she shivered, then pressed herself naked against his jacketed chest. Slowly, shudderingly she commenced to lift and fall. Just as she was on the verge of orgasm, she thought of Dawn sitting at the kitchen table, saw Dawn's small saddened face and heard her soft, sorry voice. Then she heard a faraway voice inside her own head quietly denying everything, saying, It's not true, not true; she clutched Jack and came, sobbing.

She remained on his lap, reluctant to release him, keeping her vaginal muscles tensed around him as she lay against his chest with her arms wound around his neck. His hands hypnotically stroked up and down her back. Finally she whispered, "I love you so much, Jack. Go get your things and move in tonight. I can't sleep alone without you any more. I'm awake all night. I fall asleep in the morning and when I wake up, I've missed half the day. It makes me feel so awful, so scared. As if, for every morning I lose, I'm losing something from my life. Please get your things now and come back tonight."

"All right, baby," he agreed, suddenly scared too. He held her while she wept brokenheartedly. He simply couldn't understand why she was crying. But the quality of her anguish sounded alarms inside his head.

Clinging to Jack like a life-preserver, floating mid-ocean, she suddenly thought of Ralph and guiltily realized she'd never answered his last letter and wished she had, but knew she never would. She wished, perversely, she'd just done all this with Ralph. But no. Ralph was in France now. Tiger's eyes and lion's mane and laughing letters from Spain. I did love you, Ralph. I probably will never see you again. I want Jack to marry me. He'll want to marry me. I wonder where you are now, Ralph. Jack will marry me.

Cassy telephoned to say, "Dana and I are getting married. We would like you and Jack to be with us."

"Oh, Cassy." Glenn started to cry. "I'm so happy for the two of you. So happy. I would feel so proud to be there. When?"

"Glenn, darling, would you like to come talk? Are you all right?"

"I'm fine, Cassy. It's just that I'm really so happy for Dana and for you. I know you'll both . . . be . . . so happy together."

"I'm coming there," Cassy said. "Something's wrong."

"No! Don't come here! There's nothing wrong."

"Then come here! Come to the house!"

"Everything's all right, Cassy. Jack's working. I'm going to go in and tell him. He'll be so pleased."

"Are you drinking?" Cassy asked quietly.

"No, no. I took some medication. For cramps. Bad cramps."

"All right," Cassy said wearily, defeated. "Have a nap, darling. Get some rest. I'll ring you later, we'll talk."

"I'm happy for you, Cassy. I love you."

"I love you, darling." Cassy hung up and whispered, "Dear God!" then covered her mouth with her hand and stood for a long time staring at the wall, thinking a multiplicity of thoughts, many of them conflicting. Then she looked at her unopened trunks, the boxes of books, the crate of furniture and went to find the keys to the trunks.

Gaby, most surprisingly, offered to babysit Zane so that Dawn and Corey could attend the wedding.

"Tell Dana I wish him well," she said, when they dropped Zane off at the penthouse. "Tell him I'm sorry."

Corey, for the first time in twelve years, kissed his mother.

The ceremony took less than two minutes. Then the six of them went in Jack's car to Ginetta's for a celebration lunch. Glenn drank only one drink and sat throughout the meal looking at Cassy and then at Dana, then at Dawn and Corey, then back to Cassy, thinking, you're all so happy. You all look so very, very well. Why do I feel so old, so terribly tired, so removed? My brother, my nephew. Cassy, Dawn. She turned to look at Jack. My lover. The man who lives in my house with me, who tells me he loves me, whose body urges me into astonishing performances where I have nothing of my own but everything of yours that must be given to you. I have, in every conceivable place and in every conceivable fashion, opened myself to every part of you, and taken the greatest pleasure in the giving. You comfort me. You love and make love to me. Why can't I be happy: I want so much to be happy.

She again looked at the faces. I love you all. If I had another drink, I would begin to tell all of you how very much, how deeply I love you. I think Jack will marry me. Perhaps then I will be happy.

Jack, without quite knowing why, picked up her hand and kissed it, drawing her attention to him. She bent her head and rested her cheek against his hand.

Cassy looked across at Dawn, their eyes meeting.

They both got up.

In the ladies' room, Cassy said, "You spoke to her?"

"I tried."

"What happened?"

"I felt like a murderer," Dawn said.

"What can we do?" Cassy said. "Something has to be done!"

Dawn shook her head. "There's nothing to do. Nothing any of *us* can do."

"I fear for her," Cassy said, chilled.

"So do I. But she told us she's going back to the Art College and she wants to try writing. Maybe that will help."

"God! I hope so. I do hope so."

"Hey!" Dawn smiled. "Don't get all down! It's your wedding day. And it's terrific!"

Cassy smiled slowly. "This is a remarkable family," she said. "Quite, quite remarkable. You will bring Zane and come visit, won't you?"

"Absolutely! I think we'd better get back."

"Bless you, darling," Cassy embraced her. "You *do* see."

# Seventeen

There were any number of things Jack would do, but getting married did not seem to be one of those things. She couldn't bring herself to talk about it and now resorted to Jack's previous style of subtle and not-so-subtle hints, skirting the matter more closely at every pass. He wouldn't, though, talk about marriage and plainly wasn't considering it. His consistent refusal to rise to the bait she so frequently dangled created a small knot of resentment in her belly. She carried this knot with her everywhere, often unaware of it, more often unable to direct her awareness anywhere else.

Jack was what she'd always wanted but she couldn't get him to commit himself for good, and his failure to make this commitment made her less and less eager to have him at all.

Jack.

He was exceedingly tidy about his personal belongings and the house as well. He cooked far more often than she did, vacuumed oftener, too. He convinced her to donate several pieces of her older furniture to Corey and Dawn in order that he might move in some of his things. She minded, but didn't mind. His furniture was better than hers.

They did the grocery shopping together because both had favorite foods they wouldn't for some never-stated reason, allow the other to purchase on his/her behalf. Their life together daily felt more imperfect, stranger to Glenn. She wanted it to be somehow both more and less than it was—more communication of a different nature, less sex now that her system, after more than two years, had adapted at last to regular lovemaking. It seemed the fit had ended. She was no longer desperately driven to him out of a consuming need for his sexual ministrations.

She tried over and over to get started writing but couldn't sustain any one thought or idea long enough to get past page 3 or 4. So she now possessed an 8½ × 11 manila envelope which housed her several efforts, along with an itchy malaise that sent her pacing up and down the living room while Jack's typewriter clacked away hour after hour, day after day, producing two more screenplays and another novel. All of which he sold, for ever larger sums of money.

When he went off for a nine-city promotional tour for his novel that lasted fifteen days, she had the irrational feeling he'd gone off for good and wasn't ever going to come back. His nightly telephone calls did nothing to relieve her of this feeling and she grew desperate in every way as the length of his absence grew. She couldn't sleep without him in the bed, tried masturbating, only to doze off for a few minutes and then wake up, unable to get back to sleep. She'd have one drink, two, finally a third and then at last be able to sleep.

Cassy telephoned to say, "Have you eaten?"

"No. I haven't thought about it."

"I'm coming, bringing dinner with me. Dana's down at the station working late. Some problem with dialogue or some such thing. I'll be there directly."

She came to the house with a large pizza, saying, "I've developed a mania for these bloody things. Where shall we eat?"

Glenn looked around, saying, "Where would you like to eat?"

"In here, then," Cassy decided, setting the pizza down on the coffee table in the living room.

"I'll get some plates, napkins. What would you like to drink?"

"Something soft, if you have it, darling," Cassy said, tactfully staying well away from liquor.

"I've got some Coke. Okay?"

"Fine!"

Glenn ate half a wedge of pizza, then lost her appetite. She put the remainder of the wedge down on her plate and sat watching Cassy eat.

"It's so nice having you here." Glenn smiled at her.

"It's lovely to be here. I do love this house. It's so *you*, my darling."

"What is me?" Glenn asked. "What do you see is me?"

"I see *you*," Cassy said, wiping her fingers on a napkin. "You as you are, you as you could be. You as I hope you will be."

"And who are you, Cassy?"

"I?" Cassy smiled. "I am someone who cares for you, cares to be with you. You're lonely with Jack away."

"I have this awful feeling he's not going to come back."

"Of course he's coming back!" Cassy said firmly, thinking how almost pathetically thin Glenn looked. Thin arms and tiny breasts showing through the light shirt she was wearing. "Jack loves you very much. Why on earth would you think he'd not come back?"

"It's stupid, isn't it?" Glenn smiled again, less convincingly. "Jack likes to tell me I'm very naive. But he says it's one of the things he loves about me. Do you find me naive?"

"Only sometimes." Cassy slipped down off the sofa to sit on the floor beside her. "Wouldn't you like to tell me what's wrong, how you feel?"

"Oh, I would," Glenn said. "If I knew."

"All right, darling," Cassy said, putting her arm around her. "I know."

Glenn sighed, relaxing inside Cassy's arms, whispering, "I'd like a baby."

"Yes, I guessed." She stroked Glenn's hair, feeling Glenn unbending by degrees, until her head was resting on Cassy's breasts.

"I'm glad you came," Glenn said sleepily, feeling drugged by Cassy's warmth and softness. "I was so lonely."

"I know. I know."

The night Jack was due to arrive, she planned to be waiting for him at the house. But at the last minute she felt so anxious, so hungry for the sight of him she got out the car to drive to the airport, and crushed the right rear fender backing out of the garage. She got out to look at the damage, decided it wasn't enough to become upset about, and got back in to go pick Jack up at the airport.

His plane was four hours late. She checked with the ground attendant, confirmed this, then went to the bar to have a drink while she waited. She was glad she'd come. It would have been terrible sitting at home waiting, not knowing the plane had been delayed.

By the time the bartender woke her to say they were closing up, Jack's flight had landed, Jack had hopped into a taxi and gone home. She found it close to impossible to make sense of what the airline people were telling her but finally figured it out and called the house.

She was too drunk to drive, so she left the car at the airport and took a taxi home. Jack and the cabbie got her out of the cab and into the house and Jack took the airport limousine out to the airport the next morning to bring back her car.

"Somebody smashed in the fender," he told her, waking her up with a cup of coffee after returning from the airport.

"No, they didn't," she said dopily. "I did it, backing out of the garage."

"Next time," he said gently, "do me a favor. Don't try to drive the car when you've had a few. You might get hurt and I don't like the idea of anything happening to you."

She was on the verge of being offended but looked at his smiling mouth and fell back, bringing him with her, sighing, "Oh, Jack. I'm so glad you're home."

He was wonderfully generous with his money, surprising her with bracelets or scarves, silver rings from Mexico embedded with bits of turquoise, items of silk lingerie far more expensive than anything she'd have bought for herself. He arrived home with flowers, hand-dipped chocolates, champagne. He came through the front door carrying books, delicacies he'd picked up at one of Corey's two Eaterys, a pair of outsize crystal goblets into which he'd set white, gardenia-scented candles. Generous to a fault, she faulted him. She sat drinking gin, teaching herself how to smoke because it gave her an oddly powerful feeling as well as a singularly light-headed sensation she especially enjoyed. She sat, hearing the typewriter clacking, clacking; trying to nurse her petty grievances into a full-scale series of complaints. She couldn't. She'd face him with a mouthful of angry words, see the hurt taking shape on his face, swallow the words and embrace him instead; loving him terribly yet wishing he were something he was not.

She wasn't succeeding either with herself or her future as she'd hoped she would. She came to believe that she didn't love Jack nor communicate with him as completely or happily as she had with Ralph. She felt so sick with guilt, so disappointed with herself and with Jack, too, she felt she might die from the weight of all her unfulfilled longings. She sat and drank and smoked. And sometimes, when Jack was working night and day—the heat of fevered creativity hard upon him—she'd go to visit with Corey and Dawn, volunteering to take Zane to the Indian Hill zoo or for long, rambling walks or to puppet shows; every so often—making sure Zane was safe—nipping into a nearby bar for a fast drink. Zane, four years old, raced to meet her with outflung arms; filling her with gladness.

Of course, Dawn and Corey loved her. She could feel it in their eyes, their words, the way they spoke to her, gently, with deference, including her in their happiness and occasional problems. But Zane. His joy was pure, undiluted. She did want a child of her own. A child might, once and for all, satisfy and ease the monstrous knotting inside her.

Zane. A little boy like Zane. Or a little girl. Someone who'd be glad to see her in a way no one else would. She thought and thought about it. Watching Zane eat ice cream while she had a drink, she'd think about it, replacing Zane with a child of her own.

Jack said, "Are you serious, Glenn? Is that what you *really* want? Would a baby make you happy?"

"I think so. I want one so much."

"If it's what you want, then I want it too," he said with a smile that sent her into tearful laughter as she threw her arms around his neck, relieved. She was almost thirty-one and nowhere near any of the goals she'd set for herself. A child would be someone to love her unreservedly, the way Zane did.

She telephoned Cassy to say, "We are going to try for a baby." She sounded so well, Cassy said, "I am glad, darling. Perhaps that is the answer." Glenn had her first visit with a gynecologist since having the I.U.D. put in, and had it taken out, not in the least minding the examination, scarcely aware of the proceedings. What was a little discomfort? she told herself as the speculum expanded inside her. Nothing mattered. She and Jack would make a baby.

The two of them went back to making love again with their former cyclonic dedication. Conscientiously, she at once gave up her newly formed smoking habit and cut down sharply on her gin consumption. If she were going to get pregnant, she couldn't afford to drink too much. After the initial novelty of smoking had worn off, she hadn't liked it all that much anyway, so giving it up was no hardship. It was actually a relief, one of the most rewarding things she'd done for herself in years.

She felt so newly positive, so newly tolerant she began cooking dinner regularly each evening at seven. She spent at least three hours a day trying to get something down on paper via Jack's old Smith-Corona portable. She resisted the temptation to go straight out and start buying baby things, telling herself there'd be all kinds of time to do that once she was actually pregnant.

The world looked cleaner, shinier. Jack was handsome again, tremendously appealing. She felt very well.

"You look absolutely marvelous!" Cassy exclaimed over dinner at their house. "I've never seen you looking and sounding so well."

"I feel very good," Glenn admitted. "Very energized. I think I've finally got my idea for a book worked out."

"That's great!" Dana said, glancing across at Jack, seeing that Jack also reflected Glenn's present state of well-being. "Typewriters all over your house." He laughed.

After Glenn and Jack had gone home, Cassy said, "I do

hope this works for her. She deserves to be happy."

"Why do you feel so strongly about her?" Dana asked, having been curious and just a little doubtful about Cassy's passionate attachment to Glenn from the first.

"Dana, you're not jealous, surely."

"I don't think so. I don't feel particularly jealous. I'd just like to get a little more insight into why you feel the way you do about her."

"How can anyone explain why someone else is important? I can't do that, darling. I simply care. So do you, don't you?"

"I've always cared about Glenn, about what happens to her."

"Then it shouldn't be difficult for you to understand my feelings. Actually," she said, "if you really want to know the absolute truth, I feel very—motherly about Glenn, as if she were a child of mine."

"Did you ever think about having children of your own?" he asked.

"Of course I thought about it."

"Did you want them?"

"I did, yes. As it happens, everything's always come a bit too late in my life."

"Like me, for instance."

She smiled, got up and crossed the room to sit on his lap. "Like you, for instance," she laughed, pulling his ears. "Don't resent my affection for your sister, darling. It's something quite separate from you and me, and shockingly maternal on my part. Do you know what your sister told me? That night on the pier? You remember?"

"I remember."

"All in a rush, she started saying I felt like her mother, your mother. Touching me about the breasts, crying like a lost child, saying, 'She killed herself. Threw herself in front of an automobile.' Because none of you could love her the way she needed to be loved. It chilled me right to the bone."

"My God! She believes that?"

"She did at that moment. Is that what happened?"

"Lisette threw herself at a child. Typically, she was thinking of the child. They both died."

"How sad!" Cassy sighed. "How awfully sad! And did you children love her?"

"I want to show you something," he said, setting her down on the sofa. He went to his desk and opened a drawer, pushing around through stacks of papers until he found what he wanted. Then he returned to the sofa, lifted her back onto his lap and handed her a photograph, saying, "Look at that and tell me what you see!"

It was one of the very few family photographs ever taken. Gaby had been fifteen, Dana thirteen and Glenn, four.

"What do you see?" he asked again.

"It's Glenn," she said, a little breathlessly. "It's bloody uncanny!"

"It is, isn't it?"

"And she's the tot here, of course," Cassy said, gazing at the photograph. "What was she like, your mother?" she asked, holding on to the photograph. "I'm curious."

"She cared too much. About everyone. I think, in that sense, Glenn's right. We didn't love her the way she needed to be loved."

"And how old was she when she died?"

"Fifty-seven."

She looked down again at the photograph. "Well," she said, at length. "I do hope this baby works for Glenn. I do so hope that."

With amazing ease, Glenn began writing about a Corey-like character. She wasn't serious, she told herself. It was simply something to do while waiting for the baby. She told herself that, but getting to the typewriter every day slowly became very important. She had to see how the story would evolve this day and the next day, going back to read what she'd so far done with the same hunger and obsessive need she'd had at the start for Jack. These people she was writing were so real to her, their lives proceeding in such logical directions, she was captured completely by them, couldn't keep away from them, wanting to be with them all the time, to keep them going, never to have them end and leave her. She'd discovered a source of real people—one it hadn't ever occurred to her might exist— her own brain. She could sit down and fall into a trance-like state, her eyes fixed on the page as her fingers pushed out one word after another; she stated thoughts and ideas, actions; she

created qualities and characteristics so real she frequently sat
crying over her efforts, astonished and bemused at finding
people on paper could assume more reality for her than the
people within the immediate circle of her own life.

Jack was real, certainly. So were Corey, Dawn and Zane,
and Dana and Cassy. All the people around her were real. But
was she? She'd get up from the typewriter after three or four
hours' solid, concentrated effort, to catch sight of herself in
the mirror and actually start in surprise to see she had shape,
form, substance. While she was writing, while she was at the
typewriter lost in her paper world in the act of creating real
people, she was weightless, bodyless, purely a medium through
which information passed. To see herself then was startling,
even shocking. The more she wrote, the more surprised she
was when she stopped and saw her preoccupied eyes gazing
back at her from the mirror as if to say, Why are you bothering
me? Can't you see that I'm very busy?

Jack, seeing her hard at work, not smoking, and drinking
considerably less than usual, felt very much eased. He'd been
going around for quite some time—how long? he wondered—
with held breath, fearful in some nonspecific way. The regular
meals and the sound of her working reassured him to such an
extent that he became even more prone to generous outpour-
ings, going out for between-work sessions to prowl the downtown streets, returning with fresh-cut flowers from the stall in
the Old Market, or a string of red onions, along with an armload
of fresh spinach and magnificent, unblemished mushrooms—
ingredients for a spinach and bacon salad he'd prepare to go
with their dinner. He'd go out of the house, drop by to say hi
to the kids, continue on his way after a cup of coffee, and
eventually return home with a pair of antique diamond earrings
that had just happened to catch his eyes; or three exquisite
hand-tatted lace handkerchiefs he'd found lying at the bottom
of a bin in the Salvation Army thrift shop. He went out to walk
his way through his thoughts and came back with a two-foot-
long kosher salami, just-baked seeded rye bread, and made
huge, delicious sandwiches he coaxed her into eating while
they sat in front of the fire. He spent one entire afternoon
preparing a pot of soup, then watched her diligently eat her

way to the bottom of the bowl—her eyes growing very round—
to find an antique sterling-silver brooch lying there.

She was eating, gaining a little weight, losing that gaunt,
haunted look she'd had for far too long. He felt so happy, so
pleased seeing the surprise that lit up her face when she received
his offerings, moved by the somehow melancholy passion with
which she responded to his generosity. If she'd touched him
before with gentle caring in her hands, she was even gentler,
more caring now. This period while they were trying to make
a baby was, they both agreed, the best time they'd so far shared.

He had been growing concerned about her, worried about
her drinking, scared she'd been developing a dependency. But
seeing the discipline she exercised in cutting back, stopping
smoking, settling down to work, he felt he'd perhaps been
overanxious. He loved her, more all the time. She understood
so well the creative process, the need for privacy both in which
to create and also to restore one's self. He very much valued
this in her. She didn't resent his work and read those pieces
he offered her with unfeigned interest and pride and often
responded with some piece of valid criticism or some remarkably incisive comment that altered or enhanced the perspective
he'd had, sending him back to the typewriter to emerge with
a much improved piece of work.

She was totally without pretense or manipulative tendencies.
And it was this above all that he loved about her. She seemed
to have no comprehension of the mechanics of games-playing
and noted the maneuvers of their friends with curiosity, later
telling him, "I don't understand how they can do that." Or,
"Why don't they just say what they want, what they mean? It
seems to me it'd be easier that way instead of taking such
circuitous routes." It was this quality that he'd first seen in her
as naive. Perhaps it was. He was very reluctant to overanalyze
those qualities he best liked. Analysis, he'd found, harking
back to his marriage, was inevitably destructive when too much
of it was being done. Trying to evaluate the weight and import
of every word, every possible thought, was crazy-making.
Glenn's straightforwardness lulled and calmed him. He could
talk for hours to her about his past, his ideas, random recollections and she'd listen, curled into his side, occasionally

asking a question, more often saying, "Go on, Jack. What happened then?"

He loved her. He occasionally conceived of something happening to her and became panic-stricken, terrified. He wanted her to live forever, to live forever with her. He was slowly making his way toward a consideration of marriage. He did want it. He hadn't enjoyed those runaround years after his divorce, flying from one woman to the next making love as if it were lethal, refusing to divulge his thoughts or feelings. He did like an established, settled home life, liked a certain uniform regularity to his days, liked waking up beside Glenn to lie quietly smoking a cigarette, watching her sleep, loving the look of her, the silken fall of her hair. He'd ease back the blankets to look at her body, admiring the length of her thighs and the slow curve of her spine into her buttocks, the barely perceptible lift of her breasts as she breathed. Her nipples made him want to cry, they were so pink, so beautifully soft. He'd cover her over and lay his arm protectively across her sleeping body, awed by his good fortune in having her. No one else could move him or open him up the way she could. Not because she tried to, but because she respected his right to his private thoughts. So, very aware of this respect, he volunteered himself.

He wasn't jealous of her work, or competitive. He hadn't any idea what she was writing and didn't ask, believing she'd enlighten him or not as she wished, when the time was right. He wanted most of all—beyond the range of his personal desires for her—to have her satisfied, fulfilled, at peace. Happiness simply was an inadequate word for what he wished for her. When he tried to narrow it down, define it more precisely, what he wanted was for her to be able to find contentment in the life they were building together. He wanted her to be with him, wanted her to be proud of her own accomplishments, wanted her to value the countless good things they had both individually and together. But in a remote region of his mind, he was deeply frightened by the possibility that not only might it not be within his capabilities to provide her with that contentment, but also that she mightn't be capable of deriving pleasure—from him, or from herself, or from their individual and joint accomplishments.

* * *

For a year and a half she worked simultaneously on getting
herself pregnant and completing her "story." She didn't dare
think of it in terms of a book because she felt it might be
presumptuous to believe that what she'd put down was sufficiently plotted—she couldn't quite get her mind to work with
plots—or well enough defined with beginning, middle, and
end, to be considered a book. But she finished it, whatever it
was, and sat down to read it through, and then felt wretched
because it was all over, ended. She'd wanted to go on writing
about her people forever. But they'd insisted on an ending and
she'd had to give it. Now it was done and she sat in the living
room staring at the stack of finished pages, completely at a
loss as to what to do next.

She fixed herself a drink, resumed her seat and continued
to stare at the manuscript. She'd have to ask Jack to read it
and felt reluctant to ask him, remembering their conversation
years earlier about his probably being jealous. But whom else
could she ask? She hadn't any idea how people went about
getting books published or even if what she'd written was
publishable. She did like the idea of having it all nicely printed,
bound between hard covers with a lovely jacket. She'd even
done half a dozen sketches for the jacket design, daydreaming
over her book in store windows, pyramided displays.

Jack looked at the three hundred and forty-two pages sitting
on the coffee table and laughed as he dropped down beside her
on the sofa. "I don't believe it!" he grinned, hugging her against
his side. "That's one hell of a hefty pile of manuscript."

"Would you read it, Jack?"

"Sure, if you want me to. But I warn you, I'm not much
good at that sort of thing."

"But you'll have some idea whether or not it's any good.
And maybe you'll tell me what I should do with it."

"I'll make you a deal," he said. "I'll read it. I like it, I don't
like it, I'll still pay a typist to do up a clean copy and we'll
send it to my agent, let him be the one to decide. Okay?"

"All right," she said quietly, her manner subdued.

"It's a hell of a comedown, isn't it?" he said, sympathetic.
"Finishing a book. It's like you just lost a carload of the best

friends you ever had. Let's go out tonight and celebrate! What d'you say?"

"It isn't working," she said, almost in a whisper.

"What isn't?"

"The baby. It isn't working. I'm starting to feel . . . I don't know. Making love . . ."

"Give it some time," he said sensibly.

"We've already given it quite a lot of time."

"Well, let's give it a little more. Or," he said, "if you're worried, go talk to your doctor, get checked out."

"Yes," she said distractedly. "I will."

They went out to celebrate. She got drunk for the first time in almost two years. Laughing, dancing, hilariously drunk. Not loud, or unpleasant, but very, very drunk. He felt a little embarrassed as he propelled her out of the restaurant to the car. She was giddy, reeling drunk. It bothered him, as if it were an omen, her staying sober all these months, then getting drunk now. He couldn't shake off a gut feeling something was going to happen.

When they got home, she raced up the stairs, almost losing her balance and falling. He quickly put out the downstairs lights, locked up and ran upstairs after her, following the trail of her clothing, coming to a halt in the doorway. She was sitting completely naked on the end of the bed with her legs spread, looking down at herself, touching herself as if she'd just that moment discovered an entirely new area of her body she'd never known existed.

It was too much. He tossed off his clothes and sank to his knees to bury his face between her thighs, suddenly desperate to make love to her. But she raised his head and gazed down at him, blinking, whispering, "Call me your lady. Will you?"

"My lady," he smiled, his throat lumping. "My lady lady, I love you."

Still blinking, she began to cry; she smiled, crying and wrapped her arms around his head, holding his head hard against her belly, whispering, "Jack, Jack, I love you, too. Love me more."

She waited out the second year. Be fair, she told herself. Give it at least two years. Jack's right. It takes some time.

So she waited, gradually deriving less and less pleasure from the enforced-seeming lovemaking they indulged in too often. She did want him, but her pleasure in their lovemaking seemed to diminish in direct proportion to her waning hope of becoming pregnant. The less she came to believe in the possibility of a pregnancy, the more despondent she became.

The book was typed and sent off to Jack's agent.

"I like it a hell of a lot," Jack told her. "But I warned you, I'm a lousy critic. Let's let Harry decide."

Harry, after keeping her waiting almost three months, finally agreed he'd handle the book and began submissions.

"You're halfway there," Jack said, proud of her. "I knew you'd be good at whatever you decided to do. Why don't you start another one?"

"I really don't feel like it," she said listlessly.

"How about your painting? Why don't you do some sketching, some drawing? You can't sit in the house doing nothing. It's no good for you. It's not good for anyone. You know that. At least," he said, trying not to push her too hard, "go on over and visit the kids."

The kids.

They'd opened the boutique and, naturally, were a roaring success. Corey's business instincts were one hundred percent on target. Just a few years and she and Jack were already receiving regular income from the Eaterys. Now Corey was negotiating for a fourth one, always out on the go drumming up publicity for the boutique. Zane was going to be starting kindergarten in the fall. He was almost five and a half. Corey's long-awaited twenty-first birthday had come and gone. The kids were putting off the marriage because they simply didn't have the time to go downtown and get it done. And Dawn, after asking Glenn several times without success, had had to go elsewhere for the boutique designs. Glenn didn't mind. She hadn't really felt like doing it. She really didn't feel like doing very much of anything.

Jack was—as always when finishing a new piece of work— locked in the spare bedroom preparing the final draft of what he said was far and away the best screenplay he'd done.

"This is the one that's going to make it for me!" he declared. "When you read it, you'll know what I mean. Even if it doesn't win any prizes, I know the damned thing's good and it'll make one truly beautiful film."

She took long walks, always feeling chilled. The months were slipping away from her. She returned home to sit in the living room listening to the removed clacking of Jack's electric typewriter, trying to warm herself by the fire, drinking gin or sometimes rum to try to thaw herself inside. Even as summer reached its peak she couldn't seem to get warm and kept fires going all day long in the living room, sitting on the floor with her back against the sofa, trying to read, trying not to drink; waiting for Jack to get finished working and either come down to be with her or give her an excuse to move. To get dinner or go out. Anything. She sat staring into the fire thinking, about her mother, about the old house, about Mrs. Petrov, about Cassy and Dana, about small, cooing babies, about her book.

The book was out there somewhere wending its way through the innards of various publishing houses and she couldn't think about it, didn't want to, couldn't help herself. It was finished, done. It didn't matter. Did it matter? She sat before the fire and did small pen and ink drawings, little pieces that were exercises to keep her hand mindful of its ability.

Finally, having given it two and a half years from the day they first decided to try, she made an appointment to see her gynecologist. Then, feeling even colder than usual, she telephoned Cassy.

"I have to have a series of tests," she said, her voice sounding very small to her own ears; wondering how it must sound to Cassy. "Would you come with me, Cassy? I'm so frightened."

"Of course, I will, darling."

Cassy went with her and sat out the hours in the doctor's waiting room while, with a leaden precognition weighing heavily against the back of her skull, Glenn went through test after test. She emerged, at the end of the series of tests, looking so fragile and ashen, Cassy took her home in a taxi, undressed her and put her directly to bed.

"Don't go away, Cassy. Stay with me until Jack comes home. I hate being alone here."

"All right," Cassy sat down on the side of the bed.

"Cassy, will you hold me? I'm so cold."

"Poor darling," Cassy crooned. She lay down on the bed

and gathered Glenn into her arms, stroking her down, down
into sleep.

Then there was more waiting.

The typewriter upstairs was always going. Jack was starting
something new. She paced up and down the living room, drinking without thought, waiting for the results. Deeply, critically
frightened, she could think of nothing else but those test results,
and suffered agonies every time the telephone rang; couldn't
speak to anyone on the telephone for fear the doctor might be
trying to reach her. Until finally, finally, the doctor himself
called up and she knew simply from the apologetic tone of his
voice what he was going to say.

She replaced the receiver and sat down in front of the fire,
staring into the flames, feeling her life, her hope, her spirits
dying, all dying. Her eyes felt too big for their sockets, her
hands—she looked at them, repelled—appeared large and grotesque, ugly. Her throat ached and she drank some to ease it,
without success. The typewriter went on and on. She drank a
little more. Her eyes burnt dry by the fire, her insides colder
than before, she sat listening, waiting for the typewriter to stop.
The telephone rang. She answered it. It was Cassy, asking,
"Any news yet, darling?"

She said, "I can't talk to you now, Cassy. I'll call you later.
I'm sorry. Please don't think me rude."

She hung up, picked up her newly freshened drink and went
unsteadily up the stairs and down the hall to the spare room.
She opened the door. Everything was out of focus, wavy.

For weeks, he'd watched her slowly lapsing into the old
drinking habits. He'd watched, feeling scared and irritated by
her inability to retain some kind of control over her mood-
swings. As she fell into more frequent silences, as she laughed
less and less often, she drank more and more and more. It
seemed to him that once she started she simply hadn't any idea
how or when to stop and would drink until he had to put her
to bed or else she simply stopped being there and fell asleep.
He'd been promising himself they'd talk it out as soon as he'd
finished this last screenplay. But then, he'd had the idea and
gone smack into this other thing. So he'd started telling himself
he'd talk to Glenn as soon as this one was done, talk to her

seriously about the damage she was probably doing to herself—God knows she was so thin a strong gust of wind might blow her away—not to mention their ridiculously mounting booze bills. He didn't mind a few drinks himself, but over a hundred dollars a month just for liquor was crazy, an absurd waste of money.

He heard the door open but didn't look up for a few seconds, wanting to finish reading one last bit. He was preparing a good copy himself this time, to get the dialogue in before the shooting deadline, so was painstakingly proofing and editing every page, making corrections as he went. He planned to have the whole thing Xeroxed and get it the hell out and on its way by the next evening at the latest. He'd spent far too much time working recently and not nearly enough time with Glenn.

She took a step, not watching where she was going, too concerned with how she was going to tell him, putting words together inside her head. Her heel hooked into the edge of the rug and she tripped. The glass flew out of her hand sending gin and tonic and ice cubes all over his script. He leapt up, his face scarlet with sudden anger, shouting, "Jesus *fucking* Christ, Glenn! Look what the *hell* you've *done!* Weeks of fucking work, *ruined!* I'm going to have to type all these *goddamned* pages *over again!* Oh, shit! Shit!"

She put out her hand to touch him but he swatted her hand away, furious.

"I'm sorry, Jack," she said in a whisper, swallowing hard, horrified by what she'd done and by his terrible anger. She'd never seen him so angry. "I'm sorry," she whispered, backing away. Her eyes were round, glassy.

"Damn it all to hell!" He was muttering to himself, picking up the ice cubes, using handfuls of Kleenex to blot up the liquid. "Son of a *bitch!*"

"I'm so sorry," she whispered, at the doorway, staring at his enraged features, watching him trying to repair the damage. She stood a moment longer watching, and suddenly it was all too much. Failures of one kind or another, so many of them. Everything she touched was destroyed. She backed out into the hallway, then turned, went into the bathroom and locked the door. She opened the medicine cabinet and took down one of Jack's double-edged razor blades, unpeeled the paper and held the blade carefully between thumb and forefinger as she stepped out of her shoes, stoppered the bathtub, turned on the faucets and climbed fully-dressed into the tub. Holding her wrist under the cold water, she drew the blade down across her wrist as deep and hard as she could, slicing open the tips of the fingers holding the blade in the process. No matter. Quickly, she turned off the cold water and put on the hot. Shivering, she dropped the blade, feeling the strange, stinging sensation in her wrist and fingers, mostly in her wrist, and lay down in the water staring at the ceiling. She felt quite warm really.

He finished blotting up everything and examined the pages, seeing now that the damage wasn't nearly as bad as he'd thought initially. Realizing that, he felt terrible for having shouted at her that way. But, Jesus! What a thing to have happen! No more fooling around with it. The time had definitely come to have a talk with her about her cutting down on the drinking. It was just no damned good. All right, so she was upset about not getting pregnant. Okay. But drinking wasn't going to help her chances. It wasn't helping anything. And if she didn't watch out—if he didn't start watching out with her—the next thing anybody knew, she'd have a full-scale problem on her hands. Half the time she didn't even seem aware of what she was doing, just automatically poured out drinks, drank them, then went for refills. It was as if she'd gone off somewhere, out of touch. It scared him. He wanted her with him.

He heard the water running in the bathroom, thought she was probably taking a bath or a shower to sober herself up and continued cleaning his desk, mopping up the floor around his chair. It was just goddamned incredible how much liquid, how much mess there could be from one eight-ounce glass. Checking the draft, he decided he wouldn't have to redo more than five pages, and sat down to start them right away.

He'd finished the first page when it occurred to him that the water had been running quite a long time. Listening, he rolled a second page into the typewriter. When he removed that page from the machine, he tuned back in to hear the water still running. No other sounds. Strange. Beneath the sound of the water there were no other sounds at all, only an eerie silence. Had she gone out and left the water running? He got up and went into the hall to listen outside the bathroom door and looked down to see water trickling out from under the door. He felt his eyes grow suddenly very large. He pounded on the door, calling her name, his heart gone crazy with fear as the silence seemed to scream at him.

He kicked in the door and cried out at the sight of her floating on her side in the water. Pink water, swirls of red. He ran to pull her out of the tub, frantically yanking at the stopper, turning off the water, exclaiming aloud at the sight of the blood-spurting gash in her wrist. He grabbed a roll of tape from the medicine cabinet, pinched the whitened lips of the wound together and taped round and round her wrist, his hands flying. He ripped off her blouse and made a tourniquet of the sleeve, tying it tight on her upper arm before flopping her over on her stomach to apply artificial respiration because her breathing was so faint, so shallow. He kept it up for several minutes, then dashed across the hall to call for an ambulance, ran back to tear the wet clothes off her, just pulling them to pieces, not wanting to waste time, wrapped her—thinking, My God! You're a skeleton. Why haven't I noticed?—in a blanket and carried her downstairs to wait for the ambulance. He was scared sick she'd die, sick with misery and guilt for having shouted at her, tortured at not being able to understand why she'd done this. Why? Why? Gazing at her colorless face, bloodless lips, he held her tightly on his lap; the minutes too long, too long waiting for the ambulance to arrive. Her face was a death mask, yet so young, flawless. Not a mark, not a line, not a clue as to why. Why? All the way to the hospital in the ambulance, to the emergency room where he was obliged to stand waiting, shivering in the corridor, he kept on asking why. Why, why? He telephoned Corey because Corey was his friend, Corey knew her, Corey was ageless and he needed someone to help him understand why. Then he telephoned Dana, and got Cassy.

Dawn stood, hearing Corey say, "Oh, *God!* Hang on, Jack! I'm on my way!"

"Did she *die?*" she asked him, stricken.

"She's just barely making it."

"Oh, no! *Go on! Hurry!* And let me know! I'll pick up Zane and come back, wait right here by the phone."

"Call my mother!" Corey shouted, going out the door. "Just tell her to get there!"

Cassy gripped the telephone so hard she got a cramp in her arm.

"I'll come at once," she said, then rang Dana at the station to tell him.

"Jesus!" Dana's voice was a dim whisper. "Not the Pavilion. Not again."

"I don't understand, darling. What?"

"Not now. I'll meet you there."

He ran through the station remembering every detail of that emergency room: the corridor, the bench, the door to the operating room. The death. Glenn going in through the door. The only one. He ran.

Jack and Corey sat on the bench in the corridor, waiting. Cassy was some distance away, leaning against the wall, chain-smoking. Dana paced up and down, up and down, his open overcoat billowing out every time he turned.

Jack too was chain-smoking, trying to relate to Corey what had happened. Corey heard him out, then shook his head judiciously, saying, "She'd understand your being upset about the script, Jack. That's not the sort of thing to send Glenn off the deep end. No. Something else. It has to be. Don't sit blaming yourself. Just wait."

Cassy stared at the wall thinking, I knew, I knew. Why couldn't any one of us have stopped this? I *knew*. A deep pocket of fear sat in the pit of her stomach, filling to over-flowing. Don't die! Don't die for any of this, any of us! Please don't die! Her eyes followed the movements of scurrying nurses, interns rushing in and out, blue-suited doctors in surgical garb. Such a lot of activity. Her eyes shifted to Dana, pacing back and forth, back and forth. His face was creased, his eyes un-seeing. Watching him, she knew suddenly, with frightening clarity, exactly what was going through his mind and suffered with him, thinking of a middle-of-the-night confessional conversation whispered out through tears and choking anguish. "I never told her I loved her. She died without ever hearing me tell her." Now it might happen to him again.

Gaby sat beside the telephone, unable to move, unblinking. She stared at the dial, telling herself, You've got to get up, go there. You have to, you must.

Corey found a coffee machine, and silently went about placing paper cups of coffee in their hands. Then he resumed his seat on the bench beside Jack, his eyes on the door, sipping at the coffee.

Finally, she was all right, stitched up and transfused. They were allowed, one at a time, to see her for a few minutes. Jack insisted Corey be the first.

Corey looked at her thinking she still looked young but she was old, so old her eyes seemed to him like portals through which he might have an awesome glimpse of death. He held her left hand, the fingers thickly bandaged. She clung weakly to his hand, staring at his face, seeing his impossible youth, its clarity, its beauty.

"You're so beautiful, Corey," she whispered. "I've always thought you were beautiful."

"Whatever it is," he said, "don't die for it, Aunt Glenn. Nothing's worth that. All kinds of people would rather have you live. I need you to be here. We all do. Jack's waiting. I'll come back tomorrow."

He kissed her smooth, waxy forehead and went home to Dawn feeling as if every joint in his body had seized up, so that walking, breathing, the simple act of sitting down—everything—was painful.

Cassy stood speechless on one side of the bed, Dana on the other. Dana was in tears, his chest heaving. Cassy dropped down and put her face very close to Glenn's and said, "I know. And I won't say anything at all now. But I'll stay with you after the others have gone." Then she got up and silently went out.

It was Dana's crying that seemed to hurt the most. Glenn didn't want to look at him, wished she could sink back into unconsciousness because having to see him crying was too terrible, made her feel too guilty.

"I'm sorry," she told him in a whisper. "Please, I'm sorry."

*"I'm* sorry!" he cried, pulling over a chair and sitting down. "Why don't I ever tell the people I care about that I do? I love you. I *love* you! We've never been a family for talking about our feelings. And we've been so stinking wrong. What is it that's so bad you have to die for it, Glenn? If it's something we can help with, you've got to tell us."

"I can't tell you, Dana."

"Where did we all go?" he asked, so bewildered. "What happened to the way things were supposed to be?"

"I don't *know!*" she cried out. "Please, I can't tell you!"

He realized suddenly that he wasn't helping the situation at all, that what he was doing was asking her to forgive him for unrecognized acts of omission: articulated soul-searching. He had to stop. He got up.

"Sounds stupid," he said, wiping his face with the back of his hand, attempting a smile, "but you're too young to die. So don't do it!"

Jack sat down on the side of the bed, closing both his hands over hers, asking, "Why Glenn, *why?*"

"I'm sorry, I'm sorry." She said it over and over. "Sorry, I'm sorry, Jack. I didn't mean to ruin your script. It was an accident. I didn't see..."

"I know that. Don't you think I know that? But this," he touched her wrist above the bandage. "Why? I... why?"

"I didn't know I was going to do it," she said, her eyes sunken, her face so totally without color even her lips were white. "But when I started, I wanted to do it. I've done so little for you, Jack. All your gifts, the lovely things you do and I give you nothing."

"That's not true! You give me all kinds of things, all kinds. Important things. You don't have to give someone presents as proof that you care. I know you do. And I love you. I know you've been upset about this baby business, but I thought... Haven't you...? God, I thought we were doing... I thought things were so good. The last couple of years..."

She watched him struggling for a reason, an answer to why she'd done this and felt sad for him, so sad for him, and sorry.

"I'm sterile, Jack." The sound of her voice and the words were surprising. "They did tests. I can't ever get pregnant. It's funny," she said grimly, looking past him at the wall. "If you think about it, Jack, it's funny. All those years with that bent wire inside to keep me from getting pregnant. It's really *funny*." She started to laugh but it turned to wrenching sobs. He held her thinking, This is so fucking sad, so goddamned unfair.

"It doesn't matter," he whispered in her ear. "It doesn't *matter*. Not to me and I won't let it matter that much to you. If you want a baby, there's always a way to get one. But not this, Glenn. This doesn't solve anything. It's an exit, taking you away. I don't *want* you to go away. You're important. With all kinds of future. And if you want a baby, then we'll get married and adopt one." He sat up to see her reaction.

"Not out of pity. Not because I've blackmailed you into it. That's not why . . . this happened." She forced her eyes to focus on him, feeling so drugged, so hopelessly stupid; seeing him through a haze.

"I was getting ready to raise the subject before this," he said, grieved now by his rotten sense of timing. "I've got to learn to tell you these things instead of saving them up to say at the 'right time.' You just gave me one hell of a graphic illustration about what can happen, waiting for the 'right time.' I was so scared I'd lose you. You're *everything* to me. Don't you know that?"

"I don't know how you can care," she said wearily, feeling sorrier and sorrier for him because at this moment she felt nothing, nothing at all, simply an empty ache. "It's such a long list of failures, mistakes . . . I'm falling asleep. I didn't do it to hurt you, Jack. I'd never hurt you."

"I know that."

"I did it to hurt *me*." She looked straight into his eyes, trying to bring him into sharper focus. "I'm so *tired* of me, Jack, tired."

"You're wrong. Wrong to want to hurt yourself, wrong to be thinking about failures. You've got such a lot going for you. You haven't failed. We're going to talk a lot, about everything. I'll go now and let you rest. Cassy's going to stay with you."

"All right," she said faintly, wetting her lips.

"*I'm* sorry. I love you. You're my lady and I need you around. Things stink when you're not around."

She was dimly aware of Cassy's presence, aware of her

perfume and Cassy's hand stroking her face, lightly, lightly. Cassy's voice softly saying, "I *knew*. I knew and it was very wrong of me, of all of us, not to acknowledge we knew and do something. Your mother gave it more time than you're giving it, Glenn. If nothing else, darling, give it more time. You're forcing history to repeat itself. And you can't. Darling, you *can't!* None of it may have been the way you thought it was. You've assumed. You may be wrong. Please, give it more time. Be kinder to yourself. You're not bad, but you think you are. You haven't failed but you think you have. *Please,* give it up!"

"I want to die, Cassy. I want to."

"No, no, no!"

Cassy's fingers stroked her eyelids, her lips, her forehead, tricking her out, away, gone.

She slept for a time and awakened, undrugged, the sedative out of her system. She awakened with every bone and muscle in her body screaming for a drink, howling for one. She awakened to see Gaby sitting in the chair beside the bed. Was it Gaby, or Cassy? No, Gaby. Gaby sitting like a stone effigy, looking back at her with horror-filled eyes and her mouth trembling.

Gaby asked, "What should I do for you? I have to . . . there must be something . . . You look so *ill!*"

"Gaby." Glenn could barely speak; she ached all over, her wrist pulsing and throbbing, her head pounding, hands trembling, the two stitched fingers whining with pain. "Gaby, I love you. Go away! Please, please, go away! I love you but please go away!" Oh God, it hurts, everything hurts. "I don't want you to see! I know how these things upset you so go away, I understand, honestly I do, *please,* Gaby go away!"

Nodding rapidly, Gaby pushed up out of the chair and hurried away.

Her entire body was shaking, everything rattling. She groped for the call button, wanting something, needing something to take it away, the aching, shaking demands of her body. A drink, just one, to make it all hurt less, take her out; because everything was black, black. To get almost out, nearly all the way out and have to be still alive, still here, conscious of

another failure, another one. Closing her eyes, she pressed the
button, waiting for someone, anyone to come, help her; thinking about Jack, how he'd screamed, then how he'd cried, tears
rolling down his face. Making him cry, scaring him. Can't
give you a baby, can't give me a baby, years we spent
trying... Somebody *come!* Give me something to take me away
again, I can't bear it that I'm here, still here when I should be
dead, want to be dead, have to...

When he came back, Jack made her listen to his carefully
thought-out list of optimistic possibilities.

"Your book'll probably be published. I called Harry to get
a status report and it's on its fourth reading at its third sub-
mission. That's practically as good as sold," he said. "You're
going to get published. And who knows? They might even let
you do the jacket design. It's worth a shot. You've got so many
things going for you, *so* many things. You can paint, you can
write. You know what Cassy's said about your paintings, how
good they are. And she knows. There's your book. It just isn't
that important that you can't have babies."

"Jack, I felt like such a *fool!* The tests, going through all
that. As if I should have *known.*" She squeezed his hand,
searching his eyes. "Jack," she wet her lips, "I need a drink.
I feel as if I'm going to break into a million pieces."

"Glenn, you can't! You're on medication. You can't start
drinking. You'll screw up the medication."

"Then give me *something!* Please? A cigarette, okay? Let
me have one of your cigarettes! *Look at me!*" she cried, holding
out her trembling hands. "I don't know what's *happening* to
me! The only two things I can think of are dying and a drink.
Give me a drink so I can stop thinking about dying. *Please!*"
She saw his uncertainty and squeezed his hand harder, pleading,
"Jack, if you *love* me, *help* me! One drink to get me through
the night. That's all. Please! Oh God! Jack, *Please!*"

"Glenn," he said softly, "you're hooked." Saying it suddenly made it real, and now he was very scared.

"You are." His voice was shot with misery. "I've been
making excuses for you, telling myself it's this or it's that. But
the truth is, you're hooked."

"Okay!" she cried wildly, throwing back the blankets and
trying to sit up. *"OKAY!"* There had to be something in that

bathroom, something she could use. She could break one of the drinking glasses. She'd get the bandage off. It was already done, she just had to open it up again.

Panicked, he pushed her back down, wanting help, needing help; feeling he couldn't handle what was happening. It was all out of control.

"Glenn, lie down! What're you doing? You can't get up!"

"Okay okay. I'm hooked! I am, okay. Whatever you say! But if I am, help me! One drink so I can *stand* this place! JACK!" She screamed at him, her fingernails digging into his arms through his shirt.

He couldn't stand her crying, screaming, pleading with him this way. "All right," he said, defeated. "I'm going to do it. This one time. And then you're coming home and we're going to do something about you. I mean it, Glenn. You don't know what you're doing. You're altogether out of control. You're scaring the living hell out of me."

Out of control. She was. The truth of it made him dizzy. The repercussions seemed infinite in their potential. He went out of the hospital, ran two blocks to a liquor store, bought a can of pre-mixed cocktails—not even bothering to look at what it was—and ran back to the hospital, terrified of arriving back to find her dead.

It was the worst moment of his life, watching her sit up and reach for the drink. The bandage on her wrist, her taped fingers, her eyes large with anticipation as he put the glass into her hands. She was like a starving baby getting a bottle, or a vampire finding a victim. Holding the glass in both hands, she drank down her nourishment with an ecstatic shiver that made the hair on his arms stand on end, made him go cold with despair.

"You're a drunk," he said under his breath, watching her eyes droop with an almost sexual pleasure, seeing her shudder as the drink hit her stomach. "God help us! You're a drunk and I don't know what to do about you."

She collapsed back against the pillows, smiling at him, extending her arms to embrace him. "Thank you, thank you. Oh, I love you, *love* you, you're so good to me, Jack. I do love you. Everything'll be all right now, I promise. You'll see. I promise."

He held her, feeling her bony body under his hands, for the very first time doubting the quality and depth of her professed "love." He left the hopsital shattered, no longer sure of anything—not love if it came as a token reward for contributing to her sickness, and certainly not his ability to help her. How the hell could he help her when for close to eight years she'd been drinking herself back and forth in and out of oblivion and he'd been too polite to notice?

The only drunks he'd ever known had all been other people's problems. But this drunk was his. He'd signed on, an emotional commitment made for the duration. Like it or not, they were together. What haunted him, frightening him more than anything else, was the awful possibility that she hadn't ever really cared about him, but had only wanted him close by as a some-time drinking partner. Glenn. A drunk. How? Why? Either she had no idea of the truth or she simply refused to admit to it. She was unable to think of anything but death and drinking. She drank in order not to think about dying.

He went home to start making phone calls, telling Dana, then Gaby, then Corey. "We've got to have a family conference. Here. Now. Right away. Glenn needs help. *I* need help."

# Eighteen

       She'd listen carefully to everything everyone had to say, agree that each of them was probably right, she had been drinking too much, then shake her head, insisting, "I don't have a problem. I can stop any time I want to." And "I'll cut back." Then, minutes later, she was getting up to fix herself another drink.

      She'd find herself with a drink in her hand and stare at it, wondering how it had managed to get there; then she'd drink it. A bit later, she'd look down and there would be another drink. She told herself, I've got to stop this. Maybe they're right. I am drinking too much, and she forced herself to pay attention to what she was doing, cutting back.

      It went on for months. Jack watched closely, carefully, and it did seem to appear she was cutting back. He was anything but satisfied, but figured since it had taken her quite a few years to get well inside of her drinking, it'd probably take some time before she'd be willing to admit the drinking had managed to get inside of her. He waited. She watched him waiting, watching her; resentment building.

      Then the two of them would have another heart-to-heart

with Jack trying every way he knew how to point out to her that she wasn't cutting back, wasn't in control, wasn't doing herself—or him—any good. She'd hear him out—looking hurt, looking tired, looking so goddamned painfully thin— then defeat him yet again by quietly saying, "I don't have a problem, Jack. But you'll give me one if you don't stop watching every move I make."

Exasperated, he asked Corey to talk to her. But Corey, displaying what Jack at first thought was stubborn reasonableness and came later to see as chillingly wise insight, refused, saying, "It wouldn't do any good. She's got to want to do it for herself. If she won't even admit she's not in control of the stuff, there's no way she's going to listen to anything any of us tells her. She's got to come to this by herself."

"Fine!" Jack said bitterly. "And in the meantime, she'll destroy what we have and drink herself to death. Have you *looked* at her? She doesn't eat. When was the last time you saw a five-foot-nine woman who weighed about a hundred pounds? I'm *scared!* If she doesn't pick up another razor blade, she'll just go ahead and starve herself to death. I can't stand it! I don't know what to do for her."

"Put it to her that way," Corey advised. "Try it. Take her to an A.A. meeting. Let her meet and listen to some others. But I've known her all my life and I'm telling you right out front: she won't be influenced."

She fought for more months about going to an A.A. meeting, arguing, "I don't need that, Jack. I'm hardly that far gone."

Cassy and Dana, too, tried, unsuccessfully over dinner at their house. It was an intense, soul-searching evening that had everyone in tears, but left Glenn unmoved, unconvinced.

"I know what I am," she told them. "I know." Sobbing, she walked into the wall.

Cassy put her head down on the table and wept. Glenn wouldn't be helped, and she'd die. This time she would. She'd decided. And nothing any of them did would persuade her away from it.

But then Harry telephoned to say, "We've had an offer for your book. Four thousand for the hardcover rights."

Jack said, "Grab it!"

She said, "Go ahead!" and the book was sold.

In a high, magnanimous mood that evening, she consented

to accompany Jack to an A.A. meeting. She couldn't help feeling he was pressuring her unfairly. But to humor him, she went with him to the church hall where the meeting was to be held, looking at the people assembled, making a game of trying to separate the alcoholics from the people who were there as family members or observers, failing dismally. It seemed she couldn't distinguish the people with the addiction from those who were there to help.

She listened open-mindedly to several people who got up to speak, quite moved by one or two of them, deciding A.A. obviously had a great deal to offer for a lot of people. But even, she thought, if I were a hardcore, falling-down drunk, this wouldn't work for me.

There was too much of the revivalist meeting aura about it, too much of a group-therapy feeling or a kind of semireligious fervor. She hadn't ever been able to function to any successful degree within groups and being there made her uncomfortable, nervous and angry with Jack for putting her through two hours of grinding emotional trauma. The stories of family and financial ruin, loss of friends and jobs saddened her; she could even identify with some of it, particularly the people who spoke so openly, so earnestly about their feelings of inadequacy, their failures. But she was altogether put off by the tone of the group, the mass spirit.

She did, though, as a result, arrive at the conclusion that she'd allowed herself to become too visible. She'd have to be more careful, give everyone less ammunition to use against her.

Thinking this way, she was appalled. A part of her was disgusted by her paranoia, demanding, What's wrong with you? This isn't you. What are you trying to prove? Where am *I* in all of this? What's happened to *me?*

In due course, she spoke with her editor, made the requested changes in the manuscript, received her advance, then sank into an even deeper depression, feeling hopeless, feeling trapped, feeling utterly helpless and unequipped to extricate herself from the black mud of her despondency.

"I don't understand you!" Jack said, seeing her sitting staring into the depths of a glass, afraid to ask what it was she was drinking. She sometimes tricked him by holding a glass of water or fruit juice. He had the feeling she'd finally evolved

into a games-player, with a deadly weapon. He could no longer
tell when she was drunk or when she wasn't. In fact, she was
slowly stopping. She didn't understand how or why but she
was stopping. Her self-hatred was overlapping into her drinking
habits, causing an awareness. When her hands reached out,
she could see. And most often, she didn't drink. It made her
feel too sick, just as eating made her feel sick. But sometimes
it was neat gin in the glass she'd be holding. Neither of them,
now, knew or understood what was going on.

"Look at me, Glenn!" he said, crouching in front of her,
trying to make her look at him. "You've got everything going
for you. I mean it. You've got a great house. You've got
money. You don't owe anyone a cent. You've got a damned
good income coming in from Corey's Eaterys, not to mention
your own portfolio. You've got plenty of money. You've sold
your book just like that, one two three. I mean, Jesus! Glenn.
It took me *years* to sell my first novel. D'you know that? And
here you sell yours practically on the first time out."

"I know all that, Jack. Are you going to be jealous now,
the way you said you might be?"

"I'm not! I said that then because I wasn't sure, I didn't
know. I was covering myself in case. I'm happy for you, proud
of you. Can't you see that? Don't you know? What will satisfy
you? You've got more talent than any six people I know. Cassy
must've told you a hundred times how good your paintings are,
how easily you could have an exhibition. You're beautiful,
capable, intelligent, gifted. What do you *want?*"

"I can't tell you," she said, ashamed. "I don't know."

"Glenn, you're after some kind of illusion, something I don't
think exists. Glenn?"

She didn't answer. She was thinking about her mother,
seeing herself as a little girl standing in the bedroom doorway.
Her mother was putting dots of perfume behind each ear, smiling. Then she was turning away, stepping into her high heels,
checking her seams. Looking around over her shoulder, she
smiled. Mama. Was it like this? Is this the way it is? Where
is my life?

He sat before her a moment longer, then sighed and went
back upstairs to work. He felt the pressure, too; feeling it
building, the accumulating fear, his impotence.

What do I want? she asked the space where he'd been. She thought of Ralph. Perhaps she should've gone to Spain with Ralph. The two of them would have lived a natural life, a free life; one unencumbered by cars and houses, property taxes, income taxes, emotional taxes; a life dedicated to simple pleasures: crusty loaves of fresh bread, hunks of tangy cheese, red wine from the bottle. On a hillside, they'd have looked down at the world.

But no. Wine made her sick. She didn't like cheese well enough to make a steady diet of it. And she rarely painted now, despite Cassy's encouragement. Still, Ralph, with his yellow eyes and wild-flying hair; his stocky body and large, blunt-fingered hands, capable hands. Paint stained. Perhaps they'd have been happy together. It wouldn't have been like this. She looked around the room, noticing Jack's pipe on the coffee table, Jack's tie-clip on the mantel, Jack's book on the arm of the chair beside the fireplace. Jack's things were everywhere. Jack had made his home here. And the sight of his things bent her double, hurting. Everything hurt.

She spent hours staring into the fire trying to understand the events of her life, her life itself and why she so desperately wanted to leave it. She hadn't planned to kill herself, hadn't even consciously given thought to it. It had simply been there— for how long?—at the edge of her mind, waiting. A door she could open, go through, and close with resounding finality. So, she'd done it; she still wanted to do it. There'd been such a splendid rightness to the act, a painless anticipation of having an end finally to living. And never mind what came after death. Whatever it was, it couldn't feel worse than living. Cassy had told her, You're forcing history to repeat itself. It can't be done. Am I? Again and again she relived that hideous feeling of despair that had crawled over her as she'd opened her eyes, realizing she was still alive after all. And then, the sedatives had worn off. She'd sent Gaby away so Gaby wouldn't have to see, to suffer because Gaby couldn't bear any of that: blood, sickness, illness, death. She'd sent Gaby away so she wouldn't have to witness any of the trembling, her insides jumping, quivering, racing; her body a maze containing dozens of crazed white rats searching for an exit. Shaking. She'd been unable to stop the shaking until Jack had given her that drink.

She looked at her wrist, at the raised white welt marking the end of her hand, the beginning of her arm—thick deadened tissue at the thumb and forefinger of her left hand, where there were more white seams where they'd stitched back the nearly-severed tips. There's so little to me. A cut, some blood and I die. Easy to die. Easy. Why do I want to harm myself this way? Why?

Unable to relinquish this concept of effortless death, she had visions of bodies, of Lisette throwing herself in front of a car. Dead; a battered, broken body on a stretcher, blood clotting just beneath the surface of the skin. What was the point to living if the body was so haphazardly fragile that it took so little to destroy it? Perhaps the trick was somehow managing to survive in spite of the imperfections, the weaknesses. Provided you liked living well enough to be very, very careful with your flimsy, killable body.

Sex too often now seemed a profoundly silly trick played upon her by her body. She could go upstairs to bed with absolutely no interest whatsoever, lie there and watch Jack perform upon her—amazed that he cared to—and all at once find herself involved, almost against her will, because it seemed to require such a lot of effort to return the caresses, stroke him, make herself sufficiently gentle to accept the incoming thrust of his body; so much effort to engage in the twisting, gasping, writhing exhaustion. All for a few seconds of explosive interior spasms that sent the body jerking this way and that. It ended always too soon, leaving her feeling utterly depleted and more in need of a drink than at any other time, yet somehow oddly determined to resist that need. She was unable to anyway because Jack looked so pained if she did and she couldn't bear hurting him any more.

"Why won't you give it up?" he asked her, loving her, tenderly touching her. "All of it."

"You stop smoking," she said, trying to deflect him.

"Right! Fine! Gladly! If you stop drinking."

"I'm trying. Jack, I need time. Nothing makes any sense to me. I hate hurting you. Hate it! I hate me for doing it to you."

"Stop hating yourself! You're *not guilty!*"

"I am, Jack. I am, though."

Deflated, he went silent, that sudden spurt of silly hope-fulness, subsiding inside him. He was clutching at insubstantial snippets of hope, desperate to hit upon some idea that might be the key to reaching into her, and if nothing else, succeed in getting her to admit the seriousness of her drinking problem and what it was doing to their life together.

She was rarely drunk any more. She could converse co-herently, prepare meals she scarcely touched, keep the house immaculately clean and perform everyday tasks. But there was always a glass somewhere nearby, and it was a fifty-fifty tossup whether the glass contained gin or water.

Jack watched, seeing a near-vacant expression to her eyes every so often that alarmed him disproportionately. Her eyes seemed to slide into focus when he spoke to her, as if she were pulling herself back from some place infinitely more attractive than this reality and was extremely reluctant to return. When she did look at him, he had the chilling feeling she loathed him at that moment, not only for interrupting the flow of her spiraling thoughts, but also for simply being there to witness her departures and returns.

She'd see his visible distress and hate herself even more for what she was doing to both their lives, wanting to stop all of it, everything, but unable to find her way out of herself, past the years and years of blockage.

She got up one morning, determined to talk it out, desperate to talk it out. She made breakfast for Jack, said, "I'm going out to see Cassy," and went. For the first time she didn't bother to telephone first, and encountered Dana on his way out the front door.

"Cassy's still in bed. Go on up. Are you all right? Every-thing's all right?"

"Dana, I don't know. She won't mind if I go up?"

"She won't mind. Wait a minute, okay?"

"What is it?"

"Remember, way back, one time we talked about being happy? Remember? And I said I didn't know what it was?"

"Vaguely."

"Well, I know what is is, lovey. And so do you. You've

just got to stop and see it. I know you can. I've got to run."
He kissed her on the cheek and hurried off.

Cassy was still sleeping, in the nude, with the sheets flung
away from her. Glenn stood gazing at her, her eyes playing
tricks, creating illusions. The gray slowly overtaking Cassy's
hair was the only real indication of the changes in time. You
look so healthy, Glenn thought, so wonderfully healthy. Glenn
sat down in the rocker, rocking back and forth, waiting for
Cassy to wake up, deriving a profound pleasure from watching
her sleep, from the freedom of being there, able to study the
shifting play of morning light on Cassy's body. The woman
was small and lovely, vulnerable. It was a painting, a painting
of Lisette, the one she hadn't ever been able to do.

The alarm rang. Cassy's hand went out to shut it off. She
stretched, yawning, her body arching, magnificent. Glenn
couldn't take her eyes off her. Cassy saw her and smiled,
holding out her arms. It was an automatic gesture, one without
thought, simply a welcome. Glenn got up and closed herself
into Cassy's arms, sighing deeply, shudderingly; home.

"You're feeling better, aren't you, darling?" Cassy said
softly, enjoying holding her, that maternal feeling on the ram-
page through her system. She was pleased by Glenn's head
nodding into her shoulder. "I am glad," she said. "I so want
you to be happy."

"Cassy, let me paint you. Will you let me? This way. It's
so important."

Cassy laughed, "Are you mad, darling? Why on earth would
you want to paint an aging, raddled nude?"

"You're not, Cassy," Glenn said seriously, with no idea
what she was doing. "You're beautiful, magnificent." Glenn's
hand reached out to mold itself to Cassy's breast. "You're
*beautiful.*"

"What do you see?" Cassy asked, stopping her hand. "What?
This very moment? Where are you?"

"Mama," Glenn said, her voice dropping to a whisper. "I
can do it, finally. Capture her. Through you. Please, Cassy. I
know I can. It's so important. I don't know why. I have to."

"A sketch," Cassy compromised. "Twenty minutes. Only
for you. Go on. You'll find everything you need in my work-
room."

Glenn found pencils, a sketchpad and hurried back to the bedroom, feeling excited and alive, as if she *had* been dead. She was suddenly breathing again, functioning. Cassy stood for her for the twenty minutes, stood completely motionless, watching Glenn work, thinking, There's no price to pay in helping you play out these dreams or memories or fantasies or whatever they are. No price at all. And if there is something you find here in me, something that transcends everything else, it's here for you and you must have it, must take it, I long for you to have it because it's too much to ask of all of us, too much to expect us to stand by silently, without protest, and allow you to die. *I* will not allow it. I cherish in you all that is pure and troubled and struggling to survive pain I cannot begin to comprehend. Not the reasons why or the causes. But the pain I do know. I do know.

She didn't ask to see what Glenn had done. It was enough to see the purposefulness, the newly determined set of her features, enough to embrace her before Glenn went flying off, saying, "I have to get to work on this right away. Thank you, thank you."

The painting, became an instant obsession. She worked on it day and night, not drinking at all, not eating very much, either. But not drinking. Jack carried mugs of soup in to her in the studio, made certain she drank at least part of the soup, then went away, leaving her to her work, not questioning what she was at work upon. He was glad that she'd found something she actually wanted to do.

In between sessions in her studio, she sat downstairs with Jack in front of the fireplace, idly dreaming, seeing herself signing autographs in book stores, on television talk shows, speaking at literary luncheons. She received a proof of the dustjacket from her editor and looked at the paper that would enclose her book with the oddly remote sensation she was looking at something having nothing whatsoever to do with her. She wanted to feel elated, but felt only artistically pleased by the graphics. It was a good jacket.

She read the galleys, corrected and returned them; through-out all of this feeling no involvement with these paper people she'd once loved so passionately. Her preoccupation with them

then had been so complete it had excluded everyone and everything. Now, the things these people said and did seemed stiff,
wooden, contrived. She sent the galleys off at the post office
feeling bereft and returned home to sit down in front of the
fire, helplessly crying, asking, "What's *wrong* with me? Why
can't I be happy?"

"Maybe some professional help," Jack suggested diffi-
dently.

"Am I crazy, Jack? Do you think I am?"

"Jesus, Glenn! I don't know anything anymore. For all I
know, I'm the one who's crazy."

"Don't hate me, please, please don't hate me, I feel as if
I'm drowning sometimes, sinking lower and lower, until all I
can think about is dying. I know!" she said quickly. "I know
you don't want to hear it! I don't want to be *thinking* it. I'm
sorry," she said abruptly, getting to her feet. "I'll go up, work.
Yes, yes. I must work." She went hurriedly up the stairs to
the studio, to stand in front of the half-completed painting, not
seeing it; seeing only herself dead. Closing her eyes, she imagined her book being published posthumously. Opening her eyes,
she picked up a brush.

Publication date came and went. The book was in the stores.
Some of Jack's friends bought and read it, liked it. Some of
her old friends did, too. Corey and Dawn loved it, gave the
book as a gift to favored friends and clients. Dana was impressed and said so. Cassy cried over it, finding meanings,
signposts to the interior Glenn in it everywhere. One smallish
ad appeared for the book in the newspapers. The trade reviews
were raves. There were two highly favorable reviews in national
magazines. And that was the end of it. She kept waiting day
after day for something more to happen.

"Why aren't they doing anything?" she asked Jack. "I don't
understand. They're not advertising. They're not doing any
promotion. Why?"

"That's just the way it's done, babe," he commiserated.
"The money, the big sales will come from the paperback re-
print."

"I don't care about the money," she cried. "I care about my
book. It's a good book. Everybody says so. I don't understand."

"I know how it is," he said, unable to lie to her and tell her things would be other than they were. "But look at the positive side of it. You've been published. You got great reviews. They're interested in anything else you write. That's goddamned good! Be proud of yourself, Glenn. There's no reason for you to be so down."

"It's just that I thought . . . It doesn't matter what I thought. It doesn't matter."

He winced, watching her toss down half a glass of neat gin, then lick her lips. He felt guilty and angry; he was beginning not to care, tired of coping with her ups and downs, her discontent and depression. He wanted to cart her off to a hospital or someplace private and get her dried out, straightened out, back together. Had they been married, he could've taken her and left her somewhere. But he hadn't any legal rights. He was powerless. All he could do was see it through day after day, watching her age years in just months, seeing flesh vanish from her body as she lost any last interest she'd had in food and made a manic pretense of pushing it around on her plate in an effort to disguise the fact that she wasn't eating. He wanted to hold her down and push the food into her mouth, force her to swallow it. He did nothing. He'd tried everything he could think of to get through to her but nothing worked, not words nor lovemaking nor challenges, not gifts nor bribery nor threats. He was beginning to wonder why he was there, what he was trying to prove by staying when she didn't seem to care if he was there or not. In any case, when she was drinking, the booze so successfully insulated her she saw and heard very little; she needed nothing and no one.

But when she was working. Christ! The transformation was astonishing. She'd eat a bit, stay away from the gin and, when he least expected it, throw herself at him, winding her arms around his neck as if she hoped he might physically rescue her. With a resurgence of passion, she'd aggressively make love to him, pressing urgent caresses up and down the length of his body as if she might somehow save herself through his skin.

Afterward, he'd hold her, waiting for the beating of his heart to ease, telling himself there was a solution. There had to be. Because in spite of everything, he didn't want to lose her or leave her. He thought, bitterly, that the only real solution might lie in his joining her in the bottle, the two of them holding hands as they drank themselves straight to hell.

For six months from the date of publication she tracked the book's progress, knowing with daily more certainty that the dreams weren't going to be realized. The book sold almost four of the five thousand copies printed and then quietly went to sleep. She called for and received a sales figure from her editor, had a couple of drinks and then began pacing up and down the living room. Finally she stopped and telephoned Cassy.

"It's been finished for months," she told her. "Come see it. Please."

"Are you sure?"

"I'm sure. I think I'm at the breakpoint, Cassy."

"What does that mean?"

"Something," Glenn said vaguely, and put down the phone.

Jack was upstairs working, the typewriter clacking, clacking. She had a fire going in the living room and sat down in front of it to wait for Cassy, praying to the fire, to the room, to the clacking typewriter for an answer, a crack in the door, something to provide her with a handhold.

As soon as she saw her, Cassy knew what she'd meant about the breakpoint. She took Glenn's hand saying, "Show me. And then we're going to talk."

They went up the stairs, Glenn held open the door and Cassy stepped into the studio and walked over to the painting to stand in silence for several minutes while Glenn stared out the window at the cold, gray afternoon.

"That is your mother," Cassy said, at last. "I cannot begin to imagine how you drew any part of that from me, out of me."

Glenn turned slowly, leaning back with her hands on the windowsill.

"It was the feeling I got looking at you," she said quietly. "The feeling you gave me. What I can't understand about any of you—you and Jack, Dana, Corey—is why you tolerate me. I'm a clown, Cassy, a fool. I can't stay up and I can't stay down. Part of me knows I've succeeded. Another part of me wants the success to be bigger, better, flashier. I am a fool."

"I think not," Cassy said, looking again at the portrait. "You loved her. You didn't think she loved you. Or not enough. But look what you've done! Look at the woman you've created here! Even if *you* can't love you, that woman did. That woman loved everyone. Too much, to hear Dana tell it." She turned. "To see you paint it. And you've spent all these years and years growing just like her, caring too much, expecting more love than anyone could humanly give you. Enough never being enough. I could understand it in that woman, a mother with three children, children like Dana and Gaby and you. But I will not accept it in you, Glenn. I'm convinced you think somehow you can rewrite the history, relive it and alter the inevitable course of events. You're only succeeding in destroying yourself for no reason. *Look* at it!" she insisted, pushing Glenn across the room, forcing her head around to the painting. "That is *not* you! It will never be you. You're the child, not the mother. Your mother loved you. Let her go, Glenn. You can't live her life and you can't die her death. You've such talent! God, a marvelous talent! Use it! Use your bloody life, woman! Before you lose it. Because you might wake up one morning soon and feel you do want to live after all and it'll be too late. You need fresh air. You need moving and breathing room. Go out, get out and walk it off, think it through. If my loving you gives you the incentive to do something as wonderful as this painting, just think what Jack's loving you—if you allowed it—might give you the incentive to do. Let us in, damn you! Let all the rest of this bloody misery go! Every one of you's paid the price for this fictitious guilt. It's time now to let it go. Go on, go out, take a look at the world. And if you feel you have to talk, I'll be at home."

Glenn nodded. Without bothering to tell Jack she was going, she pulled on her coat, grabbed her handbag and left the house with Cassy. Each of them went in different directions.

She walked block after block, heading into the Little Village, glancing into the windows of the boutiques and galleries, feeling chilled through to her bone-marrow, frozen, numb. The wind was like daggers of broken glass that cut into her eyes, her throat. The sidewalks sent her footsteps jarringly back through her body. She looked at shop windows, stepping out of the path of others traveling the streets, trying to force her mind to turn on. With every step she could hear her heart pounding in her ears, could see the clouds produced by her painful exhalations, could feel the cold like acid eating its way through her, turning her blood to ice.

She thought of what Cassy had said.

I am in trouble. I shouldn't be in trouble, but I am. It's all in me, in my mind, the feelings, the failures. Corey. Holding my hand, looking into my eyes, telling me, "Glenn, all my life I've known just one person I could always count on to be absolutely straight with me, play it truthfully without putting down my ideas or talking down, putting whatever you had to give into it. You've been the most important person in my life, next to Dawn and Zane. Important. To all of us, especially Jack. But there's a kind of responsibility people have to the people who love them, Aunt Glenn. It's having to play your side of the net, guarding your end of the court. God damn it! I hate sitting here having you look at me that way. Why the hell won't you listen to what we're all telling you? You've got a great big bad drinking hangup! Is there some kind of charge you get that the rest of us don't know about, sitting around half the time with a big buzz on, missing most of what's going on around you, just nodding every so often like you're paying attention? Can't you get a high just from being *alive?* Don't you know the reason why you're in such a damned funk half the time is 'cause your system's rotted out with gin? Get off the sauce and start feeding yourself and you're going to find out you feel just fine! I'm telling you! Listen!

"You'll die!" Corey warned brutally. "You're going to fucking well *die!* Listen." His features softened. "What about Jack? Have you any idea really what you're putting him through? I don't think you do. He won't stick around to watch you die, Glenn. You can't ask that much of anyone."

How did I get to be me, to be here, to be what I am? What *am* I? Jack's trying to find a way to tell me he's going to leave. Do I care? Will I miss him? *Think!* Take deep breaths, see the world, THINK? What's happened to my brain, my life? Is it drinking? Have I destroyed my brain cells?

She looked into the last of the gallery windows, deciding she'd head back downtown and find a decent place to have a drink. One very nice thing about having money, you could afford to do your drinking in nice-looking places. She stopped, retraced her steps and moved closer, her heart taking an astonished skip as she looked beyond the window into the interior of the gallery, then once more at the window, at the small poster advertising a showing of selected paintings of R. J. Greaves. She looked once more into the interior of the gallery, then went to the door, making a face as she opened the door and a bell somewhere rang. She quickly closed the door, taking another deep breath and stepped into the center of the deserted gallery, turning slowly to look at the spotlit groupings on the walls. She felt her lungs deflate and her heartbeat slow to a dull, stunned thudding. She saw the five paintings grouped together and picked up a brochure off the corner of a low-slung table to look at the titles. "Woman Vanishing." Her hand trembling, she remembered Ralph saying, "The bra, the bra. I don't want to paint your goddamned *bra!*" And here was the completed painting in thickly laid-on oils, brilliantly executed. The artist inside her nodded in assent. The rest of her went sliding Alice-like down a dark mental tunnel to arrive facing an image of herself as a very young woman, someone healthy-looking, rounded, with breasts. In the second painting—an exact duplicate of the first—most of the color was removed, leaving only a scattering of highlights in the hair, faint skin tints on the shoulder, the arm, one leg. The third—she wrapped her arms around herself, trying to absorb the impact of what she was seeing—was the same again, done this time in fading shades of gray and cream. The fourth—she was sure—was the original drawing he'd done that night. In pencil, with pen and ink. The last consisted of half a dozen India ink lines curved around an eye, a nipple, one hand. She looked back to the first painting, then again to the last, and felt faint. Woman Vanishing. How had he seen this in her all those years before? Or was it merely coincidence? How had he conceived of this? What did it mean? It was clever, but so cruel, so very cruel.

He was sitting just inside the storeroom doorway and saw her come in and stop in front of the grouping, to stand there shivering, staring at the paintings. He put down his newspaper and looked more closely. Was it her? The resemblance was there. This woman was elegant, but older, thinner, taller than she'd be. Or was she?

He stood up noiselessly, reluctant to disturb her—it might just be a customer and he didn't want to scare off anyone who so obviously had bread—and moved to the other side of the doorway to try for a better view. He knew, seeing the expression on her face, that it was her after all. The recognition was a downer. She looked terminal, as if any moment might be her last. The expression in her eyes seemed to indicate she knew this and was merely biding time, waiting for an ending. So tall and gaunt, but still beautiful. And, with all of it, dynamite elegance. No, it couldn't be.

When she failed to look at any of the other paintings, but continued to stand gazing at those five, he knew he'd been right in the first place. It was her. Never in a thousand years would he have predicted she'd turn out looking the way she did.

She turned to go, and he was going to let her leave because she was so plainly brought down by the paintings, but he couldn't, not without at least saying hello after all these years. He spoke her name.

She felt as if she'd just witnessed her own murder and was grateful there was no one else present to see her reaction. Perhaps, she thought, he didn't mean it as I've interpreted it. But whatever he'd meant, it no longer mattered. I thought you loved me. I thought I loved you. But you saw me as someone only half there, only part of a person; someone disappearing at that. I may be a lot of things, but all of me is here. How cruel! she thought again. She moved toward the door, heard her name called and stopped, startled. She turned guiltily, as if she'd been caught stealing.

"Hey!" Ralph smiled, ambling down the length of the gallery, his hands pushing air out of his way. "Thought it was you. Read about the showing?"

"I didn't," she said. "I happened to be out walking."

She'd never have recognized him had they been passing on the street. He still had long hair, but it was wild and ragged-looking. His teeth had gone quite yellow, several of them chipped. His smile was somehow obscene. And he was enormous, far bigger than she'd remembered. The flesh around his middle overlapped the fraying band of his jeans and his open-throated, paint-smeared shirt was unpleasantly suggestive. He leaned forward to kiss her on the mouth and the smell of him made her feel sicker: sweat and turpentine, tobacco in his moustache. She thought of Jack who was impeccably clean, always smelling pleasantly of cologne, pipe tobacco. Jack, in a sports jacket of wool softly pleasing to the touch. Jack. She felt dizzy, a series of small ongoing shocks jarring her.

"Noticed you didn't get all too turned on there," he said, indicating the group of paintings. "It's the big hit of the show, got a lot of heavy press. Sold the whole grouping opening night for heavy-duty bread. So, hey! What're you doing all these many moons later? How 'bout some coffee? Yeah! Let's make it over the road to Angie's and grab us a coupla cups of coffee! Come on!"

He called out to someone in the back that he'd be going out for a while, then took her arm and led her out of the gallery, down the steps and across the street to a coffee bar that was deserted except for two frizzy-headed young men playing chess at a corner table. Ralph ordered two espressos, then tilted back in his chair eyeing her appraisingly.

"Take off your coat, eh?" he invited. "Pretty hot in here."

"I'm a little cold," she smiled, forcing it. "I think I'll just keep it on." She tried not to stare at him, but couldn't help herself. Where's Ralph? What happened to that beautiful young man? He made me tea, invited me to go with him to Spain. Can this be Ralph? If it is, are his senses reeling, too, at the sight of me?

"You look real down," he said bluntly.

How had she managed to forget that about him? He'd always said whatever was on his mind, just spit it right out. "Been sick?" he pursued it.

She didn't answer. She was studying him too intently, seeing an old memory beginning to slowly disintegrate, breaking down into hundreds of tiny fragments, the fragments shifting down to ash. She felt she'd finally, for good, lost the ability to make distinctions between real and not-real. This was real: Ralph at the end of a memory. Whatever had become of that beautiful, defiant young man?

"Smoke?" he offered, extending a pack of Gauloises. She shook her head.

"Have you come back to stay?" she asked, looking down to see she was clutching her handbag with both hands. It was a handbag that Jack had given her. She forced herself to let go.

"No way!" He waved his hand about, then returned the Gauloises to his shirt pocket. "Just came back for the showing, some bread. Made a lotta bucks on 'Woman Vanishing.'" He smiled. "Anyway, end of the week, I head back home. Non-resident now, you know," he said, with pride.

"No, I didn't know."

"You married, kids?" he asked. "You look pretty heavy-duty, clothes-wise."

"No," she answered.

"No?" That surprised him. "No shit! I thought you would, man! I really thought you'd buy that whole bag. So you didn't. How about that? What're you into anyway?"

"Not very much," she said, then stopped, thinking about it, realizing that wasn't true. She'd done quite a lot. "I published a book this year," she said, for the first time taking some small pleasure from that fact.

"Far fucking out!" he laughed. "What kind of a book?"

"A novel."

"Man, that's heavy! Write down the name of it. I'll buy it, take it back home with me." He pushed a napkin at her, took a 4B pencil out of his shirt pocket and passed it over, watching as she wrote down the name and publisher of the book. He looked at what she'd written, folded the napkin and put it into his pocket with the pencil and cigarettes. "So," he said, "you're a writer, eh? Ever do any painting anymore? You were one fucking beautiful painter, man."

"Did you think so?" she asked, surprised at this.

"Oh, yeah! Beautiful!" He nodded seriously. "Nice, clean pieces. Great eye for little details. A lot of depth. Beautiful color sense. I got off a lot on your stuff. That attic you lived in."

"I've just started painting again," she said, deciding she'd start a new piece. She thought of Jack, feeling an urgency taking her over. Jack. "Why did you do that grouping, Ralph? What gave you the idea?"

He drew thoughtfully on his Gauloise and for a moment reminded her of the young Ralph who'd listened to the conversations of others, invariably throwing out one caustic remark sure to put an end to conversation.

"It was nice," he said, "writing back and forth." He paused, examining the hard prominence of her cheekbones, her knobby wrists; looking again at her deep blue eyes, her mouth, her lips. Her skin lay so close to the bone there wasn't a line, a crease. She looked so fucking young-old both at the same time. He couldn't get over it. "I had big eyes for you to come over," he said at last. "Thought for a long time maybe you would. But you never did it. Too bad."

"No," she said, "Why *did* you paint me that way?"

"I don't know. I guess because I knew you weren't ever going to come over there. And dreams kind of drift off that way sometimes, just sort of fade until you only remember a little bit here, a bit there. An eye, the color of it; a breast, the shape of a hand."

"Oh," she said softly, touched. She was seeing the young Ralph emerging now, finding more and more in him that was recognizable. And suddenly she knew that they'd make love, go somewhere to try to find the youth they'd lost in the depths of each other's bodies. And that was all right because she wasn't ready yet to leave him. There were questions she needed to ask him. And his eyes were still yellow, still extraordinary.

They talked through second cups of espresso and then Ralph said, "Got a room upstairs over the gallery. Let's go over, rap awhile. Okay?"

"All right," she agreed.

The rooms were a pleasant surprise, furnished in art deco, the walls papered in an attractively subdued red paisley.

"Guy owns the gallery lives here," Ralph explained. "But he's out. Take off your coat."

She was still cold and reluctant, too, to have him see her. She felt self-conscious for the first time and aware of how she looked. He said, "Come on. Make like you're going to stay awhile," and let his hand travel daringly from her shoulder down across her breast, enjoying the fur under his hand. "Nice," he said. "What, mink?"

"Sable," she said, wetting her lips before removing the coat, watching his eyes, knowing he was judging her now as harshly as she'd judged him. But he hadn't her politeness, and whistled through his teeth, "Jesus, babe! Thin, thin!"

She smiled, embarrassed, and looked around the room, trying to decide where to sit, what to do. He put his hand on her arm and then embraced her, surprising her again. She wasn't sure how to react. She felt a tiny excitement and an enormous curiosity. It was strange being contained within his arms, held hard against his too-soft body. Jack was solid, lean and strong. She indicated she wished to be released and he let go, easing her down beside him on the sofa, once more disconcertingly letting his hand pass from her shoulder down across her breasts. He laughed.

"No bra, eh?"

"No breasts," she quipped, then flushed scarlet. He was going to make love to her, and she was going to let him. But she couldn't stop thinking about Jack, wanting somehow to use this experience to clarify her thoughts about Jack, about many things.

"Goddamned good to see you," he said, hugging her too hard. "No shit!" She hoped he wasn't bruising her.

"It's funny," she said, unable to contain her thoughts. "Seeing your paintings has started me thinking. I think I've been needing to get back into my painting fulltime. *Was* I good, really?"

"No lie," he said. "You were good. Man!" he sighed. "I *do* remember you." He was remembering how much she'd liked it, how crazy for it she'd been.

She could feel the increasing heat from his body and wondered what she should do.

"I've got eyes," he said at length, his bluntness surprising her yet again. "You got eyes?"

She didn't answer. She was waiting.

"Come on in here," he said, pulling at her hand. "Come on!"

"For old time's sake?" she said, finding a certain humor in the idea of that.

"Maybe. Yeah." He held her, looking into her eyes as he lined his body up against hers. "Never knew anybody could do a long-distance turn-on the way you could. I used to get off watching guys at the College get terminal blue balls just following you down the hall."

"I don't understand."

"Oh, yeah," he said. "The way you were. Still are, matter of fact. Surprised the hell out of me you weren't beating them off with sticks. Couldn't believe it when you gave it to me."

"Why?"

"Why?" he repeated, his hands lifting the back of her dress, insinuating themselves down inside her tights, over her buttocks. "Why? Maybe because you were just so fucking *nice*. Not put-on or phony nice but honest-to-God genuine, real-article nice. Never talking bad about anyone. Fair. That kind of thing shows on a person. Then, you take that and put it together with some truly beautiful talent and you've got something that has the guys jerking off in the can."

She laughed. She didn't know what else to do. His hands were shaping her buttocks, around and around, over and over.

"I'm no poet or writer," he defended himself. "I never could explain things worth spit. Feel that?" he asked, urging his hips against hers and she nodded, feeling it. She had an odd sense of power combined with a helpless sense of powerlessness. She could do this—make him go hard with wanting her—but she couldn't control what either of them would do. He squeezed her buttocks—too hard, too hard—saying, "I remember you. I *remember* you!"

It was when he kissed her that the strangeness began to ripen inside her. He wasn't Jack. His mouth was totally unlike Jack's. Ralph's kiss was hotly wet, his tongue slipping into her mouth, shocked her with a gritty pleasure, the sort of pumice-stone pleasure masturbating gave her. It was as if she were engaged in some illicit performance, deriving far more pleasure than she should have from something she'd have preferred not to be doing.

He broke away for air and hurried her into the adjoining room, putting her down on the bed where he lay on top of her—forcing the air out of her lungs so that she could scarcely breathe—his hand up under her dress, his fingers, pressing on her upper thigh, squeezing. He was making bruises, she was certain. He kissed her again, causing her to ask herself, Why am I doing this? I don't think I want to be doing this. But I know I'm going to do it. Why, why? Am I mad? Is that it, really?

There were several skirmishing moments during which he awkwardly began trying to remove her from her clothing, then gave it up, saying, "You do it, eh, babe?" as he jumped off the bed and, by the time she'd removed her dress, he was back again on the bed, naked. His clothes lay in a pile on the floor. His body was round and spreading and soft: a huge, hairy baby, with pathetic-looking genitals. She didn't remember his being quite so hairy.

He watched her closely as she removed her chemise and her tights, reaching for her the instant the last of her clothes was gone. His hand went at once between her thighs, probing, giving her a degree of pleasure. She knew she was going to come for him and thought it sad, because she felt nothing, nothing but disappointment. She was sorry for Ralph; she wanted Jack, needed to be with Jack. Jack! I had to do this, had to find out.

Obliging, she thought. I'm so obliging. Yes, I am.

Ralph indicated he wanted her to do it. The gesture in itself deprived her of any remaining emotional response to him. She did it. Yet for all her dutiful effort—mechanical at best, feeling like an unpaid whore—he remained semi-erect, removing himself finally from her mouth as he rolled her around like a doll, maneuvering her down under him, licking at her lips. She hated it.

"Forget that," he told her. "I need a coupla minutes. I was out half the night last night."

"It's all right," she said, watching his head dip to her breast, feeling his tongue measuring out the dimensions of her breast, her nipple. "It doesn't matter," she said.

But of course it matters, she thought, as he disappeared down past her belly. It matters to you. It simply doesn't matter to me. Now you'll have to prove to me how much it matters to you by making me come. And I will come, too.

He spread her thighs and teased her with his fingers for several minutes—she watched, unable to look away—before putting his mouth, his tongue to her, delivering a decidedly oblique pleasure. More mechanical exercises. She lifted closer, her body responding, and he raised his head to grin wetly at her.

"You'll come, eh? I remember that too."

"Oh, I'm easy," she said sadly. "Easy." I come very easily, even for people I don't like.

"Mmmm," he agreed, gathering her up, holding her to his mouth, his tongue stabbing, his mouth sucking deliberately.

I knew it, she thought, completely connected to herself; no separation was taking place. I knew I would. She came, very gently, very quietly. So quietly, it was barely noticeable, except inside of her: a faint twinge, scarcely any external display, just an ending and an inability—an oversensitized and abraded inability to continue. She asked him to stop. She wanted to go home, needed to go home. She knew Ralph wasn't going to be able to come inside of her. She had no idea specifically why. She simply knew he wouldn't. The dream was dead. A dead dream could not go burrowing inside your flesh. A dead dream had no substance, no thrust.

He lit another Gauloise and drew her against his side, his armpit unpleasantly wet, his sweaty smell more pronounced. He and the Gauloise combined to make her nauseated.

"Man," he said conversationally, "I can't wait to get home, get back to work. This trip's been one fucking bummer, sitting around all day, making nice with the tourists, shitheads coming to do reviews. Bad fucking scene, man. Can't get a decent stick of grass anywhere. Miss my old lady, the kids, too."

"Are you married, Ralph?" How funny, she thought. All these years, she'd never thought he might be married.

"Oh, sure!" He smiled at the ceiling. "Nine years, eh? Got one boy almost eleven, the other boy five. My old lady's into ceramics. We've got this farmhouse outside Lyons. A big studio out back. Ever been to France?"

"Never," she answered, trying to picture him married, the father of two boys. She couldn't believe it, and didn't like him for being disloyal to his wife by making love to her. She didn't like herself for this treacherous disloyalty to Jack. She hadn't ever looked at or desired another man since she and Jack had begun seeing each other. She hadn't actually desired Ralph.

This was purely a matter of certain dreams needing attention, not anything to do with love or wanting or real desires.

"Seriously," he said, rolling over on his side, letting his eyes travel the entire length of her body, taking in her pronounced ribcage and almost nonexistent breasts, her sunken belly and protruding hipbones, the hollow between her thighs. "You been sick or something?"

She sat up, turning to face him, her hands resting on her thighs. Looking at him, she felt the interior dissolving, accelerating now, going faster, faster. The fanciful memories were going. The past was disintegrating, going too. Here was someone she'd considered a part of her life long, long after he'd left it. Now, here he was, a transient, someone who'd just put his face between her legs—for old time's sake—and derived a dubious pleasure from the act. Strangers. She could say anything to him. It wouldn't matter because they'd never see each other again. Nothing mattered but that he'd lost his beauty and that she looked old and ill to him. Nothing mattered but these few moments and the truth they might contain. Her curiosity was driving her to pursue these moments, see what might come of them; to grasp reality with both hands and try to keep some sort of hold on it.

"What would you think?" she asked, sitting on her heels, gripping her thighs, leaning towards him. "What would you think if I told you . . . If I said I'm an alcoholic?"

"Oh, yeah?" he said, looking very interested. "No shit?"

"*If.* What would you think of that?"

"You telling me you gotta have some juice, babe?"

"No, no. What would you *think?*"

"Think? Like how?"

"Just what would you think," she repeated.

"I'd think, I guess, I'm not surprised."

"Oh?" She lifted her head, studying his face. "You're not? Why?"

"Not the way you used to put the grape away, no. The kind of too-good-to-be-alive way you were, no. Out there, they eat people like you for hors d'oeuvres. Delicious. You into A.A. and all that?"

"None of that," she said, her nose starting to run. "I'll be right back. I need a handkerchief." She got up and walked out to the living room to dig around in her bag, searching for one of those frivolous lace handkerchiefs Jack had bought for her. *Jack!* She hurried back to the bedroom, in a fever to find out more. More what? No, no. I am finding out.

He was sitting up, leaning against the wall—the bedroom was not so finely furnished as the living room—the bed was without head or footboard. She thought of her bed, the one she slept in with Jack and wanted to hurry more now. She had to get home to Jack.

"You serious?" he asked, as she climbed back onto the bed, once more sitting on her heels, facing him.

"I don't know. Am I?"

"You're talking like a flake," he said, a little annoyed.

"Sorry. I don't know. I'm just deciding."

"Deciding what?"

"Do I look terrible?" she asked him. "Old? Do I look awfully old to you?"

"I don't know, man," he hedged. She looked a good forty, older; but he didn't want to dump on her. This whole trip was turning into a downer. He wished she'd split. She was making him feel bad. "I'm bad on ages," he lied. "You look your age, I guess. I'm thirty-seven, so you're what? Thirty-three?"

"Almost thirty-six," she said with a small smile, the answers coming to her more quickly now, more quickly. She was getting many answers. "I look terrible. I know it. And I look old. I know that, too. The world doesn't eat people like me." She felt excited, incredibly excited. "We eat ourselves, Ralph. I've got to go. We're finished here, aren't we? I didn't tell Jack I was going out. He'll be worried." She got off the bed, reached for her pants, then stopped. "May I use the bathroom?"

"Sure," he said, putting out his Gauloise. "In there."

I can't go home smelling of another man, she thought, quickly washing between her legs, under her arms, over her breasts, trying to erase Ralph's sour smell from her body. I've got to get right home, right away. She dried herself on a worn-thin towel, then rushed back to the bedroom, scarcely aware of Ralph now, in a panic to get home and see Jack, talk to him, tell about the answers she'd found.

"I'm glad I saw you again," she said, meaning it, stepping into her dress as he watched from the bed. "Really. Thank you."

His expression was one of total mystification as she flew out of the bedroom, snatching up her coat and bag as she went through the living room and on out.

# Nineteen

It had started to snow. She stood in the street, looking for a taxi. There weren't any. But there'd be taxis on the main road. She hurried, slipping, over the icy sidewalks toward the main road two blocks away, trying to run, but it was difficult. The snow got in her eyes, the wind whipped her face.

There was a taxi discharging a passenger on the far side of the main road. She dashed into the traffic, frantically waving to get the driver's attention; got it and yanked open the door, threw herself onto the back seat and gave her address. Breathlessly she sat with her hand on the door as the driver swung the cab out into the oncoming stream of traffic and drove about a hundred yards. There was a grinding, screeching, squealing of brakes; glass crashing, metal colliding against metal. The interior of the taxi was spinning, she was turning, hurled from one side of the car to the other. Finally she was on her knees, her head against the door, unable, for a moment, to lift her head. It seemed attached to the door. She heard car doors opening, shouting voices, cars stopping.

She lifted her head slowly and struggled back onto the seat, dazedly staring through the wet side window at the blur of people beyond. Snow was slowly covering over the windshield. The door beside her was pulled open and a policeman was peering in at her asking, "Are you all right, ma'am?"

She shook her head, trying to clear it, remembering Jack.

"I've got to get home," she said, moistening her lips, tasting something warm, salty.

"You just sit right there, ma'am. There's an ambulance coming."

"No, no. I have to get home. It's all right."

"That's not a good idea," he said, gently but firmly. "Now you just sit quietly. The ambulance'll just be a few minutes."

"But I'm not hurt!" she protested. "Please!"

JACK! I've got to get home. He could be gone. He can't be gone.

"We'll need your name, your address," the policeman said, taking a notebook from his pocket, flipping pages.

She gave her name, her address. "Please, I'd like to go home now."

He looked doubtful. "That's not such a good idea," he said, obviously wanting her to stay right there but if she stayed right there Jack might decide to go, she'd never see him again.

"Please let me out," she said, her voice becoming wavery with urgency. "I'll find another taxi, go home. *Please!*"

"Okay," he said, stepping away from the door. "You go see your family doctor, make sure everything's okay."

"Yes, yes," she said impatiently, climbing out of the car, almost blinded by the thickly falling snow. She turned this way and that. Traffic was stopped in both directions, horns were blaring and people were climbing out of their cars to see what the holdup was.

"You won't get a cab in this," the policeman told her, watching her scanning the street. "You want to get a cab, your only chance'll be to walk down to Old Street, try to get something going crosstown."

"That's the wrong direction," she said feverishly, thinking, I'll just have to walk. She started off, perspiring under the heavy fur, yet feeling frozen. Her shoes slipped on the wet snow. Her gloveless hands flew out in an effort to keep her balance. Unable to run, longing to run, she needed so badly to get home, get to Jack. One block, two. She waited desperately for the lights to change, then darted out into the road, heading for home. Her shoes were saturated, her feet were turning numb with cold. Her hair was soaked, dripping down the back of her neck. Her coat was turning into something atrocious-looking as the fur matted, dripped. Out of breath, a stitch in her side, she was gaining on her destination now. Two more blocks. Jack! For God's sake be there! Please be home waiting! You can't leave!

Her head hurt, just there, on the side. The front of her mouth, too. And on her right side, her ribs. Everything was starting to hurt. No matter. It was just another block. She tried to run, feeling frustrated being unable to go as fast as she wanted to. Rounding the corner, her shoes lost their purchase and she fell on her knees, her hand. She grabbed her bag, picked herself up and hobbled the last block on her broken heel.

Pushing her key at the lock, she whispered, Go in, go in! throwing open the door.

Jack was waiting in the living room, very obviously upset. More upset—he got slowly to his feet with a peculiar expression on his face—when he saw her.

"You didn't tell me you were going out," he said, his eyes taking in the damage.

She took off her wet coat, hung it up, hating herself for her habits—wasting valuable time fussing with a stupid coat—then moved to stand in the doorway, looking at him, for a moment seeing Ralph's image superimposed upon him. She blinked and Ralph went away. For the first time in too long, she saw Jack. He'd lost most of his hair. And he, too, had aged. He was almost forty-six. Fine lines had grown down into the skin around his eyes, his mouth. Jack. Please, God, don't let it be too late! I can't lose you. I won't make it without you, not after all these years.

"What happened to you?" he asked, taking in her split lip, the bruise forming on her cheek. He looked down at her bleeding knees then back up at her dripping hair.

"I met an old friend," she said, trying to catch her breath, so frightened it was all too late. This handsome, charming man had struggled through more than nine years with her for no reward. Nothing. She felt herself swaying toward him, drawn by his goodness and sometime anger and astonishing loyalty, drawn by a sudden tremendous, throbbing sexual appetite for him. She hadn't felt this way about him in so long, such a long long time. Standing looking at his mouth, his eyes, his hands, she could feel his hands on her, wanting that.

"And?" he prompted suspiciously, wondering if someone had beaten her up, mugged her.

"So many things. I have so many things to tell you." She held on to the doorframe for support, his quiet anger threatening. She felt weak, suddenly, nauseated. "Jack?" She let go of the doorframe and stepped closer to him. "Could you understand? If I told you...I have so many things to tell you. But I'm so frightened you might misunderstand. And I need you to understand. Jack, could we go to bed? I want to lie down. I'd like you to come with me, lie close to me, have you hold me. I'm so cold. Could we do that?"

"What happened?" he asked solicitously. Her eyes seemed almost too bright, too beseeching. He put down his pipe and reached into his pocket for his handkerchief, holding it over her mouth. Then he pushed the wet hair back from her face. She closed her eyes, swollen with all the revelations, the feelings; distantly aware of bruised areas in many places. She wrapped her hand around his wrist, whispering, "I need to go upstairs, to have you with me. Please?"

"Something's happened," he said again. "Where have you been, Glenn? Are you drunk? Don't you know your mouth is bleeding?"

Her head snapped back and her eyes flew open as if he'd slapped her. But what else could he think or say? What else? Bleeding? Unimportant. She felt only the weight of reality crushing down on her, bending her spine.

"I'm not drunk," she said in a low voice. "There was an accident. The taxi. I had to walk home, and I fell. Jack, please, come up with me. Don't make me beg this way, Jack."

"Is that the truth?" he asked, no longer able to trust her, the things she'd say. Her words rarely meant what he thought they did anymore.

"It's the truth. Please, come up." She was going to choke on need, the terrible yawning need to put something inside her to make up for the drink she wouldn't have if he'd just come upstairs with her, into the bed with her.

Still looking doubtful, he held her, pressing his lips to her forehead. What is it this time, Glenn? he wondered. Don't ask me to go through the wringer with you again because I'm at the end. This is just delaying the inevitable. Another stalling tactic. You grow them the way the crabgrass grows in the back yard. You're killing off all the love, Glenn.

Yet she seemed so suddenly different. The quality of this embrace was different. The way she was holding him, holding herself tightly against him, resting her cheek against his shoulder, her eyes half-closed, her hand in the small of his back; flatly pressing, urgent.

"Are you hurt?" he asked.

"No, no. No."

They went upstairs.

She said, "Let me, please," and lay with him on the bed, slowly undoing the buttons on his shirt, unzipping his trousers, piece by piece undressing him. He was so caught up in her mood, her immediacy, that he let it happen, until reality seemed to catch him across the forehead and he got up—leaving her watching him fearfully from the bed—went into the bathroom and came back with a dampened washcloth and a towel; he knelt down and cleaned the bloodied scrapes on her knees, then toweled dry her hair, returned the towel and washcloth to the bathroom, then went back to the bed, to hold her against his bared chest, looking hard into her eyes, asking, "Why? What else happened? There's something else, isn't there?"

"I'll tell you. But I want to be holding you."

She didn't seem drunk, didn't seem to be lying. But it was so goddamned hard to tell anymore, about anything. She was hurt, but she didn't even seem to realize that; she seemed, in fact, oblivious to it. He didn't know what to do. He stood and watched her rise languidly from the side of the bed to get undressed, wincing unknowingly as her ribs protested, as she peeled the ruined tights off.

Confounded, he watched as she lay down and held out her arms to him, shivering; yet smiling a smile unlike any other he'd ever received from her. As if hypnotized, he lay down beside her, wanting to believe in magic, in fairy tales, in anything that would turn all of this right again. I love you, he thought, feeling adrift, confused.

Her leg across his hip, she whispered, "Give me your hand."

He gave it and she held it fast, feeling the emotion welling, building; an infusion. "I met an old friend," she began again. "And he kept on asking if I was sick. He thought I looked sick. I do look sick. And old, too. Old and sick. Do you know what I asked him finally?"

"I can't wait," he said skeptically. "What did you ask him?"

"Don't, Jack! I know you want to hurt back. And I deserve it. I know that I do. But this is so important. Please, be patient with me for just a few minutes."

"Sorry," he said.

"He made love to me." She tensed for a blow. He felt as if she'd struck him. It hurt. He'd never suspected anything could hurt quite so much. He closed his eyes for a moment, then opened them, his hand equally hard around hers now.

"Go on," he said stiffly, prepared for the worst.

"Not properly. He couldn't. He made me come. It doesn't matter, Jack. It doesn't. Because the thing of it is, it was a dream. It wasn't real. None of it's been real. For so long. Maybe always. But you, Jack. You're real. And I kept thinking about you, about how you look, how you feel, all you've given me. All the things I suddenly wanted to say to you. So many things I've been saving for years and years, thinking I'd one day say them to a ghost. He was just a ghost but I've been keeping him alive. One of my ghosts. Others, too. Just one of my dreams. I'm ashamed of so many things. But it didn't *mean* anything, Jack. He . . . I hate telling you. I know I'm hurting you again, always hurting you. But it's important. I have to tell you because it's so important. I wanted to get out of there, had to get out of there because I wanted *you*. I wanted you so much! More than I've ever wanted you. You've been here, real, all these years. And I was carrying on a love affair with an old memory. Once upon a time, you were the memory and I had my love affair with you. For five years, thinking about you, wondering why you never came back. But it's all over now, all of that."

"I'm not enjoying this," he said, moving to disengage his

hand. He wanted to cry. It was all blowing up in his face.

*"Wait!"* she cried. "Please! Oh, God! Please, Jack! This is so hard for me. *Please!* You've got to listen, to hear. We talked. And he asked again, Was I sick? And I . . . I asked him what would he think . . . what . . . if I told him I was an alcoholic? What would he think?"

"Jesus Christ!" he exclaimed. "What're you saying, Glenn?" He felt sizzling electric charges taking off up and down the length of his spine. This was it! Was this it! Oh, Jesus! Was it going to turn right after all?

"I'm an alcoholic," she said, round-eyed, terrified now of future prospects. She hurried on. "I've never been so scared in my life. Are you going to leave me, Jack?"

"I've been thinking about it," he admitted, truthfully. "Are you conning me? Is this another trick like the glasses of water that look like gin? Don't for God's sake, con me, Glenn! I can't take any more of it. I really can't. I'll help you if you're serious. You know that. But if it's another, new kind of angle, it'll be the end. It's been too long happening."

"I have to make you understand," she cried, her eyes glued fearfully to his. "I was trying to get home to you, Jack. I couldn't get here. The snow, the accident, falling. Understand, please. I met him. It was such a disappointment, so awful. Cassy came. And we talked. And she told me the truth, sent me out to walk, look at the world. I went to look at the galleries, and saw his work. He'd done a series of paintings of me as someone in the process of disappearing. So cruel, so savage and beautiful. But cruel! I felt it didn't matter what I said to him. Nothing that went between us mattered. Making me come. It meant *nothing*. I didn't feel anything because I didn't *care*. But I thought I did, you see. All these years, depriving *you* because of someone who went away fifteen years ago and could never come back. And mama, going away, never coming back. I was so little and I thought she didn't love me. So many things, Jack. God! Can I tell you everything?

"Having you, afraid; frightened by all my imperfections, never able to be satisfied with what I have, what I can do, the love I do have. Always wanting it to be more like the dreams, more perfect; yet never believing myself to be in any way . . . good. Not good at all, at anything. Afraid to believe

in what I could do. I'm so scared, Jack. It's like that time when
Corey was spending the summer with me, years ago. We used
to go down to the big pool at the shore. And one afternoon he
talked me into diving off the high board. He climbed all the
way up the ladder and stood there behind me, saying, 'Go on,
Aunt Glenn. Just jump in! You'll like it! It's really fun!' I
stood on the edge of that diving board looking down, terrified,
knowing I'd do it but scared, so scared. Because if I landed
wrong, I'd get hurt.

"My whole life's been like that," she said, moving closer
to him, the shivering becoming worse. He automatically held
her, trying to warm her. "Do you see?" she asked. "Always
standing on the edge—of my ability, of love—terrified of
jumping in because I knew I'd get hurt. But if I only *pretended*
I was jumping in, nothing could hurt me. Maybe I'm not making very good sense. I'm so cold. Jack, I want to try to be
happy with what I have and stop thinking about the things I
don't have, or ever will have. None of that matters. Being rich,
being famous. It would be nice, but it doesn't *matter*. I don't
want to end up for-real crazy, Jack. With the D.T.'s, seeing
things that aren't there. All alone by myself, because you'll
go, won't you, if I don't stop?"

"That's right," he said softly, overwhelmed. They were
crashing through, breaking out, like two flyers in free-fall,
hands on the rip-cords, tensely waiting; yet filled with tremendous exhilaration.

"If I don't stop," she went on quickly, "things are never
going to be the way I want them to be because *I* can't be the
way I want to be. And I want to be me. I don't want you to
go. I can't let you go. I didn't think I cared. Telling you I
loved you, not thinking about it, just sort of saying it automatically. But Jack, *I love you*. I don't want to be here without
you. I don't want to be alive without you. All this time I thought
you were some kind of crazy staying on and on, telling me
how much you loved me. I was indulging myself, wasting our
time together thinking about Ralph, about being famous.
Dreams. And you've been real, here all the time. Please, help
me, Jack! Please, I need you. Don't give up on me now! If
you do, I . . . Please?"

"You know I'm going to. I've been trying to for a long time now."

"Why?" she asked, her voice breaking, all at once aware of the pain in her face, her ribs, her knees. "It's the one thing I can't understand about you. Why do you bother, truly?"

"I don't know why," he said, honestly. "Something about you that makes the day better because I know I'll wake up to the day with you in it. It's not all a pleasure trip, that's for goddamned sure. But even drunk, you're kinder, gentler, realer than anyone else has ever been for me. What else is there, Glenn? I don't know."

"I want a drink so badly," she whispered. "But I won't have one if you'll stay up here with me for a little while."

"You really *do* mean it," he said, on the road to believing.

"I do! I do so much. And it doesn't matter about Ralph, does it? Not really."

"Not if you say it didn't matter to you, no."

After putting it off and putting it off, Dawn and Corey finally found time one afternoon just before Christmas to run down to City Hall and get married. Then Corey got started on the paperwork in order to adopt Zane.

Glenn had to go into the hospital for two weeks, because she couldn't eat. She was fed intravenously. Then came trays of bland, mushy food, and finally, solids. She and Cassy talked every day, for hours. Cassy beamed, leaving the hospital.

At Christmas, Jack and Glenn invited the entire family to come for Christmas dinner and cooked for a solid week, preparing. On the day, Gaby arrived with Lloyd and asked to see the portrait of Lisette.

"Cassy talked about it," Gaby said. "And I would love to see it."

Glenn took her upstairs to the studio. Gaby looked at it for a long time, then turned to look at Glenn, taking hold of Glenn's hands.

"I haven't any right to ask you," Gaby said quietly. "But it would mean so much to me to have it."

"Why?"

Gaby looked again at the painting, gazing at it as she spoke.

"Her loving everyone killed me," she said, in a whisper. "I hated her for being so forgiving, for loving me in spite of the way I treated her. I wanted to kill her for loving me, because she forced me to love her even though I didn't want to."

"Have it!" Glenn said.

Gaby kissed her.

On Glenn's birthday, she and Jack got married. The act satisfied something in both of them. Afterward, they went home, Jack to his typewriter, Glenn to the studio.

That spring, Zane began to drop by occasionally after school or on the weekends, to sit in a corner watching her paint, or to chat if she wasn't working at something. He reminded her so much of Corey. He'd park his bike on the front walk, carefully chaining it to the picket fence before coming up the front steps to ring the doorbell.

"Zane Alan Shea!" She'd smile. "Come on in. What's new?"

"Hi, Aunt Glenn." He'd come in with that same man-inside-the-little-boy self-containment Corey had always had. "Got any juice or anything? I'm really thirsty."

"Well, let's see," she'd say, opening the refrigerator door. "We've got apple juice, orange, and grape. There's also Jack's Vichy water, if you can stand that."

"I think grape," he'd say, sitting himself down at the kitchen table while she poured out two glasses of juice. He really liked coming here. It was almost as good as home.

Sometimes, she let him help her with the cooking, explaining the recipes, and talking about things, telling him things he wanted to know. He thought she was about the best person he'd ever known, outside his mom and dad.

In April, Jack's screenplay won an Academy Award, and the entire family again got together to celebrate.

In May, Cassy and Glenn jointly exhibited their paintings to much acclaim.

And in June, Lisette's two books of poetry went into their twenty-second printing.

Turn the Page

for an exciting sneak preview of
Charlotte Vale Allen's new
novel, coming from Berkley

*INTIMATE FRIENDS*

Ross had sent freesias. Red roses would have more in keeping with her expectations of him. Freesias were a little mystifying. She felt both elated and confused. She wanted to believe the flowers were Ross's personal choice, that he hadn't had some corporate lackey call the florist. Were that the case, it signified more than professional, habitual good manners; it could mean that he was genuinely interested in her. But Ross struck her as the sort of man who'd have a cleverly skillful assistant, someone who'd instinctively sense what to send to whom. The card enclosed was simply one of Ross's business cards, which confirmed her suspicion that an assistant had done the ordering. She wondered, smiling, if the florist had files of business cards and simply attached an appropriate one to each order.

It was trivial, she told herself, of no importance. Yet it was important. Since their initial meeting the previous week she'd had the feeling that events were going to shift direction; she was standing on the brink of something. Again she felt guilty. Every time she went out on a date with a new man she felt disloyal, as if she were actively betraying Alec by accepting the attentions, no matter how slight, of other men. There were times when, angrily, she wished Alec would finally die for her so that she'd be free to live without guilt or anger. As it was, he was an unseen presence, sitting in judgment, commenting on the men she saw. Now Ross had entered her life, with his offering of freesias and his invitation to dinner, and she wanted to approach the situation with an open mind, but she couldn't stop processing Alec's thoughts and applying them to much of what happened in her life.

The truth was she'd found Ross attractive, appealing. More than that, she'd found him desirable. For the first time since Alec's death, she'd met a man who stimulated not only her brain but her nerve-endings. It seemed dangerous, as if by admitting to more than a passing interest in a man other than Alec she was revealing a treacherous, trenchant vein of weakness in her nature.

Rather than continue to go through these ennervating analyses of her actions she frequently thought it would be far safer and less exhausting simply to stay at home alone. She felt furious with Alec for dying and leaving her alone to discover territories inside herself that might have been better left uncharted. She longed to be free, to be able to go out for an evening without the seemingly everpresent doubts that turned her every thought and action suspect. Ross had sent freesias and she wished she could just relax and enjoy the damned flowers.

Ross wondered why had he failed to remark upon her good looks. He found her exquisite. Perhaps it was the all-black outfit that pointed up the silvery blondness of her hair, wisps of which escaped enticingly down the nape of her neck and in front of her ears. Her skin looked flawless, pale with a pearly sheen. When she walked across the room to pour him a drink he watched the way her body moved inside her clothes, the slight sway of her breasts, the side-to-side shift of her buttocks, and silently complimented her on her good taste, her natural attractiveness. He'd been trained to examine "product," and she was top quality. For the first time in a long while he found himself profoundly interested in a woman's potential. He sat comfortably on the sofa, taking his time to look around, perennially intrigued and charmed by the atmosphere of a woman's home. There were invariably subtle differences, a certain delicacy of scent and selection, between the homes of men who lived alone and those of women. His house, by contrast to Lynne's, was lacking in texture. He'd concentrated so much on the look of things that he'd omitted considering how those things might feel. He'd been unaware of his error until this moment, and knew he'd go home this evening to touch the various fabrics in his house, and to study the color schemes.

"This is really charming," he complimented her, turning to study the smile she gave him before she said, "Cheers," and touched her glass to his.

"Thank you for the flowers. I like freesias."

"Well, good," he said, wishing he had, for once, taken the trouble to select the flowers himself. "Good. Tell me"—again he looked around—"we didn't have much of a chance to talk the other evening, and I'm curious. What do you do? Are you a career girl?" He thought he sounded like a pompous old fart, and despaired of having to carry out this charade of ignorance.

"When I was twenty-two," she said carefully, "I was a career girl. At forty, I like to think of myself as a woman with a career."

"Point taken." He smiled, glad of her confidence. "I stand corrected."

"Asking about my career. Is this where we display our credentials for one another?" she asked, bored at the prospect of another predictable evening.

"God, I hope not," he said, stretching his legs out in front of him. "I suppose most single people have to go through that. Personally, I don't have the energy anymore. After a while you even stop listening."

"That's true," she agreed, "you do."

"What was your career at twenty-two?"

"Credentials?" she asked, with a half smile.

"Interest, curiosity."

She sighed and looked over at the fireplace, took another sip of her drink, then returned her eyes to his. "I started with the network as a secretary. An opening came up in production. I applied for the job, as a glorified errand boy with a title, and got it. Once I got the job and had a chance to be involved in actual production, I became fascinated. I started night courses in TV and film technique—editing, production, whatever was available—and began paying very close attention to what was being done, and how. I had visions of being one of the few dynamic woman producers."

"And you succeeded."

"Only to a degree." She looked closely at his eyes. There was no hint of condescension in his expression. He wasn't a handsome man; his features were all mismatched, nose a shade too large, eyes dark and deeply set, mouth too—what? Mobile. He was attractive, though, and he did have good, broad shoulders. She could hear her mother telling her years before, ". . . watch out for narrow-shouldered men. You can't lean on them, can't rely on them to be there when you need them. I've always mistrusted men with narrow shoulders; it's like a visible character flaw." Alec had had broad shoulders, but he'd always been too thin, his chest slightly concave, giving him a tubercular look when he was younger. Ned Booker had narrow shoulders. Funny, she'd never thought about that before. "I'm the only woman," she explained. "They give me a lot of the less important work, the pieces they think have a 'woman's angle.' Alec was forever telling me I was beating a dead horse, that they'd never give me a chance to do anything more. I'm beginning to think he might have been right."

"How long were you married?" he asked.

"Seventeen years. I was twenty-one."

"And how long have you been a widow? D'you mind if I smoke?"

"Not if you offer me one. I don't feel like getting up to go for mine."

He lit two and handed her one.

"Two years," she answered, accepting the cigarette. "Thank you. And you?"

"Five."

"It ages people," she said philosophically. "I used to look young for my age, but in the past two years I've caught up with myself. It's probably that, and the strain of coping with everything alone, without anyone at home to explode at."

He chuckled. "I know what you mean. Although I'd like to argue about how old you look."

"And the awful part of it," she continued, electing to ignore the implied compliment, "is all the well-meaning friends who want to fix you up, who want to see you happily married again with someone new so they can stop thinking about you, stop feeling guilty, stop having to invite another odd person so the table will be balanced at dinner."

He nodded. "Nobody *talks* about it. Have you noticed that? People are so damned dishonest. They want you off their hands, off their consciences." He stared at her for a moment, liking her more and more, then smiled. "We're off to a pretty morbid start."

"We're off to a truthful one," she said. "It's a nice change. I've grown so used to people saying one thing but meaning something else that half the time I'm afraid to believe what I'm told. This is probably the most refreshing conversation I've had in the last two years."

"I'll drink to that." Again he touched his glass to hers then reached for the ashtray and placed it on the sofa between them. "I feel very relaxed with you. I'm not sure what to think about that."

"Oh?"

"Corporate jitters," he explained. "Never trust appearances and most of all never trust your instinct to relax."

"Christ!" she exclaimed. "That's it exactly! I think you're the first man I've ever heard admit that. I think men would like women to believe that they don't feel that way, and that because we do—even if we don't broadcast it—we're inferior. Why do you keep on with it?" she asked.

"You start out as one thing and thirty-odd years later you've ended up as something else, but you've fallen into the habit. What's your work schedule like?"

"I've been off for the last few weeks. Between assignments," she explained. "Actually, I've been trying for close to two years to get the producer to let me do a segment on rape, and he's blocked me every time. Dianna . . . Do you ever watch the show?"

"'Up to the Minute'? I do, as a matter of fact."

"You already know about the show," she realized. "Did I tell you about that last week? But I must have. I'm sure I did. Why did you just ask me about my career?"

"I'm a little absent-minded," he lied ineptly, promising himself he'd done the last rundown he was ever going to do on anyone. He loathed finding himself in a position where he had to lie with every other breath. "Anyway, you were about to say something about Dianna."

"Dianna phoned about an hour or so ago to say that Ned— he's the producer—is going to pass my proposal, finally. I'm afraid to believe it."

"Why?"

"Because he's an opportunist, and an operator. He'd say something like that just to get someone off his back."

"And you think Dianna was on his back?"

"Something like that," she said cautiously, fearful of being indiscreet.

He felt her pull back on the subject, and decided to shift the direction of the conversation to help her out. "What interests you?" he asked.

"This is starting to sound like an interview," she said warily.

"I'm sorry."

"Do you have children?" she asked, then laughed. "I suppose we've got to get all this out of the way."

"I don't mind," he said. "Three sons. You?"

"We decided not to have children."

"It takes a lot of guts to defy the conventions."

"No, it doesn't. I have an old college friend who never married. We were talking one afternoon and I said I thought it showed a lot of courage on her part, never marrying. She told me it didn't have anything to do with courage. It had to do with deciding what was best at the time. When I thought about it, I still had to say I thought it took courage. Then she laughed and looked a little deflated and admitted that no one who'd interested her had ever proposed. That made me mad, and I said so. It's awful to hide your disappointments under a noble light, allowing people to endow you with qualities like courage when the truth is we're none of us any different. We don't think noble or courageous things when we do what we have to do."

"We're all cowards in one way or another," he said. "And we're all looking for someone, whether we admit it or not."

"You're still looking?" she asked, disarmed by this admission. "Why?"

"Not actively," he qualified. "There's just an awareness that's always alert, always on the lookout for the possibility. Whether or not I'd ever do anything about it is a whole other ballgame."

She felt a small stab of satisfaction. He'd just confessed to a vulnerability she hadn't thought he'd have. It made him seem more accessible, less of a cookie-cutter businessman.

"I'm hungry," she declared.

"I'll feed you." He downed the last of his drink, stubbed out his cigarette and moved to get up.

Watching him, she said in a low voice, "Don't look to me. I'm really *not* looking."

He picked up her coat from the rocker and came toward her holding it out. "Liar," he said gently. "That's the first dishonest thing you've said so far."

He wasn't, she was pleased to see, a heavy drinker. He had two glasses of wine with dinner and offered her a liqueur after but declined to have one himself. "A Scotch before dinner and a glass or two of wine and that's my limit."

"Mine too," she said. She was discovering that he was anything but predictable.

"You're not typical," she said in the car as they headed back to her house.

"Neither are you."

"No, I mean it."

"So do I." He smiled over at her. "I thought you'd be one of those women on a perpetual diet. It did my heart good to watch you eat."

She laughed. "I've always had the appetite of a trucker. My friends in college despised me. Half of them would gorge themselves on pizza and beer then slip discreetly into the nearest john and throw up. I'd eat an entire pizza, drink three or four beers and an hour later want to go out for Chinese food. A manic metabolism," she explained.

"All I have to do is look at food and I start growing a paunch," he said. "I sometimes wish I had the courage not to look like a businessman, that it didn't matter to me."

He directed the car into her driveway and put the shift into neutral before turning to look at her. He hoped she'd invite him in for a nightcap or some coffee; he wanted to spend a little more time with her. When she didn't say anything, he said, "Will you invite me in?" He took hold of her hand, startled by its coldness.

"Not yet," she said, allowing him to chafe her hand. He was very gentle in his gestures. "The truth is I haven't made love to anyone since my husband died. If I invite you in, I'll want to. And I'm not ready."

Taken aback by her directness he couldn't say anything for a moment, so he continued warming her hand, trying to find the right words. "I was only," he said finally, "hoping for some coffee, a chance to talk with you a little longer."

"I know that," she said.

"You know that," he repeated, looking into her eyes. "You're quite a woman. Are you always so direct?"

"No," she answered truthfully.

"Well." He released her hand. "I'm going to have to go home and think about all this. I'll try to call you tomorrow."

"Good. I'd like that. Let me give you my card with the office number." She opened her bag, found a card and gave it to him. "It was a lovely dinner, and I enjoyed talking with you. Truthfully, more than I expected to. If you do find time to call tomorrow, I'll enjoy talking with you again."

"Saturday night," he said on impulse. "Will you come out?"

She paused, thinking. "Out where? I'll be honest again and tell you I've come to hate all the little local gatherings for cocktails, the paddle tennis club get-togethers. I only went last week for Amy's sake."

"I see. How does this sound? I have a housekeeper who cooks like a dream. She can't clean to save her life but her dinners could inspire poetry."

"It sounds wonderful."

"Pick you up at seven?"

"Good."

She stood in the driveway watching him reverse out into the road. She waved, then moved toward the door. Neither the man nor the evening had been what she'd expected. Mercifully,

Alec had remained in the background. She let herself into the cottage considering some of what she'd said to Ross. She'd surprised herself, saying what she had about making love. Why on earth had she blurted that out? Because, she told herself, she really was fed up with all the nonsensical aspects of dating. She was tired of subtlety and innuendo, of the giving and receiving of credentials, of the feeling she usually had at the end of an evening with some man that nothing she'd said had really been heard, that she'd been indulged, patronized, in return for which she might gratefully offer her body. She didn't care if she never went out on another date as long as she lived. If Ross liked her, fine. If he didn't like her, fine. She liked him well enough to be truthful. It was up to him how he chose to proceed.

John sat on his bed and listened to the night sounds, cars passing less and less frequently on the road outside. The restaurant was closing. He heard Joe and Gina close the front door; a moment later their car started up and they drove off. Silence. He looked over at the table, at the open Random House dictionary, at the stack of yellow manila copy paper, and the completed pages. He told himself he should walk across the room and get a few hours' work done. But he wasn't in the mood.

He folded his arms behind his head and thought about the cottage near Pear Tree Point. It was a great little place, exactly the kind he'd live in if he had the money. She'd done a nice job fixing it up, hadn't made it all cute and chintzy the way a lot of women would have.

She looked like someone with a career. She had the decisiveness, the attitude of someone used to being in control. The only discrepancy was her sad blue eyes.

He yawned and slid a bit further down on the bed. Gazing at the ceiling, he tried to imagine what it would be like to have his book accepted, to see it in print, bound between hard covers. Maybe it'd be a best seller. "Hah!" He laughed aloud. Some joke. He'd be lucky if it even got a reading. No matter what happened, though, he wasn't going to quit. He wasn't going to spend the rest of his life odd-jobbing for the locals, jump-starting cars and delivering cord wood. If he bombed out with the book, he'd move into the city and start trying for editorial jobs. At least he'd make a halfway decent salary and be able to afford a better place to live.

He thought again of Lynne Craig and felt anew that expansion in his chest, an interior spasm of sorts. No one had ever had this kind of an effect on him. She was so vivid in his thoughts, so fully fleshed and intimately detailed he could almost touch her. He wished to God he had an irresistible smile, or a way with words.

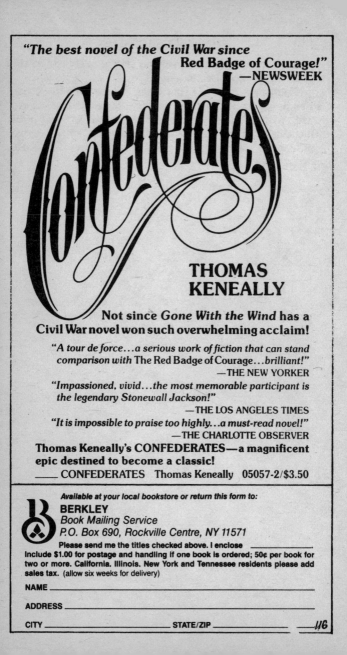